SEIZED BY PASSION

"Come here," Nick muttered in a dark, raspy voice. He never her gave a chance to move. He caught hold of her with one hand and hauled her into his arms only seconds before he fastened his mouth over hers.

He had waited all day for this. From the minute Jessica had walked out of his room that morning, he had been dying to have her back, to feel her softness under his palms, to taste her on his tongue. He had purposely pushed himself harder than usual, staying late in the fields just to temper his unruly need, but it hadn't worked. The delay had only increased his desire to have her, now.

He thrust his tongue past her parted lips. It was the exact release Jessica needed. Freed from her momentary daze, she gave herself up to her instincts and wound her arms around Nicholas's neck. His mouth plundered hers, taking, demanding, and she realized that he had been as desperate for her as she had been for him.

She arched against him, suddenly frantic to have him again. "Oh, God, Nicholas," she moaned.

He didn't bother with niceties. Hands sure and swift, he lifted her from her feet, turned and, in one fluid motion, swept the contents of the desk onto the floor. . . .

TODAY'S HOTTEST READS
ARE TOMORROW'S SUPERSTARS

ELIZABETH SHERWOOD

LOUISIANA ROSE

ZEBRA BOOKS
KENSINGTON PUBLISHING CORP.

ZEBRA BOOKS are published by

Kensington Publishing Corp.
850 Third Avenue
New York, NY 10022

First Printing: September, 1994

Printed in the United States of America

For Steven and Cathy
with love

Thank you Debbe Goddin
for gifting the world with your wonderful sense of humor

Chapter One

New Orleans, 1850

She really didn't think she was going to be able to live through this. The wretchedness of what her father was about to do set her every muscle to shaking.

Jessica bit into her lower lip, in her fear ignoring the blood she tasted on her tongue. Standing against a bookcase inside the law office of Mr. William Wyatt, she watched and listened as her father bargained with her life.

"She's a sturdy girl, even if she is on the small side," her father proclaimed to the balding attorney.

Mr. Wyatt drew in a deep breath, the gesture that of one seeking a bid for patience. "Mr. McCormick, I am sure what you say is true, but I do not handle the kind of transaction you need." His gaze slid to Jessica in a look she thought was somehow sympathetic. "I suggest you try one of the slave exchanges."

Ben McCormick screwed his ruddy face to one side and scrubbed a fleshy hand over his chin. "Now, Mr. Wyatt, I was hoping to avoid that."

"Why? That is what you're after, isn't it? You want to sell your daughter."

As though pained, Ben McCormick winced at the acerbity of the lawyer's words. "But not as some slave. Just as an indentured servant." Ben patted the air in front of him and added, "Only for a few years or so."

William Wyatt's chin came up, his eyes taking on a flinty look. When he spoke, his words were as frosty as his manner. "As I said, Mr. McCormick, I suggest you try elsewhere."

Jessica knew what would happen next even before Mr. Wyatt finished speaking, and her pulse quickened. Her father had little patience to begin with, absolutely none when he believed himself insulted. Gripping her hands tightly about her bundle of possessions, she watched her father fill with a rage she had come to know so well. Unconsciously, she pressed back against the leather book bindings, an instinctive move born of an apprehension rooted in her soul.

"If I wanted to take her into one of them trading pens," Ben McCormick grated in a dangerous growl, "I would have done so. But you and I know that I won't get a fair price for her on the open market like that."

Embarrassment joined Jessica's fear and she looked away, only to find that a tall gentleman had entered the office and was staring straight at her. Quickly, she pulled her gaze to the bare wood floor directly in front of her, oddly discomfited, and waited for her father's anger to escalate.

"What I want is a private sale, one that will bring the kind of money she's worth," Ben insisted.

"Mr. McCormick . . ."

"Just look at her, man. Manageable, quiet, good-looking in the bargain. Got all her teeth, hardly ever been sick a day in her life. She can cook and sew, and dig garden trenches all day long if needs be." Ben paused only long enough to lower his voice. "And she's a virgin. Made sure myself that she stayed that way."

With all her might, Jessica prayed for the floor to open and swallow her whole. The blush of embarrassment that had stained her cheeks only moments ago drained from her head, making her feel dizzy and a little sick to her stomach.

In all her life, she had never felt so humiliated. Every embarrassing situation, every boorish, thoughtless predicament in which he had ever placed her paled by comparison. Being discussed as though she were a piece of horseflesh made her want to crawl into herself and die.

Some composed corner of her mind told her that she should have expected nothing less from her father. This wasn't the first time he had tried to bluster and argue his way along. Nor was this the first time he had gambled himself into a corner, a very dangerous corner. No, none of this was new to her. What was unexpected, and what had her father running scared was the amount of money he had lost. One thousand dollars, to a man who would have his due or Ben McCormick's life.

Thinking it all out seemed to give the matter a certain amount of logic. Her father had lost badly at cards, he now owed a great deal of money. His only means of obtaining that money was to sell her to the highest bidder.

Her stomach knotted and desperation glazed her eyes. She wanted to run screaming from the *logic* of it all, from the building, from her father, but there was little chance of her doing any of that. Experience at her father's heavy hands had taught her that she wouldn't get far.

"She's good for at least ten years of honest labor, more if she's fed proper."

"Mr. McCormick," Mr. Wyatt retorted, "I'll have to ask you to leave."

Ben's chest swelled with the huge breath he drew, the look he levelled on the attorney laden with equal amounts of rage and stubbornness. Shaking his fist, he swore, then turned to Jessica so suddenly she jumped. "Get over here."

Dread raced up her spine. For a few seconds, she stared back at him, having no idea what he meant to do. Mr. Wyatt had made himself perfectly clear in his refusal. What could her father hope to gain by pressing the issue?

She left her place at the wall, realizing only then how much security it had offered. On shaking legs, she crossed to stand at her father's side. Not quickly enough. Two paces off, he reached out, grabbed her by the arm and yanked her the remaining way forward.

"When I say move, I mean move," he bellowed, shaking her with enough force to jerk her head backward.

She caught her breath on a low gasp. Other than that she was helpless to do anything except let her body go as slack as possible. Hard-learned lessons had taught her it was the only way to withstand the kind of physical mistreatment her father dispensed so frequently.

"That is enough," Mr. Wyatt objected, so appalled his voice rose in volume.

"Stay out of this," Ben snarled back. "She's my daughter, and I'll do as I see fit." As if to prove that, he gave her another shake. "Unless you're willing to see that I get her indentured, you can go to hell."

"Now see here," Mr. Wyatt began, but again, Ben cut him off.

"Let's go." He headed for the door, his hand still clenched about Jessica's arm.

The abrupt move caught her off guard. Already off balance by the shaking he had given her, she stumbled, tripping to her knees on her small sack. In that position, with her skirts trapped beneath her, she became a dead weight.

Ben was forced to halt his steps. He spun back to Jessica and hauled on her arm with enough power to pull it from its socket. "Get up."

Spearing pain lanced through her shoulder. Helplessly, she cried out even as she tried to right herself.

"You miserable little bitch, I said get up!"

She wasn't going to be able to move fast enough to please him. She knew that as certainly as she knew she couldn't manage to get her feet clear of her skirt and come to her feet. In an eerie foresight, she relaxed her muscles and curled into herself protectively at the same moment his hand lashed out at her.

It was a reaction of pure instinct, based on years of intuition and seasoning. She tucked her head as best she could, threw her free arm protectively over her face and drew her knees up to her chest. Holding her breath, she waited for the feel of his fist, and then the awful blow that would bring such pain.

Reflexively, she blocked out her surroundings, her mind focusing only on surviving the moment. She never heard the hoarse curses that rent the air, never saw the scuffle that went on around her. Even when her arm was unexpectedly released, she couldn't do anything more then clamp it to her side and wait, smelling her own fright mix with the odor of mildew permeating the wooden planks pressed to her face.

Strangely enough, it was the sound of a man's voice that filtered through the numbness swathing her mind. The deep, resonant tones broke into her consciousness . . . and dragged up a panic that had, up until then, lain dormant.

Ignoring the ache in her shoulder, she scrambled away, fighting the hampering folds dragging at her legs. She didn't know where her father was, or what had prevented him from hitting her. She knew only that she had to put as much distance between them as possible.

Sucking in one shallow breath after another, she backed herself up to the bookcase, then came to her feet. It was with a certain amount of surprise that she looked about and found her father at the mercy of the unknown man who had also been in the office.

She swallowed hard, seeing the tableau before her, but not quite believing it. Her father was pinned, face first, to the sturdy door, held there by the strength of the tall, commanding stranger. Standing off to one side was Mr. Wyatt, a pistol raised and ready to be fired.

"Move, and you'll be sorry," the dark-haired man grated, his voice lethal in its menace.

Her father grunted and swore, fuming at his inability to move. "You friggin' bastard. You got no right to come between me and what's mine."

"That may be true, but I won't let you lay a hand to her."

"I'll get the law."

The gentleman's mouth curled into a nasty-looking smile. "You could try, but if I were you, I wouldn't even breathe too heavily. My good friend, Mr. Wyatt, might take exception to that." With that threat, the man shoved away to plant himself like some immovable force in the middle of the room.

Ben swung about, his black eyes finding Mr. Wyatt and the pistol at once.

The lawyer spoke with great care. "I don't want any trouble, Mr. McCormick."

"That's just what you're going to get if you keep pointing that damn thing at me." However, for all of his bravado, Ben didn't so much as move. Instead he jabbed his gaze back to the other man and attacked in the only way left to him. "Who the hell are you?"

Apparently unperturbed by the demand, the man raised one straight black brow and mocked, "Ah, the social niceties at their best." He offered an equally insulting bow and added, "DuQuaine. Nicholas DuQuaine."

"I'll see you pay for this, DuQuaine."

Nicholas thrust one hand deep into the pocket of his trousers. "I don't think so. You and I have some business to transact."

That caught Ben's attention. His eyes widened in interest. "What's this?"

As though Ben had said nothing, Nicholas spoke over his shoulder to Mr. Wyatt. "I'll buy her indenture."

Wyatt's hand shook slightly. "What? Nicholas, you can't be serious."

"When have you ever known me not to be when it comes to money?"

"But . . . but this is most irregular," Wyatt sputtered. "I don't usually handle this kind of thing."

Turning his head only enough to allow Wyatt to see his expression, Nicholas smiled coolly. "You'll make an exception in this case, Will. That's what I pay you for."

William Wyatt stared at Nicholas as though trying to discern if his client had lost his wits. Finally, he lowered the pistol and shrugged. "If that's what you want."

"It is." He nodded then turned his attention to Jessica.

She watched him approach, trepidation giving her face a pinched look. Confusion and fear held her immobile. He was a formidable man, powerful enough to deal with her father, compelling enough to force Mr. Wyatt to do as he was told. She had the distinct impression that Nicholas DuQuaine could make mincemeat of her with a single glance.

He came to stand before her. "Are you all right?"

She blinked, then blinked again. He wanted to know if she was all right. It was a simple enough question, but it had been a long time since anyone had thought to bother himself about her welfare.

A little uncertainly, she nodded.

"Did he hurt you?"

Again, the considerate inquiry confused her. "I'm all right," she murmured, unable to keep from staring.

"That's not what I asked."

He reached a hand toward her shoulder, but before he could touch her, she stepped away, wariness darkening the blue of her eyes to gray. She didn't know this man nor what he was capable of. The last thing she wanted was for him to touch her.

A frown etched deep lines into Nicholas's forehead, yet he didn't lower his hand. In the silence that fell between them, he studied her carefully.

She expected him to hit her. He could see that as plainly as he could see the faint trembling of her lips. "I'm not going to hurt you." Deliberately, gently he lowered his hand and cupped her shoulder in his palm. "Does your arm hurt?"

Her sharp indrawn breath told him all he wanted to know. In that second he could have easily sent her father to hell without a single regret. Actually, he had wanted to do that from the first moment the bastard had opened his mouth. That was one of the reasons, Nicholas admitted to himself, he had involved himself in the matter. McCormick was the type of man who wasn't worth the salt from which he was made, the type of brutal, cruel excuse of a man Nicholas detested.

He scanned the girl's ashen face again. The only color to be seen was in the remarkable blue of her eyes and a small reddened bruise on her lower lip. With the exception of that

brief instant when embarrassment had flooded her cheeks
with a blush, she had remained chalk white.

His gaze continued its inventory. She was a little thing—
the top of her head reached only to his collar bone—and too
slender by far. If she had eaten a decent meal recently, he
would be damned. Disgust settled sourly in his stomach. He
wouldn't treat one of his dogs the way McCormick treated
his own flesh and blood.

"What's your name?" He kept all trace of emotion from his
voice.

"Jess . . . Jessica."

"How old are you, Jessica?"

"Seventeen."

"Do you have any other family?"

"No, sir."

"Any friends you can go to?"

She swallowed hard before replying. "No, sir."

Nicholas hadn't thought so. Which was another reason he
had decided to embroil himself in what was, for all practical
purposes, none of his business. Despite the fact that he didn't
need another slave or servant, he couldn't turn his back on
her. God only knew what kind of circumstances she would be
sold into, but servitude was the *best* she could hope for. If
that was to be her fate, he could at least insure that she had
a decent place to live, adequate food to fill her stomach.

He picked up her bundle where she had dropped it. "Draw
up the necessary papers, Will."

Jessica followed his every move with eyes rounded by a
multitude of thoughts and emotions. It was going to happen,
she was actually going to be sold into short-term slavery.
There was no other way to describe indenturing. She didn't
know what she could expect. Modest duties? Grueling labor?

Prostitution? Her throat clenched at the latter. Would Nicholas DuQuaine use her that way?

Biting on her lower lip, she watched him as he and her father settled their business. Nothing she saw changed her first impression of Nicholas DuQuaine. Everything from his intense gray eyes to the confidence with which he moved declared him to be a powerful man. Unfortunately, it was impossible for her to garner a clear impression of whether he would use that power against her.

Some part of her mind told her he wouldn't. After all, he had shown an unexpected concern for her possible injury. That said something for the man.

He was also ruggedly handsome, and that spoke of other matters entirely.

Not even aware that she did so, she let her gaze trace every chiseled line and broad plane of him. He wore his virility like he wore his dark gray jacket, effortlessly, comfortably, undeniably. With his inky black hair and broad shoulders, she was certain that women were his for the taking.

He looked up in that instant and their eyes locked for several seconds. Jessica's pulse leaped into a frantic cadence and she yanked her gaze away.

From where he stood, Nicholas could detect a trace of pink on her cheeks. In a small way, it reassured him that behind her quiet, forlorn little countenance, she was still thinking and reacting.

Settling his shoulder more comfortably against the window frame, he considered her appearance. It was a little difficult to get past the thinness of her, or the shoddiness of her faded blue dress. But she was clean, and as well-groomed as her obvious lack of means would allow.

She had a certain prettiness about her. Lord knew, she had the bluest eyes he had ever seen, and her mouth possessed an appealingly generous curve. For all of that, however, a tired-ness hung over her features like a pall, stripping her of a vitality that would have taken mere prettiness to beauty.

Her hair was arranged in a neat braid coiled about the back of her head. The color was neither red nor blonde, but an intriguing blend of the two. Fine tendrils framed her temples, their wispiness throwing the stark hollows beneath her cheeks into sharp contrast.

Beneath his breath, he swore. She had had a rough time of it. Instantly, he caught himself before he finished the thought and a rueful smile tugged at his lips.

Just like his father, he had always been a soft touch for the weak. Francois DuQuaine had taken in every stray dog and injured bird that had come his way. Nicholas knew himself to be no different. A homeless waif was a homeless waif, and all had the same effect on him, inspiring a protectiveness he couldn't deny. He supposed Jessica McCormick was one more lost little kitten in need.

"This should do it, Nicholas," William said, breaking into his musings.

Nicholas scanned the hastily written agreement and thought on a wry note that this particular little kitten would cost him one thousand dollars. Flicking an assessing glance from Jessica's profile to the avaricious gleam in Ben McCormick's eyes, he signed the paper. Only on an afterthought did he wonder what his father would have had to say about the matter. No doubt Francois DuQuaine would have done the same thing.

"Done, done and done," Ben crowed, pocketing a draft to be drawn on Nicholas's bank. "Glad to have done business with you." Grinning hugely, he rubbed his hands together before making his way to the door. Laughing for all to hear, he exited into the bright sunshine, not giving Jessica another look.

The finality of the door closing jarred her to the bone. She stared at the heavy panel feeling adrift, alone. Not for a second did she wish for her father to return, but the future lay ahead of her like a wilderness. At least with her father, she had known what to expect from her life. It hadn't been exactly pleasant, but it had been familiar, something with which she had learned to cope.

Now, here she stood, the property of Nicholas DuQuaine for the next five years and she was horribly frightened of what that would entail.

"Are you ready?" he asked from directly behind her.

Gasping, she spun and stepped back at the same time. She hadn't heard him approach. "What?" she breathed, every ounce of her dread painfully obvious.

Patiently, Nicholas repeated, "I asked if you were ready."

By sheer will alone, she calmed her breathing and then remembered to answer. "Yes, yes, I'm ready." No, she wasn't. She knew nothing about this man, where he made his home, how he earned his living. Yet because her father had signed his name to a piece of paper, she had no choice but to follow in Nicholas DuQuaine's wake.

"Come along, then." He handed over her bundle of possessions and led the way from the office.

She held the cloth sack to her chest and trailed a full step behind. If that was the proper placement for a servant, she didn't know. He didn't say or do anything to enlighten her. In any event, she didn't worry about the matter for too long. The difference in the length of their strides quickly forced her to concentrate on keeping up.

He might not take kindly to her lagging. She had seen no signs of his possessing the kind of foul temper her father had, but she wasn't going to take any chances. She would do nothing to provoke the man, least of all dally behind.

Head lowered, she hurried along, doing her best to avoid the muddy puddles left over from last night's rain. The frequent glances she sent the broad expanse of his shoulders assured her that she had kept pace. She sighed in relief, only to realize too late that he had stopped without warning. Drawing in a startled breath, she tried to halt her own progress, yet in that second, walked right into him.

"What the devil?" Nicholas exclaimed.

In a whirl of motion, Jessica skittered away, an apology on her lips, dread in her eyes. "I'm sorry."

Nicholas automatically caught her upper arms to steady her. "Easy, there."

She didn't hear the care in his voice any more than she saw the humor curving his mouth. Old habits rode her hard and she yanked back with all her strength.

"Don't!" she cried, fully expecting him to backhand her into next week. She dropped the bundle and pushed futilely at his chest. "I'm sorry. I didn't know you were going to do that. I . . . I didn't know, I'm sorry. . . ."

All trace of Nicholas's humor died. Her fear struck him hard, reminding him of the callousness with which she had been treated. Mentally he strangled Ben McCormick.

With an ease born of pure, masculine strength, he subdued her frantic struggles. "Damn it, Jessica, stop fighting me. I'm not going to hurt you." He lowered his head until he could peer directly into her eyes. "I'm not going to hurt you."

The gray of his eyes drilled into her, the smoky depths delving deep to assuage her abused instincts. Through the haze of her panic, she heard his words and stilled.

Her heart beat rapidly and she was a long way from feeling completely reassured, yet something in his manner set her at ease, at least for the moment. Silently, she lowered her gaze and waited to see if he was as good as his word.

Her quiescence was so sudden and so tense as to be insulting. Nicholas dropped his hands away and stared down at her in frustration. "You need to understand something right now," he commented in a voice hardened by annoyance. "I'm not your father. I've never struck a woman in my life and I'm not about to start with you."

It took her several seconds to get past the tone of his voice to the meaning of his words. When she did, she looked up, her expression of distrust replaced by one of hopeful skepticism.

Nicholas swallowed another curse. "Do you understand?"

"Yes, sir."

"Good. Now let's hurry or we'll miss our boat."

"Boat?" she questioned before she could think better.

"That's right. I've passage booked on the afternoon ship leaving New Orleans. If I'm going to make cabin arrangements for you, we need to make haste."

She was going to be sailing away. To where? From mind to lips, the question came forth. "Where are we going?"

"North of Baton Rouge," he answered. "To my home. Bellefleur."

Chapter Two

Baton Rouge

Bellefleur. The name tripped through Clarice's mind, conjuring up memories that she likened to a clumsy whore. The images of that plantation were far from perfect, but they were better than nothing.

Remembrances from years ago assailed her. She had stood beside her mother, on the lane leading up to the grand plantation house. Together they had stared at the pristine whiteness of the pillared structure surrounded by rolling lawns and acres of fields. The sight had captured her breath, and in the manner of the child she had been, she had pleaded with her mother for a closer look.

Josephine had smiled a sad smile and simply shook her head, that slight gesture saying all that needed to be said; that Bellefleur was not for them. It never would be.

The bitterness of that ate at Clarice's insides, so much so that there were days when it felt as if her stomach held smoldering, glowing coals. No amount of buttermilk or honeyed tea soothed the burning that seemed to reach clear to the marrow of her bones. And no amount of cajoling or reasoning or teasing from anyone alleviated the fury that consumed her mind.

Some of that anger singed her nerves now. She flung aside the gown she had been sewing and crossed to the large window of the dress shop. Shoulders rigid, she wrapped her arms about her waist and stared sightlessly through the glass. Her liquid brown gaze was turned inward to the detestable truth that had forged her past and fashioned her future.

"Octoroon." She spat the word out, its sound in the empty shop sounding hollow. As hollow, she thought, as her life. A brittle laugh escaped her when she considered just how dull and luckless her existence was. She had her mother to thank for that. Her mother and Francois DuQuaine.

"Francois DuQuaine, the once mighty master of Bellefleur." Her voice carried every ounce of resentment she possessed for the man who had given her life and nothing else. Damn his soul. His being dead wasn't good enough for her. If she could have her wish, she would see him alive just so she could stab him through his privileged, aristocratic heart.

She heaved a sigh, and shut her eyes briefly. So much for wishes. Her *father* had been dead for seven years, going to his grave without even knowing about her. To this very day, she had to wonder if things would have been different if he had known. It was far too late for her to know and nothing her mother said had ever given her any clues.

"Are you done already?" the familiar voice asked from behind.

At her mother's entrance into the room crammed with bolts of fabric, Clarice didn't bother to turn. The resentment she felt for the woman was only slightly less than what she felt for Francois DuQuaine. It didn't help that she resembled her mother to such an extraordinary degree.

Both shared the same high cheekbones, curve of lip,

almond-shaped eyes and black hair. Only the color of their skin differed, Josephine's being several tones darker to Clarice's ivory white. She thanked the heavens above for that.

"I'm not done with the dress," she jeered back. "I'm tired, so I took a break."

If Josephine Bouchard heard the scorn in her daughter's voice, she made no comment. Her own voice was as low and smooth as it always was. "Mrs. Cummins will be by shortly for a fittin'."

"Mrs. Cummings can go suck raw eggs," Clarice snorted.

Josephine's honeycolored face creased with a disapproving frown. "I don't like to hear you talk that way."

"Why?" Clarice looked over her shoulder with the single word.

"Because it ain't right."

"The only thing that *ain't right,*" Clarice snorted in disgust, "is the way you bow and scrape and 'yes ma'am' and 'no ma'am' your way around people like Mrs. Cummings."

Josephine picked up the dress Clarice had tossed aside. "It wouldn't hurt you to be a bit more respectful."

"I'm as respectful as I'm going to be to the likes of those bitches that sashay their dimpled asses around town."

"Clarice!"

Clarice ignored the sharp voiced censure and spun to face her mother. "Oh, face facts, Mama. Mrs. Cummings and her kind would just as soon spit on us as *respect* us."

"That ain't so. Mrs. Cummin's is a fine woman."

"Fine, my ass. While her husband's lying ill, ready to meet his maker, she's messing around with any man who will give her a second glance."

"That's none of our business. And it don't have anythin' to do with the way she treats me."

Folding her arms across the generous curves of her chest, Clarice taunted, "And what way is that?"

Josephine lifted her narrow chin and stared her daughter straight in the eye. "Like I matter. Maybe not as much as the next person, but at least like I'm a human bein'. That's more than some folks get."

"And you're satisfied with that?"

"Yes, and you should be, too."

"Well, I'm not. I'm not going to spend the rest of my life catering to them the way you do."

"I earn an honest livin'," Josephine argued in her own defense.

"Now. But it wasn't so long ago that Mrs. Cummings and her like didn't give you any choice but to make your living lying flat on your back."

Josephine gasped, clutching the dress to her chest. A remorse that could not be missed drained the color from her cheeks, the liveliness from her almond-shaped eyes.

"No, I didn't have no choice," she whispered. "I did what I had to do to live, but as soon as I could, I left that way of life behind me. And I saw to it that you had better than me."

Suddenly weary, Clarice threw up her hands. "Please, Mama, I've heard it all before. I've heard how you bought your freedom with the money you made from whoring. I heard how you set up this shop. I heard how you made a place for yourself among the proper folks. I've heard it all, Mama . . . including how you *loved* Francois DuQuaine."

"That's right, I loved him—"

"And he loved you," Clarice finished contemptuously.

"He did."

"Too bad it wasn't the kind of love that lasted forever."

Looking as if her shoulders carried a weighty burden, Josephine crossed to a padded chair and lowered herself with a lassitude that belied her fifty-one years. "Nothin' lasts forever, girl."

"Sure as hell not his attentions to you."

"What could he have done? He was the rich owner of a plantation. He had his own life to go back to."

"That didn't stop him from crawling between your legs whenever he had the urge."

"He was hurtin'. His wife had died. He needed someone to help him through the pain."

"That isn't love, Mama. That's fornicating."

In a twirl of flowered muslin, Josephine surged to her feet. "Don't you go slanderin' what your father and me shared! We loved each other for the time we had. That didn't make it any less real."

"Then why didn't you ever tell him about me?"

"It wouldn't have done no good."

"Maybe not for you, but what about me? Aren't I the daughter of the mighty Francois DuQuaine? Didn't I stand to gain something from that?"

The scoff that worked its way up Josephine's throat was laced with disdain. "Girl, now who ain't facin' facts? You've been starin' at yourself in the mirror for so long, you've forgotten what you are. You may look as white as any lily, but underneath, you still got blood that runs clear back to Africa."

Inside, Clarice felt her stomach begin to blister with a scorching heat. She held her breath briefly in silent self-defense and narrowed her eyes with venomous intent. "Oh, I don't ever forget, Mama. You never let me."

Josephine's eyes drifted shut then slowly opened. "I don't want to argue with you about this," she murmured, her voice laden with heavy remorse. "I love you, Clare. I did what I thought was best for you."

"You didn't think very hard, then."

"I've tried to give you a life you can be proud of." Lifting a hand, Josephine gestured to the room. "I know it ain't much, but one day all of this will be yours, if you want it."

The front door opened, putting a halt to the discussion. But it was far from settled in Clarice's mind. It would never be settled until she had her due.

"Good afternoon, Josephine," Mrs. Cummings declared, sweeping into the shop on the arm of Phillip St. James.

Phillip. Clarice balled her hands into fists. She had heard the rumors that he was Mrs. Cummings's latest lover. She had told herself repeatedly that she didn't give a damn.

She watched him steadily, despising him with a vehemence that ran hotly in her blood. He had once been her lover. Now, he could barely spare her a look. The bastard.

He was handsome enough, with his light brown hair and darker brown eyes. His height and weight were average, but he carried himself with an air that made him appear somehow bigger, more imposing, perhaps even more important than he actually was.

That attitude of prominence had attracted her far more than his handsome face. He was a powerful man who, she had stupidly thought, would be able to take her from the drudgery of her life. He hadn't. He had taken her virginity, enjoyed her for as long as it pleased him and then discarded her with an arrogant laugh and a sneering, "You pathetic little octoroon."

The ache in her stomach intensified, and she swallowed tightly. She had been a fool to pin her hopes on a man. Phillip had taught her that. He had also taught her that if she was ever going to have the kind of life she wanted, she was going to have to get it on her own. And she would, too.

Bellefleur would be hers. That was the dream she took to bed with her each night, the dream she would turn into a reality someday. In the meantime, she had to suffer through the present, tormented by her mother's kowtowing.

Josephine put forth her best smile. "Good afternoon, Mrs. Cummin's. Mr. St. James."

"Isn't this just a lovely day?" the almost-widow asked with a gaiety that never failed to grate on Clarice's nerves.

"Just lovely," Josephine agreed.

"Do you have my dresses ready?" Mrs. Cummings asked, fingering a lazy blonde curl that lay against her neck.

"Of course. All are waitin' for you to try on."

"Marvelous. Isn't that marvelous, Phillip?"

Phillip St. James offered a smile that appeared just a little too brilliant to seem sincere. Clarice mentally scoffed. She had been on the receiving end of that grin often enough to know that a mighty conceit lay at its core.

Rage glistened in her eyes, and she cautiously lowered her gaze to the floorboards in front of her. As far as she was concerned, Phillip St. James was just one more arrogant man in a world full of selfish, arrogant men. Every last one of them used women like they used their horses, for their own pleasure and convenience.

Picturing Mrs. Cummings as a tired, fat, sway-backed nag made Clarice feel a touch better. She smothered a smile and turned to make her way to the fitting room to help Mrs. Cummings into the first of the dresses. Behind her, she heard her mother say, "Why don't you have a seat, Mr. St. James."

Clarice let the curtain fall between the front room and the back, picturing in her mind how her mother would trip over herself to clear a space for the banker, how she would fetch the most comfortable chair.

Her stomach gave her a piercing jab. Damn her mother. Double damn Francois DuQuaine.

She helped Mrs. Cummings disrobe, hiding her animosity

behind a serene expression and a well-tempered composure. It was the latter that allowed her to stand at the ready as the woman spun about for Phillip St. James's inspection.

"What do you think, Phillip?" the blonde asked, eyes aglow with a flirting delight.

"I think you look quite beautiful."

It was obviously what Mrs. Cummings wanted to hear. She craned her neck this way and that, checking her appearance in the long mirror on the wall. "I do look rather marvelous." Giving into a laugh, she smiled first at Phillip and then Josephine.

"You've done wonders with this fabric, Josephine. You were right about the color, but then you're always right about things like this."

"Thank you, ma'am," Josephine returned with open pleasure.

"Oh, don't thank me," Mrs. Cummings countered, waving her hand in a dismissing gesture. "I'm only saying what's true. You're an absolute genius when it comes to clothing."

Clarice's poise slipped. The exchange was everything she despised about her place in life, and for a second she thought that she would gag if she had to watch her mother fall victim to such self-serving acclamation. She sorely wanted to grab her mother by the shoulders and shake her until she realized that Mrs. Cummings's opinion didn't count for anything.

Exercising every bit of self-control she possessed, she again fixed her gaze to a spot on the floor and pulled in on her temper. As much as she wanted to tell every person in the room what she thought of them, she knew it was impossible. For now.

She had to bide her time. She had to plan and think about what she was going to do, for she was not going to spend the rest of her life here.

Her eyes came up to find Phillip St. James leisurely examining the curves of her breasts. She drew in an outraged breath, and his insolent, knowing gaze rose to meet hers.

Oh, no, she was most definitely going to leave Baton Rouge. Where she would go, she didn't precisely know, and it didn't really matter. In the end, she would end up at Bellefleur. One day, that grand plantation with its acres and acres of cotton fields would be hers. That was a vow she was prepared to seal with blood.

As Jessica hastily brushed out her hair, she stared about her tiny, windowless cabin. It was as wide as the length of her bunk built into the wall opposite the door. The only furniture was a wooden chair, and a table nailed to the deck. She had a bucket for water, and a lantern for light.

Meager quarters to be sure, but she didn't mind in the least. Compared to some of the places she and her father had lived, this closet-like room was exceptional. It was clean, it was private, and it had a sturdy lock on the door. She appreciated all three.

In the four days she had been traveling north on the Mississippi, she had spent her time either here in her cabin, or on one of the lower decks where other servants were allowed. She had seen Nicholas DuQuaine for a few minutes every morning. Like clockwork, he would stop by just before breakfast and make sure that she was all right.

Which was why she was now hurrying with her hair. She didn't want to be standing there looking half-baked when he arrived. He probably wouldn't react one way or the other. Still, she still didn't know what would set the man off and what wouldn't. With her father, she never knew. What he overlooked one day upset him the next.

She had no way of judging exactly what time it was, however; she had slept longer this morning than she normally did. From the sounds coming from above, it was already breakfast time, and if Nicholas followed his normal routine he would be knocking soon.

She bent at the waist and brushed the waving curls down from her neck. Clamped between her lips was the ribbon she intended to use to secure the length once it was braided. Hoping the offtimes stubborn mass would cooperate this morning, she hung upside down and took a final swipe of the brush just as the knock came.

Her gaze flying to the door, she straightened quickly enough to flip the entire length away from her face and down her back. "Yes," she called a little breathlessly. "Who is it?"

"It's me, Jessica," Nicholas's voice returned clearly from the other side of the door.

There was nothing she could do with her hair now, and she wouldn't think of keeping him waiting. Brush in one hand, she released the lock and swung the door wide, only then remembering to pull the ribbon from between her lips.

"I'm sorry, I overslept," she began, not quite meeting his gaze as she tried to subdue the tumble of curls. "I'm usually not this careless about things, really I'm not, but for some reason I didn't wake up on time." She paused and chanced a look up at his face.

Her breath caught in her throat. Black brows angled into deep diagonal slashes, he stared at her, his eyes taking in every detail of her appearance. Almost afraid to ask, she whispered, "What? What is it?" But she truly didn't want to know; didn't want to hear his reproach or anger or scorn.

Unconsciously, she took a step backward, holding her breath.

Nicholas blinked at the movement and only then realized

that he had been staring. He hadn't been able to help himself. She normally had her hair tucked up in a braided coil. He hadn't envisioned it in any other way, had damn well not even thought about what the red-gold curls might look like all loose and flowing about her.

The sight had caught him completely off guard. There was something extremely sensual about the shining strands that accentuated her as a woman as nothing else ever could have. For the first time, on a very personal level, he saw her not so much as his bonded servant, but as the young woman she was.

He searched her face again, then quickly swallowed an oath. She couldn't hide her trepidation, and it all but slapped him in the face with two very real truths; one, his reaction had frightened her, and two, he had no business thinking of her as anything other than a servant.

"You don't need to apologize for anything," he said more gruffly than he intended. "It isn't as though you have any duties to keep you busy."

Little by little, Jessica let go of the tension that had held her balanced to flee. Once again, he had not resorted to using his fists. She sighed in relief, fingering the brush she still held.

"I . . . wanted to be done before you got here."

"Because you thought I'd get angry if you weren't."

The nod she gave was accompanied by a one-shouldered shrug.

"Because that was what you could have expected from your father."

There was no need for her to make excuses to him. He had seen a small sample of how her father had treated her. "Yes, sir. He is a very angry man."

Nicholas already knew that, and it galled him to be classed

with a bastard like Ben McCormick. Yet in her mind, he, and most likely all men were.

"I suppose this is going to take time," he mused softly enough to disguise his annoyance.

"What is?"

"Your coming to trust men not to hurt you."

In soothing, mellow tones he had put voice to the heart of her fear. She *didn't* have any faith when it came to men. Oh, part of her understood that they weren't all cut from the same cloth as her father, but a deeper part of her mind, the part that remembered every painful blow he had ever given her, had no cause to listen to reason.

As a whole, men were larger, stronger, more powerful. At any given moment, they could inflict pain on anyone or anything smaller, weaker or less forceful. That was the truth of things as she saw it and she had few experiences in her life to contradict that truth.

For some reason, Nicholas DuQuaine seemed to understand how she felt. No one had ever delved into her most secret thoughts before, certainly not a man. Uncomfortable, horribly insecure, she looked away from his too-knowing gaze.

There it was again, Nicholas thought. That vulnerable bearing that wiped the color from her face and changed the blue of her eyes to a deep, dark gray. It was the exact same expression he had seen on her face in William Wyatt's office.

Damn it all to hell! How was he supposed to deal with this kind of dread? More importantly, how could she? Irritated that he didn't have any answers, he turned to a matter that would prove less unsettling, the matter that had brought him to her in the first place.

Keeping the frustration from his voice he asked, "Any problems during the night?"

She was glad for the customary question. "No, sir, I was very comfortable."

He digested that for a bit longer than might have been necessary. "Do you need anything?"

"No, sir." Even if she did, she would never have dreamed of asking.

"All right, then."

She watched him leave before shutting the door, feeling that their relationship was back on its normal course. How it had gone astray was a bit of a mystery, but she sensed that for a few minutes it had definitely wandered from that of master and servant.

It was something she pondered through the morning and well into the afternoon. Through breakfast of biscuits and grits, she tried to sort through all that had been said. By the time she was standing at the rail on the lower deck of the steamboat, she decided that Nicholas DuQuaine lay at the heart of the matter. His questions had been too probing, too keen.

"Enjoying the view?"

At the sound of his voice, she spun and stared up at him in astonishment. She had been thinking about him, and now, there he stood, for the second time in one day. It was very disconcerting, made even more so by the fact that he was so superbly handsome.

She wasn't one to normally consider a man's appearance, but from the very start she hadn't been able to overlook his tall figure and dynamic features. Standing in the bright light of day, the combination was all the more startling, making her uncomfortably conscious of him.

"Hello," was all she said.

He stepped to the rail beside her. He hadn't meant to seek her out in this manner, or any manner. The day had slipped by, though, and he hadn't been able to get her out of his mind. He had pictured her again and again as she had looked that morning; red-gold curls framing a narrow little face, cascading over the subtleness of her curves. But after all, it was only natural that he should dwell on her. She was his responsibility, his servant. As her master, as one human being to another, he was concerned about her.

Or so he told himself.

"I thought you might be here."

She glanced about a little nervously. "It is all right, isn't it?"

"Of course. I don't expect you to confine yourself to your room for the entire journey."

Hearing him put it in those terms did make the prospect sound absurd. She relaxed and offered a wavering smile. "No, I suppose not. Even though the room is very nice, I like to watch the river go by. I've never been on a boat before."

"No?" He braced both forearms on the rail and studied the forested shoreline in the distance. "Where are you from?"

She hesitated for only a second or two, confused by his attention. "Georgia, originally. After my mother died, we . . . uhm . . . we traveled." That was the most polite way of explaining the transient nature of her life.

"You and your father?"

"And my sister, too."

His head snapped toward her suddenly, his gaze piercing. "You have a sister?"

"No, not any longer," she hastened to explain, seeing his sharp interest. "Bethy is dead."

The memory of that still made her ache inside. Little Beth with her bright yellow curls and somber blue eyes had been a sweet, delicate soul, too fragile to resist the fever that had taken hold of her. Within a week, she had died just one day short of her twelfth birthday.

"We were in Savannah at the time," she said, sadness tinging her voice. "It took us more than a week to carry her back to Atlanta to be buried next to Mama."

"How long ago was this?"

"Two years."

Nicholas nodded before turning his attention back to the river's edge. "How did you end up in New Orleans?"

Her bittersweet memories of Beth were quickly replaced by more recent recollections of her father. The full curve of her mouth thinned. "Father was always looking for an easy way to make money. Sometimes that involved gambling."

Nicholas nodded. "It makes sense that he would try his luck in New Orleans, then. It's difficult to take three paces without bumping into a card game somewhere."

"Father had heard he could make a fortune there."

"Instead he lost?"

"A great deal." An illogical wave of embarrassment swept through her. She hadn't been in any way responsible for her father's actions, and it certainly wasn't her fault that she had been sold to pay a gambling debt. But she couldn't control the sense of disgrace she felt about the entire incident.

Hoping to leave the matter at that, she pursed her lips and examined the churning water below with special care. Unfortunately, Nicholas didn't appear to want to let the topic rest. From the corner of her eye, she could see him staring at her with a look of dawning amazement.

"Is that why he indentured you? So he could have enough money to throw away in a damned game of chance?"

She picked at a tiny patch of peeling paint on the rail and sighed. "No. He had already lost the money. The only way he could pay it back was to—"

"Sell his own daughter," Nicholas cut in through clenched teeth. Damn it all to hell and back! He wished for five minutes, just five short minutes with Ben McCormick.

Her gaze jerked up to his. He was angry. If the tone of his voice didn't tell her that then his narrowed-eyed glare did. Dismay rose up in her in one encompassing wave. Instinct took over, disregarding logic and human decency. Frantically, she thought of how to best protect herself as he straightened from the rail.

"Pray that your father and I never cross paths again," he spat.

For the space of two heartbeats, Jessica remained still, as confused as she was fearful. She didn't like the cutting edge in his voice nor the glint of steel in the gray of his eyes. Both were enough to send a chill up her spine.

She flicked a glance to his hands. The long fingers were curled into fists, yet his hands remained at his sides. She continued to stare and finally understood what he had said.

He was angry at her father, not at her.

"If you need anything, let me know," he told her. Not giving her another look, he turned and strode away.

Too shocked to do more than watch him walk off, Jessica pressed shaking fingers to her lips. In all her life, she had never encountered a man like Nicholas DuQuaine, and she didn't know what to do, what to think.

That a handsome, powerful man would bother himself about her was amazing. Yet he had and for no reasons that she could discern. She could only ask herself why.

Chapter Three

Ben McCormick should be strung up by his balls and left out to dry.

That thought repeated itself again and again in Nicholas's mind for the next three days. Every time he thought back on his conversation with Jessica, his hand would curl into a fist.

The more he learned about Jessica's father, the more he was tempted to hunt the bastard down. Logically he understood that McCormick had had every right to treat his daughter any way he damn well pleased, but that justification didn't go far in assuaging Nicholas's anger.

As the steamboat carried him past Baton Rouge, north of Natchez, ever closer to Bellefleur, he took great satisfaction from knowing that Jessica belonged to him now, at least for the next five years. And for reasons that were rooted in self-respect and pure male pride, he would see that she was never harmed again. What was his, he took care of, whether it was one of his slaves, his land or his house.

That sense of purpose was an ingrained part of him. He normally never gave it conscious thought, but standing on the upper deck of the steamboat, watching the shores of Bellefleur slowly come into view, he was curiously aware of the streak of protectiveness he had inherited from his father and his father before him.

Bellefleur. A smile stretched the line of his mouth as he gladly relinquished his contemplations for the sheer gladness that wrapped itself about his heart. He had journeyed from the plantation often. Yet no matter how many times he returned, he still felt the most gratifying sense of welcome whenever he looked upon the line of cypress trees that hid the land from view. Behind those trees lay everything that held any meaning for him. His heritage, his future, his life, his home. Bellefleur.

Without realizing it, his gaze stroked over the stretch of shoreline that was his, the gray of his eyes softening to a deep smoky pewter. Like a man visually caressing the contours of a beautiful woman, he studied the shifting colors of water meeting land, and the sharp contrast of the wooden dock jutting out into the river.

The protectiveness of which he had been so aware earlier, descended upon him like a flow of energy to permeate his muscles. He simply accepted it, this urge to care for the land. He couldn't remember a time when needing to insure its continuance hadn't been part of him. Perhaps this absorption had been inbred, a trait not learned at his father's knee. If so, he wouldn't have had it any other way.

With all the shuddering vibrations and resounding noise of shoring up, the steamboat eventually stopped at the dock. Before Nicholas had even descended to the second deck, people had gathered on the shore, hands waving, faces smiling. Among those faces, Nicholas could see his driver, Simon.

"Welcome home, Mast' DuQuaine," the round black man called as the gangplank was lowered.

Nicholas lifted a hand to his forehead in a ritual salute he had come to share with Simon. In return, Simon beamed a bright smile and lifted his straw hat from his head. The little custom made Nicholas shake his head in wry humor. Simon had never, and probably *would* never forsake his special greeting. For all of its paltry insignificance in the grand scheme of things, it made Nicholas all the more glad to be home.

Wanting to be standing on his land with all haste, he glanced about at the people milling on deck. He spotted Jessica at once and motioned her over.

She came forward quickly, her bundle held securely in her arms . . . perhaps a little too securely. She clutched the sack as if it were her lifeline to sanity.

Nicholas lowered his head until he could peer directly into her eyes. "Are you all right?"

The nod she gave said yes. The wide rounding of her eyes said differently.

She was nervous, he realized with a shock. What for him had been a sublime experience had set her nerves to trembling. "There's nothing to be afraid of."

Jessica wanted to believe that. It was difficult, however. With her first step on to this plantation, she knew her life would be forever changed. The thought made the knot in her throat tighten.

"Come along," Nicholas said.

Swallowing repeatedly, she followed behind him, taking what comfort she could from the sight of his broad shoulders. Up ahead, a group of what she assumed were slaves crowded about the lane leading inland from the dock.

A black man separated himself from the others and came forward. "Welcome home, welcome home, Mast' DuQuaine."

"Thank you, Simon," Nicholas returned, giving the man an affectionate slap on the back.

Simon shifted from one foot to the other, redistributing his hefty weight with ease. "Miz Anna been near to runnin' in circles, makin' sure ever'thin' just right for your comin' home."

Nicholas laughed. "My sister is always running in circles, Simon." With a broad wink, he added, "But don't tell her I said so."

A deep rumbling chuckle shook Simon's frame. "No sir, not me, no sir." The dark brown gaze slid from Nicholas to Jessica in obvious curiosity.

"Simon, this is Jessica McCormick," Nicholas explained. "She'll be working with us for a while."

"Don't say?" Simon mused, his eyes rounding in genuine interest. "Well, you's goin' to like Bellefleur, yes, girl, you are."

In all her life, Jessica had never met anyone as friendly as Simon. His smile was wide and toothy, and seemed to be permanently fixed to his face.

"Hello," she said, giving him a bit of his own good humor.

Simon tipped his head to one side. "You feelin' peaked or somethin', Jess, girl? You lookin' a little peaked."

"It's been a long trip for both of us," Nicholas answered.

"I hear you, Mast' DuQuaine. I hear you." Simon nodded to a pile of luggage stacked at the end of the dock. "Let me get your things and we'll be on our way in no time, in no time a'tall."

Simon was as good as his word. In a matter of minutes, Jessica found herself seated beside Nicholas in a small open carriage, Simon at the reins. Curious, she took in her first sight of the landscape that was to define her home for the next five years.

To either side of the winding lane, trees grew in lush abundance, draped in heavy mantles of silvery moss. Despite the fact that spring was at least a month away, the green of vegetation lay in every direction, mixed with yellow hues of budding growth. The colors were pleasing, redolent of the recent and saturated with promise of the future.

To her unpracticed eye, the forests looked as if they had lain undisturbed for centuries. At a quick glance, she could see no signs of trees having been felled, no bare plots that had been cleared. For some reason, she liked the notion of such undisturbed continuity, such unrelenting permanence.

She gave a small smile just as the carriage cleared the trees and instantly, her one-sided grin was transformed into a gasp of wonder. Brilliant light poured down directly from above and shone on a house such as she had never seen before.

"Oh, my goodness," she breathed in awe, unable to look anywhere but at the pristine white structure.

"I shall take that as a compliment," Nicholas commented from beside her, pride evidenced in his every word.

A trifle embarrassed at having voiced her wonderment, she exhaled raggedly, but there was no dampening the admiration shining clearly in the crystal blue of her eyes. "It's beautiful."

But the word seemed inadequate to describe the grand, two-story mansion with it double porticoes marching the full length of the house. *Beautiful* didn't do justice to the eight magnificent columns nor the twin, curved stairways that formed a lazy horseshoe.

No, *beautiful* was only a mundane appraisal, failing miserably to express the essence of the structure that went far beyond wood and brick and mortar. An aura of abundance, of bountiful heritage and enduring decency emanated from the structure and reached clear into Jessica's soul. Home in the purest and most excellent meaning of the word came to mind, and that could never be summed up in so simple a word as *beautiful*.

By slow degrees, she became aware of the live oaks that

stood majestically to either side of the house, the wide, manicured lawn that would grow plush in the summer, and the scent of newly turned earth that encompassed it all. Glimpses of the outbuildings on the land side, and beyond them the fields, gave hints of the grandeur that awaited her.

Taken in its entirety, the scene brought Jessica to tears.

She blinked rapidly, feeling foolish at her helpless display. Hoping to gather her composure, she turned her head away, but not quickly enough. Nicholas reached out and caught her chin in his hand.

"What the devil is this about?" he demanded, concern as well as dubious humor furrowing his brow.

Hastily, she wiped at a tear that refused to be blinked away. What a fool she was, giving into such emotion. He was going to think her an idiot. For the life of her, though, she had been swept away from herself.

"I . . . I've never seen . . ." That sounded ridiculous, she silently scolded herself.

The humor left Nicholas's face and he stared at her with an intensity that frayed the composure she was so valiantly trying to restore. His fingers at her chin lingered, the light touch somehow becoming possessive.

Slowly, his smile returned, softening his expression. "I haven't met a person yet who didn't think the house was impressive," he commented, dropping his hand, "but no one I know has ever cried about the matter."

She stared down at her lap. How could she explain the emotion behind her tears when she wasn't certain she understood it herself? "I didn't mean to do that."

"Don't apologize. I—" But there his words were cut off as the carriage pulled to a stop in front of the house and a young woman hurried down one set of stairs.

"It's about time you came home," she declared teasingly.

At the first word of the remarkably melodious voice, Jessica turned her attention from Nicholas to watch the woman's joyous face.

"I haven't been gone all that long," Nicholas returned, stepping down from the carriage.

The woman laughed. "Only long enough for me to miss the odor of those obnoxious cigars you insist on smoking from time to time."

"Well, you have missed me, then. I'm impressed, Anna." Nicholas circled in front of the horses in time to catch Anna's exuberant hug.

With Simon's help, Jessica stepped down from the carriage, all the while keeping her gaze fixed on the pair. On first seeing the woman, Jessica had wondered if she might have been Nicholas's wife. Even though he had never mentioned whether he was married or not, it had been a natural assumption for her to make.

Then she remembered that Simon had referred to Anna as Nicholas's sister and Jessica saw the marked resemblance that declared the two to be siblings. Anna possessed the same black hair, gray eyes and high cheekbones as her brother. However, that was where the similarity ended, for Anna appeared to be as feminine as Nicholas was masculine.

Her deep blue muslin dress showed to advantage the slender curve of her waist and the full contour of her breasts. Movements as languid and graceful as the honeyed smoothness of her voice marked her every move.

She was lovely, Jessica thought, all smiles and charm and magnolia-blossom skin. And obviously dearly loved by Nicholas.

"Who is this?" Anna asked, catching Jessica's eye without warning.

Nicholas came around to Jessica's side. "Jessica McCormick. She's indentured to me for the next five years."

"Indent . . . ?" Anna caught herself, looking from Nicholas to Jessica and back again in such blatant shock that Jessica had the distinct impression that having an indentured servant about was most unusual.

Patiently, Nicholas placed his finger beneath Anna's chin and urged her parted lips closed. "Later," was all he said.

It was obvious enough. Anna recovered at once and turned back to Jessica. "Well, I should see that you get settled."

"I thought we could give her the spare storage room on the first floor," Nicholas said.

Again, Anna seemed taken aback, but just as quickly as before, proceeded with utter composure. "You're right. That would be perfect, although it will have to be cleaned. And we'll have to move some furniture in."

"Get Mama Lou on that right away."

Anna tapped a finger against her lips, already giving the matter a great deal of thought. "We can bring down one of the spare beds from the attic, and we'll have to air out a mattress at once if it's going to be fit to sleep on before tonight." She turned toward the front door and called out, "Mama Lou," then continued without missing a beat. "Bed linens; I'll have Betsy see to those. And a chair and one of those small tables we were going to donate to the church." She paused long enough to slant an annoyed looking brow at Nicholas. "Really, Nicholas, I wish you would have sent word. I could have seen to this before you arrived. But there's no help for it now. Mama Lou!"

Jessica watched in fascination as Anna DuQuaine worked herself into an enthusiastic fuss, and all over the simple matter of arranging for a place to sleep.

This was not at all what she had expected. She hadn't

known what was to await her at Bellefleur, but it was not this kind of attention.

"Jessica, why don't you come with me," Anna suggested kindly. "We'll see what we can do about your room."

Her own room. Her very own room. It was almost beyond Jessica's imagination. Feeling as though she had just stepped into a dream, she gave Nicholas a fleeting glance and quickly followed Anna up the stairs and into the house.

"This is the front drawing room," Anna explained, waving a graceful hand to indicate the spacious interior.

If Jessica thought the outside of the house was a marvel to behold, the inside only intensified that wonder. Splendid pieces of furniture were arranged in comfortable settings. Deep green drapes dressed the windows and complimented the pale yellow walls and the yellow pine floors.

"We use this room on an informal basis," Anna explained as she headed for a door at the left side of the room. "Through here is Nicholas's library."

Close behind, Jessica made her way into the book-lined room, then actually came to a stop in her tracks. Books everywhere, from floor to ceiling. The pattern of rows and rows was broken only by two long windows on the front wall, and a door on each of the three other walls.

In the middle of the room was a huge desk and several wine colored leather chairs. All were set on a tightly woven carpet whose colors matched the chairs and the swags on the windows.

It was definitely a room Nicholas DuQuaine would use. From every corner, it seemed to shout of a masculine presence that was so much a part of its owner.

"In here," Anna prompted, opening the door opposite the windows, "is the plantation office and next to that, at long last, is the room that you shall have." Anna propped her hands on her waist and added to herself, "As soon as we make it liveable."

From the library came the sound of a woman calling. "Miz Anna, who you talkin' to?"

"In here, Mama Lou," Anna called back.

The woman who belonged to the voice appeared in the open doorway in moments. "What are you doin' in here, Miz Anna? I heard you shoutin' all the way from the front steps."

Anna sighed and rolled her laughing eyes. "Nicholas has finally come home, and has brought us a new servant. This is Jessica."

Jessica remained silent and unmoving under the tall black woman's intense regard, and made a few observations of her own. Mama Lou was an austere looking woman. Buxom and broad shouldered, she had a no-nonsense air about her that was evidenced in the lift of her long chin and the set of her wide mouth. Definitely not a woman to cross.

"Jessica, Mama Lou is our housekeeper," Anna commented a little distractedly. She had already begun inspecting a stack of boxes set beneath the window.

Jessica nodded politely.

Mama Lou's face took on a skeptical cast. "Servant? Lord, girl, you don't look hardy enough to lift a hand. The first good wind that comes along would blow you into the next county. How old are you?"

"Seventeen."

"What kinda servant are you?"

The question widened Jessica's eyes. "I . . . I don't know."

A rumbling sort of growl emanated from the housekeeper's chest. "You been a lady's maid or a kitchen helper, laundress or what?"

Jessica caught her lower lip between her teeth before answering. "Since I was nine, I cooked and cleaned and sewed for my father, but I've never been anyone's servant before."

Surprisingly, Mama Lou laughed with enough humor to set her ample breasts to quivering. "Girl, you been servin' for the better part of your life and you didn't even know it. What does the master plan for you?"

Anna responded. "I haven't had a chance to talk to Nicholas yet, but he suggested that Jessica should have this room while she's here."

"If that's what he wants, then we better get on it." Mama Lou scrutinized the room as thoroughly as she had Jessica. "Where you want to move them things, Miz Anna?"

The end result of the question led to a thorough cleaning of the storage room. Jessica was put to work immediately helping Mama Lou and a young house girl, Betsy. Anna supervised with an easy poise that Jessica rapidly realized typified Anna's manner. Nonetheless, that the mistress of the plantation would personally involve herself in something as menial as readying a room for a servant simply amazed Jessica.

In quick order, Jessica learned the outlay of the house. To her surprise, the ground floor had no hallways. The house was four rooms long and two rooms wide. Every room had doors that led to another room beside it or behind it. The middle of the house was dominated by the front drawing room that faced the river and its near duplicate, which overlooked the circular drive winding inland from the county lane.

The second story held another eight rooms, four to each side of a long, central corridor that ran the length of the house. Above was the attic, an impressive space used for storage.

Jessica lost track of the number of times she passed from

what was soon to be her room, through the plantation office to the stairway situated between the back parlor and the dining room, carrying boxes and stores to and from the attic. But in slightly more than two hours, the first floor storage room was transformed into a living quarters, complete with a braided rug on the floor.

Narrow bed in place, window opened to let in the fresh air, Mama Lou stood with arms akimbo while Anna smiled in satisfaction.

"I never knew this room had such potential," Anna commented. "Papa always used it to keep extra supplies on hand, but I swear it's been wasted all these years."

"Made up real nice," Mama Lou agreed before she caught Betsy staring listlessly out the window. "I swear, Betsy," she grumbled, "if you had to haul ass, you'd have to make two trips."

Betsy looked up, a grimace spreading across her deep brown face. "Sorry, Mama Lou."

"You are that. A sorrier piece of work I ain't never seen."

"I'm tryin' my best."

Mama Lou humphed her opinion on the matter. "That's what I'm afraid of. Get yourself upstairs and clean out the grate in the master's room before I forget I'm a Christian woman."

Betsy twined her hands in her apron and did as she was told.

Jessica nibbled on her lower lip at the exchange. It had taken her all of ten seconds to realize that Mama Lou took her duties as housekeeper very seriously. The woman expected nothing less than perfection. Jessica had to wonder if that was a natural trait or one learned to satisfy Anna's demand for excellence.

Giving Anna a brief glance, Jessica acknowledged the fact

that behind the serene loveliness, Anna DuQuaine was a determined, forceful young woman who took extreme pride in her home.

"You hungry, girl?" Mama Lou asked in a voice that had lost none of its severity.

At the sharp query, Jessica stiffened out of sheer reflex. She didn't want to make any trouble for anyone, but it was difficult to ignore the hunger eating at her backbone. She hesitated for a long second, gazing intently at the tall housekeeper and decided that under Mama Lou's gruff tone lay a humane sentiment that was far more than anything she had ever received from her father. He had never given a damn if she had eaten or not.

"Yes, I'm hungry."

"Then take yourself out to kitchen and tell Pearl to give you somethin'. That don't mean for you to dawdle. When you finish up, you come find me here in the house. By then, we'll see if the master's decided what he's goin' to do with you."

Chapter Four

"Are you going to tell me about her?" Anna asked, gliding up to Nicholas where he sat at his desk.

She watched her brother lean back in his chair and give her a smile that could only be described as indulgent.

"I suppose you mean Jessica."

"You know that's who I mean."

He sighed and laced his fingers together over his chest. "What do you want to know?"

Anna tilted her head to one side. "To begin with, where did you find her?"

"New Orleans. Why?"

"Well, you left here for a few weeks of vacation and you return with a servant, an indentured servant, Nicholas. There hasn't been an indentured servant here since *Grand-pere's* time."

"I know."

Her eyes narrowed. "I sense a 'but' is forthcoming."

Nicholas shrugged with his brows. "*But* if you had seen what her circumstances were, you would have done the same."

Anna knew her brother well. She understood better than

anyone how compassionate he could be, especially to the downtrodden. Pursing her lips, she took a seat in one of the leather chairs opposite the desk. "How bad was it?" she asked solemnly, noting the glint of anger that flashed in Nicholas's gaze.

"Her father was trying to sell her to pay off a gambling debt."

"What?" Anna felt her stomach wrench. "Her own father?"

An expression of distaste lined his face. "By the way, that is a generous description of the bastard. When he wasn't trying to barter her to the highest bidder, he was giving her his fist."

Anna's dismay turned to anger. She had known nothing but love and care from her own father, and mother. It sickened her to hear of such callous treatment of a parent toward a child.

"You were right to bring her here."

With a nod, Nicholas acknowledged her agreement. "I thought you would see it that way."

"Have you given any thought to what she'll do?"

"I have. I want her working in the house."

In a gesture very much like the one Nicholas had given, Anna raised her brows in inquiry.

"You've seen her," he answered, lifting a hand in silent emphasis. "She's downright skinny, even for a little bit of a thing. She won't last a day in the fields. Unless you feel differently, we don't need another soul working in the kitchen or the laundry or even the dairy. She can work here in the house."

"She already has."

"Oh?"

"She and Betsy cleaned out the storage room."

Nicholas swore under his breath. "Betsy. Is she still made of molasses?"

A shaming grin pulled at Anna's lips. "You haven't been gone that long, Nick."

"No, I suppose not."

"Don't be too hard on Betsy. She's a good worker."

"If you can ever get her going."

"It was you who decided that she be a maid."

"You don't have to remind me."

Anna laughed at her brother's discomfort. Betsy was just one more example of her brother's compassionate nature hard at work. Most of day to day life was beyond Betsy's capabilities. Sweet-tempered, anxious to please, the girl always did her best . . . at a pace that would put a turtle to shame.

Most men in Nicholas's position would have sold the girl and been done with the entire matter. Not Nicholas. Betsy's entire family lived on Bellefleur and Nicholas never, *never* broke up families.

"Don't worry about Betsy. With Jessica's help, perhaps she'll improve."

Nick steepled his fingers as he considered the suggestion. "I think you're right. This will work out fine. As slow as Betsy is about things, it'll help to have Jessica with her."

Anna couldn't argue. That settled, she turned to a more amusing topic. "So, did you enjoy yourself in the big, wicked city?" she teased.

A very male smile curled about Nicholas's face. "What do you know about wickedness?"

"Nothing, but that doesn't mean I don't want to learn."

"You'll get in trouble with ideas like that, little sister."

She fluttered her eyelashes as she raised one shoulder in a pretty shrug. "I think I could stand a little trouble."

"Ladies don't get into trouble."

"Spoken like a true man who is allowed his share of *trouble.*"

He shook his head with irritating insouciance. "I'm not about to give you lurid details."

"Why not?"

The query earned her a deep-throated chuckle. "I see things around here have been quiet while I was gone."

Sighing heavily, Anna rolled her eyes. "Dull is more accurate."

Nicholas stood and came around to lean back against the front of his desk. "Don't worry. As soon as planting begins, life will improve."

"I hope so. I'm anxious for spring."

"You say the same thing every winter, Anna."

That was true, she had to admit; that didn't mean, however, that she felt any less adamant about the matter. Even though the winter was mild, she spent most of her time indoors. She still had duties and responsibilities, to which she gladly, wholeheartedly applied herself, but it seemed that the relative inactivity served to point out how stagnant her existence was.

She didn't like the sensation of standing still. At nineteen years of age she should be getting on with her life. She wanted to experience a little adventure, she wanted a husband and children, love and laughter. She wanted it all, most especially the love. She didn't want a marriage without love.

There was no telling when or if any of that was ever going to occur. Thus far, she had had her share of parties and sojourns to Baton Rouge. None of those, however, had brought her closer to fulfilling her dreams and she was growing impatient with waiting, with the uncertainty of things.

The only certainty she could count on was the piece of land she had inherited from her grandmother. Seven hundred acres of prime field adjoining Bellefleur and worked right along with the rest of the plantation. The legacy had been hers from birth, and she fully intended to pass it on to her own daughter. If she ever had one.

"You're going to hurt yourself," Nicholas commented.

Anna shook herself mentally. "What?"

"You're going to hurt yourself if you keep thinking that way."

"Oh, you." For good measure, she stuck her tongue out at him. "You have no idea what I was thinking. And stop trying to ignore my original question. Did you have a good time in New Orleans?"

"Yes, I did. And I even managed to take care of a little business."

She eyed him curiously. "Did you?"

He made a murmurous sound of assent, his entire bearing becoming more sober in that instant. "Cotton prices are expected to remain at eleven cents a pound. I had hoped that we could have expected better this year, but at least there won't be a decline."

Which Anna knew was good news, indeed. There were years when the price of cotton dropped as low as six cents a pound. By the time a planter accounted for his initial investment, he could be lucky for a profit of five percent. With prices holding steady again this year, Nicholas, and every other planter up and down the Mississippi and the Red, could expect a sizable profit.

"This should be a good year, then."

One of Nicholas' brows arched. "As good as any we've had, barring rain or drought or insects or hurricanes or . . ."

Coming to her feet, Anna sighed, "Enough, Nick." He was being nothing less than honest, but Bellefleur had withstood all the elements and then some, and had always managed to survive. Part of the success of that lay with the men in the family, from great-grandfather Raynard right down to Nicholas. Each had a soul-deep commitment to the land that was almost humbling. Were Nick to cut his arm, it would bleed Bellefleur.

The other part of the success of the plantation was Bellefleur itself. Twenty-five hundred acres of rich, fertile earth. It seemed to have a kind of energy of its own, changing and growing from season to season, year to year, yet remaining steadfast and durable.

"*Now* what are you thinking?" Nicholas asked when her silence grew.

She smiled, feigning a snobbish mien she was far from feeling. "I shall keep that a secret."

"You're being awfully saucy for someone who was only moments ago complaining of boredom."

Her nose elevated. "And you're awfully impertinent for someone who has been home only a few hours. If you want your dinner on time, you had best mind your manners."

"You're sounding more and more like *Maman.*"

With a swish of her blue skirt, she made her way to the side door connecting to the front drawing room. "And just like *Maman,* I see right through your charm and cajolery."

Nicholas's laughter trailed behind her, bringing an answering curve to her own lips. It truly was good to have him home. The house seemed too quiet and still without him, as though it had lost its heart in his absence.

She continued on into the back drawing room, exiting the house through a wide central door. The kitchen lay situated off to the right at the end of a brick-paved path. It was there that Anna was headed to check on Jessica.

The sound of an approaching horse checked her progress. Lifting a hand to shade her eyes against the sun, she recognized the rider as Mathew Bennett. Questions as to why their friend and nearest neighbor would come calling quickly formed in her mind. The answer she settled on was that word of Nick's arrival had already spread upriver as far as Mathew's plantation, Hartford Grove.

"Hello, Mathew," she called, leaving the path for the drive.

Mathew Bennett reined in his gelding and lifted his hat respectfully. The blond of his hair reflected gold in the sun's rays.

"Afternoon, Anna."

"I would ask what brings you here, but I can guess."

"Oh?"

"Nicholas is in the library. I know he'll be glad to see you."

"How can you be so sure of that?" he asked, his brows lowering over serious blue eyes.

"He's always glad to see you, Mathew. You're his best friend."

For what seemed an inordinately long time, that serious blue gaze rested on her face. Anna was half-tempted to lift a hand and check if she had a smudge across a cheek. Instead, she dismissed the notion. Mathew Bennett had been giving her that exact same look for months and months now. If she didn't know better, she would say he needed to be fitted with a pair of spectacles.

"He'll want to tell *you* about his trip to New Orleans," she said, watching him tether his horse to the wrought iron post nearby.

Obviously hearing the odd emphasis behind her statement, Mathew slanted her a curious look. "Is there some reason he wouldn't confide in me?"

"Certainly not. It's me he won't say a word to."

Mathew strode to her side, his expression more serious than usual. "I'm sure he has his reasons, Anna."

"Of that I have no doubt. He's being his typical self, acting the big brother, thinking he can protect me from whatever the world has to offer."

"That is what a brother should do, especially when there is no father about to see to your welfare."

It was the very kind of staid comment she would have expected from Mathew, the same kind of safe, comfortable remark she had heard from him ever since she had known him. Offered with good intentions, it nevertheless served to prick her ire.

Unable to keep the impatience from her voice, she said, "It's no wonder you and Nick are such good friends, Mathew. You think so much alike."

"There's no need for you to take offense, Anna."

She led him up the stairs and into the drawing room, her irritation beginning to spiral in on itself. "If you didn't want me to take offense, then you shouldn't have said something to offend me."

Hands spread wide, Mathew asked, "What did I say?"

"It's what you didn't say," she explained, not explaining anything at all. How could she possibly make him, and her brother, understand that she didn't want to be protected until she knew what it was she was being protected from? She wanted to make up her own mind about life, and not forsake her opinions to their charge.

"You and Nick might be shocked to know that I'm not going to melt into a puddle of offended sensibilities at the mention of the word gambling or brothel or . . ." she paused to spin about and pin him with a heated glare ". . . whore. I have heard those words before, I know what they mean. I also know that my brother is man enough to not only comprehend their definitions but to utilize them to the fullest extent of his masculinity."

Mathew's normally tanned face took on a reddish tint. "Anna, you're upsetting yourself."

She looked him straight in the eye. "No, you and Nick are upsetting me."

By the second, Mathew was becoming increasingly more solicitous, and it plainly showed all over his hard-jawed face. "Do you think you should lie down? Do you want me to send for Mama Lou?"

Anna clamped her mouth shut, her gray eyes nearly black. For such a handsome man, Mathew Bennett was too obtuse for words. Shaking her head, she stared at the grim line of his mouth, the concern in his blue eyes, the rigid set of his broad shoulders and wondered what he would do if she were to hit him over the head with the nearest vase. Probably nothing more than cautiously flick the shards of glass from his jacket, pat her on the head and excuse the entire matter as some kind of mental anxiety brought on by her monthly affliction.

"No, I don't need to lie down," she got out from between stiff lips. "I'm going back out to the kitchen. You can find Nick in his library."

She turned on her heel, just as Nick stepped into the room.

"Did I hear my name?"

Mathew grimaced as Anna slammed the door, then heaved a sigh.

Nick looked from the abused door to his friend. "Do I want to know what that was all about?"

A little helplessly, Mathew turned to Nick. "I'm not quite sure myself. One minute we were talking about your trip to New Orleans and the next she was going on about sensibilities and whores."

"Whores?" Nick could not suppress his smile. "She really got her dander up this time."

"But I've never been on the receiving end of it."

That surprised Nick as much as it amused him. "No? You mean after all these years, this is the first time she's loosed that temper on you?"

"You needn't sound so pleased about it."

"Sorry. I'm just glad it was you instead of me."

Still wearing the bemused lines of a man who had weathered a sudden, unexpected storm, Mathew gave the door another glance. "Is she always like that?"

"Like what?" Nick's nonchalance was genuine. He was well accustomed to Anna's deep running passions and didn't see anything unusual about the flaring spirit he had just witnessed.

"All fire and rage just waiting for an outlet."

Nick's shoulders rose with a shrug. "More often than not. My mother was the same." He gave into a one-sided grin. "My father used to say it was her most endearing quality."

The comment sent Mathew's blond brows upward.

Nick laughed, and took pity on his friend. "You look like a man who either needs a drink or fresh air."

"Fresh air, I think."

"Good. I wanted to check the south fields. You can ride along and fill me in on how things have been here while I've been gone."

It was the only way, Nick knew, to distract Mathew from his sober musing. Ever since they had been boys running along the banks of the river, Mathew had possessed a serious streak that had only intensified over the years. From long experience, Nick was certain that his friend would ponder the issue of Anna's temper in grave detail and at great length.

A surge of humor rose up within him. Anna was an extraordinary combination of fiery temperament and limitless love. Her beliefs and opinions were based on a sense of righteousness, devotion and oddly enough, an almost absurd need for independence. He had to pity Mathew for tackling a puzzle as tangled as Anna. The man didn't know what he was getting himself into.

Moments later, sitting astride his favorite mount, Nick flicked a speculative gaze to Mathew. The man wasn't one to waste time or energy on anything he didn't deem important, yet there he sat, reins held securely in hand, and it was extremely obvious that he was already hard at work on the issue of Anna. The question now was why?

"How have you been, Matt?"

As though startled from his thoughts, Mathew blinked back to his surroundings. "Fine."

"Right about now you don't look it."

Mathew lifted his hand in a gesture that was somehow defenseless. "No, actually, I've been busy with the usual. It's just that Anna . . ."

His voice drained to nothing, the silence telling Nick a great deal. Narrowing his eyes slightly, he asked, "What exactly is going on with Anna?"

"I wouldn't know," Mathew was quick to assure him. "Why do you ask?"

With seeming indifference, Nick shrugged. "No reason other than I come home to find her yelling at you, something she's never done before."

A faint hint of red colored Mathew's cheeks. "I swear I don't know what got into her."

Nick believed him. Mathew was as honest as any man could possibly be. In this case, however, he was also ridiculously transparent and it was all Nick could do to keep from laughing.

So that was the way of it. Mathew had finally gotten around to noticing Anna. Nick had long thought the two would be a good match. Mathew's solemn bend was the perfect steadying force for Anna's impassioned ways, while that very same nature was the exact dash of spirit Mathew needed. Despite all this, Nick had always kept his opinion to himself, believing that it was something for Mathew and Anna to decide.

A smile actually came to his face. Knowing his sister, he didn't envy Mathew at all, not at all.

"Well, I wouldn't worry about her."

Mathew's head came around sharply, his gaze searching and direct. "No?"

"No. Once she's vented, she's not one to brood over things. By the time we get back to the house, she'll be asking you to have dinner with us."

"Do you think that would be wise? I don't want to upset her further."

Personally Nick thought that if Mathew was seriously going to pursue his sister, he was going to have to learn to handle her temperament. And the sooner the better.

"You won't upset her. And even if you do, I'm inviting you to dine with us. We can discuss the latest market for cotton and corn."

Relief and pleasure washed over Mathew's face in equal doses. "I didn't ride over here to capture a dinner invitation, but I will stay." For the first time that afternoon, he smiled. "You haven't said anything about New Orleans. How did things go?"

"All right, but I'm glad to be back."

"Doesn't sound like you enjoyed yourself."

It was both a statement and a question. "I wouldn't say that. There were the usual diversions."

"Such as Marie?"

At the mention of the name, the exotic image of dark sultry eyes and generous curves infiltrated Nick's mind. As whores went, Marie Germaine was extraordinary. She owned her own brothel and reserved her attentions for a select few men. A *very* few. Nick strongly suspected that he was the lone recipient of the woman's erotic regard.

He had no qualms with that. In fact, he preferred the arrangement as it was. Yet he had found something unsettling about it this time that he had never felt before and when he spoke, something like displeasure tinged his words.

"Marie was her usual, amazing, diverting self."

Mathew gave him one of his long serious stares, the only hint of humor evidenced in a slight curl at the corner of his mouth. "Paradise gone sour?"

"Not exactly sour. More like overly ripe. And it was never paradise." No, the closest thing to heaven on earth was Bellefleur.

Heaving a sigh, he gazed out over the fields. In his absence the ground had been turned according to the instructions he had given his overseer. The rich brown hues lay waiting for the new green of this year's crop. Those colors would slowly deepen and then alter to the gold of corn and by summer's end, cotton's white.

He breathed deeply, taking into his lungs the pungent odors of the soil. In his mind he could picture how the land would look a month from now, two months, five. The images were satisfying, even necessary to his peace of mind, if he were completely truthful about it. He could not conceive of his existence separate from Bellefleur. It was his paradise.

And it needed a mistress.

The unexpected thought drew his brows into deep diagonal slashes. He hadn't seriously considered taking a wife before now. Like the changing of the seasons, it was something he took for granted as being inevitable, but slated for some time in the nebulous future. Now, for the first time, he seriously contemplated the notion.

He wanted a wife. Surprisingly, he realized the feeling had been with him for some time, remote, peripheral, but steadfast for all of its reticence. Perhaps that was why his time with Marie had left him feeling as if something had been lacking. What they shared was pleasurable but momentary, expectancy and permanence completely lacking.

Staring at the acres of tilled earth, the uniform rows seemed to mock him for falling victim to the comfort of a habit left over from his youth. It was time, the soil told him, to lay aside the senselessness of the kind of relationship he had with Marie. It was time to look to marriage and all it offered.

As if he had studied the issue for years instead of mere minutes, the necessary traits of a wife, *his* wife, sprang full-blown to mind with such speed he was nearly stunned. He wouldn't have thought he would have been able to describe the ideal wife, but he could with absolute assurance. And even more shocking was the realization that physicality took a decided second place to personality.

He had always been partial to beautiful brunettes, with slim hips and full breasts. Now, that didn't seem to matter. To be sure, he would *like* to awaken each morning for the rest of his life beside a winsome smile and teasing dimples, but he *needed* to go to sleep each night gratified by love, and a devotion to him. And Bellefleur.

The latter went without saying. The woman he married would have to have an unwavering loyalty to Bellefleur. She would have to be willing to sacrifice and labor, and love the land as he did.

The future of Bellefleur, generations to come lay between them, this nonexistent wife and himself. She was out there somewhere, amongst the gently bred daughters of the planta-tion owners, or waiting amidst the upper crust of society. He was eager to start looking.

Chapter Five

Clarice gave her reflection in the mirror one last look before she turned her back on the image and strode from the dress shop. She was looking in fine form this morning. Her hair was coiled up beneath a silk bonnet that matched the deep rose of her walking dress. The richly tinted fabric suited both her coloring and her mood.

Despite the fact that it was barely March, she flipped open her parasol as she made her way down the street, past the rows of shops. It was only minutes after ten o'clock. Nonetheless, she was careful to keep the protective shade between her and the already-brilliant sun. This wasn't just a matter of habit or fashion, rather one of grave consequence.

Her mouth turned down at the corners a tiny bit. The sun was her enemy. It took only a few minutes in the bright sunlight to see her white heritage reduced to nothing. The remnant of her black ancestry made itself known with a darkening of her skin that shouted reality for all to see.

More than anything else, the yellow-white orb hovering in the cloudless sky cruelly reminded her that she was caught between two worlds. She was of neither class, and of both. That was all about to change. She longed to take her place in the ranks that had belonged to her father, and that was exactly what she intended to do.

Determinedly, she headed for the shipping office, the first step in her progress toward making a new life for herself. In the back of her mind, she knew she would eventually come to reside at Bellefleur. That was in the future. How far in the future, she couldn't guess. For now, she simply needed to leave.

New Orleans was the logical choice of destination. The city offered everything she needed, opportunity, diversity, and most especially a social elite. The brown of her eyes glistened when she thought of the rich Creoles throwing their money about on lavish balls and extravagant dinners, hotels catering to one's most luxurious needs, and the limitless supply of people just waiting to be taken advantage of.

She smiled broadly. Yes, New Orleans was where she would go.

An hour later, her lips were still curved into a satisfied line as she made her way back to the dress shop. Day after tomorrow she would be sailing south. If she thought that almost too incredible, she had only to look in her reticule for proof. The receipt she carried was for passage for one to New Orleans aboard the steamship *Mississippi Queen*. First-class passage.

A bubble of laughter tickled her throat. The transaction at the shipping office had been ridiculously easy. She had inquired into transportation, had laid out her money, and as easily as that, the clerk had added her name to the passenger list. He had given her no sneers or condemning glares, no remarks about being uppity or remembering her place. The man had never once mistaken her for anything but the lonely widow she told him she was. The lonely, *white* widow her appearance presented.

As a result, she was indeed leaving Baton Rouge behind,

and in grand style. It was an exhilarating thought, rife with a symbolism she clearly understood. All that she despised in life was here, in this city. Ahead lay the promise of untold fortune. Everything was possible.

Anticipation put a fine trembling in her hands. She did nothing to curtail the slight quivers. She had never felt this alive, this excited about anything.

Savoring the sensation, she entered the shop. At the familiar sight of the darkened, cluttered interior, she half-feared that some small portion of her excitement would be tempered, even sacrificed to the wretchedness she had come to associate with the place. She held her breath and then found to her amused satisfaction that for the first time ever, she could look about and feel nothing, not hatred or resentment, not even bitterness.

"What are you grinnin' at?" her mother asked, coming in from the back room, arms laden with a stack of fashion plates.

"Was I grinnin . . . *g?*" she returned, stressing the *g* her mother habitually dropped.

Josephine ignored the slight censure as she laid the drawings out on the counter. Not even bothering to disguise her interest, she studied Clarice. There was something about her daughter this morning worthy of note; a bearing of poise or joy or peacefulness. Perhaps all three combined. Whatever the manner, Josephine was pleasantly surprised.

"You were grinnin', and it was a fine thin' to see. You don't smile enough."

Clarice tipped her head to one side and sauntered across the room. "Perhaps because I've had very little to smile about. However, I think that's about to change."

"Really? What brought this on?"

"Nothing you have to worry yourself over."

Josephine's hands stilled, the deep brown of her eyes filling with a concern that could not be concealed. "I'll always worry over you, girl. Don't you know that?"

Almost as soon as her words were out, Josephine answered her own question. No, Clarice didn't know how much she was loved. More often than not, her offspring looked at life and saw the negative side of things. She was never content, not with her life or her situation, and certainly not with the greatest gift Josephine had to offer. Her love.

For a time, that had been all Josephine had had to give. Poor freed slaves didn't have much in the world, but that hadn't affected how she felt about her daughter. She had showered her babe with every ounce of care and affection beating in her veins.

"I love you, daughter."

Clarice turned away from the penetrating stare, and the devotion underscoring it. She didn't want to have anything to do with sloppy emotions any more than she wanted to have anything to do with her mother. She was finished with all of it, Baton Rouge, the dress shop, Phillip St. James. From the second she had decided to begin a new life for herself, she had severed whatever bonds had been forged in the past.

"I'm going upstairs and lie down for a bit. I've got a headache."

Not giving her mother a chance to reply, she passed through the fitting room to the stairway leading to the second story apartments. With the same sense of eagerness that had carried her home, she shut her bedroom door behind her and tugged off her white gloves. She had serious business to tend to beginning with packing without her mother's knowledge.

That didn't present an overwhelming problem. Still, she narrowed her eyes while she contemplated the situation. As long as she pleaded a headache, her mother would leave her alone. That would give her time to pack carefully, lightly. What she didn't take with her, she would purchase in New Orleans.

Of course, she would need money. This posed only a minor difficulty, but not because she didn't know how to come by the funds. She knew exactly where to get the money; under a loose floorboard in her mother's bedroom. No, the problem lay in getting into her mother's bedroom undiscovered.

Josephine Bouchard was a frugal, *cautious* woman, trusting no one with her money. Hence, a lifetime's savings was contained within several tin boxes beneath her bed. Night after night, she closed up the shop, then routinely pulled one of the boxes from its secret hiding place and deposited her coins. At any given moment, she knew exactly how much money she had squirreled away. If so much as a dime were to be missing, Josephine would know.

Clarice sat on the edge of her bed, her lips pursed tightly. Timing had suddenly become crucial. The ship's departure was scheduled for early in the morning. Long before dawn, she would need to be ready to leave. Somehow, she was going to have to take the boxes of money after her mother's nightly deposit and sometime before she made good her escape. And an escape it was, right down to the clandestine nature of the act. She was seeking her freedom, and for that she would risk everything.

The strength of that conviction saw her through to the next day, but by late afternoon, her nerves were charged with a raw kind of energy. She chafed to be gone, and with the exception of the money, all was in readiness.

Sitting down to dinner with her mother, she mentally reviewed her preparations. She had made arrangements for a driver to collect her by six o'clock. Her clothes case was packed and hidden in her closet. Now, if only the night would be over and done with.

She looked up from her plate to her mother sitting opposite her and a sense of predictability nearly overwhelmed her. How many times had they enacted this very scenario? Dinner at seven, bathing by eight, into bed by nine. It never changed, and until this evening, it hadn't ever mattered.

Tonight it mattered.

"You feeling all right, Mama?"

Josephine raised startled brown eyes to her daughter. "Yes. Why?"

Shrugging with one shoulder, Clarice cut her chicken into small pieces. "No reason. I thought you might look a little out of sorts, is all."

"I don't feel out of sorts."

"You sure?"

Lines of dubious humor formed along Josephine's brow. "Yes, I'm sure. Why are you askin'?"

Clarice blinked in feigned concern. "Don't I have the right to ask?"

"Of course. It's just that . . . well, you don't usually take note of how I feel."

The remark was a statement of fact, void of censure or judgement. It nonetheless unraveled Clarice's rapidly fraying nerves. A blistering rejoinder rose to her lips. She suppressed it by the expedient means of taking a bite of chicken.

Swallowing past the anger clenching her throat, she managed a convincingly wounded look. "I'm sorry I brought it up. I simply thought you could use a bit of fresh air."

Josephine's hand stilled in the act of raising her fork to her lips. That Clarice's manner had taken her by surprise was clearly evident. "I . . . I don't need . . . It's nice of you to worry."

Clarice silently cursed. She was worried, all right. She wouldn't be able to get into her mother's bedroom if she couldn't get the bitch out of the house. "You're my mother. I don't always show it, but I care about you. That's why I mentioned your getting out tonight. I thought you could stand a little amusement." She waved a hand to indicate the room. "You never go out, you hardly ever take any time for yourself."

Slowly, Josephine laid her fork down, her eyes filling with a blatant mixture of wonder and love. "That's real nice of you, Clarice."

Hope swelled in Clarice's veins. "It's a pretty night. You could take a stroll or . . ." her eyes lit up with sudden inspiration ". . . visit Altha. How long has it been since you visited with Altha?"

Mentioning Josephine's long-time friend was a fine touch. Clarice could tell from the gentle curve beginning to curl her mother's lips that her ploy had worked. Unfortunately, as quick as Josephine's smile began, it faded away.

"Oh, I don't know, Clarice. I would like to step out, but Altha ain't about these days. She's gone off to visit her mama."

It was all Clarice could do to keep from lunging across the small table and shaking her mother silly. "Well, isn't there anyone else you could call on?" she pressed, striving to keep the desperation creeping through her from her voice. "After all, Altha isn't your only friend. There's got to be someone you want to gossip with."

For a long moment, Josephine seemed to consider the suggestion. In the end, she shook her head and sighed. "Maybe tomorrow night. I think I'll just finish dinner and then go to bed."

And that, Clarice knew, was that.

Hot, spearing pain jabbed at her stomach, and she reached for her glass of water. From long experience, she knew the cool liquid would provide her with little relief. She drank anyway, needing the moment to collect her precarious temper.

What was she going to do? She had counted on her mother's absence tonight. In hindsight, she realized she should have prepared for this, should have arranged for her mother to be called away on some pretense or another. It was too late for that now.

Going through the motions of finishing her meal, she frantically searched for a possible course of action. Nothing came to mind, but she would be damned to hell and back if she would let her mother keep her from her chosen path.

In less than a half-hour, Clarice paced the confines of her bedroom, biting her thumbnail down to nothing.

"No, no, no," she murmured to herself. "I'll get the money. I will." And she didn't care what she had to do to make that a reality.

She came to a stop by the foot of her bed, a certainty at the back of her mind gradually making itself known. Like a blinding shroud falling away from her eyes, she suddenly saw exactly, precisely what she would have to do.

Spinning on her heel, she glanced about, her sight directed inward as she weighed the issue of choices. As far as she was concerned, there were no alternatives. Her course of action had become a matter of destiny. Fate directed her actions.

"You'll just have to understand, Mama," she whispered.

To the sound of her own fanciful laughter, she laid out the dress she would wear the following morning when she sailed away from her existence as an octoroon.

* * *

Josephine came out of her sleep in slow stages. Something had woken her, although she wasn't conscious enough to wonder how she knew that. She drew her lips inward over her teeth and sucked in a deep, long breath. Languidly, her body still weighted by the remnants of slumber, she rolled onto her back and finally opened her eyes.

The room was defined by the uniquely murky grays that exist only in those moments before dawn. Shapes were distinguishable for what they were; all were painted in a hue not far from black. Through the shadows, she peered about, unknowingly tipping her head to one side.

It occurred to her after the fact that she was listening for a sound. Instantly, she held her breath, her eyes widening against the dimness of the room.

"Who's there?" she asked, her sleep-cracked voice both fearful and demanding. She levered herself into a sitting position and reached for the oil lamp on the bed side table. "Anyone there?"

A sound, subtle and low, came from the far corner of the room. Josephine abandoned the idea of lighting the lamp and lunged from the bed, driven by a bone-deep fright.

"Who is it?" But she truly didn't want to know. Instinct impelled her to flee, to be gone from whatever danger lurked too closely, to protect Clarice and see them both to safety. Giving free rein to the reflexive impulses, she extended her cold, trembling hands for the door, her legs moving automatically in the same direction.

"It's me, Mama."

Like a balm to her soul, Clarice's voice washed the fear from Josephine's body. She pressed one hand to her forehead and one to where her stomach should have been.

"Girl, what are you doin' creepin' 'bout my room this

way? You just scared ten years from my life." She turned with her words and squinted to see her daughter more clearly.

"I'm sorry, Mama. I wished you hadn't woken up."

"It's all right, now that I know it's you." She closed the distance between them. "Is somethin' wrong? What are you doin' in here?"

Clarice's reply was a long time coming. When she did speak, her voice was nearly musical in quality. "I didn't want it to be this way, Mama."

"Be what? What are you talkin' about?"

"You should have stepped out last night like I told you to."

Josephine didn't understand. The last bit of her fright gave way to confusion. "What are you goin' on about?" As if light could shed reason to the moment, she crossed to the lamp and lit it with efficient moves. She turned, then came up short at the sight of Clarice dressed for traveling.

"Where are you goin'? It ain't even dawn yet."

"I'm leaving."

The words stunned Josephine with all the impact of a fist to her lungs. Her breath caught and she had to wheeze to draw in air. "You're goin' away? Where?"

"Away. That's all you need to know."

Josephine shook her head in denial. "No, you're my daughter, my own flesh and blood. You can't just be walkin' out in the middle of the night without tellin' me more than that."

"Yes, I can."

"I don't understand." A little desperately, she lifted a hand in a gesture of appeal, a hollow feeling beginning to take hold of her senses. Eyes filled with dread, she scanned her daughter's beautiful face.

This was her baby, her own sweet child born of love. She wasn't ready to see her go, especially so unexpectedly. Oh, realistically she knew Clarice wouldn't remain forever, but in the back of her mind she had associated that leaving with marriage, not in the middle of the night with no warning.

"Are you in trouble, Clarice?" It was a sudden thought, prompted by the tumult of racing emotions.

"No, Mama," Clarice sighed.

" 'Cause if you are, I'll help you any way I can."

"I'm not in any trouble. I'm just going."

There was something about the utter assurance in Clarice's words that gave Josephine pause. It was a quality that brooked no argument, allowed no discussion. She stared hard at the young woman she loved above all else and saw an almost odd kind of serenity in the brown eyes.

"You're scarin' me with this talk of leavin', Clare," she got out around a nervous chuckle. "Why don't we talk about this in the morning and maybe we can decide what we can do."

"We? This doesn't involve both of us, Mama." Clarice pressed a fist to her chest and spat, "This is about me, not you. Not ever *you,* not ever again."

They were hurtful words, made even more so by the raw venom reflected in Clarice's eyes. Josephine bit on her upper lip, for the first time ever, feeling a complete failure as a mother.

Tears threatened. "What do you want me to do?" she got out on a choked whisper.

To her surprise, her query met with a trill of laughter.

"I want, Mama of mine, for you to crawl under your bed and get me the money boxes."

Josephine blinked in shock. "What?"

"The money, Mama. Get the money."

Josephine had seen traces of malice in her daughter before. It had been nothing compared to what she witnessed now.

Lines of revulsion hardened Clarice's mouth and her eyes seemed to glitter with dangerous intent.

Searching in her mind for some cause for this swelling of her daughter's spite and hatred, Josephine remained unmoving, until Clarice reached into her reticule and pulled out a compact pistol.

"Oh, my God!" Josephine cried. "Where did you get that?"

"It doesn't matter." Clarice nodded toward the bed. "Get the money."

The most devastating sensation of loss overwhelmed Josephine. Every drop of blood seemed to sink out of her body, taking with it her joy, her purpose, her resolve. She wanted to deny what was happening. It was impossible with Clarice pointing a pistol straight at her heart.

The pain of that knowledge was too awful to bear. She had withstood her share of suffering in her life, but nothing, *nothing* wounded her like Clarice's betrayal.

Tears flooding her eyes, she whispered, "Clare, why are you doin' this? That money is for my old age, for our security."

"That money is mine," Clarice hissed. "That and a whole lot more."

"I don't understand."

Clarice stepped closer, the pistol clenched hard in her grasp. "I'm Francois DuQuaine's daughter. I should have been living up there in the big white house, but you took that from me."

"No . . . no, I didn't."

"It would have taken only one word from you and I could have had a good life."

The pistol waved erratically. Josephine watched its movements with a growing fear.

"It's all your fault, Mama. I'll have my due—"

"Clare—"

"First from you and then from the DuQuaines."

Josephine's fear escalated to terror. Clare was talking madness. Unable to control her nervous reaction, she glanced to the door. If she could only run . . .

In that second, the blast of the pistol rent the stillness in the room. Tearing agony ripped into her chest, stunning her with its force, holding her captive while her mind scrambled to take in reality.

Eyes huge and round, she stared in disbelief at her daughter, and then burning pain consumed her, ate at her chest, spreading in every direction. She dropped to her knees, pressing icy hands to the blood rapidly soaking the front of her nightgown.

The floor tipped, swayed and finally rose up dizzily. Josephine labored for breath, writhing in an agony that was as much of the mind as it was the body. Everything she had done in her life had been for her precious daughter. The scrimping and saving, the toiling and laboring. And the whoring. That too. All had been for Clarice. Her beloved Clarice.

Through blurred eyes, she stared up into that beloved face. Clarice looked down, her face lacking emotion of any kind.

"I should have done that years ago, Mama."

It was the last sound Josephine heard.

Chapter Six

"You up yet?" Mama Lou asked.

Eyes still shut, Jessica nodded against her pillow. "Almost."

"Get to it, girl."

Behind her closed lids, Jessica heard the housekeeper shut the door to her room, and gave into a sleepy smile. In the week since her arrival at Bellefleur, Jessica had come to realize that Mama Lou was a creature of habit. The tall, imposing woman had set a pattern for herself that never seemed to change, with the possible exception that her morning routine now included waking Jessica at dawn.

Opening one eye, she glanced to the window. Weak sunlight already tinted the sky with the first wash of color. Nearly everyone on the plantation would be up and about soon. From the youngest field hand to Nicholas DuQuaine himself, all worked from sun up to sun set. It was a demanding way of life, one to which, Jessica told herself, she needed to apply herself at once.

She flipped back the covers and dressed quickly. It was only a matter of minutes before she was tying an apron on over her faded gray dress as she made her way to the kitchen.

Like Mama Lou, she had her own routine to follow, starting with breakfast.

"Good morning, Pearl," she said, stepping into the cook house.

The plantation's rotund cook turned at the greeting. "Mornin' back to you," Pearl replied, giving one of her beaming, toothy grins. "Grab yourself a hunk of dat cornbread what left over from last night while I get dese eggs to fryin'."

Jessica gladly did as she was told, taking a seat on one of the wooden stools near the huge stone fireplace. In all of her life she had never eaten food as wonderful as that prepared by Pearl. From grits to beef, the woman had a magic touch with a wooden spoon and a cast-iron skillet.

Watching Pearl work a little bit of her culinary sorcery on a half dozen eggs, she contemplated the last few days. Surprisingly, she had been readily welcomed into the domain that Pearl considered hers alone and somehow a definite kinship had sprung up between them. Jessica ate all her meals in the kitchen, although she wasn't certain how it had come to be.

Perhaps it was because of the very nature of her presence on the plantation. Being neither black nor a slave, her place was not down the row of whitewashed shacks. Yet neither was she a free white woman to take her meals in the manor house.

Her station lay somewhere in between, undefined, but no less real for its lack of a title or distinction. That didn't bother Jessica, nor did she seem to think that Pearl minded. In fact, Jessica believed Pearl appreciated the company despite the fact that the cookhouse was never lacking for people. As much food as she prepared, her helpers were almost always about, peeling potatoes, churning butter, or kneading flour and water into the absolute best bread Jessica had ever eaten.

She glanced down to the bread she held in one hand, and was helplessly reminded of other times, other morsels of bread. Deep within her, she felt the ingrained need to save the bit of food, to tuck it into a pocket so she would be assured of having something to eat later on in the day. For too many years, that practice had been more than a habit. Never knowing for certain when or if she would eat again, she had taken to reserving a portion of her meal and hoarding it. All too often, she had had to rely on that little supply to ward off her hunger.

"It ain't gonna get up and walk away," Pearl laughed, setting her pan of eggs on an iron trivet.

Jessica shook off her musings. Sternly, she reminded herself to leave the past where it belonged. She didn't need to worry over what she would eat that day or where she would sleep that night. There was constancy in her life now. She simply needed to get used to that.

There was an oddity to be found in the situation. She was the property of another human being. That should have been a terrible reality. It wasn't, and she was honest enough with herself to admit that in her bondage to another, she had discovered a certain peace of mind. Of course, that state was solely due to Nicholas DuQuaine. At the hands of another, she doubted she would be faring so well.

Offering Pearl a lopsided grin, she popped the last bite of bread into her mouth.

The cook laughed in pleasure as abundant as her girth. "Dat's what I like to see. You eat up all you like."

Jessica pulled at the waist of her dress. "If I keep eating this way, I'm going to burst my seams."

"Shoot, girl," Pearl scoffed. "You got you a long way to go before dat's a problem. Dat dress of yours is still hangin' loose."

"But not as loose as it used to be."

"Good. I aim to fatten you up like some pretty little pigeon."

"Then I'll have to waddle my way around the house."

"Nothin' wrong with dat." With an expert hand, Pearl flipped the contents of her pan. "Life's too short to be frettin' about how you walk or talk. It's what you got goin' on in your heart dat counts. Like Master Nick. He's a fine man, a right fine man with a monstrous fine heart."

Jessica's brows rose at hearing her own opinion voiced. "He is very kind."

"Dat he is, just like his daddy, always takin' care of what's his."

Jessica needed no confirmation of that. All around her, she could see signs of the extraordinary attention given to every facet of the plantation. No corner of the house was left in disrepair, no shrub allowed to grow untrimmed. The slaves were clothed and fed far beyond mere adequacy and from the little she had seen of the fields, the fertile earth received equally discerning care.

"And proud?" Pearl continued. "Lord, dat man is proud. Got dat from his daddy, too." She chuckled at some private thought. "Francois DuQuaine was like some grand king rulin' over his land." She turned the eggs out onto two tin plates. "Here, put your mouth to dose."

Jessica shook her head. She'd never be able to finish three eggs. She'd do her best, though, if for no other reason than to please Pearl. "How long have you been here?"

The cook settled her cumbersome weight on a stool beside Jessica. The copious curves of her belly prevented the formation of a lap, but she managed her plate nonetheless. "For always. I was born here. Same for Mama Lou and a whole mess of us." Again, she chuckled and her eyes took on the light of fond memories. "I remember dose days when de old master was about. Seemed like he was always goin' off in three directions at once, takin' care of the cotton, keepin' an eye on his children. And, of course, lovin' his wife." Rolling her eyes, she whistled low. "Now, dere was a couple to try the patience of all the saints what live in Heaven."

"Why do you say that?" Jessica asked, her curiosity undeniably pricked.

" 'Cause Miz Emilee was as proud as her husband and dey both as stubborn as all get out. He get mad, she get mad and dey both take to arguin' in dat French dey talked. Whew, but dey could argue." She smiled a smile of delighted wickedness. "But, oh, lord, could dey make up. Never did see no man and wife so in love." The corners of her smile drooped, her brown eyes losing their sparkle. "Life just went right out of him when she passed on. For a while, we thought he might just shrivel up and follow her, but he come around finally, saw the light of things, he did."

"What do you mean?"

Pearl's brow puckered deeply. "Why shoot, girl, don't you know? He had him his children and his land. To de DuQuaines, dat's what life is all about." She waved her fork at the one uneaten egg remaining on Jessica's plate. "You goin' to eat dat?"

Jessica blinked at the change from one topic to the next, glancing down at her plate. "No, my stomach is already protesting."

Like a mother hen fretting over her runt of a chick, Pearl clucked her tongue. "I don't know how you manage to work up to the house with nothin' inside you."

"I've eaten more than I'm used to," Jessica insisted, finding the woman's fussing wonderfully endearing. She set her plate aside. "And if I don't hurry up and get to my work, Mama Lou will come looking for me."

"Like to see dat," Pearl declared, her lips pulling into a sour moue. "She knows better dan to mess with me. I say you need to sit and finish your eggs, you gonna sit and finish your eggs." She came to her feet and grumbled, "I stay out of her house, she better stay out of my kitchen."

Jessica wasn't about to debate the matter. From the sound of things, not all was in accord between cook and house-keeper, and she had no intentions of getting in the middle of whatever strife existed between them.

Assuring Pearl that she could not eat another mouthful, she hastily made her way back to the house and the chores that awaited. As she expected, Mama Lou was waiting for her in the dining room.

"About time, girl," the housekeeper stated, her wide mouth tightening into its usual stern line.

"Am I late?"

Mama Lou set her hands on her hips. "Now, that all depends."

"On what?"

"Whether that old Pearl's been feedin' you or talkin' your ear off."

Jessica wasn't one to lie. However, in this instance, she saw the wisdom in stretching the truth. "I was hungrier than usual."

That earned her a shrewd look. Her eyes rounded slightly in self-defense against the twinge of guilt tugging at her in-sides. Thankfully, Mama Lou spun about and headed for the parlor.

"Come on, then. We got windows to clean."

Hours later, Jessica ruefully wondered how one house could have so many panes of glass. For the entire day, she scrubbed the windows with a mixture of vinegar and water, ridding the glass of winter's grime. Time and again, she toted wooden buckets out to the well for fresh water and tore up muslin for rags. Standing on a stepladder, she took down curtains and stretched up on her toes to reach the highest glass corners.

By nightfall, she was wearied, but filled with a sense of satisfaction when she took a moment to view her accomplishment. Fourteen of the twenty-four windows downstairs were polished inside and out to a shining gleam. She fell asleep that night, smelling faintly like a pickle, but feeling remarkably pleased.

That pleasure was with her the next day as she worked her way from one room to the next. Mama Lou checked on her every now and then, but even the woman's sharply scrutinizing eyes and acerbic tongue couldn't dampen Jessica's spirits.

She couldn't explain why, but the painstaking act of applying cloth to glass rewarded her in ways she found amazing. Not that it was something she would wish to do every day. Her arms and back ached and the sting of vinegar had reddened her hands. But there was something, some sensation she derived that she could only describe as *right*.

By the time she entered Nicholas's library to start on the last three windows downstairs, she decided that her feelings had not so much to do with pride in achievement, but rather everything to do with caring for this particular house. Bucket in one hand, a bunch of rags in the other, she gazed at the book-lined walls and realized she felt somehow connected with the house.

Her blond brows lowered at the unexpected thought. There was no earthly reason for her to feel anything in particular for the structure. It wasn't hers, and she had only been there for a short while. Still, she had to dismiss logic for the overwhelming emotions generated in her heart.

Riding those emotions, she set her supplies down and hurriedly fetched her ladder. It was just past noon and Nicholas would be in from the fields for lunch soon. As was his habit, he would spend a portion of his afternoon behind his desk, and she wanted to be finished before then.

She set her ladder before one of the floor to ceiling windows, careful not to scratch the nearby mahogany table with its collection of decanters. With the ease of practice, she removed the burgundy swags, set them aside, then climbed the ladder once more with a wet rag.

Later, she would never be able to tell exactly why she lost her balance. She didn't know if she hadn't been paying as close attention as she should have or if she was distracted by something she viewed outside. Either way, her foot missed the rung and halfway up the ladder, she lurched to one side.

Reflexively, she thrust one arm out and was able to deflect the worst of the fall. However, her hip struck the corner of the hard wood table and her hand crashed against the collection of decanters. She landed on her knees as bottles toppled to the floor. Brandy and bourbon splashed in every direction accompanied by the sound of crystal smashing into hundreds of pieces.

Pain shot out from her hip and radiated up her arm. She ignored the dual assault, staring at the scattered shards in instant, growing horror.

"Oh, no," she whispered. Fear churned in her stomach, tearing through her muscles and nerves. Whatever faith she had in Nicholas Duquaine's kindness was instantly fractured along with the bottles. He had always treated her well, but she had never done a thing to cause him to do otherwise. She couldn't begin to guess how he was going to react to this. All she knew, the basis for any anticipation she had, lay in the certainty of how her *father* would respond.

Her gaze jerked from one door to the other, then back to the mess she had created. The broken decanters glared back at her, accusing her in silent, menacing sparkle. Surely the bottles had been costly. Were they also precious heirlooms ripe with sentiment?

"Oh, *no!*" All color draining from her face, she swallowed hard as she grabbed a rag and tried to soak up the spilled liquor. Only then did she notice the copious bleeding from her left palm. From wrist to knuckle, a deep slash tore her flesh open.

She surged to her feet and bound her hand in a dry scrap of muslin, wincing at the piercing pain. All the while, distressed, apprehensive thoughts tumbled one on top of another in a chaotic tangle. Should she run to Mama Lou now or after she cleaned up the floor? Maybe she should go directly to Anna and confess to her clumsiness. She was trying to decide when the decision was taken from her and Nicholas entered the room.

"Is everything all right in here?" he asked.

Jessica whirled to face him, stepping back in the same motion. As though the sight of the blood even now soaking through her makeshift binding would make matters worse, she tucked her left hand behind the folds of her skirt in a purely instinctive gesture. Eyes rounded to enormous proportions, she watched the dawning of comprehension settle over Nicholas's face.

His black brows slanted as he took in the sight at her feet. "What happened?" He strode forward with his query, his black boots sounding ominous on the wood floor.

At his first move, she took another step back, observing his approach with dark, wary eyes. "I'm sorry," she choked out, somehow finding her voice. "I fell. I didn't mean to . . ."

He stopped a mere arm's length away, giving her an assessing look. "Are you all right?"

"Yes." Her reply was immediate and abrupt to the point of being brusque. The deep angle of his brows increased. Her heart thudded and she sidled further away. "I'm . . . I'm sorry. I'll clean it up." Again she swallowed with difficulty, giving into the fear she had learned at her father's hand. She had no way of knowing that every bit of that alarm was engraved into her face and carved into the lines of her body.

Nicholas squinted slightly, taken aback by the fright that practically emanated from Jessica in palpable waves. In a mixture of surprise, annoyance and concern, he realized that she fully expected him to explode with anger.

"You don't have to worry." He kept his tone carefully modulated. "It was an accident. Just clean it up and be done with it."

She nodded woodenly.

Her awkward response was rife with enough doubt to shove Nicholas's annoyance to the forefront of his emotions. "I'm not going to hurt you, damn it. Do you understand?"

Even though his tone was slightly barbed, his avowal had its desired effects. If he were going to resort to violence, Jessica reasoned, he would have done so by now. Slowly, the tension drained from her body. She nodded in response, the contour of her shoulders softening.

"I'm sorry."

"Stop apologizing."

"Yes, sir." But that was easier said than done. The abating strain of the moment gave rise to a profound relief. Her nerves trembled anew with a quivering kind of energy and suddenly, the need to rattle off explanations and apologies became too overpowering to deny. "I should have been more careful. I suppose I wasn't watching my step, but I promise I'll not be so careless again." Her left hand, bound so tightly, throbbed painfully with the tremors that seized her limbs. "I'll clean it up at once."

Nicholas found himself neatly caught between the dire urge to take her by the arms and shake her until she ceased her nervous chatter and the equally fierce impulse to draw her close to still her shaking. To do either was out of the question.

"Jessica," he intoned slowly. "Calm down." Bending low from his great height, he stared directly into the blue of her eyes. "You're working yourself into a stew for nothing. There's no great loss here. It was just a few bottles."

She stared back and took a deep breath. He meant what he said. He honestly was not upset with her.

One corner of his mouth quirked upward. "Better?"

"Yes, sir." And with the exception of her hand, she truly was. His gentle reassurance had slain the last of her trepidations. "I'll fetch a mop and broom." With her words, she stepped away and headed for side door only to be stopped by Nicholas's imperative query.

"What the devil is this?"

Uncertainly, she turned, her line of vision following his to a small puddle of blood staining the floor. Her gaze slowly raised to his and in the gray depths she saw the unequivocal, unrelenting demand for the truth.

"I . . . uh, I cut myself." As slowly as she had looked up, she lifted her hand in an awkward move. She was unprepared for the sight of so much blood. The entire piece of muslin was dyed crimson.

Nicholas was across the room in an instant, taking her hand between his own. Seeing so much blood, he cursed soundly. "Damn it all, Jessica. What were you trying to do?" He didn't wait for a reply. Instead, he scooped her into his arms and strode for the door.

Jessica's breath caught in her throat. His move was so unexpected she spent several seconds simply waiting for her mind to play catch up with the reality of the situation. He was kicking open the door to her room when she finally found her wits and her voice.

"What are you doing?"

"Seeing that you don't bleed to death," he growled.

"I'm not going to bleed to death." More likely, she would expire from the surge of emotions making hash of her insides. The feel of him was unlike anything she had ever experienced, beyond anything with which she was prepared to deal.

The entire right side of her body was pressed snugly to the heated strength that fashioned the wall of his chest. All along her back and beneath her thighs, she felt the muscle and sinew of his arms holding her effortlessly. Her forehead grazed the steely edge of his jaw and with every breath she took, she drew in the scent of man and power.

His presence surrounded her, unnerved her. "I can walk. Put me down."

He did set her on her bed, but only because that had been his intention all along. Coming down onto his haunches before her, he once again took up her hand and carefully removed the length of bloodied cloth to reveal the wicked gash in her palm.

"Son of a . . ." He clamped his jaw tight, practically chewing on the words he thought were best left unspoken. His eyes, though, showed every blazing sign of his loss of patience. That fine sentiment had been replaced by a displeasure rooted in concern.

"Did you think you would be able to leave this untended?" he asked in a tight voice.

As gentle as his ministrations were, pain lanced up Jessica's arm. Her muscles flinched involuntarily and she bit down on her lower lip. "I didn't think about it at all," she whispered at last.

His gaze shot to hers. "How could you not think about it? It has to hurt like the very devil."

Under his stern disapproval, her shoulders rose with a shrug. "It didn't seem that bad at the time."

He saw the partial truth of that for what it was and his eyes narrowed to dangerous looking slits. "More likely, you believed this as some kind of punishment you thought you deserved. And for what? A couple of pieces of glass that can be replaced?" He swore beneath his breath and came to his feet, every inch the master of Bellefleur. "Don't move," he ordered, thrusting a long, commanding finger beneath her nose. "Don't even *think* of moving."

Back straight, eyes wide, Jessica watched him leave. Not for a second did she contemplate disobeying him. The man was in a temper, and it was directed solely at her. She would have to be a fool to cross him under normal circumstances, ten times the fool to do so now.

She exhaled a long, slow breath, shaking her head in wonder. She had anticipated Nicholas DuQuaine's anger, but she had assumed the cause would lie in the broken carafes. Her assumption was wrong. As far as she could tell, he was angry with her for having ignored the cut on her hand.

She looked from her palm to the door and back. She had never met such a man, one who was as benevolent as he was compelling, as compassionate as he was handsome. The sound of his approaching footsteps drew her bewildered gaze upward. In seconds, he appeared in the doorway, Anna followed behind.

"Oh, my goodness," Anna exclaimed, rushing to Jessica's side.

"I think it'll need to be stitched," Nicholas advised from just inside the door.

Jessica stared up at him as if seeing him for the first time. Who was this man that he would take such an interest in a mere servant? On one level she understood that from the very start he had acted on her behalf, yet that awareness had been tempered by a wariness that was ingrained into the fabric of her being. Now suddenly, she felt as if he had broken through the barricades she kept firmly about her, reaching deep inside her to emotions she couldn't define.

"Are you all right?" he asked. Stepping near, he peered closely into her eyes. "You've lost a lot of blood. Perhaps you should lie down."

Some part of Jessica's mind told her to answer . She shook her head to clear her thoughts and lifted her hand slightly. "As long as I don't move, it doesn't bleed."

Anna laid a gentle hand on her shoulder. "We're going to have to sew it up, Jessica." Clearly feeling upset about the task, she added, "If we don't, it'll never stop bleeding." The words sounded innocent enough, but Anna's expression told Jessica all she needed to know about the prospect of having her hand ministered to.

The silent preparations by brother and sister only added to her misgivings. The low table by the head of the bed was hastily cleared while Anna fetched a basket of needed supplies. And then like some puppet on a series of strings, Jessica found herself shifted and settled so that she sat on the edge of the bed with Nicholas seated directly behind her, his long legs spread wide to encompass her thighs. With her back pressed against his chest, and his hands holding her left arm pinned to the table, she felt the beginnings of a true panic.

"Just relax," he told her, his voice low and smooth in her ear.

If she lived forever, she didn't think she could possibly relax. Being held immobile stripped away any manner of defense that might be hers. She was left nervous and vulnerable and to make matters worse, Nicholas literally surrounded her with arms, legs, even his head above hers. *And* the juncture of his thighs was snuggled intimately to the curves of her bottom. Through the fabric of her dress, she could feel the bold, intimate masculinity of him.

The blood of an excruciating blush filled her cheeks. If he hadn't held her so securely, she would have bolted from the bed. As it was, his hands anchored her firmly in place. Her only defense was to close her eyes and bow her head.

Before she could take her next breath, though, burning pain gripped the nerves and muscles of her hand and ripped up her arm. Her eyes snapped open, her head came up and her entire body jerked back against Nicholas's solid form. Dragging in a breath laced with a low, strained cry, she realized that Anna had poured a liberal dose of whiskey over the ragged cut.

"Easy, Jess," Nicholas murmured, his breath fanning her temple.

The embarrassment she had felt only seconds earlier was slain before the onslaught of heated agony. She was suddenly thankful to have Nicholas pressed close, for without his support, she would have crumbled.

"I'm sorry, Jessica," Anna said, her face lined with regret. "It's the only way I know of to make sure it's clean."

"I know," Jessica managed to get out through gritted teeth. "I . . . I just didn't expect it."

"That should be the worst of it."

Jessica truly hoped so. She had experienced her share of pain, but not this type. Her body trembled in silent reaction.

"Let all your weight rest against me," Nicholas instructed.

She didn't even think to question him. Her body simply responded on its own accord and she leaned back.

Drawing in a deep breath, she released it slowly. It was the pattern she followed as Anna applied needle and thread to her palm. Each stitch brought fresh pain and Jessica tried to steel herself, to concentrate on rhythmically filling her lungs, but within minutes, a sheen of moisture glazed her forehead and her entire body had all but crawled into Nicholas's to escape the pain. Through it all, Nicholas held her carefully, securely, confidently. Without knowing it, Jessica drew on his strength and made it hers.

Finally, Anna snipped the thread and bound the hand with fresh bandages.

"It's all right, Jess," Nicholas murmured.

Feeble tears of relief filling her eyes, she simply nodded.

"I think you should lie down now," Anna suggested. "And I don't want you up for the rest of the day."

Jessica didn't argue. She was suddenly frighteningly weak. Her strength seemed to have deserted her and her mind struggled to make sense of its thoughts.

All she wanted at that moment was to sleep and hope that the insistent throbbing in her hand would go away. Yet she couldn't summon forth the energy necessary to rise and move out of Nicholas's way, which was truly odd. She didn't like being this close to a man. Normally she went out of her way to avoid such contact. Yet there she sat, comforted rather than repelled, secure instead of nervous.

Why was that? And why couldn't she think of an answer? Did she really want one? Would her hand ever stop hurting? And why was the light in the room suddenly growing so dim?

The last thought she had was of how wonderful it felt to be in Nicholas's arms.

Chapter Seven

It was time. Standing on the back steps of the house, Nicholas squinted slightly against the morning sun shining down from a cloudless, cerulean sky and once again silently declared that planting the corn seed would begin this morning. He had surveyed the grounds and knew the timing was right.

The air was just warm enough, the ground plowed and trenched. The nights had relinquished the last of their killing frosts and the spring rains had not yet begun in earnest. It was definitely time.

A rush of anticipation vibrated along his spine, and he had to smile. No matter how many times he began a new season, he always reacted this way. The promise of bounty lay ahead, beckoning to his senses, reaching deep within him to a fundamental part of his being. He liked the process of growing, of watching the land give up her fruits to his labor. The rewards he garnered from that were immeasurable, and harbored, he knew, in his soul.

His smile turned a bit wry. He did have a tendency to muse on things profound, especially when it came to Bellefleur. For one hundred and fifty years, the plantation had been the home of the DuQuaines. Four generations had lived and loved and died here, and he wasn't entirely convinced that the house and the grounds and even the dirt itself had not collected the temperament of all who had called Bellefleur home. In return, the plantation seemed to bestow the collective spirit of ancestors past on each succeeding generation, endowing each new master with a love and appreciation for the essence of all that had preceded him.

Nicholas caught the trend of his thoughts and gave a mental shake. It was a perfect morning for reflections, but an even more perfect morning for planting corn. Bellefleur's primary cash crop might be cotton, but the plantation would never survive without corn.

He descended the stairs and made his way toward the stables, letting his gaze wander at will. Out of the corner of his eye, he caught a flash of pale blue amidst a field of green.

Jessica. She sat beneath a huge crepe myrtle whose limbs were graced with fresh spring leaves. Across her lap lay a quilted spread, a basket of sewing supplies at the ready. With her head lowered over her task, she was not aware of his presence.

His pace slowed as his eyes made a studied inventory of her figure. She presented a fetching picture, sitting in the dappled sunlight, her blond hair swept up to reveal the elegant line of the nape of her neck. Her right hand worked quickly, taking stitches in the quilt while her bandaged left hand rested palm upward.

He gazed at the white binding that had been applied the day before, and frowned. The sight of the linen dressing dragged to mind a host of very startling impressions, some with which he was not entirely comfortable.

There was no denying that Jessica McCormick was a most remarkable young woman. She had gotten through what amounted to minor surgery with hardly a whimper. He admired that kind of fortitude, especially so in a woman. And, he admitted, she possessed a resilient character. Her life had changed dramatically over the course of the last few weeks, yet she had adapted with apparent ease.

But—and he confessed to this with great reluctance—she had an arousing effect on him that he seemed helpless to control. Instantly, his mind recalled the feel of her in his arms as he had held her securely. The smoothness of her skin beneath his fingers, the gentle curves of her breasts against his forearms, the rounded softness of her buttocks cradling him. He had wanted nothing more than to continue to hold her snuggled close, and absorb her body's trembling with his own.

He swore beneath his breath, and his thoughts took a chiding bend. For the love of God, she was his servant. His mind understood that, his body did not. Even now, the mere memory of the touch of her made his blood begin to pound.

He lengthened his stride in a useless attempt to ease the suddenly uncomfortable fit of his pants. Not for the first time, he told himself he had no business thinking of Jessica in terms other than that of a servant. Unfortunately, she chose that second to look up from her sewing and their gazes locked. His resolve dissipated like so much dust in the wind.

Knowing he was making a huge mistake, he changed his course and headed for the crepe myrtle. With each step he took, he was reminded of how he had wanted to ease her suffering, of the way she had swooned in his arms . . . of how perfectly her body had conformed to his. For far too many reasons, it wasn't wise of him to appreciate any of that.

"Good morning," he said, coming to stand at her feet. She started to rise and he waved her back into place. "Don't get up. I just wanted to know how you're feeling this morning."

Her gaze dropped briefly to her left hand. "It still hurts, but it's much better than yesterday."

He, too, glanced to the thick bandaging. "Make sure you don't do anything to tear out the stitches."

"I don't think I'll have the chance." She smiled a little crookedly. "Sewing is as strenuous a task as I've been given until I'm completely healed."

The upward curve of her smile caught his attention. He wasn't used to seeing her smile. It was something she rarely did. A good thing, too, perhaps, for the nerves about his stomach knotted in response. "Make sure you do as you're told," he ordered more forcibly than was necessary.

All traces of the smile vanished. "Yes, sir."

Inside he squirmed. He had snatched away her meager joy and now felt like a heartless beast. Damning his own idiocy, he sought to make amends. "What does Mama Lou have you doing there?"

"This?" She instantly fingered the quilt. "Repairing a hem. Some of the stitching has worn loose."

"And she sent you out here?"

"No. She didn't care where I worked so I chose to be outside."

"I don't blame you. On a day such as this, it's difficult to be confined to the house."

She drew a breath and tilted her head to look out over the fields in the distance. "It's so beautiful here. All the land and the gardens stretching out until it seems they'll never end." A look of undiluted wistfulness caressed her face. "I think this is as close to Heaven on earth as anyone can get."

Nicholas was stunned into silence. Her longing struck him hard and for several seconds he was reduced to merely staring at her profile. There had been many who had paid their compliments to Bellefleur, but he had never heard anyone voice his own beliefs so accurately.

Bellefleur was indeed his Heaven on earth. All he wanted

in life was here. He hadn't thought that anyone else, Anna included, felt the same.

"I'm glad you like it here."

She turned back to stare up at him, a blush of unmistakable self-consciousness coloring her cheeks. "I probably shouldn't have spoken so freely, but I've never been anywhere even half as nice."

Nicholas knew it to be a compliment given straight from the heart. She truly meant what she said.

"Would you like to see the rest of Bellefleur?" The question was out before he even realized it, however, he wouldn't have recalled the words for anything. It was suddenly very important to him that she experience Bellefleur in its entirety.

"Come with you?" Her eyes rounded into two disbelieving blue orbs. "You want me to come . . . along . . . along with you?"

"I think you'll enjoy it."

"I know I will." She looked guiltily to the quilt. "But I'm supposed to finish my work."

This time he thought to temper his dictate. "Leave it until later." A touch of humor crinkled the corners of his eyes. "I give the orders around here, remember? If I say the quilt can wait, then it will wait."

She hesitated for only a long second. "All right."

"Good. Go tell my sister or Mama Lou where you'll be and I'll meet you right back here in five minutes."

She watched him stride off toward the stables, absolutely entranced. There was nothing more she wanted to do than to accompany him. From the minute she had stepped foot on the plantation, she had yearned to explore every corner of this wonderful land. Until now she hadn't thought she would ever be given the opportunity.

Quickly, she gathered her things, ever mindful of her hand.

It did ache terribly, but she overlooked the discomfort in light of the excitement racing through her. She felt as if she had been given a rare and utterly remarkable gift, and she wasn't about to let an annoying pain impair her enjoyment.

She caught up with Anna in the plantation office and made her explanations. Anna's response was what Jessica might have expected, a ready smile and a wave of her hand to shoo her on her way. In less than five minutes, Jessica stood beneath the crepe myrtle waiting for Nicholas's return.

Heart thumping madly, she smoothed the creases from her dress, then scolded herself at once for her nervous gesture. She was carrying on like a silly child about to take her first outing. Some remote closet of her mind laughed at the thought. Only a portion of her giddiness was due to this unexpected tour of the grounds. The ultimate reason for the trembling of her fingers was Nicholas DuQuaine.

The truth of that was like a dash of ice water in the face, and she sobered in the next heart beat. Part of her was uneasy about going off with him and part of her was elated. She was comfortable with the former, absolutely unnerved by the latter.

She normally didn't react this way to men. To keep her distance was an instinct she had developed long ago, and a condition by which she lived. Now, she was almost tingling in expectation at the idea of spending time with the most compelling man she had ever met.

If she had any sense at all, she would heed the warnings being given off by her brain and politely decline his offer, make any excuse, or even find some place to hide. She had to be sadly lacking in reason, then, because as he rode toward her on a giant of a stallion, she stood rooted to the ground and let her gaze slide over the lines and planes of him.

He reeked of masculinity. His manner was of bold male

power, his appearance of virile strength. The combination was frightening. So why was she waiting there, drinking in the sight of him as if he could quench an excruciating thirst?

Because, her wayward mind replied with brutal honesty, she was undeniably attracted to Nicholas DuQuaine. On some deep level, she was drawn toward him and led into the realm of trust.

She blinked at the notion, and then examined it carefully. She supposed she was beginning to trust him, and with good cause. Not once had he demonstrated any of the tendencies that typified her father. That more than anything else helped alleviate some of her anxieties about him as a man.

Staring at his muscular thighs gripping the horse, she silently declared that he was *definitely* a man. And yet, yesterday she had given herself over to his keeping, her fears and apprehensions be damned. And the pain was no excuse. She wouldn't have yielded to his arms if she hadn't wanted to, no matter how badly she had been hurting.

He brought his horse to a standstill and she tipped her head back to gaze into the gray depths of his eyes. Smoky richness swirled with a lighter network of silver. The complex mixture in those orbs echoed the tangle of feelings that swirled about within her.

"Ready?"

His voice came as though from a great distance. A little taken aback, she collected her wits, realizing only then that she had been staring at him like a besotted little fool.

"Yes, of course," she answered, sounding in control, but she wasn't. He had the most profound effect on her and she had no idea how to handle it. "Lead and I'll follow." Belatedly, she remembered to summon forth what she hoped passed for a natural smile.

"Lead?" One of his black brows shot upward. "You have

it wrong, Jessica." He extended his left hand down to her in both invitation and command.

She clamped her upper lip between her teeth. He meant for her to ride with him. On the same horse.

"Up you go," he coaxed. Before she could utter a sound, he took hold of her right wrist and lifted her as easily as he would a child. When she came to rest, she was seated across his lap, her legs draped to one side while he held her securely in place.

Out of sheer reflex, she grabbed hold of his steely forearm. A split second later, she was infused with the impulse to jump to safety. She was so conscious of their positions she could barely swallow. Along every inch of her, she felt the shift and play of his muscles, felt the startling warmth of his skin permeating his layer of clothing and her own. With every breath she took, she drew in the spicy scent of his cologne mixed with the essence of the man himself.

He was completely male. Nothing was more glaring to her than that. His hollows fit her curves, his great height complimented her diminutive stature, and where she knew herself to be soft, he was iron honed.

All the contrasts that shaped and molded each of them were there. His masculinity as opposed to her femininity. It was natural, it was normal. It scared her half to death.

"Relax," he said. "I won't let you fall."

She almost wished he would. Then at least she could regain control of her body and her senses.

Horribly self-conscious, she made a murmurous sound that could have been interpreted for anything, and concentrated on not concentrating on him.

"I've . . . I've never been on such a . . . tall horse," she stammered. Given her circumstances, she believed that a plausible thing to say.

"It's no different than being on a smaller horse except for your distance to the ground. Don't let that frighten you."

Beneath her thighs, she felt him set the animal into motion with a commanding squeeze of his legs. The stallion moved forward with a powerful gliding stride that only increased the contact of her body and Nicholas's. Thankfully, the movement also required that she attend to the business of retaining her seat. Even though they moved at a leisurely canter, and Nicholas held her firmly in place, the horse's gait was ground eating and forced her to pay close attention to her balance.

Gratefully, she let herself be distracted from the disturbing intimacy of being cuddled against him in so suggestive a manner. It truly was for the best. If she didn't divert her attention from him, she was going to be reduced to a trembling idiot.

"Where are we going?" she asked, not looking up.

"To the fields, of course."

She should have known. At the very heart of Bellefleur lay the fields. "I don't know anything about cotton."

"It's a bit early yet for the cotton. Right now, we've got to worry about the corn. That goes in weeks before any other crop."

"Why?"

"To save our sanity come August."

"I don't understand."

"It's really quite simple. We can't possibly harvest both crops at the same time. There aren't enough hours in the day. So we put in the corn first so we can have it completely picked by the time the cotton is ready to be brought in."

The soft line of her lips stretched into a smile, and unconsciously, she relaxed slightly. "That's very clever."

Nicholas tipped his head to one side to garner a clearer picture of her face. If he hadn't felt the ease of her body, her expression would have told him that she was not as nervous as she had been. For that he was glad. He didn't want her afraid of him.

"I wouldn't call it clever so much as practical."

She wouldn't have dreamed of disagreeing with him, but she thought the plan had more merit than mere practicality. "What do you do with the cotton after its been picked?"

"It's ginned."

She looked up quickly, forgetting her reticence at the mention of this. "You mean in a cotton gin?"

"Exactly. Does that surprise you?"

"Yes, even I've heard of Mr. Whitney's wondrous machine."

Nicholas chuckled as much from her reaction as to the thought of the cotton gin housed in its own shed. Mr. Whitney's machine cut the cotton processing time by a third. "It is a wonder."

For some reason that Jessica couldn't put a name to, everything involved with the cotton crop intrigued her, the gin in particular. She had first heard about it years ago in Charleston. Even then, she had marveled at the ingenuity that went into the invention.

Eyes alight with every ounce of delight she felt, she said, "I read about this cotton gin. Does it really do everything it's supposed to do?"

"That depends," he replied with a laugh. "If you've read that it will prevent blight or fill the river with fish, the answer is no. On the other hand, it does separate cotton lint from the seed."

"Yes, yes," she insisted, giving free rein to her enthusiasm. "I think that is absolutely remarkable."

Her tone of voice gave Nicholas pause and his black brows slanted upward curiously. He hadn't expected such eagerness from her, especially not over something as commonplace as ginning cotton. Fifty years ago, her reaction would have been in keeping, but these were modern times. Machinery was making a place for itself in the world.

Though, apparently, not hers.

His insides stilled with a melancholy. He had a fair idea of what her circumstances had been, and yet he had to wonder at the true extent of her hardships if she was so overwhelmed by a half-century old contraption.

He slanted her a long stare. Damn, but she was a remarkable little thing. With each passing day, he discovered that there was so much more to her than he had first realized. For all intents and purposes, she had been deprived of the most meager niceties life could offer. Things he took for granted, gave her cause for elation.

Nonetheless, she still had a zeal for life. It was normally hidden under a skittish wariness learned at the hand of life's more cruel injustices. But when she forgot the effects of her past, when she let go of her inhibitions as she did now, it was easy to see that she had a dogged capacity to put one foot in front of the other without ever doing so at someone else's expense. Somehow, through it all, she had held onto a spark of optimism.

Startled, he saw that a multilayered strength of character lay beneath her too-thin frame.

He shifted her slightly in his arms, and considered that frame. It wasn't nearly as thin as it had been in New Orleans. Jessica had put on some weight and those pounds looked good. She could stand to gain a bit more, but the angles and hollows that had comprised her face had begun to take on a healthy softness. The sunken depression between her shoulder blades had become less prominent. Even her hands had lost their gaunt cast.

Like dry tinder claimed by quick fire, his mind pictured her slender curves filled out to an abundant fullness. Not fleshy opulence, but feminine richness able to cradle a man's body with warmth and softness and take him to paradise.

The picture expanded. All too easily, he saw her belly swollen with child, *his* child, her breasts enlarged to accommodate that child.

His entire body jerked. The stallion danced to one side. Mentally swearing, Nicholas fought to bring the horse under control as he yanked in on himself. Mind and body, his wayward senses had taken command once more.

"What happened?" Jessica gasped, clinging with her one good hand to his arm.

"The horse is a stallion," was all he said. It was all he could manage. In his mind, he was firing condemnations and curses at himself as quickly as he could.

"What does that mean?"

"What?" He checked the horse's shifting movements with a determined hand.

"What does his being a stallion have to do with anything?"

Nicholas dragged in a deep breath. "He fights for control of the bit. If I don't keep a ruling rein, he'll slip free to do as he pleases." Scoffing silently, he decided not to consider the similarities between himself and his horse.

It took a shift of his weight and a readjustment of the grip of his legs to gather the horse beneath him. As Nicholas urged the mount into the first of the fields, he damn well wished it would be that easy to settle himself. He was thankful for Jessica's silence as she openly studied the land.

She scanned the acres of tilled earth with something close to awe. The land rolled like gentle waves, cresting slightly before slanting into the next umber trough and the one beyond that. Just looking at the vastness of the land filled her with an eager sort of energy and she was helpless to pull her gaze away.

All her life, she had been moved from one locale to another, accompanying her father as he searched for some undefinable goal. The majority of the time, they had lived in one city or another where space was reduced to crowded blocks of buildings and roadways. Grand expanses of land were something with which she was not familiar, nor was it something she could take for granted.

The richness of it was almost humbling, tugging hard at the heart of her.

"Will all of this be corn?" she asked, nodding to the tract that stretched to a grayish-green border of trees.

"This field and four others just like it."

"How many acres is that?"

"A little over five hundred."

"That leaves the rest for cotton?"

"Not all of it. Fourteen hundred acres are allotted for cotton."

Jessica ran the numbers through her head. "What about the remaining seven hundred acres?"

"It's used."

"How?" She truly wanted to know, and had she been thinking as much about her manner as she was about the workings of the plantation, she would have realized that her questions could have been considered impertinent. As it was, she felt as if a whole new world had been opened up to her and she was anxious to saturate her mind with as much knowledge as she could. "How does it all work?"

The tinge of impatience that raced through her was reflected in her voice. Nicholas flicked a glance at her and couldn't suppress a smile. She was practically vibrating with curiosity and it plainly showed in the soft parting of her lips and the brightness of her eyes.

In the face of such eagerness, his temporary annoyance of moments past dissolved, to be replaced by a contented indulgence. He liked nothing better than to discuss Bellefleur. In Jessica, he had an appreciative audience.

"The house and outbuildings, stables, barns and sheds take up space. Then there are the gardens and the pastures, the acres set aside for growing grain for the livestock. The forest acreage takes up the rest."

She looked eastward where a line of trees hid the river from view. "What happens when the river floods?"

And so her questions continued. Never relinquishing her gaze on the sight she found so inspiring, she plied Nicholas for answers. He gave them with a readiness rooted in pride.

They raised their own sheep to have wool for warm winter clothes. They constantly replenished the growth of trees to insure a continuous source of lumber. Hogs were fed grains grown on the land, only to be slaughtered and smoked with hickory wood taken from one of the stands.

Manure gathered from the livestock was turned out into the garden to fertilize the vegetables that would be pickled or dried. Ice cut from the fresh streams and stored in the winter saw them through the long, sweltering summer months. A host of artisans turned out saddles and blankets, barrels and plows.

With every response Nicholas gave, her need to know grew right along with her admiration for the land. By the time they had ridden over the better part of the fields, Jessica had a clear understanding that nearly all and anything that was needed to survive was there on the plantation.

"Bellefleur is its own little community," she averred in amazement.

"As close to that as possible," Nicholas returned, liking her wonder as much as the gleam in her eyes. "What we don't grow, raise or build, weave, cook, or sew ourselves, we trade for. We call in the doctor or dentist when needs be, import a few liquors, buy glass, paint and a few metals when it's necessary, but other than that, Bellefleur is self-sufficient."

Jessica considered that for a moment, and when she spoke, her voice was laden with a yearning she couldn't hide. "You can live your whole life here and never have to leave to go looking for anything." She gazed longingly about the secluded glade into which they had ridden. Circling a wide expanse of lawn, a profusion of bushes stood beneath towering elms draped in delicate, silvery moss. "The plantation, Bellefleur gives you everything you need."

Nicholas absorbed the look on her face, caught by the sight of her raw hunger. "That's the beauty of Bellefleur," he explained slowly, once again taken aback by the many facets of this woman. "We take care of the land so that it will take care of us so that we can care for the land *ad infinitum.* Self-perpetuation."

She had never experienced that kind of state before, where her life was so directly related to the land. Nicholas, however, had known no other existence.

Turning to stare directly into his eyes, she confessed, "I think I envy you."

"What," he returned, unable to conceal his surprise. "Why?"

"Because you've had the chance to experience all of this." She swept her hand wide to indicate the beauty of the glen about her. "Everything here, even this out of the way meadow, has meaning, a certain importance in the scheme of things. You've been able to share of yourself with something that has true purpose."

She glanced away, her gaze coming to rest on a rose bush in full bloom, red blossoms bursting forth with the vivid promise of expectancy. She smiled broadly. Where else but on this wondrous property could one find roses blooming in March? Nowhere. Somehow, that didn't surprise her.

Tipping her head back to look at him again, she whispered, "Bellefleur is truly a home."

The soft reverence Nicholas witnessed in her velvet gaze shot straight into him with all the speed and accuracy of an arrow released from a straining bow. In the region of his heart, his chest clenched until his lungs ached and he felt his blood pound through his veins.

She was mesmerized by the plantation. In return, he was mesmerized by her. Her thoughts and beliefs and perceptions were uncannily intimate, touching him deeply and on an extremely private level that no one, at any time, had ever reached before.

Longing rose up from the core of him. For a few mad seconds, he was beyond reason. He forgot the reality of their stations in life, reined the stallion to a halt and captured her lips with his own.

Chapter Eight

He was kissing her. Jessica's mind registered that fact several seconds after she felt the firm pressure of his lips on hers. But during that brief moment before she actually became consciously aware of his actions, time became suspended and all she could do was absorb the wonder of feeling his mouth move over hers.

The warm touch of his flesh robbed her of will. Without the slightest warning, her bones became useless and her heart thudded painfully in her chest. She melted into the heat and strength of him, helpless to do anything but experience him in every pore of her.

Every impression she had ever had of him dulled by comparison to the newest feelings generated in that instant. His power, compassion and virility seemed magnified, intensified. The effect on her was as overwhelming, as all consuming as Bellefleur itself.

Her senses quickened and flared to life . . . too quickly, too turbulently. In a blinding flash, time resumed its normal state and alarm snaked its way through her.

"No," she gasped, tearing her mouth away. She shoved at his chest, desperate to put as much distance between them as possible. In her haste, she forgot the injury to her left hand and cried out in pain. "Stop! Let me go."

At her first protest, Nicholas raised his head. Awareness returned in a wild, disorienting rush. The need she inspired within him demanded that he ignore her protests, that he claim her for his own.

That he plant his seed.

The thought came out of nowhere. Again. And he was appalled. Twice in the past hour, his mind had betrayed him in this manner.

What the devil was the matter with him? He was no untried youth whose body made demands to conquer his better judgement. He was a man in his prime, at ease with and in command of the sensual side of his nature. There was no excuse for his behavior.

"Jessica, I'm—"

"Let me go," she insisted, struggling to reach the ground.

He caught her by the waist and held her in place. "Hold still before you hurt yourself."

She was beyond listening. Every insecurity she harbored surfaced, choking her with dread and doubt. Too many years of mistreatment at a man's hand obliterated the logic that this man had never hurt her. Too many years of jeopardy suffered because of a man's neglect negated the reality that this man had given her shelter from life's cruelties. Too many years spent mistrusting men overshadowed the fact that *this* man's kisses had stolen deep inside her to make her feel things she had never felt before.

She squirmed and twisted, fighting for an even breath. When the pressure of his arms only increased, she pulled in on all her defenses and went utterly still.

"Let go of me."

Nicholas cursed under his breath, wondering what in the hell he could possibly say to her. "I had no right to do that."

"I want to get down." She stared straight ahead, her attention focused solely on removing herself from his lap.

The unnatural stillness of her body pricked his concern. "Jessica, there's no need for you to get down."

"I don't want to ride any further. I want to go back to the house."

"Fine, I'll take you back at once."

"No."

"Damn it all! I made a mistake. It won't happen again."

As reassurances went, it sounded believable, but she was in no frame of mind to put store in such promises. "Please, let me down," she insisted, speaking each word in precise intervals.

Her tone was uncompromising, her body literally inflexible. The combined effects told Nicholas that he would not be able to make her see reason. At least not now. To push her further would only make matters worse.

Once again, he swore liberally, damning himself for a fool. "All right," he grated between tightly clenched teeth. His instincts rebelled at leaving her to her own care. Just as quickly, his mind jeered, wanting to know where his good intentions had been a minute ago.

Carefully, he lowered her until she was standing on her own two feet. It didn't help his temper at all to see her hastily back away. "The house is that way." He indicated the direction with a nod of his head. "I'll tell Mama Lou that you'll be along in about a half hour."

Nibbling on her upper lip, she nodded.

At her wide-eyed response, Nicholas's temper escalated another notch. "Don't get lost." With that, he urged the stallion out of the grove, leaving Jessica to stare after his retreating figure.

When he passed from view, she released her breath in a long, slow exhalation. Her eyes closed slowly while conflicting emotions tumbled riotously about within her.

Nothing happened, she told herself. He hadn't pawed and grabbed at her as she had seen men so often do to women. There had been no force or brutality. He had simply kissed her.

Logically, she accepted that. Men kissed women every day and the world did not come to a screeching halt. That wasn't the end of it for her, though. Nothing in her life had ever been normal when it came to men. Consequently, being kissed by a man fell into that realm of not being quite normal.

She had been kissed before. All too easily, she recalled those few times when some man had dared to inflict his attentions on her. She had always panicked at that kind of intimacy, and she knew that was partly due to her wariness of men in general. More specifically, however, was that the only men who had ever tried to kiss her had been crass, boorish chums of her father. To this day, she shuddered at the memory of fleshy lips claiming her own.

Nicholas's kisses had been completely different.

She opened her eyes, her blond brows elevating at the unexpectedness of that revelation. Despite the fact that he had had no right to do as he did, she hadn't been repulsed by the touch of his mouth. In fact, for several moments she had been quite entranced by his kiss. That is, until her mind had taken over and unconsciously dragged up old reflexes.

Her hand rose to her lips to trace the soft contours. All the wonder of Nicholas's caress swamped her, sending a jab of sensation racing to the core of her. Amazed, she stared down at her waist, then lower. Dear Lord, what was the matter with her? Her body was behaving with a will of its own.

She yanked her hand away, swallowing hard. Completely flustered, she wanted to pretend that nothing out of the ordinary had happened, but she couldn't. No, she had always dealt with plain, bald truths and the truth of the matter was that she liked being kissed by Nicholas.

The admission sent a groan of despair up her throat. She didn't know what to make of the situation, if it was good or bad. Worse, she didn't even know how to handle it. Regardless, she could not deny that to kiss Nicholas DuQuaine was quite extraordinary.

A crooked smiled wobbled about her lips. It flattened almost as quickly as it formed. There was too much for her to think about and she couldn't stand where she was. Nicholas had given her thirty minutes to reach the house. In light of their exchange, she did not want to do anything to further test his good will. And she did *not* want him returning for her.

Spinning about, she headed for the house, then stopped when her gaze fell to a nearby rose bush. The lush color silently beckoned, and she approached the beautiful shrub to breathe in its floral perfume.

The smile that came to her lips this time was full and sure. For one of the rare times in her life, she gave into a sudden impulse, plucked a small, perfect rose and tucked it into her pocket. Then she hastened back to the house as quickly as she could.

"I was gettin' ready to send someone out for you," Mama Lou informed her. "You all right?"

Jessica looked away from the searching glint in the housekeeper's eyes. "Yes. I'm fine."

Mama Lou weighed her reply with apparent skepticism. "You don't look so good. Your hand troublin' you?"

"No." Not wanting to dwell on all that had occurred, she said, "I need to finish the quilt."

The nod Mama Lou gave her was a deliberate, pensive-looking move, filled, Jessica was certain, with a liberal dose of disbelief. Thankfully, the housekeeper kept all thoughts to herself, and Jessica sighed in relief.

Sewing kept her hands busy for the remainder of the day. Sitting beneath the crepe myrtle once more, she mended seams, taking extra pains with her stitches. To do her best was inherent to her nature, but she had to wonder if the exceptional attention she had paid to the bed covering wasn't a mental ploy to keep from thinking of Nicholas.

By late afternoon, she gave up the struggle and faced the issued head on. She should have never allowed him to kiss her. She should have never ridden with him. She should have never gone off with him in the first place. If she hadn't, she wouldn't be sitting there right that minute, besieged by guilt and indecision and uncertainty.

And heaven only knew what he must think of her. Even though he did apologize, he had been angry. She didn't want him, or any man, angry. She much preferred him as he had been at the onset of their ride, gallant, humorous and indulgent.

As if lured by some inner voice, she reached into her pocket and retrieved the rose. Wilted, discolored to a deep burgundy, she stared at the once exquisite petals and felt a pang of loss. The perfection of the blossom had been fleeting.

"What have you got there?" Mama Lou asked.

Jessica looked up in surprise. She hadn't heard the woman's approach. "It's a rose I picked earlier."

"A rose?" Mama Lou squinted for a better look. "What's it doin' out there at this time of year?"

"I don't know. I found an entire bush in bloom earlier."

The lines of Mama Lou's face elongated in astonishment, her brown eyes rounding to enormous proportions. "Where'd you find this bush?"

Jessica hesitated at the housekeeper's reaction. "On the other side of the south fields, in a small, out of the way meadow," she explained cautiously. "Is there something wrong? It was all right for me to pick a flower, wasn't it?"

"Damn," Mama Lou exclaimed in growing delight. "Cut off my head and call me shorty. If that ain't the sweetest sight I've ever seen."

Jessica took in the huge smile that suffused Mama Lou's face before glancing to the rose. "It is amazing, isn't it?"

"That it is."

"I've never seen a rose so early in the year."

"Girl, you'll never see the likes of that rose ever again," Mama Lou chuckled.

"No, I suppose not."

"There's no supposin' about it." Mama Lou shook her head, still plainly enjoying the moment. "That's the most special rose you'll ever come across."

"It is?" A shiver of apprehension raced over Jessica's skin. "I didn't know it was rare. If I had been told, I would have never touched the bush."

Mama Lou burst into a rare laugh, the deep, throaty sound confusing Jessica all the more. "Jess, you can pick as many flowers from that bush as you want. In fact, I may take a walk myself and gather up an entire bouquet and set it right in the front drawin' room."

Jessica gave into her own one-sided grin. "Why is this rose so special?"

Sighing in a satisfaction too blatant to contain, Mama Lou plopped her hands on her ample hips. "Not bein' from these parts, you don't know the legend of the Bellefleur rose."

"No, no one's told me about a legend."

"Well, there is one, and it goes back to the first Master DuQuaine, Master Nick's great-granddaddy, Raynard. He came over from France and made this land his. This was way back before my time, about 1730, or so." She laughed in glee, then amazed Jessica by lowering herself to sit on the soft grass. "I never knew the man, but the stories still go on about him and his Amiee."

"Amiee?"

"That was his wife. She came over from France, too. Raynard took one look at her and couldn't look nowhere else ever again. He built this place for her, put his heart and soul into it, all because he loved her somethin' fierce."

The sentiment touched Jessica deeply. "And the rose?"

"Hold your water, I'm gettin' to that. It was Amiee who brought the rose plants with her from her home over in the old country. She planted them to make some kind of a special rose garden."

"Is that where I found the bush this morning?"

"That it is. But the sad thin' about her little bushes; they never bloomed. No matter what she did, Amiee never could coax a single flower into the sun."

"Never?"

"Not a one. In fact, it wasn't until their son, Ettienne, was grown that roses bloomed, and then, only one time. Later that year, he met and married his wife. They died never seein' another flower from those bushes, but their son did. That would be Master Nick's daddy, Francois. The rose bushes came to life one winter and sure enough, he found his Emilee a short while after. I remember that. I was just a little girl at the time, but I can still see the red flower as clear as day." Brows arched, she gazed at the single bud Jessica held. "Those bushes have been still all this time. Until now."

The loveliness of the tale filled Jessica with a tender yearning. And even though she knew it was a legend, she indulged herself with the wish that it could be true. "Every time the rose bush blooms, the master of the plantation marries."

Mama Lou came to her feet with an ease that belied her commanding stature. "Not just marries," she clarified. "He finds the one true love of his life." She set her shoulders and brushed off her hands, her no-nonsense manner back in full force. "That's the legend, girl. Now, you get that quilt finished before you get your supper."

Jessica shook off the dazed feeling generated by the enchanting story. "Yes, ma'am."

"And don't sit out here too long," Mama Lou commanded. "Once the sun sets, the ground takes on a chill. The last thin' we need is to have you come down with the ague." She turned away for the house, but not before Jessica noticed her smile of pure, undiluted delight. That simple upward curve of her lips was telling.

Mama Lou believed the legend of the rose. And if all went according to legend, some time soon, Nicholas DuQuaine would find the one woman he would love forever.

For all the tender romance of the notion, Jessica found it oddly depressing.

Nicholas strode into his bedroom, feeling the strain of the day in his shoulders. Shutting the door with a well-placed heel, he kneaded the tension from the back of his neck, a gesture that did little to ease the ache settled there. The hot bath he had ordered to be sent up would help.

Crossing the room, he peeled off his shirt. The brisk dusk air breezing in through the open windows felt good against his skin. After having spent the entire day working under the sun, he appreciated the subtleties of things like cool air, calming solitude and the taste of French brandy.

He poured himself two fingers of the amber liquid and lounged back in a dark blue wing back facing one of the windows. It was the first time since dawn that he had stopped to rest, and he took several seconds to simply absorb the sensation of relaxation.

The long lines of his body eased, his posture slipping lower into the comfortable cushions. Setting his snifter on the table close at hand, he removed his boots and socks, crossed his legs at the ankles and propped his feet on the window sill. A sigh of pleasure stole past his lips as he reached for his drink.

The brandy worked its way down his throat, spreading its warming essence over his chest and lower to his stomach. Languidly, he rubbed a calloused palm through the mat of hair on his chest, the pleasurable friction only adding to his growing comfort.

Damn, but he had worked hard today. All he wanted now was to forget about the miles and miles of fences he had inspected, the huge boulder he had helped move, the bushels of corn seed he had examined, the mare who was about to foal, the endless decisions he had made.

And the taste of Jessica's lips.

"Damn," he muttered, his gray eyes narrowing to misty slits. Just thinking about the sweetness of kissing her robbed him of a good portion of the contentment he had been seeking.

In search of relief, he took a healthy swallow of the brandy. The gesture was futile. Jessica invaded his mind with a strength as undeniable as she was herself. More times today than he would like to acknowledge, his mind had fallen victim to that strength.

Knowing it was useless to do otherwise, he gave himself up to his thoughts of Jessica McCormick. What was it about her that attracted him so? She was not the most beautiful woman he had ever met. With her red-gold curls and almond shaped blue eyes, she was pretty enough, growing more so by the day, but physical attributes alone had never been enough to spur his interest in a woman.

No, there was something about her that had, from the first moment he laid eyes on her, pricked something deep inside him. He wished to God he knew what that was, because he had been responding to it ever since.

Another sip of brandy brought him no closer to the answers he sought. Instead, the headiness of the liquor served to remind him of the feel of her lips.

She hadn't been kissed often, of that he was dead certain. Before she had remembered to panic, her response had been shy and untutored, but no less stirring for all of the underscoring artlessness involved. He rather liked that, and the more he examined the notion, the more he discovered that Jessica's sexual naiveté epitomized what he found so intriguing about her.

There was a goodness within her that appealed to him greatly. In the course of her difficult life, she had not given in to the hardships that could have broken her. She had not bartered her body or her ethics, she had not compromised her integrity.

Those options could have been hers. She could have become a bitter, jaded, seventeen-year-old replica of her father. She hadn't. With a rare inner fortitude, she had clung to a decency that seemed an innate part of her, paying with the only thing left to her; trust and self-assurance. Both had been dearly sacrificed.

At heart, she was a good person. At heart, he was undeniably drawn to good people.

He wanted her.

His body jerked upright, his feet hit the floor. "Damn it all."

He did *not* want to *want* her! How many times would he have to remind himself that she was his servant, that he had no right to picture her lying beneath him, soft and receptive? Another man might ignore her circumstances and surrender to the need she inspired, but he couldn't take advantage of her that way.

"Bath is ready, Master Nick."

Nicholas blinked, his valet's voice yanking him out his absorption. Grateful for the interruption, he came to his feet.

"Just in time, Jessup," he told the aging black servant.

"For what?" Not bothering to look up, Jessup pointed a bony finger to a precise spot before the fireplace. All the while, he kept a sharp, albeit rheumy eye on the three young boys toting in a large brass tub.

"In time to save me from myself," Nicholas jeered.

Tub in place, Jessup drew himself up to his full five feet of height and gave Nicholas a shaming look. "I can't help you wid dat, Master Nick. Gonna have to talk to de good Lord above about dat."

"I think you're right."

Jessup muttered a sound that could have meant anything as he turned to the boys. "You get on out to de kitchen and hurry back wid dem buckets of water like I told you."

Amused, Nicholas watched the youngsters hurry off, glad for the distraction they and Jessup provided. "How do you do that, old man?"

"Do what?"

"Get people to jump at your simplest word."

Jessup made his way to the massive four-poster where Nicholas had dropped his shirt. "I don't do no such thin'."

"Yes, you do."

"If you say so."

Nicholas scoffed in wry humor. "I do say so."

Jessup nodded his white head like some wise, old sage, his gnarly hands folding Nicholas's shirt. "You de master round here."

Master of everything but himself, Nicholas thought. When it came to Jessica, he was master of nothing, most especially his damnable response to her. "I sometimes wonder, Jessup."

"No need to do dat. Everythin's gonna be just as right as can be."

Hearing the certainty in the servant's voice, Nicholas raised one black brow. "You sound like you know something I don't."

"I knows what I sees."

"And what's that?"

"Your time is comin'. Mama Lou's been talkin' all about dat rose."

Nicholas paused in the middle of unfastening his pants. "What rose?"

"De rose dat Jessica picked from your great-grandmammy's rose bush."

For several seconds, Nicholas couldn't make sense of the comment. Then suddenly, he remembered exactly where he had drawn his horse to a standstill to kiss Jessica. The old rose garden. At the time he had taken note of little other than Jessica. Now he realized that the flash of brilliant red he had seen had been one of the bushes in full bloom.

"I'll be damned," he muttered.

"No, sir, Master Nick. You be blessed. You know how de legend goes."

Nicholas did. It was a fanciful tale, full of romance and charm. He had never given it much credence. He sat to remove his pants. "You superstitious old goat."

Jessup eyed him indignantly. "You doubting young stud."

Nicholas burst into laughter at the man's irreverence. "I don't know why I put up with you."

"Cuz you could never get on widout me, is why. Cuz you know I's always right. And I'm right about de rose."

"Is that a fact?"

"Yes, sir. Every time de bush gives up its roses, the master of de place takes him a wife."

"Coincidence."

"Fate."

"Nonsense."

"No, sir, you mark my words. By de end of de year, you gonna find you de woman you gonna love forever, through dis lifetime and into de next. By de end of the year, you gonna take you a wife."

Chapter Nine

"Bloody hell."

Mathew Bennett shoved the curse out past thinned lips. If there was one thing he could not abide, it was waste and that was exactly what his morning had been, a complete waste. Of time.

Furious with himself, he adjusted his low crowned hat, shifted irritably in his saddle and tried to remember why he had ridden all the way to the ends of his property. He was supposed to decide whether this tract of land would be planted with corn or wheat. That was not what he had been doing. Instead, he had been sitting there like a besotted swain, staring at the bordering acres, the acres belonging to Anna.

"Bloody, *bloody* hell." There was no need for him to question the state of his mind. He knew exactly, precisely, why he was so distracted. He was in love.

He exhaled in a short, broken sigh. This wasn't the first time he had admitted he loved Anna DuQuaine. No, he had made the confession to himself months ago. Still, he was no closer to feeling comfortable with his emotions now than he had been when he first discovered how he felt. That had been in August, and for the past seven months, he had been carrying the secret of his love inside him.

Well, his secret was about to take him over the brink. There were only so many times he could catch glimpses of her at church and not picture her as his bride, only so many times he would hear her voice and not yearn for those sweet tones to carry him through the course of his day, only so many nights he could go to his empty bed and not go a little insane with wanting.

And he did *want* her, in all the ways a man could possibly want a woman, as his friend, his confidant, his lover, most especially his lover. Yet, there he sat, gazing at her land as if that could bring him one step closer to having her, but he didn't know what else to do.

Another admission with which he was all too familiar. This one made him clench his teeth together in self-disgust, for he was a grown man, in his prime, well-respected, considered passably handsome, and for the life of him, he didn't know how to approach Anna. For him, it wasn't as simple as—

". . . I love you, Anna. Marry me."

Surprisingly, speaking the words aloud struck the edge from his anger. He settled back into his saddle and scanned the newly plowed fields again. The troughs of soil were uniform, their unbroken order marching to the horizon offering a certain serenity. No answers lay in the umber furrows; only a sense of harmony.

If only his life of late could be so amenable. It would be if he could find the right way to approach Anna with his feelings. The nature of their relationship prevented that. They had been friends since childhood. She looked at him no differently than she looked at her own brother.

"You've got Nick for that," he told the absent Anna.

How was he supposed to overcome that obstacle? A firm

declaration could prove to be an embarrassment for them both if she was not inclined to share his feelings. In the end, the friendship they did share would never be the same. He could well imagine the awkwardness that would prevail between them.

The subtle approach was less of a gamble, but infinitely more frustrating. The elemental male within him demanded that he take her into his arms and claim her for his own, and damn whatever protests she might offer. The gentleman he was cautioned that Anna had been raised a lady, and no lady would appreciate that kind of barbaric behavior. A lady was supposed to be wooed and courted *after* she had offered encouragement in that direction.

Anna had never done that.

"Bloody, bloody hell."

The horse beneath him sidestepped, forcing Mathew back to the present. He filled his lungs and decided that he was going to accomplish nothing that morning by sitting there. If he was ever going to make any progress, he was going to have to move. Literally. To that end, he put his heels to the horse's sides and rode for Bellefleur, never once stopping until the majestic white mansion came into view. Only then did he rein in and dismount at the stairs.

"Mornin', Mr. Bennett," Mama Lou called, exiting the house.

Mathew gave the housekeeper a nod. "Mama Lou."

"Mr. DuQuaine ain't here, right now."

Adjusting the brim of his hat, Mathew looked away briefly. "I've come to see Miss Anna, actually."

Mama Lou's brows arched for a quick moment. "Well, she ain't here either."

Disappointment grabbed Mathew in a cruel vice. When he had decided to call on Anna, he had anticipated her being here. Forget the fact that it was perfectly logical for her to be elsewhere. At that moment, his emotions didn't give a damn about logic.

"Has she gone into town?"

"No, sir. It's wash day. She's gone down to the laundry."

Mathew mulled that over, and condemned his timing. Talking to Anna while she was in the midst of boiling water and lye was not conducive to a private discussion.

"You goin' to stay for a bit, Mr. Bennett?"

He really shouldn't, he told himself. He should ride off and come back another day when he and Anna could be alone.

"Yes, yes. I'll stroll over and see what Miss Anna is about."

And having declared as much, he matched actions to words. Moments later, he wondered what in the hell he was doing. With every step he took, he felt his stomach tighten with a nervousness that made his palms sweat. He was being a fool for proceeding like this. His only excuse was that where Anna was concerned, he was a fool.

The sounds and smells of the laundry reached him from a short distance. He spotted Anna at once amongst the women, vats and drying lines. His pace slowed as he stared at her. She was the most beautiful woman he had ever seen. Standing in the sunlight, her dark hair tucked up under a wide-brimmed straw bonnet, she wore a smile despite the taxing nature of her task.

He studied that smile and felt its counterpart curve his mouth then wrap itself about his heart. Bloody hell, but he loved everything about her. The low drawl of her voice, the gentle curve of her brow, the air of vitality that graced her every move. Even dressed for the drudgery of work, she exuded a gracious femininity that appealed to him greatly.

"Are you sure you should be out here breaking your back?" he asked, coming within speaking range.

Anna turned, her surprise apparent. "Mathew, what are you doing here?"

"Having my shirts washed?" he asked in an attempt at humor.

She laughed and cast him a shaming glance. "We have enough to do, thank you, without adding your clothes to the pile."

"I was jesting."

"So was I."

"Were you? You mean you would actually see that my shirt was laundered if I asked."

"Of course," she averred. "How can you even ask such a thing? You're practically family, Matt."

The smile dropped from his face. Once again he was sorely reminded of his place in her life. "I'm not a member of the family, Anna."

Hearing the tension underscoring his words, Anna tipped her head to one side. "Perhaps not, but you're as close as if you were."

Mathew held up a hand in self-defense. He didn't know what he would do if she actually came out and said that she thought of him as a brother. That was the last thing he wanted to hear, the last thing he wanted her to feel.

"Do you have to do this?" he asked a little irritably, waving a hand at the activity going on around them. "Can you get away for a few minutes?"

Anna looked about. "I shouldn't. We're about to start on the linens and I like to keep an eye on the amount of soap being used."

Mathew's jaw worked with his mounting frustration. "Can't you get one of these women to do that?"

"I prefer not to. Too much soap and we'll spend the rest of the day having to rinse, and the sheets will be stiff in the bargain." She gave a teasing grin. "Then I'll have to listen to Nick complain about scratchy sheets, and I'd rather not have to do that."

"I promise for only a short while, Anna."

She hesitated, scanned his face and finally nodded in agreement. "All right. For a while."

He exhaled and rubbed his palms on his pants, once again not quite certain how to proceed. A reckless kind of bravado had carried him to this point. What was he supposed to fall back on to continue? The confidence he wished he had was absent.

"Is there something wrong?" Anna asked, falling into step beside him.

"No, everything is fine." He directed their path toward the peach orchard just coming into bloom. "Why do you ask?"

"It's a busy time to pay a call. I know how demanding the fields can be."

Mathew knew only too well. Anna had him so distracted, he still hadn't decided whether the south tract should be planted in wheat or corn. "The land can wait for an hour or so. I simply thought to ride over today and . . ." *And what?* he mentally asked himself. *And ask you what your feelings might be about me, and ask you to marry me?* He cleared the constricting tension from his throat. ". . . and spend some time with you."

"With me?" Her gray eyes lit with curiosity. "I would have thought you'd visit with Nick."

"Why would you think that?"

She shrugged her hands. "Because that's what you normally do."

"Well," he declared a touch fiercely, "today I wanted to visit with you."

She blinked at his tone. "Thank you, I think."

"You're welcome." Silently, Mathew cursed. This wasn't going well at all. He was supposed to be easing into a courtship and instead he was practically harping at her. Collecting his composure, he softened his tone and offered, "I haven't seen you in a while."

Anna gazed about the peach orchard. "It hasn't been that long. You were here last week."

"Last week?"

"Yes," she returned, her brow knit with lines of confusion. "Don't you remember? Nick returned from New Orleans with Jessica."

Of course he remembered, but it had felt like months since then. "Time seems to have slipped past."

"I know exactly how you feel."

"Do you?"

"Most definitely." She stopped beneath a tree and reached up to pluck a blossom from its limb. Staring at the delicate flower, her face took on a wistful cast. "There are days when I feel as if the days are rushing by."

"Why do you say that?"

"I don't know. Probably because it's the truth."

"Are you in a hurry about something?"

She tossed the blossom aside, giving into a sigh of impatience. "Sometimes I feel as if I'm stuck in place."

He scanned her features, looking for a clue as to what meaning lay beneath her words. "Bellefleur is not such a bad place to be stuck."

A delicate scoff parted her lips. "I'm not saying differently, but . . ." Her words trailed to nothing, her gaze turning inward to visions at which Mathew could only guess.

Without thinking he took her hand between his own. "But what, Anna?"

For several seconds, his query met with silence. Finally, she shrugged. "You'll think I'm silly."

"Nothing you say or do is silly."

"Thank you for that, but I think you're a little biased."

"No, I'm not." She had never confided her personal thoughts to him. He nearly held his breath fearing that she wouldn't do so now. "Please, tell me what you're thinking."

She gave into a smile as reluctant as her manner. "Only if you promise not to criticize."

"I promise."

She looked at him with equal amounts of skepticism and embarrassment suffusing her face. "I want to go exploring."

Mathew waited . . . and waited. That was her confession? She wanted to go exploring?! What in the devil did she mean by that? "I don't understand. Go exploring where?"

Again, her shoulders rose with a shrug. "Anywhere." Drawing her hand from his, she gestured to the world in general. "Wherever my heart desires. There's so much in the world to see. I want to experience it all."

A sick feeling began in the region of Mathew's stomach. While he was consumed by passion for her, she was filled with wanderlust. "What about a husband?"

Her dark brows arched. "What about it?"

"Don't you want one?" he asked, stating what to him was the obvious.

"Of course I want a husband."

"And a family?"

"Yes, and a family."

"Well, how in the hell are you going to manage those if you *go exploring?*"

Anna thrust her hands onto her hips, the heavy censure in

his tone putting a feral gleam in the gray of her eyes. "How am I ever going to find a husband with which to have my children if I *don't* go exploring?" She shook her head in high annoyance. "Really, Matt, I swear I can not fathom the workings of your mind. I've lived my entire life on this plantation, miles and miles from anyone. Potential husbands simply do not drop out of the sky."

"No, they come riding up to your door."

"Not lately."

Her retort was like a blow to his self-esteem, and his temper began to unravel. "When was the last time you looked?"

Anna raised her chin a notch. "You're not making an ounce of sense. And why am I explaining myself to you? You promised not to criticize."

"I'm not criticizing."

"Yes, you are."

"No, I just think you don't need to go off to some wild city to find what you want. You can find contentment here at home."

A flush of anger tinted her cheeks. "Spoken like a true man." She poked a finger at his chest. "Pat the little woman on the head and make up her mind for her. Well, let me tell you something, Mathew Bennett, if all I wanted in life was what I have now, I'd be sitting in the parlor with my embroidery, going on in blissful ignorance."

Mathew felt his insides sink to his toes. She was well and truly wound up, and becoming increasingly more irate by the second. Bloody hell, but he didn't know what to do with her when she got that way.

"Calm down, Anna, there's no need—"

"I'll tell you what there's a need for. There's a need for me to get back to the laundry, the very wellspring of my contentment, while I wait for the future father of my children to crash the gates of my boredom on his white steed." In two quick gestures, she thrust her sleeves up to her elbows. "And while I'm at it, I'll design a few new patterns for my stitchery. Perhaps then I'll meet your standard of what a woman is supposed to be."

"Anna, listen to me," he demanded, trying to take her hand again. "I never meant to upset you."

"You have upset me, Mathew. And you've lied."

"Lied?" That stung his sorely abused honor. Squaring his shoulders he declared, "I did no such thing."

"You most certainly did."

"How?"

"You said nothing I said or did was silly."

"It isn't. You're not."

"You think my dreams are silly."

Striving to hold on to his shredding temper, he spread his hands in surrender. "Anna, I promise I do not think you are silly, but I am trying to make you see reason."

"I am perfectly capable of seeing reason."

"Damn it, Anna, I didn't say you weren't. Stop twisting the meaning of my words. All I meant was that as a man who has seen some small portion of the world, I have more experience, and I think I know what is best for you."

The very instant he spoke the words, Mathew would have given anything he owned to recall them. In silence, he watched Anna spiral right out of control.

"Of all the arrogant, self-absorbed, masculine things to say!" she cried. "You don't have an inkling of what's best for me, what I might need or desire. When it gets right down to it, you don't know one damn thing about me!"

"I know more than you think," he yelled back.

"Then you should already know that I'm not going to stand

here another second." In a whirl of muslin, she turned and stalked away, leaving Mathew simmering in his own anger.

"Hell, hell, bloody hell," he swore through gritted teeth. Fuming with pent up emotions, he yanked his hat from his head and slapped it against his thigh. He took two paces in one direction, spun about and paced back. All the while, he tried to figure out what had gone wrong.

"Goddamn it." He shoved his hat into place and made for his horse. "Corn. I'll plant the damn fields in corn."

"Mathew Bennett is the most insufferable, arrogant, mule-headed excuse for a man I have ever met."

Anna's voice echoed off the walls as she stomped her way up the stairs to her bedroom. A remote corner of her mind was horrified at her unladylike ascent, but she didn't care. In all her life, she had never been as angry as she was right then.

"Knows what's best for me," she declared, throwing open her door. "I'll show him what's best for me." She had half a mind to pack everything she possessed and sail for New Orleans right then . . . or Atlanta. "Why stop there? Paris and London are just waiting."

"I beg your pardon?"

Startled, Anna looked up and discovered Jessica standing at the far end of the room. She ceased her rantings at once. Her emotions, however, were still churning unfettered.

"I didn't know you were in here," she gritted out, snatching her hat from her head and throwing it on the bed.

"I was dusting." Jessica lifted her rag and gestured to the room.

"That's wonderful. Simply wonderful."

Jessica nibbled on her upper lip, clearly caught between caution and curiosity. "Would you rather I leave?"

Anna stepped to one of the windows and stared out at the landscape spreading out below her. It was the exact same scene she had witnessed every day of her life. Nothing new, nothing exciting.

"No, don't leave on my account," she muttered. "Finish with whatever you were doing."

Several seconds passed as Jessica considered Anna's distraught manner. In all the time she had been at Bellefleur, she had never known Anna to be anything but perfectly civil. A touch on the emotional side, but always sweet-tempered.

"Is anything wrong?"

Anna's lips curled in a derisive, one-sided grin. If ever there was a question, Jessica had just asked it. "Oh, there's something wrong, all right, and his name is Mathew Bennett." Every bit of resentment she felt renewed itself tenfold.

"I swear I don't know what is the matter with him." Flinging a hand wide, she paced from the window to the rosewood armoire and back again. " 'Stay home and wait for your knight in shining armor,' he says. 'I know what's best for you,' he says. He's just like my brother. They're all alike, every last one of them."

"Who?"

"Men." She came to a stop and turned to face Jessica fully. "I swear, God has to have a sense of humor to have created men as He did. Just because they pee standing up, they think they own the world!"

At the outrageous declaration, Jessica's eyes rounded, her mouth formed a silent O. She stared at Anna.

Anna stared back . . . and continued to stare and stare until finally, the ridiculousness of the entire matter overcame her. She burst into laughter, unable to contain her humor which was in most part directed at herself.

"What a silly dolt I am," she got out between laughs.

Jessica gave into her own humor and followed suit, laughing as much at Anna's mirth as at the irreverence of the woman's comment. "That was a scandalous thing to say."

"I know," Anna giggled, striving for an even breath. "And do you know what else?"

"What?"

"I don't care."

A second surge of laughter seized them both. Anna pressed her hands to her stomach. Despite the ache brought on by her uncontrollable chortling, the laughter felt good. The tension Mathew had created was completely gone.

She relaxed into one of the chairs before the fireplace, feeling almost too serene to move any further. Taking a fortifying breath, she leaned her head back against the cushion and trailed her hands over the chair's arms.

"I haven't laughed like that in a long time," she confessed.

"Neither have I," Jessica returned. "I'm glad you're feeling better."

"So am I. I don't like being angry." Certainly not at Mathew.

A soft feeling captured the region of her heart just thinking about him. Most of the time, he was very sweet, very dear. She couldn't figure out what had prompted their argument.

Jessica tipped her head to one side. "I hope it wasn't anything serious?"

Rolling her eyes, Anna scoffed lightly. "Not really."

It was mystifying that Mathew could infuriate her as he did. They had been friends for as long as she could remember, and when he wasn't rousing her ire, she liked him a great deal. More than that, she admitted. He was a striking man with his blond hair and wide shoulders. He was good and kind and dependable, although he did tend to be a touch too serious about life.

"I get anxious sometimes. It doesn't help to have someone patronize me."

"Is that what this Mathew Bennett was doing?"

"Yes."

"By telling you he knows what's best for you?" At Anna's seeking look, she explained. "You mentioned that."

"I suppose I did. And yes, he thinks he is a veritable fountain of wisdom when it comes to my welfare."

"That must be the way of men."

That little bit of wisdom, offered so easily, brought Anna's head up, her smooth brow knitting delicately. "Why is that you suppose?"

Unable to resist, Jessica replied, "Because they pee standing up?"

This time, Anna's laugh was laced with scorn. "The trouble is, they do own the world. I've never seen anything that would prove differently. All men seem to believe that they alone know what is best for women, whether they do or not."

"They don't, you know."

"You've been in a better position than I to judge that."

Anna studied Jessica with exacting care, seeing beneath her fragile, blond exterior for the first time. "Why don't you sit down," she suggested, indicating the vacant chair beside her own.

The line of Jessica's back straightened. "Oh, no I couldn't. It wouldn't be right."

Anna waved the protest away. "Of course it would. Some would say our laughing the way we did isn't right or our sharing confidences isn't right." When Jessica continued to hesitate, she added, "Please, Jess. It would mean a great deal to me."

Jessica didn't know what to make of the request. For it was exactly that, a request, not a command given by the lady of the house as if no differences in social standings existed between them. The respect inherent in that touched Jessica deeply.

Crossing to the fireplace, she perched on the edge of the chair facing Anna. "Thank you."

"Oh, don't thank me." Anna leaned back again and dismissed the matter. "If we're going to talk, we should both be comfortable."

"What do you want to talk about?"

"Men."

Jessica fingered the bandage on her left hand. "I don't know much about men except what I've seen as we traveled about."

Nothing could have snared Anna's attention more. "You've traveled? Where? When?"

There was too much eagerness in Anna's manner for Jessica to miss. "For the last ten years we moved from one place to another. Richmond, Atlanta, Charleston. Throughout a good portion of the south, actually."

"How exciting," Anna exclaimed, her eyes alight with vitality. "What was it like?"

Anna's joy was nearly tangible, and Jessica had no desire to squash it. But she had to tell her the truth of things. "My circumstances didn't allow for a gay time."

"But you got to see different sights, meet different people."

"I would have preferred to have had a permanent home to return to each night."

Anna sighed heavily. "That isn't always as wonderful as it sounds. Nothing ever changes."

"That's what's so appealing about it. The permanence is to be treasured."

"It can also be frustrating."

"So is moving about."

A slow, wry grin came to Anna's face. "What a pair we are. You've spent your life roaming the country, searching for a home, while I've spent my life at home wishing to search the country."

"Why don't you then?"

The question drew Anna up short. "Excuse me?"

Jessica spread her hands wide. "Why don't you do as you wish? You'll pardon me for saying so, but I can't see anything stopping you."

Anna shifted her gaze from Jessica's face to stare sightlessly at the pale green drapes framing the windows. For as long as she could remember, she had wanted to take an extended trip. And for as long as she could remember, she had felt as if she wasn't allowed.

Her lips pursed, her gray eyes darkened as she thought about that. Why *couldn't* she do as she pleased? Jessica was right, there was absolutely nothing stopping her. Nick had never said she couldn't go. He had never said she could, either, and because of that, she had assumed that she shouldn't. What a foolish, *female* way of thinking.

What was she waiting for? Nick's approval? It might never come, but she would never know until she pressed the issue. And even if he did oppose the idea, that didn't amount to anything. He wasn't her keeper. He was her brother.

"You're right," she breathed in awe. She came to her feet, feeling more alive than she had in months. "You are absolutely right. I can go wherever I want."

Jessica rose, smiling. "It seems logical to me."

"Of course it does. You're a woman." She laughed in unbridled glee. "Where should I go, Jess?" She didn't wait for a reply. "Money won't be a problem. I have an allowance from *Grand-mere's* will that I've been saving. I'll send a letter to Aunt Sophia at once. She'll want to accompany me."

"Where are you going?"

"I don't know. Does it really matter?" Anna grabbed Jessica's uninjured hand and squeezed it hard. "I can't thank you enough. You have no idea what you've done."

"Good, I hope."

Beaming, Anna averred, "No, it's better than good. It's wonderful, tremendous, perfect. You're perfect." Giving into the joy suffusing her from head to toe, she threw her arms about Jessica and hugged her close. "I can't wait to tell Nick."

Chapter Ten

"You're what?" Nick asked.

Anna heaved a dramatic sigh and faced her brother from across his desk. "You heard me. I said I'm going to New Orleans."

"Why?"

"Because I haven't been there since I was a child. I have friends there I haven't seen in years and years and this will be the perfect opportunity for me to do things I've been wanting to do." A smile wreathed her face. "Just think of it, Nick, New Orleans."

Nick scrubbed a hand across his jaw. "Can't this discussion wait until after I've cleaned up and had my dinner?"

"No, I've waited for you to come in from the fields all day to tell you my news." Some of the gaiety in her eyes gave way to a lethal load of determination. "And we're not going to have a discussion. My mind is made up. I'm going to New Orleans for a while."

Nick took in his sister's set jaw, the glint in her eyes, the line of her shoulders, and recognized her conviction for what it was. "If you've made up your mind, then so be it."

His easy acceptance surprised Anna. While she had been

adamant about not wanting to explain herself, she had anticipated that she would have to do so. Thoroughly annoyed
with herself for such second-class thinking, her chin came up.
"I didn't come to you for your approval, Nick. I'm telling
you this because I thought you should know."

Her tone carried just enough defensiveness to straighten
Nick's spine. "Don't get all testy on me, Ann. You've never
done anything like this before. Humor me if I'm concerned."

Given that explanation, Anna had to relinquish her pique.
"You're right. I'm sorry if I sounded abrupt—"

"Cross."

"Very well, cross, but I swear, Nick, I'm so excited about
this, I'm afraid something is going to happen to spoil it all for
me. I'm going to ask Aunt Sophia to accompany me and I
have to see about packing—"

Nick shook his head as he studied his sister. This was
Anna at her best, all enthusiasm and emotion running unchecked. "What brought this on all of a sudden?"

Anna spun away from the desk and answered over her
shoulder. "This isn't something I've dreamed up recently.
I've been restless for months and months."

"I know, but why make the decision now? Why not last
year or even last month?"

Coming to stop at one of the many bookshelves lining the
walls, Anna turned. "In all honesty?"

"Please."

"If you must know, it was something Jessica said."

"Jessica?"

"That's right. She asked me what was stopping me from
doing as I pleased." Still awed that so simple an idea could
have been so overlooked, Anna raised confused eyes to her
brother. "I didn't know what to say, but the more I thought
about it, the clearer the answer became." She glided back to

the desk, her eagerness firmly back in place. "The only person stopping me from doing what I want has been me. And for the life of me, I don't know why."

Nick's dark brows slanted over intent gray eyes. "You're a grown woman, Anna."

"I think I'm only beginning to realize that."

"It's about time."

"What does that mean?"

He strode out from behind his desk with a low rumbling laugh. "Have you looked in the mirror lately?"

She returned his smile. "Of course I have. Why?"

"Because the reflection is very definitely that of a woman, not a little girl." Draping an arm about her shoulders, he gave her a brotherly hug. "I'm surprised you didn't see that when you were fixing your hair."

"Is it that obvious?"

"To most of the men in the area."

"Really?" As elated as she was shocked, Anna pressed, "Have men actually been looking my way?"

Nick flicked a wayward curl off her neck. "Haven't you noticed?"

She had seen a few men glance at her, but she had never attached any significance to the matter. "I've seen Ben Hutchens gazing in my direction, and Clyde Morrison, but I swear, Nick, I thought they were just being nosy or something. After all, I've known them all my life. We've been looking at each other since we were children."

"Trust me. When they look at you now, they do not see the skinny, pigtailed terror you used to be."

"Ben and Clyde?" she asked, amazement raising her voice by two octaves.

"And several others, as well."

"Who?"

Nick gave another laugh. "What a greedy little flirt you are."

"Tell me, Nick."

Feigning an exasperation he was far from feeling, he dropped his arm away and headed for the door. "I'll probably regret this, but you should pay attention the next time you happen to see Simon DuBois, Tom Fouchet or Mathew Bennett."

The last name hit Anna square in her temper. "Mathew? If I never see him again, it will be too soon."

Half way across the room, Nick came to a stop, turning just in time to see all of Anna's ebullience give way to hot indignation. "Something the matter that I should know about?"

"Nothing." She crossed her arms beneath her breasts.

"That doesn't sound like 'nothing' to me. What's this about?"

Lifting her chin, Anna sniffed in royal disdain. "I told you, nothing. I'm angry with him right now, and I don't wish to talk about it."

Nick remained silent for a bit, trying to fit together all the pieces of what to him was a very intriguing puzzle. "You're still angry with him from last week?" he asked slowly, searching Anna's face carefully.

"No, I'm angry with him for what he said to me this morning."

"He was here?"

"Yes, he was here." Feeling her irritation escalate, she flung her hands wide and twirled for the opposite door. "I said I don't want to talk about it. I have too much to do and I am *not* going to let Mathew Bennett ruin my day."

With that, she shut the door firmly behind her, missing the knowing grin that stretched her brother's lips.

"You are truly blind, little sister," he whispered, chuckling to himself. It was going to prove interesting to see how things developed between the two.

He made for his bedroom still contemplating Anna and Matt. Ahead of him lay the night with its customary routine, a bath, dinner and a good book. Clinging to his muscles was the toll of the lengthy day spent on horseback and he looked forward to his moments of solitude. He wasted no time in divesting himself of his shirt as he entered his room.

Two strides into the blue and green interior and he stopped in his tracks. Shirt in hand, he came face to face with Jessica who appeared as unprepared to face him as he was to face her.

"Oh, my," she gasped, arms laden with cleaning supplies.

He hadn't seen her in two days. That had not been by design, rather accident. His work had kept him from the house until odd hours, something for which he had been grateful. It was too easy to remember the feel of her curves, the taste of her mouth, the scent of her skin.

Instantly, the sweet memory of that kiss charged brazenly into his mind. Mentally, he swore. He had tried to rationalize the episode, condemn it, laugh it off and even forget it entirely. Not seeing her had helped, yet there she stood and he was as affected by her as he ever was. In fact, taking in the slight flush on her cheeks and her softly parted lips, she was more appealing than ever.

"Hello," he commented in a slightly stiff voice.

Jessica hugged her rags and feather duster to her chest, unable to force her eyes away from the sight of Nicholas's naked torso. Broad shoulders gave way to a chest defined by steely muscles. The contour of his narrow waist was a straight line that gradually became hip and thigh.

In every respect he was her exact opposite, sculpted of

hard-edged angles and planes to her tender curves. He was a study of changing textures to her soft smoothness. The sinew that fashioned his body was well defined, molded to a strength that would never be hers. He was completely masculine and it all seemed epitomized by the mat of dark curly hair that spread from one flat male nipple to the other before tapering to a thin line of hair coursing downward.

Courtesy demanded that she look elsewhere. Her unruly heart laughed at the notion and silently decreed, *look your fill, see the man and rejoice in the differences between you.*

"I'm sorry," she blurted out, apologizing to him, to herself. Never had she experienced such unhindered thoughts about a man. Always before, her impressions had been tainted by insecurity. Amazingly free of those doubts and uncertainties, she could only stare in wonder at not only the form, but at the man within.

What she saw sent her pulse racing. He was a good man. Her heart told her so. He was a magnificent creature. Her eyes verified that. The combination had her mentally scrambling to understand her own feelings. Again, she murmured, "I'm sorry."

"For what?" he grated out, feeling the stroke of her gaze like the sultry touch of a lover's hand. That's all it took for his body to respond. An aching need curled in the pit of his belly and an instant later, he felt himself begin to harden and swell.

Damn it all to hell and back. She was the most vexing temptation to ever cross his path, and the effect she had upon him was growing more pronounced by the day. He had only to look at her and he was lured to forsake any good intentions he may have ever harbored toward her.

Desire etching into his features, he continued to stare at

her, all the while speculating on what she would look like minus that ugly dress and apron she wore.

Jessica swallowed hard and dropped her line of vision to the floor. "I'll come back later."

Let her go, Nicholas told himself. *Step aside and don't even watch her leave.* "That isn't necessary. Stay and finish."

"No, no," she whispered, so aware of him she could hardly breathe. "I should have finished up sooner, but I'm . . . I'm still a little awkward because of my hand."

"How does it feel?"

"Better."

"You're not doing too much, are you?"

"No." She edged toward the door, afraid to look at him again. If she did, she knew she would be swamped by the same headiness she had experienced for a few precious seconds when he had kissed her.

Her stomach seemed to close up like a tight fist. She didn't want to think about the feel of his mouth, the touch of his arms. What she wanted didn't seem to matter, though, for the memories had haunted her through the long nights and disturbed her peace of mind during the day. To be near him again only intensified those sensations.

Desperate to find a plausible excuse to cling to, she remembered the bucket she had left on the far side of his massive bed. "I forgot my bucket," she exclaimed, hastening away. "What a silly thing to do. I use the bucket to carry my supplies in. Not . . . not all of them, a mop wouldn't fit. But you know that . . . of course you know that."

She knew she was rambling, but she couldn't seem to stop. Her mouth was running unchecked and the muscles in her arms and legs were quivering like jelly. Regardless, she didn't take the time to ask herself what was the matter. She already knew. The prospect of Nicholas kissing her again had her losing control.

The thought was tantalizing, it was forbidden. It was delicious, it was wrong!

Dropping her rags into the wooden pail, she picked the thing up, turned . . . and stepped right into Nicholas, her body colliding with his with a soft impact that choked the air off in her lungs.

His hands settled on her waist drawing her close. "This shouldn't be happening," he murmured thickly, his breath caressing her temple.

Jessica went utterly still. She wasn't accustomed to being this close to a man, and certainly not for seductive purposes. Her first reaction was to run, oh, but the heart of the matter was that she had never *wanted* to be this close, until now.

Confusion hit her hard. Innate wariness warred with newfound feelings. The conflict made her lightheaded. Neither her body nor her mind were prepared for the sensations created by the very proximity of him. His heat bathed her skin, the musky scent of him filled her senses. A thrilling kind of fire raced out from where his hands touched her sides. Out of habit alone, she wanted to pull away in fright. Amazingly, she didn't, realizing that his touch created a pleasure too rich to deny.

"What's happening?" she choked out.

"Can't you tell?"

"No."

Tipping his head to one side, Nicholas gazed down at her, taking note of the myriad emotions registered on each of her features. "There's no need to be afraid," he coaxed.

"I am."

"I won't hurt you."

She gave a nervous laugh. "I know. I think that's why I'm frightened. I've never felt this way before."

"What way is that?" He already knew, but the elemental male that ran so strongly within him wanted, nay, needed to hear her say the words aloud.

"I feel as if . . . as if I'm not comfortable with my own body. You make me feel things . . ." Breaking off, she tipped her head back and searched his gaze for understanding. ". . . things I've never felt before."

The muscles in Nicholas's chest constricted painfully at her words, words sweeter than he would have ever imagined. He skimmed his fingers around to the small of her back, drawing her closer, and damned himself in the process.

For all the reasons he had reiterated to himself time and time again, he had no right to embroil her in this. She was an innocent, he owned her papers of servitude . . . the list was endless and he knew it by heart. Well, damn the list and the reasons. He wanted her as he had never wanted another woman. Ever. And he knew she wanted him. She might be inexperienced and wary, but she did want him. No woman could look at a man with such burgeoning awareness and *not* want him.

Lowering his head, he slanted his mouth over hers, catching her gasp and making it his own. The small vibration of sound tore down his throat and raced to a spot deep in his gut. His arms tightened about her, molding her to him until he felt her along every inch of him. The feeling was a bliss of the mind and spirit.

"Open your mouth," he urged, resenting that little bit of herself that he could not claim.

Reflexively, Jessica did as she was told, giving him what he sought. The second his tongue thrust past her teeth, she arched upward, helpless against the intimacy of the caress, helpless to her own response. The pleasure was overwhelming, doubling in on itself, expanding in every direction until all she felt, all she knew or was aware of was the essence of the kiss itself, of his mouth fastened to hers, making her ache and yearn.

"Nicholas," she sighed in wonder. Without conscious thought, she let the bucket slip from her nerveless fingers and pressed her palms to the flat of his chest.

Eyes darkened to black, Nicholas gloried in the feel of her hands. For too long he had dreamt of her as she was now, wrapped in his arms, sharing the same passion that coursed through him. He pressed his mouth to the fragile column of her neck and felt her heart's cadence. It was a wild pulse that matched his own.

Blood pounded in his veins, pooling thickly between his legs. Instinct demanded that he plunge heedlessly toward satisfaction as quickly as possible. Prudence cautioned him to be patient, to remember all she had endured in her life. He wanted her willing and unafraid. For that, he would have to progress slowly.

He kissed her again, silently rejoicing when her lips parted eagerly. The unspoken invitation was not wasted and he caressed her tongue with his own, savoring the exquisite taste and feel of her.

She was like the headiest brew, intoxicating his mind and body. Unable to help himself, he lowered one hand along her spine and pressed her against the intimate proof of his desire. Shivers of near painful pleasure unfurled in waves, and he deepened the kiss, hunger threatening to burn out of control.

Like a wild blaze consuming everything in its path, his desire swept over Jessica, singeing her clear to her soul. A gladness of the senses such as she had never even imagined robbed her mind of will and her body of strength.

"Nicholas . . ." Her words splintered to nothing as his hand captured her breast. Then whatever she had been about to say was swept away by the onslaught of her first real taste of desire.

Newly born instincts came to the fore. She wanted to give of herself to this man; heart, mind, body and soul. If she could lose herself within him, she would and gladly so. On the one hand, she found that exhilarating. On the other, she found it terrifying.

It was all too much too soon. She tore her mouth from his, the blue of her eyes dewy with a mixture of passion and dismay. "Don't, you must stop." Forgetting the injury to her hand, she took hold of his wrist, then grimaced at the resulting pain.

"Jessica." Her name came as a groan torn from the depths of him. The brief flash of pain that marred the perfection of her features jabbed at his conscience, reminding him of the foolishness of his actions. Reason returned in an abhorrent rush, igniting his temper to a torrid level.

Damn it all! What had he been thinking? He hadn't been thinking at all, that had been the problem. He had surrendered to the desire she so effortlessly evoked within him.

In the next heartbeat, he dropped his hands away and stepped back, his jaw as unyielding as cast iron. Furious with himself, he spat, "Get out."

The order came like the lash of a whip, stripping Jessica of her defenses when she was most vulnerable. She plunged to reality so quickly she was literally held immobile while she tried to gather her wits.

As if understanding could be found in the gray of Nicholas's eyes, she searched the glittering orbs. What she found chilled her blood. Anger and condemnation stared back at her.

Unconsciously, she reared back in a reflexive move that was born of habit. A steady voice inside her told her that Nicholas would never hurt her, but a lifetime of conditioning could not be ignored. She didn't know what she had done wrong. It didn't matter. At the moment, she knew only that he was angry, and that she had good cause to fear an angry man.

"Don't," she whispered, retreating until her back met the wall. Not so much as blinking, she waited for him to make his next move. All the while she prayed that she hadn't been wrong in thinking he was different from other men. She hoped with all her heart that his fury would not take a physical means of expression. "Don't hurt me."

"I'm not going to touch you," he ground out. That she would think he would raise a punishing hand to her irritated him all the more. "I may not have the sense God gave me, but credit me, please, with having some decency."

He stepped away, thrusting both hands back through his hair. Staring at the ceiling, he could feel her unwavering gaze bore into his back. Damn, he had made a mess of things, but what she did to him ought to be against the law. And it didn't help one whit to know that he should have never touched her to begin with.

His mind jeered at the uselessness of such hindsight. Over his shoulder, he ordered, "Pick up your things and leave."

Jessica did as she was told. Bucket hugged to her chest, she gave Nicholas a wide berth when she circled around him on her way to the door. The move did not go unnoticed.

"Jessica."

She spun instantly and faced him, her face pale, her lower lip caught between her teeth.

Seeing such evidence of her trepidation made Nicholas feel like the worst kind of heel. Taking a deep breath, he shoved his hands into his pockets, a gesture that was as much for his benefit as hers. He would reassure her if he could, but he would also restrain himself from touching her again. She had denied him, and with good reason. That didn't make him want her any less. Just the opposite was true. Having tasted a small sample of her passion, he desired her all the more.

"I shouldn't have kissed you."

She gave a silent nod.

"I don't have any excuse for my actions."

Again, she dipped her head in acknowledgement of his words.

"Well, say something, damn it."

She flinched. "Please, don't swear at me."

"Oh, hell." His hands came out of his pockets with his expletive. "Is that all you have to say?"

"What . . . what should I say?"

He didn't want her reticence. He deserved her anger. "How the hell should I know? Yell at me, call me a cad, make demands."

"I couldn't do that."

"Why not?"

Her lips worked for several seconds before she could actually voice her words. "I . . . you own . . . I work for you. You have all the power to do as you please."

"Not in this case. What's happening between us has nothing to do with master and servant. This is between a man and a woman."

"I'm sorry," she murmured.

"What," he snapped, "are you apologizing for?"

"I don't know."

"It just seemed like the right thing to say?"

One of her shoulders rose in a shrug. "I've made you angry. I didn't ever want to do that."

Nicholas's muscles clenched, his eyes narrowing to hard,

gray slits. A terrible suspicion gripped him hard and added a grating edge to his voice. "Is that why you kissed me back? Is that why you responded? To keep from *angering* me?"

That had never entered her mind. Incredulous that he would even think such a thing, she breathed, "No. I kissed you because . . ." A bright stain crept up her neck clear to her forehead.

"Because why?" he pushed, coveting her answer. He stared unflinchingly into her eyes, silently making demands she was helpless to resist.

"Because, I . . . it felt . . . right."

A thick, pregnant, silence vibrated between them, the lack of sound teeming with awareness and intimacy. As if her lips were soft and giving beneath his again, Nicholas felt the shivering sensations of lust streak through him.

"It was right." His words were a low, husky promise of ecstasy. "Heaven help me, I wish it weren't so, but I can't deny that there is something between us."

"You feel it too?" she asked without thinking.

"Of course I feel it. I'm not a damned block of wood."

She knew that firsthand. He was an unusually perceptive man, however, until that moment, she thought that the emotions she had been experiencing had been hers alone. It had never occurred to her that he might be sensing the same inner turmoil.

She swallowed the lump of emotion lodged in her throat. "What are we going to do?"

The gray of his eyes turned to a rich smoky velvet. "What do you wish to do?"

"You're asking me?" Tears stung the back of her eyes and sadness pulled at the corners of her mouth. "I'm a poor excuse for a woman."

"Don't say that."

"It's true. I'm not stupid. I know where your questions are leading, I know that you want to . . . to take me to bed." Her gaze finally fell. "I wish I was a different kind of woman. Then perhaps I wouldn't be such a disappointment to us both."

He took a step closer. "You didn't disappoint me."

Her head came up. "I didn't?"

"No."

"Then why did you get angry?"

Heaving a sigh, he sought to make her understand. "Jess, I was angry with myself, not you."

She blinked rapidly, several times. "Why?"

A crooked smile softened the tense line of his lips. "For noble intentions gone awry." The enigmatic response furrowed her brow and he laughed. "I'm not in the habit of seducing innocents, especially if one happens to be my servant." The smile left his face, leaving behind lines of strain and self-reproach. "I don't want to want you, Jessica, but it can't be helped. Knowing that I am responsible for you, for your welfare, your livelihood, knowing how you feel about men . . . none of that makes a damn bit of difference when I look at you. And when I touch you . . ."

The words dangled in the air, no less potent for not having been completed for Jessica knew exactly what happened when he touched her. She felt the same thing.

Suddenly, it all made sense to her. They were irresistibly drawn to each other. And for reasons singular to each, they were both trying to disavow the attraction.

The revelation slammed into her consciousness. She had never been attracted to a man before, not on a sexual level. But that was what was happening to her and she was so astonished, her blood actually began to pound out from her heart.

She had begun to think that she would never look at a man as a possible friend or husband or lover. Now, she was, for the first time in her life, behaving like a normal woman and regarding a man—she scanned Nicholas's superbly virile form—as the opposite sex, complete with all the inherent ramifications.

She was a woman, he was a man. Men and women . . . well, they did what they did. Together. And she was not in a panic over the notion! Mildly nervous . . . very nervous, but she wasn't frightened. Not if that man was Nicholas.

A rare happiness flooded her being, and not only because of this newly discovered understanding. Her instincts about Nicholas had been right. He was not a brutal man, and that more than anything gave her the courage she needed.

"I'm glad I didn't disappoint you."

Nicholas stilled, stunned and even a touch afraid to believe that he had heard correctly. In her own innocent way, she was bridging the distance that separated them. "Are you truly glad?"

"Yes." Completely aware of what she was offering, she clutched the bucket with all her might.

"Do you know what you're saying?"

Oh, yes, she knew that in essence she had told him that she was his for the asking. She nodded quickly, the underlying nervousness impossible to miss.

Nicholas arched his back slightly, at last giving into the strain in his shoulders. "I won't force you, Jess. You'll have to come to me." He stepped close and pressed a light kiss to her lips. "When the time is right for you, when you're completely ready, I'll be waiting."

Chapter Eleven

It had been the longest three days of her life. Removing the breakfast dishes from the dining room table, Jessica considered every hour that had crawled by since that fateful moment in Nicholas's bedroom.

The hours had been a sluggish progression of seconds and minutes, each comprising days that seemed longer than any other days in her life; longer than when her father had left her locked in a hotel room in Richmond while he schemed to find a fortune, longer than the night when he threatened to prostitute her out to a farmer in Mobile, longer than when she had held her sister in her arms and watched her precious life drain away.

Knowing that Nicholas was waiting for her to give herself to him had somehow delayed the normalcy of time as Jessica knew it. And she didn't know what to do about it.

The ultimate answer was that she seek him out. She wasn't ready for that, not yet. In her heart, she dearly wanted to be his, but something was holding her back. Remnants of die-hard fears, she was certain, and until she could overcome the last of those fears, she would wait. When she gave herself to Nicholas, she would do so as the woman he deserved, not some sniveling, frightened pretense of a woman.

She paused in the act of lifting a platter of ham and smiled just as Mama Lou turned away from the buffet.

"I hope you have a good reason for grinnin' at yourself, girl."

Jessica shook off her musings, but not the delight underscoring them. She did have good reason to smile. She fully intended to give herself to Nicholas. Perhaps other women would take the matter in stride. She couldn't. For her, this was a huge step, nothing less than astonishing. In her whole life, she had never thought to feel so normal.

Turning, she carefully balanced the tray so that she carried the bulk of its weight with her right hand. "It's a lovely day, isn't it, Mama Lou?"

The tall black woman humphed her opinion. "It'll get better when we can finally have Miz Anna packed up and on her way." She gathered the linen table cloth into a tidy bundle. "Runnin' in five directions at once, she's goin' to give me a dozen more gray hairs if she doesn't leave soon. That Miz Sophia better hurry up and get here."

Jessica followed Mama Lou from the house toward the kitchen. She had heard a great deal about Anna's aunt, Sophia Marcheaux, ever since Anna had announced she was going to New Orleans. The widow lived in the next county and was to accompany Anna.

"Nice woman, that Miz Sophia," Mama Lou muttered, shaking her head a little mournfully. "Kindest thing that ever did live, but she has got to be the ugliest woman God ever created."

"Ugly?" Jessica asked, amazed by the description.

"No other word for it. A real shame, too, seein' as how there isn't a mean bone in the whole of her."

Jessica was still struggling with "ugly." She didn't think that anyone was truly ugly. Everyone had some redeeming facial quality; a smile or the shape of her eyes or the texture of her skin. "Is she truly—" she hated to even use the word, "ugly?"

Mama Lou stopped and levelled her with an implacable glare. "Enough to knock a buzzard off a shit wagon."

Jessica's mouth actually dropped open.

"Close up, girl. You asked, you got your answer. And don't go thinkin' that I'm talkin' mean. Everyone in these parts knows Miz Sophia for what she is, and Miz Sophia will be the first to tell you that when it was her turn to get a dose of beauty from the good Lord above, He took a nap."

Sophia Marcheaux nearly did that very thing hours later when she stepped down from her carriage and practically blustered her way into the house.

Anna was there to meet her in the drawing room. *"Tantia,"* Anna exclaimed, throwing her arms about the impossibly round woman.

Sophia hugged her niece back with all the love for which she was renowned. *"Anna, mon petite."*

Cupping her aunt's jowly face between her hands, Anna's eyes glowed with a love that originated in her heart. *"Très heureux de vous voir!* How are you? *Ca va?"*

Sophia shrugged and rubbed at what should have been the small of her back. *"J'ai tres mal ici."*

"Is it very painful? *Est-ce grave?"*

Again, Sophia shrugged in a reply that could have meant either yes or no.

Standing to one side, ready to help in any way, Jessica watched the greeting with a pang of wistfulness. She didn't understand a word of French, but to be so obviously loved was heart-wrenching. Never mind the fact that Sophia

Marcheaux was as Mama Lou had described. Love and devotion more than made up for pitted skin, a bulbous nose and fleshy lips.

"Perhaps you should lie down for a bit," Anna suggested.

"Non," Sophia declared. Disengaging herself from Anna's embrace, she crossed the room to stand directly before Jessica.

"À qui est-ce?" she asked, eyeing Jessica from head to toe.

Jessica glanced from Sophia to Anna and back again. "I'm sorry, I . . . I don't understand."

It was Anna who replied with a generous laugh. "Don't worry, Jessica. My aunt is just being difficult."

"I am not," Sophia returned in perfect English.

"Yes, you are. You choose to speak French only to vex those around you."

Sophia squared her shoulders into as straight a line as her portly curves would allow. "I speak French because it is so much more civilized than this English you insist on uttering. Words ending in the most ridiculous drawls, vowels all sounding the same. Your father, my brother, would have been horrified." She gave Jessica another long stare. "Now, who are you?"

"Jessica McCormick."

"What are you?"

Anna stepped forward. *"Tante,"* she rebuked kindly.

Sophia turned innocent eyes to her niece. "I have a right to know who this is. After all, she's standing there, staring at me."

Jessica drew a breath to explain, but Sophia forestalled her with a wave of her hand. "It's all right. I am long past the age where curious gazes offend me."

"I wasn't staring at you, ma'am," Jessica said.

"No? I could have sworn you were looking straight at me."

"Tante Sophia." Anna's voice carried more the reprimand this time.

"I did not mean any disrespect," Jessica offered.

"Of course you didn't," Sophia agreed. "But neither could you decide if my face was real or not."

Jessica was growing more horrified by the second. This conversation was full of snares, complete with pitfalls. She could not get around the fact that Sophia Marcheaux was indeed a very unattractive woman, but she hadn't been staring for that reason. It had been the affection that existed between aunt and niece which had held her enthralled.

"If I was staring, ma'am, it was only with envy."

"Envy?" Sophia crowed in humorous disbelief.

"Yes, ma'am. For the bond you share with your family. Such devotion is a blessing."

Sophia's dull gray eyes lost a good deal of their assertiveness, filling instead with a lovely tenderness that took Jessica by surprise.

"We are nothing, young lady, if we do not have love." In the next instant, her brusque elan returned. Chin elevated, she demanded, "You have not told me what you do here, Jessica McCormick."

"I'm a servant."

Doing nothing to hide her astonishment, Sophia asked Anna, "A servant? When did this happen? I wasn't aware that Nicholas needed any more domestics, white or otherwise."

"It's a long story, *Tantia,"* Anna explained.

"I'm sure it is. Where *is* that brother of yours?"

"Right behind you," came Nick's deep voice.

The women turned as one to find Nicholas standing just inside the doorway. Dressed in a billowy white shirt and buff colored breeches, he appeared as handsome as Jessica had ever seen him. His black hair had been tossed by the spring breeze and the white of his smile shone a startling contrast to the tan of his skin.

"Nicholas, *mon bebe.*" Sophia lifted her arms for a hug, happiness etched into the deep lines of her face.

"I haven't been a baby for over thirty years, *Tantia,*" Nick said, using the nickname he and Anna preferred for this favored of all relatives.

"Faites venir un médecin, s'il vous plaît," Sophia mocked.

Nicholas's brows slanted downward. "Why do you wish me to fetch a doctor?"

"Because there is something wrong with my hearing. I thought you said you are no longer my babe."

Unable to resist his aunt's gentle badgering, Nicholas gave into a good-natured laugh. "You are shameless, *Tantia.*"

She pursed her lips into an unrepentant smirk. *"Oui."*

"And as tyrannical as ever. Leave Jessica alone. I won't have you hounding her."

Jessica did everything she could to keep from gazing at Nicholas. It was useless. Her eyes met his, and all the emotion generated by the simplest thought of him flooded her gaze. Hastily, she looked down at the floor, very aware of Sophia's avid interest.

"What is this?" Sophia asked, speculation lacing her words.

"Plus tard," Nicholas drawled, telling his aunt that any explanation he would make would come later. Not that he intended to tell her anything that mattered. What he shared with Jessica was private. "Why don't you go upstairs, *Tantia,* and freshen up."

Anna slipped her hand around the elder lady's elbow. "You really should. If we're to leave by this afternoon, you'll want to take a little rest."

Sophia let herself be escorted away, but not before she cast

Jessica and Nicholas a last look over her shoulder. Jessica felt her skin heat up at the blatant curiosity shining in the woman's regard.

"She means well," Nicholas said.

Jessica continued to stare at her feet. Feeling as she did about Nicholas, she didn't have a clue as to how she was supposed to act.

"Are you well?" he asked.

She looked up at that. It was a mistake. Desire and panic collided in the region of her heart. "Yes, no . . ."

A soft light glazed Nicholas's eyes with a silvery sheen. "Ah, sweet, I know what you're feeling."

"You do?"

"Yes." Two steps brought him close. He dipped his head to murmur against her lips, "You're feeling as if your entire body is holding its breath." Ever so lightly, he kissed the corner of her mouth. "Just know that while you are coming to terms with yourself, I am quietly going insane waiting."

Before she could utter a sound, he was gone, leaving the house as quickly as he had entered. Jessica frantically wondered if that was not a good thing. She felt stripped of all the defenses that had sustained her all her life. Sensing that his embrace would offer focus as well as passion, she was half tempted to run after him and throw herself into his arms.

She pressed her hands to her cheeks at that shocking admission. If it weren't for the fact that Nicholas had come to mean a great deal to her, she would have denounced herself as a hussy. Perhaps some would think her improper, even immoral. In her heart, though, she could not condemn herself for what she felt was so utterly right.

She had no delusions where Nicholas was concerned. He was not offering marriage, nor love, for that matter. But he shared her belief that there was a very special bond between them. She could not turn her back on that tie, on Nicholas, or on herself. If she did, she would live with the worst kind of regret for the rest of her life.

Bolstered by her conviction, she hastened up the stairs to help in the last of Anna's packing. It was Sophia, however, that requested her assistance.

"Entrez, entrez," the squat widow insisted, waving an imperious hand into the guest room.

"Is there anything I can get you?" Jessica inquired, already checking to make sure there was enough water in the porcelain pitcher.

"Non, nothing. I just wanted to get a closer look at you."

Jessica spun about. "Ma'am?"

Sophia shut the door with a decisive-sounding click. "You heard me. I want to get a good look at you."

Puzzlement pulled at Jessica's brow. "Why?"

"Because," Sophia declared, plopping her hands onto the mounds of her hips, *"you* have caught my nephew's eye, and any woman who can do that is worth getting to know."

Chagrin replaced Jessica's confusion. Had she and Nicholas been that obvious that people could detect the undercurrent of their emotions? She could well imagine what his aunt was thinking.

"Oh, dear. I . . . I don't know what to say."

"Start by telling me if you really are his servant?"

"Of course," Jessica breathed. "What el . . . else would I be?"

Sophia ambled to the bed and sat on its edge. "Why, his mistress, of course."

Jessica didn't like the word. It implied an arrangement meant for financial profit. Any gain she would derive from Nicholas would be emotional, an enrichment of the heart.

"No, ma'am, I am not his mistress."

"Do you intend to be?"

The questioning finally struck Jessica as far too personal. "Mrs. Marcheaux, I have already come to realize that you are close to Mr. DuQuaine—"

"Very close."

"As you say, very close, but—"

"But, but but . . . I know, you don't have any intentions of giving me any answers." Tilting her head to one shoulder for one of her habitual shrugs, Sophia heaved a sigh. "Very well, keep your secrets. I saw enough with my own eyes to know what is going on." Surprisingly, she gave a devilish smile. "I must say, I am pleased by Nicholas's behavior—taken aback—but very definitely pleased."

"Ma'am?"

Sophia's smile grew to the point that she almost appeared pretty. "You don't know my nephew, little Jessica. This is very out of character for him."

"What is?"

"His being so obvious about a woman he wants. As mindful of the proprieties as he is, he would never do anything to insult anyone with evidence of his . . . shall we say, more private inclinations. He's normally extremely circumspect about that, yet the minute he came into the house, he had eyes only for you."

Jessica's own eyes rounded. "Me?"

Sophia scoffed lightly. "Jessica, *ma petite,* I've never witnessed such an open display of hunger in all my life. Positively snatched my breath, it did." She shook her head in blatant disbelief. "Don't tell me you couldn't see that? How absolutely naive."

Jessica shut her eyes, mentally declaring that if Sophia's intentions were to embarrass, she had succeeded on a grand level.

"There's no need for that," Sophia laughed. "I assure you, I'll not stand and make judgements on you or Nicky. As I said, I was pleased to see him step out of his usual behavior. Gives me faith in his common sense."

Almost afraid to know what Sophia meant, Jessica opened one eye. "How so?" she asked miserably.

Sophia's answer did not come immediately. For several seconds, she gazed at nothing in particular as if trying to find the right explanation. "You must understand that Nicholas has always been the picture of decorum and propriety when it comes to the fairer sex. Not that he hasn't dallied along the way. He is very much a man. But the women in his life have always been categorized into neat little compartments in his mind." Lifting her hands, she sliced off segments of air. "His mother, his sister, his aunts and cousins. And of course, those who have shared his bed. I expect you will fall into this last group."

Hearing herself pegged in that manner brought a crimson stain to Jessica's cheeks. "I don't understand what point you're trying to make."

"Of course you don't, which only proves that you haven't known Nicky long enough to know that he never, *never* allows his feelings to show when it comes to, ah, certain women in his life. Like I said, my dear, he is the height of propriety.

"But now, for once in his life, he is obviously acting on something other than logic. No neat categories of women are coming into play here. He wants you, but he has apparently forgotten to keep his feelings well-hidden as he is used to doing." Her smile turned absolutely angelic. "I would say, my dear, that you have blind-sided the man."

There was so much glee in the woman's voice that Jessica considered the woman at great length. Sophia was indeed delighted by the situation. That in itself, raised another round of questions.

"Mrs. Marcheaux, why are you so happy about this? I mean, you don't even know me."

Sophia shrugged. "Ah, yes, well, I suppose my enthusiasm may seem strange. In all honesty, I am a very forthright woman. You may not like to hear what I have to say, but what you hear from me will always be the truth." The gray of her eyes softened. "The truth here is that I've longed for Nicky's happiness. I have worried that he will be locked into preconceived ideas of what *la femme,* a wife should or should not be. That is no way to find love."

For the life of her, Jessica wondered how the conversation had come to this end. An interrogation or condemnation would have been more expected. Instead, they were discussing that most sought after of emotions, love.

A pang of melancholy nibbled at her heart. What she knew about love was limited to her memories of her mother and sister. With their deaths had come the loss of any love Jessica had ever known.

Feeling ill-equipped to say anything on the subject, she scored her lower lip with her teeth, and finally gave what she hoped was a suitable response.

"I'm sure you are right. Everyone deserves to be loved."

"Nicky more than most. He is too good a man to squander his life away on a socially correct, pretty face. He deserves a woman who will love him, regardless of what her background might be."

In the depths of her, Jessica felt her heart turn over. "Are you saying that I am that woman?"

Sophia hopped up from the bed. "Not at all. What I am saying is that you have shaken him from his customary reactions to women. That has given me hope for his happiness. If he should find that happiness with you, then so be it."

The tolerance of this woman's opinions was beyond anything Jessica had ever known. "Mrs. Marcheaux, you have me confused. By rights, you should be aghast at the mere hint of anything going on between me and your nephew."

"True." A tinge of yearning dulled Sophia's gaze. "Then again, if my husband hadn't looked past the obvious, he and I wouldn't have known the happiness we did."

Jessica knew the "obvious" in this case was Mrs. Marcheaux's far from pretty face. "I don't know what to say."

Sophia's audacity came back full force. "Then be quiet," she sassed, opening the door with a flourish. "There's nothing worse than people who rattle on for no purpose at all. Besides, I have more than enough to say for the both of us."

The interview was unmistakably at an end. Jessica stepped out into the hall, feeling as if she had survived a whirlwind. Unthinkingly, she pressed fingertips to her forehead.

"What happened to your hand?" Sophia asked.

Jessica stared at the bandage as if seeing it for the first time. "I cut it."

"Nasty things, cuts. Make sure you take care of it."

"Yes, ma'am."

"And make sure you take care of my nephew while we're gone." With that, Sophia firmly shut the door, but not before Jessica saw the rakish glint in the woman's eyes and the teasing lilt to her grin. Both gave Jessica more than enough to contemplate, and as she went through the rest of her day, her mind insisted on dredging up fragments of their conversation.

While she watched Anna finally make her farewells and ride off with Sophia, Jessica silently heard, "take care of my nephew." As she carried stacks of linens from the laundry to the house, she recalled "he deserves a woman who will love him." And when she finished the last of her supper in the kitchen, she heard all too clearly, "never witnessed such an open display of hunger."

It was this last statement that played havoc with her peace of mind in the days to come. The notion of a man's *hunger* as referred to by Sophia was startling. That the hunger belonged to Nicholas was sobering. That she was the object of that hunger was overwhelming, not because she had never been desired before, but because she was pleased by the fact that it was Nicholas who desired her.

The thought had her gasping for breath, and after six long days and even longer nights she was a mass of strained nerves as she faced the evening ahead of her. Feeling in dire need of air to settle her tumultuous emotions, she left her room. Bucket in hand, she made her way to the well behind the kitchen, telling herself every step of the way that she had to stop thinking about Nicholas. And desire and love. Tending to the cut on her palm would occupy her mind for a while. She hoped.

Dusk had claimed the land an hour before. Muted grays blended with the last remnants of color, shapes defined more by shadow than by form. In the eastern sky, the early moon barely bestowed its pale radiance, forcing Jessica to squint hard to see her way back to the house.

The structure appeared an intricately carved silhouette. From various windows, beckoning light spilled forth, weak in its contrast to the night, but sufficient enough to cast a tall, indistinct shape in eerie profile. The shape moved from the concealing darkness and was almost upon her before Jessica realized it was Nicholas.

"You gave me a fright," she gasped. Even though she had thought of little else than him all day, she was not prepared to see him.

"I'm sorry," he murmured, his deep voice all the more resonant in the imprecise shades of the night. "What are you doing out here?"

"Getting water. I thought to change the bandages on my hand again."

He paused for only a moment, then relieved her of the bucket. Taking her right hand in his, he led her into the house, not stopping until they were in his library.

"Do you have fresh bandages?" he asked, placing the wooden pail beside a damask-covered sofa.

"In my room."

"Why don't you get them while I light a few more lamps?"

Jessica hurried to fetch the strips of linen and returned to find the area surrounding the sofa lit by a cozy arrangement of lamps. The light bathed Nicholas in a mellow glow that cast his features into stark relief, his bearing into one of infinite power.

"It doesn't really hurt any longer," she got out in a low voice. As usual, she had only to look at the man and she felt as if she was melting from the inside out. "It itches more than anything."

"That's a good sign." He took the bandages and gestured for her to sit. "Let's have a look at it." Sitting beside her, he carefully unwrapped the long strip of cloth, then just as carefully inspected the red scar with its network of sutures. "It's healed nicely. In fact, the stitches can come out."

Jessica pulled her gaze from the top of his bent head to her hand. "Really?"

He made a sound in his throat that she supposed was an agreement. That was the only sound he made as he crossed the room to his desk, returning with a small pair of scissors. Once again, he sat and cradled her hand within his.

"Hold still," he muttered, his attention focused on his task.

Jessica felt nothing more uncomfortable than a gentle pressure each time he brought the scissors into play. In no more than a minute, the stitches Anna had sewn so scrupulously were removed.

"Good as new," Nicholas announced.

A crooked, crimson stripe ran the length of her palm, breaking the lateral lines that creased her hand from side to side. Experimentally, she flexed her fingers, making a loose fist to test for any lingering pain.

"How does it feel?" Nicholas asked.

She lifted her gaze to his. "A little stiff, but it doesn't hurt."

"I'm afraid you'll always have a scar."

"At least I have my hand, all my fingers."

The positive nature of her statement impressed Nicholas greatly. He leaned back into the corner of the seat as he leisurely, exactingly examined the woman and her attitude. "Where did you come by this manner of yours?"

There was a liberal dose of wonder underscoring his words. Sitting sideways to face him, Jessica shrugged with her brows. "I wasn't aware that I was possessed of any manner in particular."

Nicholas gave a humorous growl low in his throat. "You most certainly are. You're the most resilient, undaunted person I have ever met."

"Is there anything unusual about that?"

"Given what your circumstances have been, I'd say yes. Most people in your shoes would be bemoaning their existences, casting blame or at the very least, whining." His gaze narrowed as he propped his elbow on the sofa's arm and lightly scrubbed at his chin. Slowly, he mused, "I've never once heard you so much as complain."

The intensity of his stare was unnerving. Tracing the scar's path, Jessica said, "Complaining doesn't serve any purpose. All we can hope for in life is to make the best of our fates."

"Spoken like a true optimist," he chuckled. "And what do you think fate holds for you?" He waggled his black brows in a suggestive manner. "Adventure, intrigue?"

"No," she laughed in return, liking his humor. "I don't know what lies in wait for me, but I think coming here was the first step."

"Toward what?"

"A better life," she replied instantly, easily. There was no question in her mind that Bellefleur was the best thing to have ever happened to her.

Nicholas shifted so that his long frame rested more comfortably along the cushions. "It has been that." When he thought of how miserable her life had been, he mentally strangled her father.

He thrust the image away, and focused on the immediate, most especially the happiness shining on her face. Joy was a rare emotion in her, one he could not overlook.

"So tell me, Jessica McCormick, what do you think is a good life?"

Again her response came quickly, and with an ease that spoke of utter assurance. "A home, one's heritage. A family." His Aunt Sophia immediately came to mind and she could not suppress a smile.

"Something tickle you inside?" he drawled, visually tracing the contours of her lips.

"Yes, your aunt."

He laughed outright, the rich tones doing more than tickling Jessica's nerves. "She is rather amazing."

"She feels the same about you."

"Who told you that?"

"No one, I could see it for myself, but she did make a point of telling me as much."

His face pulled to one side in a mock grimace. "That doesn't surprise me, and I can probably even tell you what she said."

"Truly?" Jessica's eyes rounded. She certainly hoped he could *not* guess at the entire conversation she had had with Sophia. In her mind, she could still hear echos of the woman's voice, ". . . his mistress . . . love . . . open display of hunger . . ."

"Oh, yes." Warming to the subject, Nicholas laced his hands over his chest. Eyes closed, he concentrated on deducing his aunt's thought processes. "To start with, she mentioned that I am a good boy, possibly a man, and that we are closer than most family members. She worries over me, my future, my happiness." He opened his eyes and asked, "Am I right?"

She laughed in response. "Yes."

"I'm sure she also made a point of mentioning that she did her best to be a mother to Anna and myself after our mother died."

Some of Jessica's laughter died. "She didn't say anything about that."

"No?"

"Not a word."

"That's unusual. She's normally very vocal about that."

"I'm sure it's too personal a matter for her to discuss with a stranger. A death in the family is very painful, a mother's passing doubly so."

Although it had been nearly twenty years since his mother had died, Nicholas recalled all the heartache he had experienced on that long-ago day. It wasn't something on which he generally dwelt. Surprisingly, he found himself wanting to share it with Jessica.

"My mother died giving birth to Anna. It was a very sad, dismal time for all of us."

Seeing the remnants of his misery, Jessica murmured, "Sophia stepped in to help?"

"She did her best. Of course, Anna never knew our mother. I was fourteen, thinking myself too old to cry when I was actually too young to behave like the adult I was trying to be."

"That had to have been difficult for you."

"It was difficult for all of us."

"What of your father?"

Nicholas sucked in a breath, releasing it slowly as he said, "He was devastated. You have to understand that he had gone through life bending it to his own satisfaction. He fashioned all around him as he saw fit. True, he had his disappointments; he and my mother lost three children before they had Anna. But even those losses couldn't destroy his zest for living. I didn't think anything ever could until *Maman* died."

"How terrible," Jessica whispered.

"He left for a while. He couldn't bear to be here, reminded daily of the woman who had meant everything to him."

"Where did he go?"

"Baton Rouge." Nicholas's mouth twisted mockingly to one side. "Into the arms of a mistress."

Before Jessica could think better, she asked, "A mistress?" She caught herself and stammered, "I'm . . . sorry. I had no right to ask."

Nick waved the apology away. "A woman by the name of Josephine Bouchard. Years later, when he told me of her, I was furious, I didn't understand. In the end, I had to face the fact that he returned here a sane, almost-whole man again. That wasn't something I could disparage."

His voice softened to nothing, leaving Jessica with a deeper understanding of Nicholas and his life. His feelings for his past ran deep. Despite the good and the bad, a loving family had been his.

"You were very lucky to have your aunt, then and now. It is apparent that she cares very much for you and Anna."

"True." Nicholas tipped his head to one side, scrutinizing Jessica carefully. It wasn't often that he confided as he just had. He wondered what was it about this woman that could prompt him to such behavior.

The gray of his eyes darkened to a flinty silver, the line of his shoulders straightened ever so slightly. "My aunt is also a very shrewd woman. She always has a purpose for whatever it is she has to say."

Under the power of his stare, a lump born of consternation caught in Jessica's throat. "Oh?"

"Mmm." He nodded, the gesture an indolent, challenging dip of his chin. "Aunt Sophia had no logical reason to speak to you about anything, yet she did. Why is that?"

She had hoped to avoid having to tell him about the personal nature of her talk with Sophia. "I'm sure I . . . I don't know."

"Don't you?" he drawled.

Jessica swallowed hard, the lump sliding from her throat to lodge thickly in her chest. Unable to look at him any longer, she stared at her lap, practically feeling the potency of his conviction like a bold force.

"Your aunt didn't tell me why she chose to speak to me," she whispered.

"No?"

"No, and you've already guessed at what we did discuss. Then she asked me about my hand and I left."

Nicholas reached out and lifted her scarred hand. Slowly, he caressed the jagged line that marred her skin.

"She told me to take care of it," she blurted out, her heart racing at his touch.

"I will try my best," Nicholas murmured. Lowering his head, he pressed his lips to her palm.

Jessica's entire body flinched at the heated contact of his mouth. The warmth he generated raced up her arm, then straight to the pit of her belly. Along every inch of the way, her nerves contracted in a response she savored in her heart, and everything she felt for this man surged to the fore.

He made her feel like a complete woman, his masculinity peeling away the layers of her femininity to reach a strength she was only just discovering within herself. It was that womanly strength she relied on now to overcome the last of her hesitation.

Undeniable feelings of trust and tenderness swirled unchecked with the desire he alone had taught her. She wanted him. Right or wrong, she knew in her most secret of hearts that she belonged to him. The thought made her shudder.

Feeling the tremor, Nicholas stared deeply into her eyes. "Jessica?"

It was a question, a plea, a demand.

She took a deep breath and curled her fingers about his. "Yes."

Chapter Twelve

"Do you know what I'm asking?" Nicholas queried. In an instant agony of anticipation, the muscles in his stomach clenched. *Say yes,* he mentally demanded, wanting more than some vague promise for the future. He needed her now, and he didn't know how much longer he was going to able to wait and keep his sanity.

He had promised not to push her into making a hasty decision. He had graciously given her all the time she required, but God almighty, part of him dearly regretted having made that promise. There was only so long he could go on picturing her without her clothes, imagining the feel of her surrounding his flesh. More than that, he had to experience this woman in his every pore and understand once and for all why she touched him as she did.

"Jessica." Her name came out as a low, cracked murmur.

Jessica sucked in another bracing breath of air, digging deep for her newfound strength. "Yes." From the heat and feel of him, she drew a measure of *his* strength. Her heart urged her forward. "Yes, I know what you're asking, and the answer is yes. I want to . . ."

His heart lunged against his ribs. "Are you sure?"

"Yes, but I . . . that is . . ." She swallowed the groan of embarrassment that threatened. "I mean, I've never . . ."

He stroked the satin smoothness of her cheek before cupping her chin in his hand. Her hesitancy was not due to fear, but an innocence intrinsic to her nature. That purity of the heart had guarded her virtue, a virtue she was offering to him.

Humbled by her genuineness, he mentally waged a brief internal battle with his conscience. He could deny himself, in fact, he should get up that instant and walk out, leaving her untouched. But the longing he felt for her was like an ever-burning blaze, ready to consume him. The hunger she instilled in him demanded that he accept her gift or forever carry the scars of regret seared into his heart.

There was no logic to that reasoning. He didn't even seek to find any. What he felt went beyond reality or passion, to where, he could not define. All he knew was that Jessica was his.

Slipping his fingers around to the nape of her neck, he stroked the delicate skin there. "I know, Jessica." Ever so lightly, he applied just enough pressure to draw her near as he leaned forward. "I know you're a virgin."

His whisper caressing her lips was like a balm to her soul. Her eyes drifted shut, the lack of the visual adding to the heightening of her other senses.

All along her exposed skin, the heat of his body warmed her. With each breath she took, she drew in the faint spiciness of his cologne and the muskiness of the man himself. Against her mouth, she felt the firm pressure of his lips, coaxing, luring, finally demanding, as his tongue thrust into her mouth. Shivers spiraled out in all directions, making her sway slightly where she sat.

His hands steadied her, one slipping down to her back, the other settling possessively on the curve of her hip. Even then, she didn't open her eyes, too caught up in the wonder of the moment. She wanted only for the bliss to continue uninterrupted forever.

It didn't. Without the slightest warning, Nicholas pulled away, only to scoop her up in his arms and stride from the room. Surprised, she looped her arms about his neck, caught by the taut expression on his face.

"Nicholas?"

He took the stairs two at a time, the only concession he would make to the urgent demands his body was making. Throwing open the door to his room, he had to remind himself, again, to temper his hunger for her sake.

It was difficult, *damned* difficult. Her acquiescence had released a tidal surge of desire that had him gritting his teeth. And kissing her, feeling and tasting her had nearly obliterated the tenuous hold he had on himself.

With a well-placed heel, he shut the door, then quickly locked it. Initially, he might have to proceed more cautiously than he would like, but he planned to have Jessica with him the entire night. The last thing he would tolerate was an untimely interruption by Jessup or Mama Lou.

He crossed the room to his bed in three long strides. There he let Jessica slide down the length of him. It was a mistake. The sensation of her softness caressing him took him one step closer to the edge of his control. His hands closed around the sweet fullness of her bottom and he thrust impatiently against her.

"This isn't going to work," he grated, tasting the flesh of her neck.

"Why?" she asked, tipping her head to one side to accommodate his mouth.

"Because," he breathed against her ear, "I want you too much. I'm afraid I'm going to move too quickly and take you before you're ready. I don't . . ." He pressed his face into the hollow of her neck. "I don't want to frighten you."

About the only thing that could have frightened her was if he stopped what he was doing. Everywhere his mouth touched, her skin came to life, sending ungovernable frissons into the core of her.

Naively she thought she had a clear understanding of passion. Clearly, she did not. A little dazed, she realized that the kisses they had shared up to now had only been a prelude, a tempting indication of . . . she had no idea, but she wanted to find out.

She spared herself only a few seconds to wonder at her yielding, at the total destruction of past apprehensions. There would be time later for her to search for answers. What consumed her thoughts just then was a yearning that had her trembling, and a need to please Nicholas.

"If I were another woman . . ." Her voice frayed to a husky murmur. His hands stroked up her back, drawing her ever closer to the muscled wall of his chest. The pressure against her breasts brought on a heady kind of languor and she had to fight to remember what it was she had been saying.

"If I were another woman, what would she be doing right now?"

He searched her eyes, seeing passion and an innocent kind of eagerness shining back at him. "You aren't any other woman, Jess. That's the problem." His arms tightened about her. "I've never met another woman like you, I've never wanted a woman the way I want you."

The admission broke the last of his restraint. He kissed her hard, opening her mouth to his demands and took all she offered. As if his life depended on it, he relished her earnest response, moaning deep in his throat when her tongue met his in ardent play.

His hands moved over her curves, seeking out her breasts, stroking the sweet fullness through the layers of fabric. Suddenly her clothes became an intolerable barrier.

Quickly, he released the buttons on the front of her bodice, lifting his mouth from hers only when the dress parted for his searching fingers. He stared down at the chemise-covered flesh bared to his view.

"This has to come off," he murmured, spreading wide the dress and slipping his fingers under the straps of her shift.

Jessica's sigh caught in her chest. The feel of his hands sent torrents of pleasure out in every direction. Her head felt light, her bones as useless as water.

"Nicholas, I don't think I can stand up much longer."

He tugged her free of her dress and threw it aside. "You won't have to, sweet." Just as quickly, he rid her of her chemise and coarse stockings, then stood back to fill his gaze with the sight of her.

"My God," he rasped. He wasn't prepared for the slender perfection of her. From shoulder to ankles, she was a play of flawlessly pearly skin and graceful lines. Irresistibly, his eyes were drawn to the curves of her high breasts, the indent of her waist and the gentle flare of her hips. At the juncture of her thighs rested a thatch of reddish curls, beckoning his body silently, irrevocably.

She was the quintessential woman; softness combined with strength, pride complementing delicacy. Everything that was male within him responded and for an instant he felt rocked to the core of him.

Heart thudding painfully in his chest, he said thickly, "You're beautiful."

True or not, Jessica simply could not stand there while he stared in open pleasure. She had never been naked with a man before and ingrained shyness overwhelmed her. Her arms came up to shield her from his view, but he caught her wrists and held them away.

"Don't." He stroked his fingers up her arms to her shoulders, absorbing the feel of her skin and committing it to an untouched niche in his heart. "I want to see all of you."

He gave her no time for a reply or for further reticence. His mouth took hers once more and then she forgot about being embarrassed. She kissed him back, matching his fervor, deepening the kiss as her arms circled his neck and clung fiercely. The move brought her body flush to his and pleasure, rich and abundant, flooded her being.

In the next instant, her world tilted. He secured her in his embrace and lowered her to his bed.

"Nicholas," she whispered when he lifted his head.

He didn't say anything. Lips thinned to a straight slash, eyes shot with heated silver, he yanked off his clothes then blanketed her with his body.

In all her wild imaginings, Jessica could have never guessed at the multitude of sensations created by the feel of his body on hers. She had never suspected that such soul-deep pleasure nor such contentment of the mind were possible. Eyes drifting shut, she tried to consume the stunning fulfillment of the moment. Instinctively, she lifted her mouth to his, seeking culmination for the myriad feelings.

Any hope Nicholas had that he could prolong this first union was dashed by the sensuality inherent in her silent offering. The last of his restraint died, and unable to help himself, he kissed her with all the pent up passion tearing at him. Parting her thighs with his own, he settled himself firmly against her and claimed the soft territory as his.

"You're mine," he declared against her softly bruised lips. He caught her face between his hands and stared into her velvet blue eyes.

In answer, Jessica wound her arms about his neck, digging her fingers into his resilient flesh. Against her chest, she could feel the heavy beat of his heart, a rhythm identical to the insistent throb of his manhood pressed so intimately against her. Instinctively, she adjusted herself to accommodate that heated flesh, then gasped when it slid into her moist folds.

Her eyes flew wide and were immediately captured by the silver gaze boring down at her. She stared back, relentlessly pulled into the depths of him as he surged into the depths of her.

She arched at the brief, intruding pain, her nails dug into his back, but she never once blinked. Taking ragged little pants, she returned his stare, the unbreakable eye contact only intensifying the reality of his possession. She gave herself to him, body and mind.

Little by little, she gradually became accustomed to the too-full feeling of his body within her. The reality of that was a staggering bliss not to be believed.

"Love me, Nicholas, make me yours," she breathed, shivering, trembling, knowing with absolute conviction that this was the most *right* thing she had ever done in her life.

"Ah, Jess."

That was all Nicholas could manage. Being sheathed in her incredible heat and softness was ecstasy incarnate. Shaking with the effort of the restraint he held over himself, he ground his eyes shut and at last gave into the hunger that had gnawed at him for weeks.

His hips surged forward, a groan worked its way up from deep in his gut and it was all suddenly out of control. He filled her again and again, drowning in the feel of her muscles clenching him, straining for the completion that was coming all too quickly.

Wrapping her in his arms, he called her name repeatedly, a litany torn from his soul and rooted in a primal instinct. As if his life hung in the balance, he knew he absolutely had to spill his seed within *this* one extraordinary woman.

He did in the next blinding instant. Tumultuous waves of almost painful pleasure tore through him, stripping him down to his most basic, vulnerable essence of man. Repeatedly, he surged into her until the last of the tremors ceased and all he could do was hold onto Jessica, feeling as united with her as he did with Bellefleur.

Reality came back slowly. By small degrees, he became aware of the ragged sound of his breathing in the hush of the room, the flickering light from the one lit lamp, and Jessica's warm softness beneath him. But more than anything else, he was conscious of the supreme sense of contentment that permeated his senses and body. He knew that he had never experienced anything even remotely similar and he knew with even greater assurance that Jessica was responsible.

Jessica. He lifted his head from the crook of her shoulder and scanned her features. He was still no closer to understanding the extraordinary affinity he felt toward her than he had been before. He had assumed that once they had made love, the puzzle would have been solved. It wasn't and that bothered him. He didn't like unsolved puzzles, especially if they pertained to himself. The result was that he felt slightly at odds with himself, and conversely, increasingly engrossed with Jessica.

He took in her closed eyes and the slightly parted lips, and mentally squirmed with regret. He hadn't satisfied her. That wasn't normal for him, as he knew himself to be a considerate lover, taking care to insure a woman's pleasure as well as his own. Then, too, his mad dash for completion had not been typical either, but the desire he felt for her had been unimaginable.

"Jessica." He levered himself onto his elbows to ease her of the burden of his weight. "Are you all right?"

She stirred and her eyes slowly opened. "I think so." Her voice was as mellow as the softness of her gaze.

"I'm sorry. I should have taken better care of you." A purely masculine smiled curled his lips. "But you made that impossible." He shifted slightly and smoothed an errant curl back off her forehead. "I promise this time will be better."

"This time?" Her blond brows angled with her confusion.

His smile grew sultry. "This time and the next, and the next."

Jessica was held in shock for a long moment. She hadn't thought they would . . . She had assumed that once . . . Her thoughts splintered at the commanding touch of his mouth on hers again.

She met the play of his tongue and gloried in the sweet ache that renewed itself deep inside her. It was the same restless need that had begun to grow earlier, expanding with every move of Nicholas's body. Now, once more, she felt the almost desperate yearning for some kind of assuagement.

Helplessly, her hips arched, the move inadvertently tightening her hold on Nicholas still sheathed thick and solid within her. She clung to his broad shoulders, instinctively seeking more.

"Nicholas. I . . . I need—"

He slowed released a groaning sigh and met her thrust. "I know what you need, sweetness." More than anything, he wanted to give her the ultimate joy. "In a while, love."

His mouth skimmed down her neck to nibble a path to her breasts. There he kissed and suckled on a rosy nipple, and Jessica cried out in stunned pleasure. Her insides clenched reflexively, yet the tension low and inside continued to build until she didn't think she could bear much more.

"Please, Nicholas." She clasped his head tightly to her, not knowing what it was she asked for. She only knew that she had no defense against his mouth or hands.

They roamed over her body, creating warm tremors that made her body tighten in on itself. Her muscles strained until she simply could not remain still. Again and again, she lifted her hips, needing Nicholas with all of her being.

He met her thrusts, repeatedly. Levering himself upward, he drove into her with powerful strokes that tore purring moans from her lips. All the while, she clung to his steely arms and gave herself up to his keeping.

It was the ultimate act of trust. Despite the sensations besieging her, she intuitively realized that every protective barrier she had ever erected was gone. She trusted Nicholas with her body. Her heart followed suit, rejoicing at the splendor of being one with him.

Spurred on by emotions raw and new, she kissed him boldly, gladly, fervently taking him into her body. The joy in that carried her to the apex of ecstasy.

Pleasure burst upon her, radiating out in pulsing waves. What breath she could manage, emerged on tiny sobs murmured against his mouth. She cried his name and held him to her, enraptured to share with him the stormy attainment of his release.

She floated back to herself on a cloud of tranquility that transcended body and spirit. Happiness such as she had never known in her life saturated her being, and she had Nicholas to thank for that.

Without warning, a bubble of the most wondrous wellbeing blossomed and emerged as a delighted laugh. All she could do was hug Nicholas, grinning while tears glistened her eyes.

He frowned at her expression. "What is it? Did I hurt you?"

Her smiled broadened at his sudden concern. "No, no."

"Then why these?" He caught a drop of moisture on the tip of one finger.

"Joy," she said simply.

By slow degrees, the furrows melted from Nicholas's brow. Eminently pleased, he carefully slipped from her body, rolled to his side and gathered her close. "Are you all right?"

"You already asked that once," she replied, distracted by the luxury of having his shoulder as her pillow.

He tucked his chin to get a clearer view of her face. "I know, but I'm asking again. The first time can be painful."

Tipping her head back slightly, she met his gaze. "It was, but only for an instant." Then she had been transported into the realm of incredible ecstasy. "I never knew," she confessed, her voice a husky murmur. "Is it always like this?"

"No, not always."

"Why not?"

The question was innocent enough, asked, Nicholas was sure, out of virginal curiosity. For all of its artlessness, however, the query promoted a reply that was fraught with a multitude of complex considerations.

Toying with a long strand of her hair, he pondered the matter. Disregarding technique and style, the act itself was the same, no matter who was involved. Experience had taught him that it was the emotion involved that took the matter from a banal expression of carnality to something of infinitely greater meaning. Experience also told him that what he and Jessica shared had ascended to a pinnacle he had never reached before. What emotions had inspired *that?*

"Did I say something wrong?" she asked.

His gaze sliced back to hers. "What?"

She nibbled on her lower lip. "You look irritated. Should I not have said anything?"

He shook off his troubled thoughts. "No, you asked a perfectly valid question. I was trying to find the right answer. The truth is that sometimes people have sex and sometimes they make love. It's all a matter of the feelings involved, what each person brings emotionally to the act."

Relying on nothing but her own limited knowledge, she offered, "We made love."

He turned onto his side to face her fully. "Most definitely." More than she would ever know. More than he was comfortable acknowledging. Yet, he wouldn't have it any other way.

Sliding his hand over her shoulder, he threaded his fingers back through her hair. Now, more than ever before, he marveled at her. She was as unique in the aftermath of love's play as she was in its throes. The appeal of that was irresistible.

"Stay with me. I want you here beside me all night."

Jessica blinked at the statement. In her thinking, she hadn't gone past the immediate. And she had no way of knowing if there was some special etiquette that governed what she should or should not be doing right then. Regardless, he made it plainly obvious that the decision to leave or not was up to her.

He could have commanded her to stay. That was his right, but as he had once told her, the situation between them was that of a man and a woman, not master and servant. Apparently, he respected her enough as a woman to leave her to her own decision.

Her happiness deepened, becoming a deep satisfaction. No one had ever held her in such regard. Unable to help herself, she stroked her hand along the planes of his chest, and lifted her mouth to his. "Yes, I'll stay." Forever, if she could. Nothing would make her happier.

She envisioned the two of them together every night for the rest of their lives. It was an image of husband and wife and everything that entailed; babies, a family, growing old in each other's arms. It was her dream for the future, and she realized in that second that she wanted that dream with Nicholas.

Chapter Thirteen

New Orleans was a dream come true for Anna. Seated in one of the many drawing rooms of the St. Charles Hotel, she was struck by the luxury surrounding her. Everywhere she looked, she saw an extravagance and excitement that reflected a grand American elegance. Tempered by European influences, the hotel possessed a richness which epitomized the very best of New Orleans.

Adjusting the drape of her sleeves, she cast *Tantia* an indulgent smile. They had had a heated discussion as to where they would stay in the city. *Tantia* adamantly desired the St. Louis, declaring that the hotel's French Creole hospitality was the only touch of civility in a city that was far too *bourgeois*. Only the fact that the St. Charles bordered the *Vieux Carre,* the French Quarter, appeased her aunt's French ancestry.

"This is certainly a mad crush," Sophia declared. Waving her fan, she kept a vigilant eye on the steady stream of people parading from one salon to the next.

"I think it's wonderful," Anna returned. The sheer number of people socializing was breathtaking. She had never seen such a congregation, all talking and laughing. Countless beautifully dressed ladies on the arms of equally dashing gentlemen milled in and about. Servants in dark formal garb hastened as quickly as possible, bearing trays of beverages or *petite* delicacies.

Anna's eyes sparkled with an enthusiasm she couldn't hide. No matter in which direction she turned, she was met with a scene that tempted her senses. From the heavy drapes framing the windows to the wide variety of evening dresses, color abounded. Perfumes filled the air and mixed with the heavy, sweet scent of magnolia blossoms decorating the rooms. And underscoring the din of hundreds of voices were the strains of violins.

"I can hardly hear myself think," Sophia complained, applying her fan with vigor.

Anna laughed. "I don't think we're supposed to think. I believe we're supposed to experience and enjoy." She intended to do exactly that.

Dressed in an gown of vivid blue organdy, her hair parted neatly in the middle and secured at her nape with a froth of lace and flowers, she was ready to plunge headfirst into the social whirl that was different from anything back home.

She thought of Bellefleur and then for no explainable reason, Mathew. Regret tugged at her heart. They had parted with a terrible strain between them and she wished it hadn't been so. As his friend, she would never do anything to hurt him, but he made her so mad at times, she could chew nails.

It hadn't been that way until recently. For months, he seemed to have been on edge, not at all like his usual affable self. His serious bend of thought was as prevalent as always, yet a tension hovered over him, so that no matter what she did, he was displeased about it.

As annoying as that was, it was also disheartening. She didn't like the discord between them; sadly enough, it would probably continue as long as he did not accept this restless eagerness she felt toward life. He didn't understand her feelings, and it was, for some reason, important to her that he did. And if not understand, then at least accept . . . impossible, irritating man that he was.

"When did you say we were supposed to meet Fionna?" she asked, repelling Mathew's annoying invasion of her mind.

Sophia snapped her fan shut, only to flip it open in high agitation. "At nine, but if I know my cousin, she'll be late."

"You're right, *Tantia*. It's already nine-thirty."

"Neuf heures et demie?!" Sophie launched into rapid fire French, complaining about her cousin Fionna's apparent inability to tell time. Anna smiled and let the criticisms roll off her back. Nothing could diminish her delight. She was far too ready to make her own happiness.

Giving the impression that she was hanging onto her aunt's every word, she scanned the crowd. More than once, she caught the eye of a gentleman looking back.

"Well, don't you agree?" Sophia wanted to know.

Cheeks blushed pink, Anna jerked her attention to the elder woman. "Yes, of course."

"I should hope so." Sophia's gaze turned sharp. "Is something wrong? Your face is flushed."

"I'm fine," Anna laughed. "In fact, I've never felt better." Memories of the conversation she had had with Nick pervaded her mind. He had assured her that she attracted her share of masculine attention. How wonderful to know that her brother had been right!

"It wouldn't do for you to swoon in here," Sophia advised, genuine concern replacing her pique. "Are you sure you don't want to go up to our rooms?"

Anna patted her hand. "I'm sure. Please, *Tantia,* don't worry."

Sophia gave one of her shrugs. "It can't be helped. I have worried over you for a very long time."

And, Anna knew, her aunt would continue to do so for a long time to come. She turned to slip her arm about Sophia's shoulder for a quick hug when the overdue Fionna Hampton made her appearance.

"Here you two are," she exclaimed, slightly out of breath. The gray-haired matron laid an unsteady hand to her sunken chest. "I've been looking for you for at least forever."

Sophia pressed her cheek to her cousin's and made the introductions.

"So, you're Francois and Emilee's daughter," Fionna sighed from her diminutive height. "You are the very image of your mother, my dear, the very image."

"I will take that as a compliment," Anna returned. Her mother had been one of the most beautiful women anywhere in Louisiana.

"She should only be here to see you now. She would be very proud, Anna, very proud."

"Well, of course she would," Sophia insisted. "As would my brother. You forget, Fionna, just how full of pride Francois was."

Fionna's lashes fluttered in apparent consternation. "I haven't forgotten a thing, cousin. Why, it's terrible of you to even suggest such a thing. My memory is as sharp as it ever was." As if to prove that point, she gave Anna her full attention. "There are at least a dozen people who want to meet you, my dear. There's Celeste LeBlanc, and Margaret Hackworth and . . ."

One by one, she named off a list that far exceeded a dozen. Anna did her best to contain her humor, especially when she happened to glance Sophia's way and found her aunt doing nothing to hide her annoyance.

"Why don't we stroll for a bit," Anna suggested.

Fionna's discourse abruptly halted. "That's a wonderful idea."

The three made their way from the parlor into another, stopping repeatedly to nod or smile or exchange a pleasantry. Anna was amazed by the number of people with whom Fionna was acquainted. By the time they had managed to cross the room, Anna's head was awhirl with names and faces. One in particular.

"Fionna, who is that gentleman?" she asked, nodding to a tall, riveting man staring boldly at her.

Fionna glanced over her shoulder, and drew in a hasty breath. "Arturo Trudeau. Don't look at him."

"Why not?"

"He has quite a way with the ladies, and naughty rumors follow him wherever he goes."

"Is he disreputable?"

"No, not entirely. He is very charming, but some say he can be . . ." she lowered her voice to a whisper, "wicked."

"Wicked?' Sophia repeated.

Fionna shrugged with her hands. "I don't know how much of it is hearsay and how much is fact. I would hazard a guess and say that a great deal is overlooked because he is so handsome."

The 'wicked' gentleman in question was indeed handsome, with his dark wavy hair and sultry blue eyes. Anna could not resist another look his way, only to discover that he was gazing directly back at her. Her heart lurched in her chest. To think that a man as virile and dashing as Arturo Trudeau would spare her a second, and a third glance was heady stuff.

Collecting her poise, she nodded politely, smiled *politely,* and forced her attention back to her companions, but it was a struggle to pay attention to anything either lady was saying.

There was something almost dangerous about Mr. Trudeau, something forbidden that touched off a responsive spark inside her.

Restless energy vibrated in her veins, and she suddenly did not want to stand there with these two wonderful relatives. She wanted Arturo Trudeau to rush over, sweep her into his arms and carry her off.

The romance of that made her pulse race. Far too easily for propriety's sake, she pictured herself clinging to his broad shoulders. His arms would be powerful, his stride smooth. And when he kissed her . . .

A touch at her arm spun her about. Half-expecting to see Mr. Trudeau's tall form, she dragged in a hasty breath, and actually had to blink to clear her vision of her fanciful reverie.

"Excuse me," a lovely young woman offered. "I didn't mean to give you a fright."

In the several seconds it took for Anna to find her voice, Fionna interceded. "Oh, Clarice, how good to see you again. Let me present you to my cousin and her niece."

Anna recovered at once, but out of the corner of her eye, she could still see Arturo Trudeau looking at her. "How do you do," she said, nodding to the woman Fionna had introduced as Clarice Johnston.

"What a pleasure to meet you," Clarice intoned pleasantly. "Fionna has spoken of you for days and days. I feel as if I already know you."

Anna returned the woman's smile, and made several instant observations. Clarice Johnston was a beautiful woman. Widow, to be more exact. In a room where extravagant color was the standard for dress, Mrs. Johnston's black gown could only have one explanation.

Nonetheless, the lack of color did not in any way detract

from the woman's beauty. The black satin served to set off her brown eyes and hair most attractively while making her skin appear milky white. The contrasts were stunning.

"Clarice has come to us from Virginia," Fionna explained.

"Oh?" Sophia queried, openly studying Clarice. "Where in Virginia?"

"Richmond," Clarice returned, lifting her chin ever so slightly.

Sophie's mobile brows arched. "I know several Johnstons from Richmond. Are you one of *the* Jamestown Johnstons? They go back for close to two hundred years."

A smooth smile stretched Clarice's mouth. "No, I'm afraid not. My husband's family was originally from Maryland. They're not directly related to the blue bloods of Richmond, although I've often thought that if we traced the lineage back far enough, there's bound to be a connection somewhere."

"I think you're absolutely right," Fionna concurred. "After all, there can only be so many people with the name Johnston."

"My point exactly. One never knows how one is related." Clarice directed a pointed look at Anna. "Wouldn't you agree?"

Anna wondered if she imagined the odd emphasis Clarice gave her statement or if the woman intended some hidden meaning. Deciding that she was letting her imagination get away with her, she shrugged off the impression. "Every family is bound to have members it doesn't even know about."

Clarice gave a laugh, trailing her fingers across the fullness of her breasts. "Oh, Anna. You don't know how right you are."

Anna warmed to Clarice's ready humor, liking the woman more with each passing moment. It wasn't everyday that you found a woman as lovely and amiable as Clarice, especially in light of her bereavement.

"How long will you be in New Orleans, Mrs. Johnston?"

"Please, call me Clarice. And I really haven't decided what my plans are." Some of her gaiety faded. "Since Joseph died, I find that I am at times without direction."

"Joseph was her poor, dear husband," Fionna clarified in a hushed voice. "Poor man passed on in the prime of his life leaving our darling Clarice to fend for herself."

Clarice was quick to dismiss the seriousness of the situation. "It isn't as bad as it sounds. Joseph left me a tidy sum." She bestowed Fionna with a benign smile. "And I have friends like you, Fionna, to gladden my days."

"You are so sweet, my dear, to say that."

"Fionna has been a godsend," Clarice explained to Anna and Sophia. "I've only recently come to New Orleans. I thought it would help ease the pain of my loss. Fionna was good enough to take me under her wing."

Almost blushing at the compliments, Fionna fussed with her graying curls. "It was my pleasure. I lost my own husband several years back so I know what you're going through. I relied on my friends to help me through that troubling time."

"You are indeed a very dear friend, Fionna."

"And now that Sophia and Anna are here, they shall be your friends as well."

Clarice smiled brightly. "I will count on that."

It was all Clarice could do to contain her glee. Her mother should only see her now; dressed as elegantly as any of the pampered rich Creole ladies, drinking the most expensive champagne, mingling with the creme of society.

People in Baton Rouge would drop their jaws. She'd like to see that, and then spit in their faces. Phillip St. James's in particular. That arrogant banker would rue the day he deemed her less than worthy.

His rejection still made her stomach burn. She'd make him pay for that someday, and that was no idle threat. Since coming to New Orleans, she had discovered that she was a very resourceful woman.

If she had had a hand in fate herself, she couldn't have designed the present situation to be any better than it was right then. Of course, she had to credit herself with having done an excellent job of playing Fionna Hampton for the old fool that she was.

In the three weeks that Clarice had been in New Orleans, she had been inching closer to her ultimate goal of claiming Bellefleur as her own. Now, success loomed closer than she would have imagined, especially given the relatively little amount of effort she had expended.

She had been fully prepared to make her contacts amongst the city's elite planter community, to discreetly inquire about the DuQuaine family. From there, she had planned to eventually work herself into the family's intimate circle of friends.

The plan had never gotten past a few casual inquires when chance had placed her and Fionna side by side in the same salon for the same musicale. Discovering that the woman was related to the DuQuaines had been a stroke of luck, and now having Anna DuQuaine handed to her on the proverbial silver platter was a slight miracle, if one believed in such nonsense.

Clarice did not. She believed in the hard realities of schemes and plans and making the most of a situation. Hence, her ploy as a grieving widow. That persona suited her purposes well, as it allowed her a social freedom denied to young, unmarried women.

She could come and go as she pleased, take a lover if it struck her fancy, and any behavior that might be construed as suspect could always be attributed to grief. More importantly, widowhood presented her in a light that hadn't failed to touch Fionna's ridiculously sentimental heart.

The lies concerning her "husband" had come easily enough, and hadn't been questioned by a single soul. Only Sophia Marcheaux had bothered to delve into the nonexistent man's past with her snooping about lineage and families dating back to Jamestown. Wherever that was. She would have to find out. After all, if she was supposed to be from Richmond, it wouldn't do for her to get caught not knowing something every Virginian took for granted.

Sipping champagne from a graceful flute, she thrust the matter aside for the time being and studied Anna DuQuaine's aunt. Damn, but the woman was as ugly as sin. And almost as dangerous, if Clarice didn't miss her guess. There was an underlying shrewdness about Sophia Marcheaux that pricked every one of Clarice's instincts, cautioning her not to overlook the woman as a possible threat.

It would be imperative to separate Anna from the old cow as soon as possible. Sophia's influence on Anna, regardless how insignificant, could prove to be disastrous.

Playing on Fionna's eagerness to help out in any way possible and Sophia's eagerness to see that her niece was a dazzling success, she quickly maneuvered Anna into another salon.

"Have you been enjoying your stay?" she asked Anna, taking a seat in one of the vacant chairs set in a cozy little alcove.

Laughing, Anna sat facing Clarice and arranged her skirt in becoming folds. "Yes. I'm almost embarrassed to tell you just how much."

"This is your first time in New Orleans, then."

"My first time since I was a child."

"Ah, you were too young, then, to have appreciated the city's finer aspects."

"I am beginning to realize that." Anna looked about with a casual air. The increased color on her cheeks, however, betrayed her seeming indifference.

Clarice noted the subtle reaction and instantly found its cause in Arturo Trudeau. He had followed them into the room, and it appeared that the impressionable Anna DuQuaine had discovered the handsome planter, and that Arturo had discovered little Anna.

An interesting development, to be sure. Clarice had heard several rumors concerning the suave, appealing Arturo. His reputation bordered just on the edge of being scandalous, without ever quite crossing over. Giving him a covert glance, she wondered just how disreputable he was beneath that polished facade.

"So where is this plantation of yours, this Bellefleur?" Clarice asked, all smiles and deceptive artlessness.

"Just north of Natchez."

"In Mississippi?"

"Oh, no, on the western banks of the river, in Louisiana."

Clarice laughed, not at her intentional mistake, but at the ease with which she was able to gull Anna. "I'm still learning my way about this part of the country. It's so different from Virginia and the Carolinas."

"Louisiana has a beauty all its own."

"I've seen a small sampling of this in several plantations in the area."

Anna smiled and rolled her eyes in good-natured defense of her home. "There's no place more beautiful than Bellefleur."

"You say that because it is your home."

"Possibly," Anna returned, borrowing one of her aunt's sassy shrugs. "But Bellefleur is truly magnificent."

Clarice silently agreed, then dropped the topic at once. She had pressed her interest far enough for now. To appear overly inquisitive could only make Anna suspicious.

"I don't mean to be impertinent by mentioning this, and I caution you not to turn around, but there is a gentleman in the far corner to your left staring at you."

Anna's eyes rounded.

"I couldn't help but notice, because I saw him in the other room casting you the most remarkable glances." Clarice allowed a sly grin to curl her mouth. "It seems you are to be congratulated. Arturo Trudeau is quite the catch from what I've been told."

Doing everything she could to keep from looking over her shoulder, Anna eagerly asked, "Do you know him?"

"We've met."

Anna snapped open her fan and applied it to cool her warming face.

"I can see that he has made an impression on you."

"I think he's incredibly handsome."

"Of course he is." Clarice leaned closer to whisper, "Between you and me, that's what makes looking at him so appealing."

It was the type of intimate confidence shared between friends. As Clarice intended, Anna responded with heartfelt laughter.

"That was almost naughty of you, Clarice."

"True, but why shouldn't I be honest? The man is handsome. What a waste not to appreciate that."

Anna paused, a look of dawning amazement spreading across her features. "You're absolutely right."

"I have no intention of apologizing for indulging my feminine curiosity. Neither should you."

Anna sat back in her chair and gave Clarice a long, thoughtful look. "Oh, Clarice, I am so glad I met you."

Tilting her head to one side, Clarice summoned forth a beguiling little grin. "How nice of you to say that."

"It's more than words," Anna insisted gently. "You're fresh and alive and unafraid to say what's on your mind."

"Aren't you?"

Anna's gaze wavered. "Not always."

Patting Anna's hand, Clarice advised, "There is a time for caution and a time for impudence. If given my choice, I would prefer to be carefree and do as I please."

"That is exactly how I feel. Time and time again I have wanted to dismiss convention, meet exciting people, journey to undiscovered lands."

"Alas, a woman's lot doesn't readily allow for such," Clarice commiserated with just the right touch of melancholy.

"No, it doesn't."

"But it does allow," Clarice added, a knowing glint of devilry shining in her brown eyes, "for us to take advantage of whatever opportunities come our way."

"It does?"

"Of course. And if opportunity presents itself, I think you should take advantage of the moment and further your acquaintance with Arturo."

Anna's mouth rounded into a startled o, but as the seconds passed, the line of her lips softened into a flirting little smile. "I think you're right. I would very much like to meet him. In truth, I believe he is the exact kind of man I have been waiting to meet." A tender light softened the gray of her eyes. "Thank you, Clarice."

"For what?"

"For listening, for being so wonderful."

"I'm hardly that, Anna."

"Yes, you are. And I know that we could become great friends."

Clarice reached out and gave Anna's hand a gentle squeeze. Inwardly, she crowed in silent satisfaction. *This* was far easier than she would have ever imagined. With a few carefully chosen words, she had the impressionable Anna DuQuaine exactly where she wanted her, right by her side and believing in a bond of friendship.

Gaining entrance to Bellefleur was now just a matter of time. From there, she had only to contend with Nicholas DuQuaine.

Chapter Fourteen

Lust had never been as magnificent. Nicholas came to that conclusion as he watched Jessica sleep. By the muted light of early morning filtering around the heavy drapes, she looked impossibly lovely, and so erotically arousing he was tempted to awaken her with all haste. He didn't. She was exhausted and with good reason.

Thinking of the night just past, a very male smile tugged at his mouth. They had made love repeatedly, and while he *had* planned to have her with him for the entire night, he *hadn't* expected that they would make love more than once or twice. After all, she had been a virgin.

Leaning back against the pillows, he ignored his body's urge to follow the night's course. He inhaled deeply and instead, studied the matter of Jessica McCormick; more specifically how she related to lust. Good old-fashioned, feel-good, man and woman lust.

He broke into a smile at that. She was certainly an eager little thing, wanting to experience as much as she could. That ardor had been exceeded only by her desire to please him. She had definitely done so, and with a selfless sincerity that had spurred his own need to please her in greater measure. It had been a sumptuous circle that left his body sated and his mind bathed in contentment.

It had been a long time since he had felt such peace of mind.

No. In all honesty, he had never felt this way. Ever.

He looked down at her sleeping form again. Curled on her side facing him, her hair was a wild golden tangle spread about her shoulders. She appeared an untamed, erotic sprite. She was that in part, but she was also a warm, generous, loving young woman. Perhaps that was why the night had been so special.

She stirred, as if his silent perusal had intruded into her slumberous bliss. Slowly, her eyes opened and he was caught by the blue of her gaze.

"Good morning," he murmured.

Her lids drifted shut only to open with equal languor seconds later. "Good morning."

He rolled to his side and leaning on one forearm, slid his other hand over her waist to settle possessively on the curve of her hip. "How do you feel?"

"Wonderful."

"No lingering aches?"

Jessica shifted experimentally, testing muscles. When she turned onto her back, a slight grimace marred her features. "Nothing that I can't live with." What was a little discomfort in comparison to the glory she had experienced in Nicholas's arms? She would gladly suffer a few twinges to feel the same again.

Sighing deeply, she slid one hand up the hard plane of his chest, marveling at the crisp texture of his hair and the vital warmth of his skin. The combination was as intriguing as the heavy shadow of beard tinting the lower half of his face.

She trailed her fingers over his jaw and cheeks, liking this evidence that was so essentially male. Then again, she liked everything about this particular man.

He had been a considerate lover, exercising special care when needed, introducing her to more lusty pursuits with what she suspected was timely expertise. Even though she had nothing by which to judge, she believed that he was a very accomplished lover. Just thinking of what they had done, the mastery with which he had handled her body, brought a bright stain to her face.

"What is this?" Nicholas asked, one black brow quirking upward at the sight of her blush.

"Nothing." She tucked her chin, trying to evade his searching fingers. His hand stayed her movements and forced her gaze back to his.

"Jessica, are you embarrassed?"

"No, not really."

"Then what is it?"

It was difficult for her to explain. She didn't regret what they had done. However, her emotions were still raw enough that she wasn't prepared to lie there and have an open discussion. In fact, harsh reality invaded at the moment as she suddenly realized that Mama Lou would be looking for her at any time.

In a flurry of motion, she slid from the bed, holding the sheet about her protectively. Looking past the veil of her hair, she turned a tight circle searching for her discarded clothes.

"What the devil are you doing?" Nicholas sat up and watched in growing amazement as she bent to retrieve her chemise.

"I have to leave," she answered quickly, not looking his way. He was naked, something that had given her only momentary pause last night. This was morning now and having him casually sit there when she was feeling so inexplicably vulnerable was unnerving.

Truly taken aback, Nicholas took hold of the trailing end of the sheet. "You aren't going anywhere." He tugged her back onto the bed and into his arms.

Instantly, she tried to squirm away, but only got as far as a comfortable seat on his lap. "Nicholas, please, I have to go. Mama Lou usually wakes me up at first light."

"So?"

She flung her hair back off her face and faced him squarely. "So, I . . . I don't want her going to my room and not finding me there."

Understanding hit Nicholas hard. Too hard, and he was a touch insulted. His jaw grew rigid as his arms tightened about her. "She's going to find out sooner or later."

"I know, but I'm not ready for that."

"You haven't done anything wrong."

"I know that, too."

"But . . ." he prompted.

She sighed heavily. "This is all so new to me, Nicholas. You have to give me time to become comfortable."

The silent appeal in her eyes went straight to his heart. He had come to think of her as belonging beside him, and to such a degree that he had forgotten that this was a momentous time for her. It wasn't every day that a woman gave up her virginity. She had to be feeling different about herself.

Relaxing back on the bed, he drew her down on top of him. Already the feel of her went far in diffusing his irritation. Carefully, he eased a long golden curl back over her shoulder. "You're not sorry about what you've done, are you?"

"No," she was quick to assure him.

"Good, because you have nothing to be ashamed of."

Her brows shrugged in contradiction. "Some people would say I do."

"Some people are self-righteous prigs who don't have anything better to do than go about casting judgement on others."

Uncertainty played over her face. "What will Mama Lou think?"

"Do you care?"

"I don't want her thinking less of me."

"She won't."

"How can you be sure?"

"I know the woman. She's one to let others do as they will. And even if she weren't, it shouldn't make any difference to you. This is a private matter that doesn't concern anyone other than you and me."

She knew it was far more complicated than that. He could feel as he did because he was the master of Bellefleur, and because he was a man. Not only was he secure in his own sense of self-worth, but society allowed him options that were denied to her and to all women. For what she had done, she would be labelled a slut. He was a man simply behaving as a man.

The injustice of that was galling. It was the way of things, though and she wasn't about to dwell on it. She had made her decision and felt no remorse or regret. What she *did* feel was a need for discretion. She would eventually come to grips with being Nicholas's lover. She would never be comfortable flaunting that fact. As he said, what they shared was most private.

"Please, be patient with me," she murmured.

"I will, darling."

She sank into the comforting strength of him, letting herself absorb the feel of his body beneath hers. "I have to go."

His hands strayed along the delicate curve of her spine. "It's still early."

"I have chores."

"They can wait."

All along the length of her, his body braced hers with heat and muscle. The sensations created tugged at her willpower. "You're making it hard for me to leave."

He smiled, a roguish, one-sided grin that made him look impossibly rakish. "You're making it hard for me, too," he whispered, lifting his hips into the softness of her thighs.

Her eyes widened at the blatant evidence of his arousal. "I . . . I didn't mean that."

"I know." His hands captured her hips, rotating them against him. "But I did."

"I . . ." She swallowed hard, unable to find any words when her body was responding of its own accord to his. Her heart beat heavily while her limbs felt leaden. Still, she tried once more, "I think I should—"

He pulled her more tightly against him. "—stay exactly where you are."

And she did as Nicholas once again claimed her with a fiery expertise that swept them both into a sensuous realm where only the two of them existed. For Jessica, their union was a joyous sharing of mind and body, and she gave of herself freely, wholly, wanting Nicholas to feel all that he made her feel.

He did, as never before. The richness of the pleasure he experienced touched his soul, nearly humbling him before this one small, courageous young woman. Perhaps it was because of that courage, or because of her indomitable spirit on her enduring generosity; for whatever the reason, she once again made him feel as united with her as he did with Bellefleur.

The feeling was breathtaking.

When Jessica finally slipped from bed nearly a half hour later, it was with lips tenderly bruised and eyes as soft and blue as a misty ocean. Under Nicholas's watchful eye, she gathered up her clothes and donned them with lethargic movements.

"You need something better to wear," he commented easily. Sitting on the edge of the bed, he scanned the small bundle of clothes she had collected and dismissed the lot as worthless. Her skin was perfection itself and should be touched by silk and lace, not muslin that was threadbare and some coarse fabric that resembled burlap.

"No, I don't," she smiled back.

"Yes, you do, Jess."

She paused in the act of tying the front of her chemise. "Why?"

"Your things are ragged." Reaching out, he flicked the frayed hem of the undergarment. "How old is this?"

Her gaze dropped to the tattered muslin. "I don't know. Several years, I suppose."

He gave a scoff. "I'll have some new things made up for you."

"No." Her head came up, her spine stiffened. "I don't want you doing that."

At her rare, imperious tone, he cocked his head to one side. "Why the devil not?" he asked with enough humor to crease his face with a grin.

"I just don't want you to."

"You can't go around dressed like that."

"I have up until now. There's no reason for that to change." She reached for her faded gray dress and quickly slipped it on. Gone was her easy languor. In its place was a brisk determination born of pride.

At her heart's urging, she had given herself to Nicholas.

To accept even one article of clothing would denigrate her actions to that of a whore.

"I don't want anything," she stated, her fingers worked diligently to fasten the buttons on the front of her bodice.

A good deal of Nicholas's humor drained away at her solemn insistence. "Jess, I don't like seeing you dressed in rags."

"These are my clothes."

"That's no argument."

Holding the mass of her hair out of her face, she searched about for her shoes. "Please, I don't want anything."

Lines of frustration creased his brow. "You need new clothes."

"That didn't bother you before now."

"You didn't share my bed before."

She whirled to face him, clutching her weathered, worn shoes to her chest. "Exactly, and you'd turn me into your paid whore."

The accusation was unjust and spurred his temper. He surged to his feet. "What nonsense is this?"

Instinctively, she started to step back from the anger she could feel emanating from him, from the ire sharpening every line of his magnificently naked body. But she held her ground, placing her trust in the bond they had forged, placing her trust in him.

Clutching her courage as hard as she held on to her shoes, she explained, "I didn't go to your bed in order to gain a few new dresses."

"I didn't say that you did."

"But that is what you would make of the situation. If you gift me with a dress, if I accept, it will be the same as my taking money in exchange for my body." Her eyes filled with tender entreaty, her voice lowered to a husky whisper. "I gave myself to you because I wanted to, because in my heart I knew it was the right thing to do. Please, don't demean what we shared. It was the most wonderful . . ." Tears rose swiftly to balance on her lids. "It was the *only* perfect thing in my life."

The depths of her feelings went far beyond what Nicholas could have imagined, to levels that stole straight into his heart and left him feeling oddly vulnerable. The sensation was disarming, but even as he grappled with the resulting discomfort, he was powerless against its cause, Jessica herself.

His hands shot out and grasped her by her arms. In the next second, he hauled her forward until she was pressed tightly to his chest, one hand at the small of her back, the other tangled in the length of her hair.

"God above, what you do to me," he ground out, pulling her head back with gentle force so he could kiss the tears from her eyes. "Don't cry." He couldn't stand the thought of her being hurt. "I'm sorry, I never meant to insult you. I want only wanted to make you happy, to give you what you deserve in life." He pressed his mouth to her temple. "We'll forget about the clothes. Walk around naked if that makes you happy." He buried his face in the cloud of her hair. "Just don't be upset."

Held so protectively, it would have been impossible for her to feel upset. That, coupled with his understanding, brought her a happiness that permeated her being, a happiness that shined brightly on her face.

Mama Lou was the first to take notice moments later. "What's wrong?" she asked, meeting Jessica half-way to the kitchen.

Jessica fussed with the ties of her apron, trying and failing miserably to keep her face expressionless. "Nothing. Why should anything be wrong?"

"No reason." The housekeeper's deep brown eyes scrutinized every inch of Jessica's face. "Where have you been? I looked for you a bit ago, but you weren't in your bed."

"I was . . . already up."

Mama Lou nodded in what appeared to be the wisdom of the ages. "And havin' a grand time, from the looks of you."

Jessica's hands stilled. "What?"

"You heard me. You look like you've swallowed the sun and you're just achin' to burst at the seams."

It was all Jessica could do to keep from touching her cheeks. Having looked in the mirror only minutes earlier, she knew her hair was neatly braided and coiled, her face scrubbed. There was nothing unusual about her appearance.

"It's a nice day. I feel good."

Mama Lou sent a knowing look to the windows of Nicholas's room. "I just bet you do." She gave a quick shake of her head, then asked, "You eaten yet?"

"No, ma'am."

"Well, get a move on. We got to begin strippin' the wax from the floors and layin' down new polish today."

Jessica hurried to the kitchen for a quick bite of corn bread, glad to be out from under the housekeeper's sharp gaze even for a few minutes. She suspected that Mama Lou had accurately guessed where she had spent her night. Thankfully, the woman hadn't made an issue of it.

Unfortunately, Pearl took up where Mama Lou had left off. "What's put dem roses in yo' cheeks dis mornin'?" the enormous cook wanted to know.

Jessica swallowed before answering. "If I have roses in my cheeks it's because I'm late and I've been hurrying. Mama Lou is waiting for me."

Pearl waddled over to the blazing coals in her hearth. "Shoot, let the old goat wait. You're lookin' mighty fine today, and I'd say it's 'cause of my cookin'. Finally gettin' some color in yo' cheeks and some meat on dem bones."

Jessica did not dispute the matter. Nor did she linger for more inquiries into her state of health. As soon as she drank the last of her milk, she hastened back to the house, finding Mama Lou and Betsy in the front parlor.

"It's about time that fat old cook turned you loose," the older woman grumbled. "Let's get this furniture moved."

Between the three of them, they carried the chairs and tables into connecting rooms, then began the back-breaking task of scrubbing the pine floor free of last year's protective wax. Jessica applied herself with more enthusiasm than was necessary. It couldn't be helped. She was feeling as wonderful as Mama Lou had described earlier, full of sunshine and bursting at the seams.

"You're smilin'," Betsy observed when Mama Lou had gone off on another chore.

"I am?" Kneeling, Jessica dipped her brush into a bucket of hot water, vinegar and lye.

"Yep."

"I suppose that's because I'm happy."

Betsy frowned, her round face creasing with her obvious amazement. "You like strippin' floors?"

Jessica chuckled. "No, not especially."

"Me either. I like standin' in the sun. That makes me happy. What makes you happy?"

In her own simple way, Betsy had asked a weighty question. The answer, however, was easy enough for Jessica to find. Nicholas made her happy.

Without meaning to, she paused to peer through one open doorway into the dining room and then through the other doorway to the front drawing room. Only then did she realize she was looking for Nicholas.

Of course, he wasn't in either room. At this time of day, he was in the fields, or the barns or stables, watching over things. He normally didn't return to the house until lunch, sometimes later. His afternoons were generally spent in his library.

Knowing all of this did not in any way prevent her gaze from straying again and again as she worked through the morning and into the afternoon. At every sound, she looked up, hoping to catch sight of him. She didn't know what she would do if she did find him. She only knew that she felt compelled to look.

By late afternoon, the floor had been cleaned and the first layer of polish laid down. Stiff and sore, Jessica pressed a hand into the small of her back as she headed for her room. Disappointment weighted her shoulders as much as physical exertion. Nicholas had spent the entire day somewhere other than the house. She hadn't had a glimpse of him since he had pulled her into his arms for one last kiss in his room that morning.

Perhaps it was silly of her to fret about it, but it wasn't something she could control. She genuinely needed to be with him, to have him hold her, if even for a few precious seconds.

Sadness tugging at the corners of her mouth, she crossed from the front drawing room into the library and from there into the plantation office behind . . . and came to an abrupt stop. Nicholas was seated at the desk. He looked up at her entrance and she froze with her hand on the doorknob.

"Oh," she got out on a breathy gasp. She had pined for him for hours; there he was and she was at a loss. A little lamely, she gestured vaguely toward her own room next door. "I was going to wash up."

Nicholas came to his feet, his body uncoiling in a smooth

play of muscle. From the look of him, he had only just come in, and to Jessica, he had never appeared more handsome. His black hair had been tossed by the river breeze, his clothes wrinkled from hours on horseback. Even the tan of his face seemed more pronounced, as if the sun had lovingly kissed his skin.

"What have you been doing?" he asked, skimming her figure with a bold eye.

She looked down at her wet and stained skirt. "Cleaning floors." Self-consciously, she smoothed stray tendrils of hair back off her face. She was a mess. "What about you? I didn't see . . . I mean, have you been out all day?"

"All day."

His gray eyes bore into her, glinting and hungry. The silvery sheen made her swallow, and she was suddenly swamped by confusion. Part of her dearly wanted to fling herself into his arms, but uncertainty held her immobile, waiting for him to do something, anything to break the inexplicable tension that vibrated between them.

Her gaze locked with his. Inside, she could feel heat twist in the pit of her belly, as if he touched her intimately. She drew a shaky breath, then held it locked in her throat when he moved from behind the desk and advanced, his eyes never releasing their hold on her.

"Come here," he muttered in a dark, raspy voice. He never gave her a chance to move. He caught hold of her with one hand and hauled her into his arms only seconds before he fastened his mouth over hers.

He had waited all day for this. From the minute she had walked out of his room that morning, he had been dying to have her back, to feel her softness under his palms, to taste her on his tongue. He had purposely pushed himself harder than usual, staying late in the fields just to temper his unruly need, but it hadn't worked. The delay had only increased his desire to have her, now. That second.

He thrust his tongue past her parted lips. It was the exact release Jessica needed. Freed from her momentary daze, she gave herself up to her instincts and wound her arms about his neck. His mouth plundered hers, taking, demanding, and she realized that he had been as desperate for her as she had been for him.

She arched against him, suddenly frantic to have him inside her again. "Oh, God, Nicholas," she moaned, straining against him.

He didn't bother with niceties. Hands sure and swift, he lifted her from her feet, turned and in one fluid motion, swept the contents of the desk onto the floor. Her legs parted even as he laid her on top of the desk. Quick tugs released him from his pants, another tossed her skirt up and then he sheathed himself within her, plunging forward heavily.

He gave himself up to the urgency that had been riding him all day. Feeling alive as never before, so unbearably in need of another human being, his body ached with pent-up desire, and he ground his hips against hers, nearly mindless with the kind of hunger that went beyond anything in his experience.

Distantly, he realized that he was taking her like some conquering barbarian of old. He couldn't have stopped himself if he tried. He didn't want to, and from the sound of the tiny, rapturous sobs breaking over Jessica's lips, neither did she.

She lifted her hips to receive him, caught in the same storm of emotion that blazed within Nicholas. The desk allowed for little comfort. She barely noticed as her insides coiled with tension, tighter and tighter until it finally snapped and she arched upward in ecstasy. All around Nicholas's thick, male flesh, she convulsed and shivered, and took him to his own shattering release.

Only the echos of their heavy breathing broke the hush in the room. Jessica lay sprawled in sweet wanton abandonment, Nicholas's head rested in the curve of her shoulder. Dusk's shadows played over their entwined figures.

"I missed you," he said at long last.

"I missed you, too." She lifted her mouth to his.

He turned the kiss into something more ardent, breaking off only when it threatened to belie the passion just spent. "This desk isn't very comfortable. We need to get cleaned up."

Jessica was content to lie where she was. "If we must."

Carefully, he slipped from between her legs, then helped her to sit up. His gaze trailed over the slim curves of her thighs; his hands followed. "I didn't mean for this to happen," he said, smiling ruefully as he smoothed her dress down over her legs. "At least not here. I thought to at least make it to my bed."

"I didn't mind."

"I must smell like the fields." He dragged a hand back through his hair.

"You smell wonderful, like hay and clean air and sunshine and you." And she loved it. She loved everything about him, his voice, his face, his laugh, the commanding way he did things, his thoughtfulness, the way he kissed her, the way he made her feel secure and whole. She loved everything there was about Nicholas DuQuaine.

She loved him.

Chapter Fifteen

"This is so very exciting," Anna declared behind her fan. Eyes sparkling with silver highlights, she gazed about the *Théâtre d'Orléans*.

"The opera is always exciting," Clarice said. "Tonight, more so than usual, *Les Huguenots* is a favorite here in the city, from what I've been told."

Fionna Hampton leaned forward in her seat to declare, "Oh, yes, Clarice. Not a season goes by that we don't have *Les Huguenots*. Why, I think the city would riot if it wasn't performed at least once a year. And anyone who is anyone will attend."

From where she sat in Fionna's box, Anna could only surmise that the dear lady was correct. Attending this particular opera seemed to be a social must. A great many of the acquaintances she had made were seated in the rows of boxes. Or at least they would be once the lights were dimmed. At present, visiting friends appeared to be the order of things. Several people had already stopped by Fionna's box to pay their respects, and to invite them to assorted amusements after the performance.

"It's a shame Sophia could not attend," Fionna sighed.

Anna pulled her attention away from the glittering sight of the milling throng below. "She has been complaining of a headache all day. I think she needs some time to rest."

"We can all use a good night's sleep. Alas, that can be difficult to find here in the city."

Again, Fionna was right. Anna had found that hardly a minute had gone by that she hadn't been whisked away to this party or that ball, a soiree or a dinner. And at every one of those functions, she had hoped to see Arturo Trudeau.

Just thinking about him sent her pulse tripping. She had only seen him that one time in the hotel and then at a distance. She had never gotten the chance to actually meet him, and ever since then he seemed to have disappeared.

She searched for him now, scanning the boxes hopefully.

"Anna, dear, did you hear what I said?" Fionna asked.

"I'm sorry," Anna apologized. Shaking off her distraction, she turned back to her aunt's cousin, becoming aware then that several people had stepped into the box . . . among them, Arturo.

Her heart flipped over in her chest. Belatedly, she remembered to school her features into not betraying her. The last thing she wanted was to look like a silly little girl, smitten for the first time.

But oh, dear Lord, that was difficult! She was smitten, or at least, entranced. Standing tall and broad shouldered, Arturo Trudeau was so handsome it made her knees weak. The edge of his jaw was a hard line, his lips were full and smiling. His hair was a deep umber while his eyes were the bluest she had ever seen, containing a hint of danger that seemed inherent to him.

He wasn't menacing; rather his manner exuded an earthy sensuality that was forbidden. She had had this same impression the first time she had glimpsed his sultry smile, and she felt it again now as she watched him talk to the others. His movements were a pleasing glide of muscle beneath his black jacket, his voice a deep vibration that acted on her nerves. And when he turned his gaze on her, trills of heat curled deep inside her.

He was deliciously dangerous, and she was enthralled by him.

The introductions went on around her; she paid them half a mind, until Arturo took her hand in his. Then she came alive.

"Mr. Trudeau." *Did she sound too breathless?*

"Miss DuQuaine," he drawled, his eyes boring relentlessly into hers. "I hope you are enjoying your stay in New Orleans."

"I am, thank you."

"This is Anna's first time to our city," Fionna interjected.

"Ah, then the pleasure is all the more keen for you."

Anna blinked, taken aback by hearing this godlike man mention pleasure. It brought to mind all manner of scandalous insinuations. "New Orleans and its people are most remarkable."

His smile grew, creasing his face with twin dimples. "I have always found it to be invigorating. I was recently called back to my plantation unexpectedly, but as you can see . . ." Still holding her hand in his own, he stroked his thumb over her knuckles. "I could not wait to return."

Anna swallowed hard. With her fingers held in his for an unseemly amount of time, she couldn't think of a suitable reply. She could barely think at all. Clarice came to her rescue.

"You have returned not a minute too soon, Mr. Trudeau," Clarice teased lightly. "We were all about to expire from not seeing your handsome face."

He released Anna's hand, offering Clarice a brief nod of

his head. "You flatter me, Mrs. Johnston. In such beautiful company, I am humbled." His gaze encompassed the three women, but settled with insistence on Anna.

She stared back, helpless to do anything but let the conversation drift away from her. She caught snatches concerning the weather, the night's performance, the latest tidbit on a particular dancer in the chorus. None of it was significant. Standing so near Arturo, she felt swathed in a blissful haze that made everything but him seem mundane. Suddenly, the prospect of sitting through hours of operatic song became uninspiring.

It wouldn't be if she were to sit with Arturo. Of course, it was out of the question and already, he and his companions were departing for their own box. Her heart started to sink, only to jolt to life when he made a point of taking her hand once more.

Heated blue eyes holding her captive, he murmured, "I look forward to seeing you again, Miss DuQuaine."

Somehow Anna scraped together enough poise to reply with what she hoped passed for equanimity. "I would enjoy that, sir."

She watched him take his leave, and with a casualness of which she felt rather proud, regained her seat and waved her fan before her heated cheeks.

"Oh, my goodness," Fionna started in the second they were alone. "Did you see the way he looked at you?" She waved her own lace fan as if she intended to take flight. "And he held your hand far too long, my dear, far too long."

"Do you think so?" Anna asked, knowing full well that he had.

"Oh, my yes." Her gray head bobbed in silent agreement. "I'll have to mention this to Sophia. This could be a predicament. The man's reputation is outrageous."

Anna was eternally grateful that the opening strains of the opera's overture sounded just then. Her emotions were tumbling one on top of another and she didn't think she had the wherewithal to listen to Fionna warble on like a protective hen watching over her chick, a chick who was about to be swallowed up by a wolf.

Thankfully, the singers took the stage and Anna used the moment to hug her feelings close to her heart. The music became a backdrop for her thoughts that swirled and circled around Arturo.

No one had ever looked at her the way he had, his eyes filled with silent, amorous intent. And he *had* held her hand too long, but she didn't care. His touch had been warm and firm and exciting. He was exciting, more than any person she had ever met.

She was even more convinced of her opinion three hours later when she found herself at a party given by one of Fionna's friends and Arturo strode into the salon. His presence seemed to fill the room and she could not drag her eyes from the sight of him.

All the excitement she experienced earlier surged to the fore. Delightful tremors attacked her stomach, and it took a concerted effort to keep her breathing steady. A little wildly, she thanked her stars above that Fionna was entertained elsewhere. The protective woman would have jumped on this with both feet.

"Are you all right?" Clarice asked.

There was no possibility of keeping the truth from Clarice, nor did she wish to. Clarice more than anyone would understand. "Arturo is here," she whispered. That said everything that needed to be said.

Clarice looked to the doorway and found the man at once.

Wish You Were Here?

You can be, every month, with Zebra Historical Romance Novels.

AND TO GET YOU STARTED, ALLOW US TO SEND YOU

4 Historical Romances Free

YOU'RE GOING TO LOVE GETTING
4 FREE BOOKS

These books worth $18, are yours without cost or obligation when you fill out and mail this certificate.
(If the certificate is missing below, write to: Zebra Home Subscription Service, Inc., 120 Brighton Road, P.O. Box 5214, Clifton, New Jersey 07015-5214

Complete and mail this card to receive 4 Free books!

Yes! Please send me 4 Zebra Historical Romances without cost or obligation. I understand that each month thereafter I will be able to preview 4 new Zebra Historical Romances FREE for 10 days. Then, if I should decide to keep them, I will pay the money-saving preferred publisher's price of just $3.75 each...a total of $15. That's $3 less than the publisher's price, and there is no additional charge for shipping and handling. I may return any shipment within 10 days and owe nothing, and I may cancel this subscription at any time. The 4 FREE books will be mine to keep in any case.

Name _____

Address _____ Apt. _____

City _____ State _____ Zip _____

Telephone ( ) _____

Signature _____ LF0994
(If under 18, parent or guardian must sign.)

Terms, offer and prices subject to change without notice. Subscription subject to acceptance by Zebra Books. Zebra Books reserves the right to reject any order or cancel any subscription.

An $18 value.
FREE!

No obligation
to buy
anything, ever.

ZEBRA HOME SUBSCRIPTION SERVICE, INC.

120 BRIGHTON ROAD

P.O. BOX 5214

CLIFTON, NEW JERSEY 07015-5214

She pursed her lips as her brows elevated. "So I see. This *is* interesting. The man is obviously pursuing you."

Anna was afraid to hope. "Do you think so?"

"Why else would he be here?"

"Because he was invited."

"I'm certain he was, and to a host of other gatherings as well." She patted Anna's arm. "After the way he looked at you at the opera house, my friend, I would say that he is here because you are."

Anna considered that rationale while she watched Arturo wend his way through the crowd. It could be a coincidence that he should attend the same party as she. After all, they ran in the same circles, so to speak; they were bound to be in the same place at the same time. She could very well be getting ahead of herself by thinking he would pursue her.

In that instant, he lifted his head and stared across the room at her with those smoldering blue eyes and her reasoning shattered.

"Oh, dear." Her voice, barely audible, trembled with a mixture of delight and shock.

Clarice laughed. "Oh, yes, he wants you, Anna."

Anna jerked her head about. "*Wants* me? You mean in . . . in . . ."

"His bed," Clarice clarified. Her head tipped to one side in a consoling gesture. "He's a man, Anna. From the looks of things, a virile man with a virile appetite."

Anna knew about men's "appetites." She understood the basic nature of things between a man and a woman. She had never applied either to herself, however. To think of herself in those terms was to delve into sexual matters, something she associated with marriage.

She clasped her hands together to still their shaking. Was

Arturo seeking marriage or a romp between the sheets? With all her heart she hoped it was the former.

Oh, but a small, niggling voice in the back of her mind was intrigued by the latter.

"I think I need something to drink," she told Clarice.

They made their way to the refreshment tables, but the punch did nothing to quell Anna's tumultuous feelings. Try as she may, she could not tame her wayward eyes and they strayed to Arturo with shocking frequency. And the closer he advanced toward her, the more agitated she became, for there was no doubt that he was carefully, slowly making his way to her side.

The anticipation of waiting for him had her blood practically humming. The sound of voices and violins didn't help, nor did the thousands of candles overhead. The light was somehow too bright, the noise an unwelcome distraction. By the time Arturo actually stood before her, her body was alternately bathed in waves of heat and trembling chills.

"We meet again, Miss DuQuaine."

Pulse beating frantically, Anna smiled and nodded, keeping her face as pleasant as possible . . . while her heart and her lungs behaved without any normalcy at all. "Mr. Trudeau."

He looked about, his dark brows arching in interest. "You're standing here by yourself?"

Surprised, Anna noted that Clarice had taken herself off somewhere. "It would seem so."

"This is to my benefit, then."

"Oh?"

He stepped close enough so that he could whisper in her ear. "I have wanted to have you to myself since the moment I first saw you."

His breath fanned her cheek, stirring loose tendrils at her

temple. Every nerve along the nape of her neck prickled, and she closed her eyes briefly in silent self-defense.

The heat of him was intoxicating, the scent of his cologne a catalyst to her senses. All manner of warnings sounded in her brain, and she resented that. Wasn't this what she had yearned for? Hadn't she left Bellefleur seeking just this type of thrilling, extraordinary adventure?

Bolstered by that strengthening reminder, she opened her eyes to reprimand lightly, "You are very forward, Mr. Trudeau."

The smile he gave her curled his mouth suggestively. "I make no apologies, Miss DuQuaine." He directed his gaze to her lips, then ever so slowly let it slide along the column of her neck and down to her breasts. There it lingered. "No apologies, whatsoever."

To her dismay, Anna felt her nipples pucker beneath her layers of clothing. "You are a cad," she muttered, but her words lacked true sting. In truth, she was mesmerized.

"You will forgive me, won't you, little Anna?"

The cobalt beauty of his eyes was her undoing. Any pretense that his attentions, reputable or otherwise, were unwelcome, dissipated in an instant.

"Yes, I forgive you." Her chin came up. "I shouldn't, but I do."

He threw his head back and laughed, a deep vibrant sound. "I'm glad to hear that. My heart would be broken if you were to reject me outright."

"My reputation will most likely be 'broken' by my talking to you."

His smile slowly faded, a hint of steel glistening his eyes. "The gossips have been busy."

"Is the gossip true?"

One broad shoulder lifted into a negligent shrug. "That depends on what you have heard."

"That you're just short of notorious."

"And yet you haven't gone running for your chaperones." He bent near her ear once more. "What does that make you, little Anna?"

She wasn't certain she wanted to reply. Then again, she didn't think she could. He was so close it was difficult to contemplate stringing two words together.

He watched her struggle for her composure. "Who are you, Anna DuQuaine?" he asked, a kind smile striking any hint of irritation from his features.

Glad for the mundane query, Anna quickly seized the topic. "You already know who I am."

"I know your name, not the woman. Are you someone's sister, mother, wife?"

Her back stiffened. "If I were someone's wife I wouldn't be standing here having this conversation with you." She held up her left hand and wiggled her bare fingers for his inspection. "But you already knew that before you asked your question."

"A wedding ring signifies nothing."

"Because it can so easily be slipped off?"

"No, because of the lack of faith that usually accompanies the ring."

His reply was cynical enough to be telling. Anna's brow furrowed. "You don't think very highly of marriage."

"I don't believe in marriage at all."

She wouldn't have thought his remark would have hurt her, but it did. Any girlish notions about his seeking her for a wife were demolished, leaving her with the cold hard reality that his interest in her was temporal.

"Have I offended you?" he asked.

"I don't know. I've never met anyone like you. It's difficult for me to determine what my feelings are."

"They can't all be disagreeable," he teased. "If they were, you'd be halfway across the room this very instant."

He was right. Even though she would have preferred him to be more respectable, she was still so intrigued by him that she didn't want to leave his side. "Are you always this astute in your opinions?"

"Yes. It's in my nature to be aware of subtle nuances. It makes life's pleasures so much richer." His voice a dark murmur, he whispered close in her ear, "The moon is beautiful tonight."

Not trusting her voice, she nodded, the gesture stroking her cheek against his chin.

"The air has a hint of gardenia. I'll wait for you."

For the briefest second, she thought she felt the tip of his tongue on the rim of her ear, and then he was gone, striding away to leave her shaking and wide-eyed.

Reality rushed back, as if its absence had been held at bay too long and was suddenly released. *What on earth am I doing?* Nothing in her past had prepared her for dealing with a such a man. Propriety demanded that that not even be an option. He was worldly, sophisticated, and so blatantly masculine that it made her mouth go dry.

Why, then, was she seriously thinking about following him? To do so was reckless and potentially dangerous. He wouldn't hurt her, she instinctively believed that, but he had done nothing to hide his male hunger. And by his own convictions about marriage, it was plain that he was not going to behave as a gentleman.

Watching him slip through one of the French doors, her eyes narrowed. He hadn't *suggested* anything. He had assumed, taken it for granted that she would meet him. The arrogance of that was beyond anything. It was irritating, provoking. It was exhilarating.

Arturo stretched his chin up above his silver cravat and drew in a deep breath of the night air. It was indeed laced with the scent of gardenia. He had to smile for he had fabricated that inducement for Anna's benefit.

Anna. What a rare morsel she was. Instinct told him that she was ten kinds of passion bottled up, waiting to be freed. It was there in the tilt of her head, the spark in her soft gray eyes, the way her magnificent chest heaved when she struggled for breath.

He had noticed that particular asset, too, along with the sweet curve of her waist, the rich silkiness of her deep brown hair and the flowing tone of her voice. She was one of the most appealing women to come along in quite a long time.

Making his way along the brick-lined path, he considered the number of women he had found appealing through the years. One might, and many did, find fault with his appreciation of the weaker sex. What could he say? He truly enjoyed women. He liked everything about them, including their temperaments. It was easy enough to be taken with a comely face or a soft set of thighs. It wasn't so easy to bear up under a woman's pique or her quicksilver moods.

He did, and gladly so. Women were fascinating creatures, entirely different from men. He wasn't about to berate himself because he delighted in celebrating those differences.

This was a philosophy of long standing with him, one that he had come to terms with years ago. By nature he was a sensualist, relishing life's more opulent offerings, whatever they may be. For him, making love to a beautiful, willing woman was life's greatest offering. Not that he indiscriminately took every beautiful woman he met. He prided himself on having some standards, amongst them that he like the woman to whom he made love.

He liked Anna DuQuaine, but he didn't plan to have her tonight. For one thing, waiting could be as satisfying as fulfillment. Beyond that, however, was that someone as unique as Anna should be enjoyed with all the luxuries at hand; wine, soft pillows, limitless hours. She should be pampered, indulged, lingered over. She should be given the time to bask in her own senses just as much as he would in his own.

He glanced back at the French doors, his eyes narrowing in anticipation. He hoped he had not misread her. Quite modestly, he considered himself to be an excellent judge of character. In his judgement, Anna was at that moment warring with herself, pulled between the more impassioned side of her nature and the temperate, well-bred side. In the end, he could only trust that she would surrender to the sensuality he sensed ran deep and hot within her.

A movement near the house caught his eye. Satisfaction unfurled in his chest. Anna wended her way along the path, outlined by the moon's pearly light. Even from where he stood he could see the hesitancy of her posture, as if she were about to flee even as she searched for him.

He made her search easier, circling closer so that her path intersected his. Then, out of the darkness, he loomed over her, his hands reaching out in a flash to pull her behind the concealing ivy-covered lattice work. Instantly, he captured her startled gasp with his mouth.

The world swung crazily for Anna. One second, everything was where it should be, and the next, the ground was gone from under her feet and she was plastered against a tall, unmovable form. She cried out in surprise, only to have her breath snatched when a hard mouth came down on hers.

Arturo. Her senses whirled. The feel of him was more than she could have ever imagined. Hard, vital, commanding, his body was unyielding, his arms powerfully wrapped about her. She struggled for breath as his lips parted hers, his tongue thrusting into her mouth repeatedly with an expertise that even she in her innocence recognized. And responded to.

Moaning low in her throat, she clung to his shoulders as if that could still her reeling senses. It was a futile gesture, for his hand slipped upward to caress her breast, and pleasure such as she had never known tore through her.

"Little Anna," he muttered, his voice as thick and dark as the night. "I knew it would be like this."

For one crazy second, she actually thought she could reply. His mouth sought her shoulder, bare above the scooped neckline of her bodice, and words fled her mind. His lips worked in a tantalizingly lazy pattern, kissing, sipping, descending slowly, irrevocably toward the breast he caressed.

"Let me," he demanded smoothly. "Let me taste you."

The words meant nothing to her. Her insides were coming apart under the heat of his passion, and there wasn't a thing she could do about it save put an end to the sweet magic. She wasn't ready to do that. Not yet, not until she experienced this small fragment of the forbidden . . . and maybe not even then.

She didn't know. And then it became impossible to think at all. With deft fingers he bared her breast, lowered his head and took her nipple into his mouth.

Shock and pleasure shot through her. A muted cry broke over her lips as her entire body arched into the caress, seeking more, wanting everything.

"Arturo." Her voice was a husky murmur, barely recognizable.

He lifted his head to stare down at her. Even by the translucent light of the moon, he could make out her heightened color. "You are magnificent." He sealed the avowal with a drugging kiss. "I knew you would be."

"Did you?" Emotions tumbled on top of sensations on top of newly-awakened desire. "I . . . I never thought of myself . . . I had no idea."

He saw the brief flash of maidenly uncertainty in her eyes, and knew that she had reached her limit for tonight. His mouth curled into a soft smile. He would do nothing to frighten her.

With far less haste than he had bared her breast, he covered the tempting flesh, taking his time to trail his fingers over the sweet curves. "The depths of your passion have not even been touched, little one."

"No?"

He shook his head to the negative.

She blinked, then blinked again. If what he said was true, then she was in dire trouble. Her entire being, body and mind, had been overwhelmed by sensations so powerful, she hadn't been able to do anything other than feel. And that was just an inkling of the passion of which he thought her capable?

Oh, dear Lord, she was definitely in trouble, for she knew she wouldn't be satisfied until she understood all there was to know about this passion of hers.

Chapter Sixteen

"You doin' anythin' from gettin' a baby in your belly?"

Jessica's head whipped about, her eyes rounding as she stared at Mama Lou. *"What?!"*

Mama Lou drew in a huge, chest-swelling breath, and continued her way along the path winding through the densely choked forest. "I said, are you doin' anythin' to keep from gettin' yourself a baby?"

A blazing ruby blush suffused Jessica's face clear to her hairline. The question was not only unexpected, coming from this offtimes austere woman, it was also extremely embarrassing. Totally unprepared to answer, she jerked her gaze back to the dirt lane and concentrated on the first thing that came to mind. Church.

It was Sunday morning, and she and Mama Lou had just attended the meeting at the chapel set up for slaves. A bit frantically, she tried to recall what the sermon had been.

Mama Lou humphed into the silence. "That answers my question. I hope you take to bein' a momma."

Jessica's embarrassment gave way to a certain degree of dismay. She wasn't an idiot. She understood how babies were created, so the likelihood that she would eventually end up pregnant was very real.

"I don't see that I have a choice." With that one statement, she openly confirmed to the housekeeper that she was indeed spending her nights with Nicholas. Until that moment, Mama Lou hadn't referred to the matter in any way, and Jessica had preferred to maintain her privacy on the subject.

The housekeeper scoffed. "Girl, you got plenty of choices."

"I do?"

"Hell, yes. You can keep your knees crossed."

Jessica gave her a slightly pained look.

"I didn't think you'd like that notion," Mama Lou chuckled. "You can always say no. Master Nick ain't goin' to force you."

He didn't need to, Jessica thought. She loved him. Sharing her body with him was a natural expression of that love. No, she wouldn't say no to Nick, or to herself. All her life, she had wanted to feel the way Nick made her feel. Cherished, cared for, special.

He had destroyed her fears, and in the process given her a sense of her own self-worth. Perhaps she wasn't as confident as the next person, or as trusting, but she was no longer besieged by numbing insecurity. She felt as if her life had some value.

Scouring her upper lip with her teeth, she stared out over the murky stream that ran parallel to the path. Her thoughts turned pensive as she further considered her relationship with Nick. It was a strange situation, where lines of propriety and convention blurred, and while she knew exactly how she felt about him, she wasn't certain what he felt for her.

His actions proclaimed that he respected her, liked her, enjoyed her company. There was absolutely no doubt that he desired her. At times, he would claim her with a swift, fierce intensity that left her breathless. Then there were those times when his lovemaking was prolonged, stretching out for hours until her mind and body were sated beyond reason.

She wouldn't have had it any other way, with one vital exception. She wished that Nick would love her as she loved him. She wished that the Bellefleur rose had bloomed for her, that she was the one woman Nick would love for his lifetime.

In this one precious instance, her usual optimism failed her. Reality could not be ignored and when she sorted through all the facts—the differences in their upbringing, their present circumstances, the division in their social standings—she was left with the truth. She would love Nicholas until she drew her last breath on this earth, but she would never be his wife. He would look elsewhere, to a proper born and delicately raised lady, to fill that position.

Some part of her had known that all along. That hadn't stopped her from giving herself to him. Her love didn't come with the kind of conditions that said, "you can have my body only if you give me your name in return." Her love sprang forth unburdened by dictates and expectations. She loved him freely, wholly, and she was honest enough to admit that, honest enough to know what her future held for her.

"Is there anything else I can do?" she asked, her words unsteady.

"From gettin' pregnant?"

"Yes."

Mama Lou's chest expanded again with another huge sigh. "You sure you want to do that?"

"Yes." A dull pain clenched in the region of her heart. There was nothing she would like better than to bear Nicholas's children. She could picture a sturdy little boy with

Nick's dark hair or a smiling little girl with his gray eyes. She would love them as much as she loved their father.

But children deserved—needed—more than that. Hadn't her own childhood taught her that very lesson? Children should have the security of a home and the devotion of two parents. They should be raised with love and laughter, content in the bond that existed in a family.

She couldn't guarantee that for her children. She was indentured to Nicholas for five years. When her term was satisfied, she would be free to leave, and he had never given her any indication that that would change. She would be an unmarried, twenty-two year old woman, with no money and no place to call home. Her livelihood and that of her children would depend solely on whatever kind of employment she could secure.

If Nicholas allowed her to take her babies with her. For all she knew, he would insist that they remain with him, raised as his bastards. She could well imagine how his wife would take to that. Worse yet, Jessica knew she would die if she had to give up any child of hers.

"What do I have to do?" she asked. This time her voice broke with all the pent up emotion of dreams realized and lost.

In a surprising move, Mama Lou slipped her arm about her shoulders for a brisk hug. "We'll make you some wild ginger root and thistle tea. Tastes nasty as all get out, but you won't have you no babies."

She wouldn't have Nicholas's babies. Jessica's heart broke.

"You're frowning," Mathew Bennett observed. Standing next to Nicholas, he propped his shoulder against a pristine white column and surveyed his friend with ill-concealed curiosity.

Nicholas dragged his gaze from the group of people milling about Mathew's carefully tended lawn. "Was I frowning?" he asked, honestly unaware that he had been scowling.

"Yes. Your bourbon not sitting well—or is there something else putting that look in your eye?"

"What look?"

"The one that makes me think of decapitation."

Nick stared down at the glass in his hand as though just remembering its existence, and mentally swore. Taking a healthy swallow of the smoky liquor, he ignored his friend's needling.

"You're supposed to be enjoying yourself," Mathew hinted broadly.

"What makes you think I'm not?"

"The fact that you're here," Mathew pointed out, gesturing to the pillared terrace behind his house, "and not out there." He lifted a hand to indicated the gathering of people enjoying the Sunday afternoon outing.

"I'm enjoying the view," Nick contended with a restrained smile.

"You've barely noticed the view—more specifically, its more interesting feminine aspects."

It was in Nicholas's mind to turn the comment back on Mathew. He didn't. He knew Mathew was pining for Anna. Any looking Mathew planned on doing in the future would be in Anna's direction alone.

"The view is the same as it's always been, Matt."

"That doesn't make it any less appealing."

"Appealing isn't the same as worthwhile."

Mathew threaded his fingers back through his blond hair at

the critical comment. "This sounds serious. Care to discuss it?"

For a long moment, Nicholas considered the offer. Through the course of their friendship, he and Mathew had shared confidences often. Childhood fears, adolescent insecurities, adult concerns. But this was different. His thoughts were a tangled snare, intrinsically private.

"Thanks, I don't know if there's anything to discuss." Nonetheless, he felt a need to be alone. "I think I'll take in the view from a different angle."

Setting his glass on a nearby table, he made his way to the formal garden, seeing none of the artistry of the isolated setting, the sound of his footsteps on the brick walk not even a distant distraction. Through the network of limbs and Spanish moss overhead, the sun shone with all the promise of the sweltering summer months to come. Already the April air had taken on the humid heat that lent a sheen of moisture to Nicholas's skin. It all went unnoticed.

He came to a stop at a wrought iron bench, taking a seat out of habit and not any conscious decision. There he leaned back and wondered what was wrong with him. He hadn't been aware that anything was until Mathew had mentioned it. Now that he was alone, the chorus of laughter a vague, irksome sound in the distance, he admitted that something was definitely wrong.

His movements reflecting his bend of thought, he stretched his legs out before him and thrust his hands deep into the pockets of his trousers. Chin tucked to his chest, shoulders arched back, it was the pose of an irritated man.

He supposed he was irritated. At himself. The day should have held a certain interest for him. Friends and acquaintances, neighbors and business associates had gathered for an impromptu Sunday afternoon party. It had been the perfect time for him to discuss the latest news on cotton prices, the conditions of the soil, and to even catch up on local gossip.

The men were in good humor, the women gaily flirtatious. Food and drink were plentiful and delicious. Why, then, wasn't he enjoying himself? The only answer he got was an obscure, unsettled feeling that something was missing. Somehow, he felt incomplete.

He didn't like the feeling, not one damned bit. Surging to his feet in a controlled play of muscle, he shook off the sensation and called himself a fool. He had given into the histrionics of the moment and placed far too much significance on what amounted to nothing more than a temporary need for respite. There was nothing wrong with him that good food and better conversation couldn't cure.

Toward that end, he strode from the garden, determined to enjoy the day, particularly, "the view, more specifically, its more interesting feminine aspects."

"There you are," Mathew greeted him as he neared the buffet table.

Nicholas spread his hands wide. "In the flesh."

"Everything all right?"

"Perfect."

Mathew seemed to weigh that. "Good. I wanted you to meet someone."

Nicholas gave him a wry look. "Playing matchmaker?"

"No, nothing like that. There's a banker here from Baton Rouge I think you should talk to."

Together they crossed the lawn to a group of people gathered by the gold fish pond. "Phillip St. James," Mathew began, "I'd like you to meet Nicholas DuQuaine of Bellefleur."

Phillip St. James turned with a pleasant smile, extending his hand in greeting. "Mr. DuQuaine. It is a pleasure."

Nicholas returned the hand shake. "Mr. St. James. What brings you north?"

Cocking his head to the side, Phillip laughed. "Profit, Mr. DuQuaine."

The comment met with a round of laughter before Mathew explained. "Mr. St. James is thinking of starting up his own bank in the area. He has some interesting ideas that you might want to discuss."

"I'm always interested in finances and profits," Nicholas commented.

"Perhaps, then, you would care to meet sometime next week," Phillip suggested smoothly around a wide smile.

Nicholas studied that smile, finding something misleading about it. "Perhaps."

"At your convenience, sir."

The course of the conversation moved on to more entertaining matters, which suited Nicholas. He wasn't sure if he liked Phillip St. James. There was something about the man that didn't set quite right.

Then of course, Nicholas reminded himself, he hadn't been in the best of moods today. His perceptions could, and very likely were, off base. He needed to get a grip on himself and make the most of the day.

If he thought about the fact that he had to work at enjoying himself, it never showed on his face. As the afternoon slipped past, he smiled and laughed, conversed and in general behaved as any of the other guests. The niggling feeling that all wasn't as it should be persisted, but Nicholas congratulated himself on ignoring the thing into submission.

He ignored it so well that by the time the day came to an end and he rode for home, he was convinced that whatever had been bothering him didn't exist.

"How are things here?" he asked Mama Lou when he stepped into the cool hush of the drawing room.

"The same as always. Quiet for a Sunday."

"No problems in the fields?"

"Not that anyone came up here to tell me about. Far as I know, everythin's fine."

"Good." He headed for the stairs.

"I'll send Jessup up," Mama Lou called after him.

Nick stripped off his cravat as he ascended to the second story. The day had turned increasingly hot, making the fine muslin of his shirt cling uncomfortably to his skin. He wanted to be out of his more formal garb and into something cooler. Nudity would suit him just fine. With Jessica beside—beneath—him.

Anxious to find her, he entered his room, removed his clothes, washed, then donned a pair of black pants and a loose white shirt, its billowing sleeves rolled back several times. He bothered with boots only because he intended to personally choose a bottle of Madeira from the wine shed adjacent to the spring house. Of all the wines in his collection, it was his favorite, and he wanted Jessica to sample its heady flavor.

"Have you seen Jessica?" he asked Jessup, fastening the row of buttons on the front of his shirt.

"Not in a little while. Dat's kinda unusual, too."

Nick gave the old man an inquiring look. "Why?"

Jessup's rickety shoulders moved in something that resembled a shrug. "Cuz she's always somewhere about, a smile here, a laugh dere, but I ain't seen her in a bit. Course, Mama Lou might know better."

She didn't, much to Nick's frustration. "She went for a walk about an hour ago," his housekeeper informed him at the foot of the stairs.

"Where?"

"I don't rightly know." She nodded eastward. "I saw her headed that way, though, over toward the river."

"Why would she walk all the way out there?"

Mama Lou lifted her chin the tiniest bit. "Can't say, Master Nick, but she looked like someone had just been funeralized."

One of Nick's black brows arched. Was that a note of censure he heard? "Are you saying she was unhappy?"

"No, sir. I'm just tellin' you what I saw." She crossed her arms over her ample chest in a gesture of finality.

Nick weighed the woman's manner. He had never known Mama Lou to dissemble about anything. "Is there something you're not telling me?"

"Nope."

"Is Jessica all right?"

"You'll have to ask her about that."

The enigmatic reply made Nicholas bristle. Swearing under his breath about cantankerous old housekeepers, he made his way to the stables. If he was going to go searching for Jessica, he would do it in the easiest way possible.

As he urged his mount forward, he told himself he could wait for Jessica to return, but impatience hummed through his veins. And it wasn't just a case of a raging desire to bed her. Yes, he most definitely wanted to make love to her, but more than that, he wanted to be with her. It was as simple . . . or as complicated . . . as that. He wasn't about to determine which.

Jessica wasn't anywhere near the river. Nick scanned the banks in both directions and found no sign of her. His eyes strayed to the water itself and a chilling fear gripped him. This far from the house, no one would have heard her cries for help if she had fallen in.

"Damn it all." He had no reason to assume the worst.

Jessica could be anywhere on the plantation. The best thing for him to do would be to go back up to the house and wait for her.

That's what he told himself as he rode over the land, searching out any other likely locations where she might be. Goading him the entire way was the fact that he didn't like not knowing where she was, and the more he looked the more helpless he felt.

Nearly an hour later, he pulled his horse to a halt, swearing in a steady stream of curses and blasphemies that were as furious as the rage etched into his face. Fear and frustration rode him as hard as he had ridden his horse. He had gone out to the north cotton fields, to the ice house, and even to the cooperage, and still no Jessica.

"Where the hell are you?"

His grating voice was caught by the gust of a cooling breeze. The air around him was suddenly filled with the scent of hickory smoke, garden herbs, and roses.

Roses!

His head snapped about toward the nearby stand of trees. The old rose garden was on the other side of that grove.

Certainty surged up inside of him in powerful waves. Jessica was in the rose garden. Why he hadn't thought of it before now baffled him, but not enough to warrant a second thought. All that mattered was that he found her.

His conviction was so profound that he wasn't the least bit surprised to discover her sitting on a swath of green grass on the edge of the old garden. He *was* very relieved. And furious. He had imagined her injured or dead. The thought that she might have run off had also assailed his mind.

This last was a bitter thought too vile to contemplate. Yet unspoken was the truth that if Jessica were to run off, she would be running from him.

She turned at the sound of his horse. Surprise bathed her features as surely as the sun cast its rays on the red-gold of her hair.

"Nicholas. What are you doing here?"

In excruciatingly precise tones, he replied. "I would ask the same of you."

The corners of Jessica's smile drooped. She hadn't intentionally set out for this spot, with its untamed air and heady scents. When she had left the house, she had been seeking solace for a melancholy she hadn't been able to shake. Her path had been guided here as though pulled by the long-ago memories of the woman who had planted the rose bushes. Jessica had found if not the consolation she sought then a quiet solitude that eased her spirit.

It had been dashed since early morning. No matter how many times she told herself that it was for the best that she not have Nicholas's children, her heart didn't believe it.

"I came for a walk. This is where I ended up."

Nick dismounted and strode toward her, his movements underscored by the tension seething within him. "You might have thought to tell someone where you were going."

For the first time, Jessica became aware of his mood. Sitting very still, she scrutinized his face and saw the irate gleam in his eyes, examined his actions and noted the rigid set of his shoulders.

"What's wrong?" Apprehension raced up her spine.

Planting his fists on his waist, he stood over her, glaring down into her upturned face. "What's wrong? I'll tell you what's wrong. I've been over a good portion of this plantation looking for you."

"I'm sorry—"

"I had no idea where you were," he went on as if she had said nothing. "Mama Lou couldn't tell me, neither could anyone else I asked. No one had seen you." His voice gained volume with every word until he was shouting. "What the hell were you thinking? Or weren't you thinking at all? I came home expecting to find you and instead spent the last hour half out of my mind with fear."

Jessica's eyes snapped wide. "Fear?" She openly stared at him, doing nothing to hide her confusion and shock. She couldn't imagine him fearing anything. "Why were you—"

He yanked her to her feet, answering her question before she had the chance to finish it. "I was worried about you, you little fool." He caught her to him and his mouth came down on hers.

It was like having her feet knocked out from beneath her. Stunned, Jessica clung to his arms, trying to comprehend what had just occurred. For a second, she felt the old alarm snake along her nerves, dragging to mind an inbred fear of angry men. He was well and truly angry with her, yet he was kissing her. No, it went far beyond mere kissing!

His mouth plundered over hers with bruising force as his hands coursed repeatedly from her neck to her thighs. He ground his hips against her softness, all the while his arms continued to tighten.

"Nicholas," she gasped, wrenching her mouth from his. He ruthlessly captured her lips again, leaving her helpless against the onslaught of his passion. His tongue plunged into her mouth, again and again in a pagan rhythm, and any thought that she might be able to tell him that there was no need for worry—that she might be able to tell him anything at all— was destroyed under the savage pressure of his mouth.

He was caught in a terrible storm of emotion, fear-born concern, anger firmly rooted in worry. That he would feel this way for her was overwhelming, and made her love him all the more.

"Don't ever do this to me again," he demanded, kissing her temple, her ear, the slim column of her throat. "Do you understand?"

Her senses were swirling. She managed a nod. It wasn't enough for him. He caught her face between his hands and drilled his fiery gaze into hers. "Jess, do you understand?"

"Yes," she breathed. Why he would exact such a promise from her, she didn't know, not any more than she knew why he felt compelled to behave as he did. All she knew was that he needed her and she needed him.

They made love right there in the grass, with the setting sun bathing their twisting bodies in brilliant radiance. It was a fierce sharing that brought Jessica to tears and Nicholas a supreme peace of mind and body and spirit.

As he lay sprawled in naked splendor, Jessica wrapped in his arms, he drew in a satisfying breath and realized that the niggling discontent that had plagued him all day, the sensation of being incomplete, was gone. Truly gone, not just ignored or disavowed because he had convinced himself it was so. For the first time all day he felt whole, and it had nothing to do with sexual gratification.

It had everything to do with the fact that Jessica was with him for the first time that day.

Chapter Seventeen

"Are you sure you're all right, *Tantia?*" Anna posed her query with true anxiety marring her lovely features. For three days, Sophia had been listless and pale, her effervescent temperament tamed to an indolent moodiness.

"Je me sens un peu mieux," Sophia proclaimed from her bed.

"You might feel a little better, but that doesn't say a great deal, *Tantia.* Why don't you let me send for the doctor?"

"Non, un medécin," Sophia declared, drawing herself up as best she could given her half-reclining position against her pillows.

Anna folded her arms across her chest and gave her aunt stare for stare. "I'm worried about you. You have not been eating well."

"Nonsense."

"What did you eat this morning?"

Sophia shrugged and pretended an interest in the bed clothes. "I don't remember. And you're being impertinent."

"If I am, it is because I'm worried about you." Anna sat on the edge of the bed and took Sophia's hand in her own. Years of devotion and love surfaced in her plea. "Please, Aunt Sophia. Let me send for the physician."

Anna's concern as well as the softness of her touch had Sophia twisting her mouth in reluctant capitulation. "Which doctor? I don't want some strange man poking at me."

"Fionna's doctor. I'm sure he's commendable."

"Bah! He's probably some voodoo-crazed imbecile."

"Then you choose one."

"I don't know any doctors in New Orleans."

"You're making excuses."

"I don't care."

"I do! *Tantia,* please."

Sophia regarded the young woman whom she had loved as a daughter, and her expression softened. "All right. I'll see your doctor *if* I'm not any better by tomorrow."

"Tonight."

Showing every sign of protesting, Sophia worked her mouth this way and that, but finally gave in. "We'll do it your way."

"Thank you." Anna pressed a kiss to the woman's brow. "Is there anything I can get you? Are you hungry?"

"No, to both."

"You're sure?"

"Yes. I just want to be by myself for a while and rest." She patted Anna's hand. "Aren't you supposed to be off to one of the parks today?"

She was, and at Arturo's insistence, they were to rendezvous. Given their tryst after the opera two days past, she could well imagine what he had in mind. Her pulse leapt.

"Yes, yes, we're supposed to ... to view the flowers," she stammered.

"Fionna will enjoy that."

"And Clarice."

At the mention of the Clarice, Sophia's face scrunched up in blatant disapproval. "I don't like her very much."

"Why not?" Anna asked, taken aback. She found it difficult to understand why anyone would not like Clarice.

"I don't know. There's something about her that grates on my nerves."

Anna sat back, a weak, crooked grin of disbelief flitting over her lips. *"Tantia,* how can you say that? She's perfectly lovely."

"To look at, yes, I'll grant you that." Sophia shook her head slowly. "But inside? I don't know."

To Anna, the notion was so absurd, she laughed and hugged Sophia at the same time. "You've been lying in bed too long, silly. Clarice is a marvel."

"Do you think so?"

"I do."

"It strikes me as strange the way she's latched on to you. You don't go anywhere without her."

"I don't go anywhere without Fionna, either."

"Ah, but Fionna is *famille,* she's family. You've known Clarice for only a short while. Doesn't she have any other friends or acquaintances in New Orleans?"

Anna spread her hands wide. "Yes, but she and Fionna are very close, from what I can tell."

"Too close if you ask me."

"I think you're too hard on her, *Tantia.* She's a wonderful woman. I've never met anyone like her. We struck up an instant rapport, and she's been very sweet to me."

The look in Sophia's eyes said that she had her doubts. "If you say so, but I want you to take care."

"I will," Anna promised. "And you have nothing to worry about."

"I'll worry if I want to."

Anna rolled her eyes in good-natured exasperation. "I know you will, and that won't help you get better." Tilting her head to one side, she studied Sophia intently. "Are you sure you don't want me to keep you company?"

"I'm sure. Go off and enjoy yourself."

Anna was hesitant to do so. It wasn't like Sophia to take to her bed. Anna hated to leave her aunt not knowing if her condition could worsen.

Sophia settled the matter for her. "Anna, if you do not go at once, I will not agree to see the doctor."

"That's blackmail!"

"That's right. Now, shoo. *Au revoir!*"

Eyes narrowed at being routed, Anna rose. "Very well. I won't be gone too long, though."

"Do not hurry on my account."

"To use your words, 'I will if I want to.' "

It was twenty minutes later before Anna felt assured of Sophia's comfort. Only then did she go below to meet Fionna and Clarice.

"How is Sophia today?" Clarice asked.

"About the same," Anna sighed. "She insists that she is simply tired. I think if she isn't better by tonight, she might need a doctor."

Fionna fluttered her hands nervously. "Oh, my, a doctor?"

"Is there one you could recommend?"

"Of course, my dear, of course. My very own is excellent, and he's very, very charming."

"That will be a help. Sophia is not partial to physicians."

"I know how she feels," Fionna commiserated. She twisted her hands again. "Oh, I feel just awful about this. Perhaps I should go up and check in on her."

Fionna debated with herself, with Anna, with Clarice; her deliberation, Anna thought more of a venting of concern than an actual dispute of ideas. In the end, the elder lady was adamant about remaining.

"You two go off and enjoy yourselves. Besides, I'm getting too old for strolling through parks for no reason. I much prefer to sit if I can."

"Your aunt will be fine, Anna," Clarice insisted. "There is nothing to be gained by the both of you keeping a vigil." Offering a smile meant to sway, she added, "Come, enjoy the park."

While concern tugged Anna in one direction, logic pulled her in the other. Clarice was right. Nothing would be gained by her remaining, and she felt much better knowing that Fionna would keep an eye on Sophia.

And also, the lure of Arturo beckoned her. She would never neglect her aunt, but the temptation of being in Arturo's arms was stunning. Not for a second since she had last seen him had she forgotten the feel of his mouth or the heated strength of his body.

She and Clarice arrived at the flowered garden park to find the air was moist and warm, a condition which, for Anna, was intensified by her agitated state. After no more than ten minutes, she suggested that they take a seat on one of the park's benches.

"You seem nervous," Clarice noted, tipping her black parasol to a more protective angle.

Anna eyed her friend anxiously. "I am. A little." She attempted a smile as she toyed with the trailing ribbons of her bonnet. "Arturo is supposed to meet me here."

"Ah, that explains it then."

"Explains what?"

"The flush on your cheeks. It's very becoming. Arturo will be delighted."

"You don't think I'm wicked for agreeing to meet him here?"

"Of course not. Why would I think such a thing?"

"Because others would. What I'm doing is scandalous."

Clarice gave her a level look. "Anna, I am not your aunt, nor her cousin. They might not understand, and certainly never approve of what you're doing. I not only understand, I think it's wonderful."

"Truly?"

"Truly."

Anna sighed, giving into a smile of joy and relief. It was difficult for her to comprehend why she possessed this proclivity for brazenness. To know that someone was supportive and understanding helped alleviate her tension.

"Thank you. I feel better all ready." Spurred by genuine affection, she hugged Clarice close. "You are such a dear. I don't know what I would do without you."

Clarice returned the hug as effortlessly as she kept her expression free of the joyful malice roiling within. How easy it was to dupe this ridiculous, pampered little idiot into believing them friends. Clarice wouldn't have thought Anna to be as naive as that. Then again, she wouldn't have thought the chit capable of such indiscreet behavior. Her half-sister had shown surprisingly improper inclinations for a woman of her station.

So much the better. It made taking advantage of her child's play. Anna wanted someone to lead her to ruin? Clarice would gladly assist in any way she could. At some point, Anna would realize her folly in dallying with Arturo Trudeau and then she would be at her most vulnerable, desolate to be without her dear friend, Clarice. And where Anna went, Clarice would go, most especially back to Bellefleur. Once there, she would deal with Nicholas.

Clarice had given him a great deal of thought. Since he alone stood between her and Bellefleur, the answer to the problem was really a simple matter. She would marry the fool.

The cogs of her scheme tumbled into place, filling her with glee. She'd marry Nicholas, send him to his grave and Bellefleur would be hers as it should have always been. It was all so very, very simple.

"I've become quite fond of you, too," she returned, setting Anna at arm's length. "Now, you have to tell me, what were you planning to do about Arturo with Fionna in tow?"

Anna shrugged in a helpless gesture. "I don't know. I've never done this before. I assumed Arturo would somehow arrange for a few private moments."

"You presumed right. He is a worldly man." Clarice feigned a mien of concern. "Anna, I would never think of telling you what to do, but you will be careful, won't you?"

Anna beamed a smile born in her heart. "Yes, you don't need to worry."

"What are friends for?"

"You are just too good to me, Clarice."

"Only because you are so wonderful to me. Now, smile prettily. Arturo is here."

Anna cast a quick look over her shoulder and felt her pulse lurch. Arturo made his way along the path toward them.

"He's very handsome," Clarice whispered.

He was that and so much more, Anna thought. He made her feel things she had never felt before, reckless, beautifully alive and so very, very conscious of herself as a woman. She had only to gaze into the blue of his eyes and her body responded in the most carnal manner.

"Ladies," he intoned. Stepping before Anna, he raised her hand to his lips. "Miss DuQuaine. You're looking more beautiful than I remember."

"Mr. Trudeau." Anna succeeded in keeping her voice steady, until she felt the tip of Arturo's tongue on the inside of her wrist. Then her words emerged far too loudly. "It's a pleasure to see you again."

"The pleasure is all mine," he replied, laughter playing at his mouth. There was nothing humorous in his gaze, however. His eyes gleamed with bold intent that snatched Anna's breath.

She inwardly chafed and fumed. Never had she detested the constraints of polite society more than she did at that moment. They carried on with proprieties, forced into banal conversation for the sake of passersby or the curious few who strolled at a distance.

"You flatter me, sir," she said, remembering to retrieve her hand from his firm grasp.

Clarice regarded the pair as she settled her parasol on her shoulder. "I was just saying to Anna that the flowers along this path are extraordinary. Perhaps, sir, you would wish to escort Miss DuQuaine for a closer look."

Arturo didn't even spare Clarice so much as a glance. "By all means." Extending his arm, he assisted Anna to her feet and led her away. "I take it your widowed friend is, shall we say, open-minded?"

Anna sent her gaze to his. "Clarice is my friend, not my keeper."

Again, his lips twisted with a wry humor. "I'm very glad to hear that, little Anna. How did you arrange for her to accompany you instead of your normal armada of chaperones?"

"I didn't. My aunt is not feeling well."

"Nothing serious, I hope."

His concern was genuine and it touched her. She curled her fingers more snugly into the crook of his arm. "I don't think so, but Fionna decided to remain behind."

"Which left you with Mrs. Johnston." They rounded a

bend in the path, their figures shielded from view. "I can not say that I am sorry."

Anna was also glad, although she couldn't give voice to her sentiments. Expectation was making a shambles of her poise. She knew why he had chosen this out of the way course, she knew that he intended to take up where he had left off two nights ago. She had understood that from the moment she had agreed to meet him today.

Intuitively, she sensed that he wouldn't make love to her here. Common sense confirmed that a more private place and a more leisurely time would be necessary. Nonetheless, the gravity of her actions suddenly hit her hard and she had to question the nature of her character that she would knowingly, *willingly,* give into this kind of temptation. Was this indicative of her need for excitement, or was she simply wanton?

Her only answer was a tremor that shook her frame.

"Is anything wrong?" he asked, turning to face her.

"No."

Catching her chin on the tip of his finger, he searched her gaze. "So beautiful," he murmured. "So sensitive to life." His fingers skimmed her cheek. "I can feel you trembling, little Anna. Don't be frightened, you know I won't hurt you."

An even breath seemed beyond Anna's capabilities. "I wouldn't be here if I thought you'd hurt me."

Her answer pleased him. "But still you tremble," he murmured in a dark voice made of liquid heat. He drew her into his arms, turning her so that her back rested against his chest, his arms about her. "Let yourself feel at ease. Let yourself enjoy the moment, feel what I can make you feel."

Anna closed her eyes, her senses bewitched. He surrounded her with the muscles of his body, the scent of his cologne, the sound of his voice. She felt, heard, *knew* him at every turn, seducing her mind and body, and she helplessly did as he bade. She gave herself up to the moment, and to his ministrations. For seemingly endless years, through frustrating nights and lusterless days, this was what she had yearned for, this heady rousing, this thrilling inflaming of her entire being.

"Sweet, sweet Anna." His mouth trailed along the column of her throat, licking, biting, nipping the most vulnerable spots.

Racked by the most delicious shivers, Anna let her head fall back against his shoulder. Captive to the sensation, she remained unmoving while he untied the ribbons of her bonnet and cast it aside. His mouth returned, this time to tease the rim of her ear.

She gasped.

"Easy, sweet," he calmed, then brought his tongue to her ear again.

Anna thought she would melt. She grasped his arms, not at all certain if she would be able to stand.

"Arturo."

He nuzzled the hair at her temple. "Say my name again."

She did, letting the syllables slide over her tongue.

"Again."

His name came out as a husky whisper, only to turn into a low moan of desire when his hand settled over her breast. Her entire body arched at the contact, the movement bearing her hips closer to his. The arm about her waist tightened.

"You are so perfect." Deftly, he parted the front of her bodice and slipped his hand within. "Do you like this, little Anna?" His fingers found her nipple and stroked it to a pouting bud. "Shall I stop?"

She didn't want to answer. She didn't want to do anything

that would interfere with the pleasure he was bringing her. "No," she managed. "No, don't stop."

He gave a deep laugh, full of rich, masculine satisfaction. "Do you want more?"

"Yes."

She didn't see the result of her reply. The heat of passion lent his jaw a hard edge and turned the blue of his eyes to an inky cobalt. But what she didn't see, she felt. The muscles along his chest flexed as the tension in his arms increased. The legs that braced her own shifted, forcing her legs wide to accommodate this new stance.

In the back of Anna's mind, she could picture them as they stood; her head thrown back, his hand delving into her clothes while her legs straddled one of his. It was a decidedly lewd pose. She didn't care. She wanted lewdness, she wanted the risqué and lustful and any of the hundreds of other words associated with desire.

Her blood was racing, her heart thumping a mad cadence. Wave after wave of pleasure washed through her. She had longed for this. During the months of necessary routine that had turned to years of tedium, this was what she had wanted. To feel beautiful, and womanly, and special, to feel her body come alive, to feel her senses reeling . . . to *feel*.

Her breath escaped her in a ragged moan. It got no further than Arturo's mouth. She parted her lips and eagerly returned his kiss. Reality began to whirl away, leaving her unaware of her surroundings, of sound, of his hand that left her waist to raise her skirt and petticoats.

It was the feel of his hand at the apex of her thighs that jolted her back to herself. The intimacy of the caress, this most intimate of all caresses, shocked her to the core. She tore her mouth from his, her legs instinctively trying to close, but his knee stayed her movements.

"No, Anna," he coaxed in a thick voice. "Don't fight it." His fingers sought the slit in her silk drawers. "This is what you were made for. Let yourself feel this, too."

And then his hand breached the feeble barrier of her underwear, claiming her softness, and there was nothing left for her to do except feel. A spurt of panic told her that she was making a huge mistake. That brief alarm died pitifully at the hands of passion.

Her chest heaving, she clung to his forearms, their sinewy strength her only anchor. She was beyond her depth now, shaken by the intensity of pleasure building low in her belly. Ragged pants worked their way up her throat, escaping as tiny mews. As though she had no control of her body, she found herself undulating, caressing the length of Arturo like a cat in heat.

"God almighty," he swore beneath his breath.

"Arturo," she moaned.

His hands continued to stroke her intimately, skillfully. "We have to stop, sweet."

"Yes." She knew that. She didn't want that.

"Tell me to stop."

"Stop." It was a reflex answer, lacking strength or conviction.

"Someone could come by at any moment."

It was a tiny, paltry bit of reality, nearly nothing compared to the tempest of aching pleasure she felt. But for all of its insignificance, it could not be ignored. Anna stiffened in reaction. The instant she did, Arturo dropped his hands away and turned her to face him.

Breathing hard, he stared down into her glowing face. "Oh, my sweet Anna." He pulled her close, enfolding her in his embrace. "Are you all right?"

"I . . . I don't know." Her mind was in chaos, she couldn't

make sense of what she was feeling. Deep inside, she was left yearning, discontented. As if solace and understanding could be found in the depths of his eyes, she looked up into the blue orbs.

He read her confusion at once. "I'm sorry, Anna. I hadn't guessed at the depths of your passion. You overwhelmed me." He cupped her face in his hands. "Forgive me. I didn't mean for us to reach this point, not here, not today."

Strangely, his explanation provoked her temper. "What did you intend?" she blurted out, her tightly strung body making a shambles of whatever composure she had left.

"A few stolen kisses. A taste of your body."

"You had that."

"Not as much as I wanted." He grabbed her wrist and pulled her hand down to the straining mound beneath his pants. "Not as much as I need."

Against her fingers, Anna felt the outline of his manhood, and swallowed hard. "Let . . . let me go."

"No, not yet." He thrust his hips into her palm. "You aren't the only one affected. I'm as frustrated as you."

"No, you're not."

He laughed gently. "Believe me, I am, and were we in my bed, I would satisfy us both." His mouth drew into a serious line. "You will come to my bed, won't you Anna? You will let me love you?"

She had known it would come to this point. "I . . ." She broke off, incapable of giving an answer one way or the other.

"You want to, Anna. Your body tells me so. Let me put an end to this unfulfilled desire that burns inside us both."

He was impossible to resist when his words stroked as effectively as his hands. "Yes, but I need . . . I need time."

His face lit with indulgence. "As much as you need." He

brushed his mouth over hers to whisper, "As much as you need."

Between the two of them, they restored order to Anna's clothing. When she returned to Clarice's side, her appearance was so meticulously unruffled, that Clarice had to wonder if Arturo was losing his infamous touch. That was, until she noted the brilliant sheen in Anna's eyes and her softly bruised lips.

So he had used her well, Clarice mused. Not well enough, given the short amount of time they had been gone. No bother. It would happen soon. In the end, Anna would come seeking solace and counsel and sympathy for her heartache and confusion.

Clarice had her advice ready.

Let me take you home, Anna, let me take you to Bellefleur.

Chapter Eighteen

"We're going home, Clarice," Anna stated, her anxiety sapping all the color from her cheeks. Standing in the parlor off Clarice's bedroom, Anna's shoulders slumped tiredly.

Clarice rose from her chair and took the younger woman's hands in her own. "What is this about?"

Too agitated to note Clarice's stunned expression, Anna paced to the window and back. "The doctor just left Sophia. He says she is ill."

"Oh, no. How badly?"

"I don't know. He can't find anything truly wrong with her, but she's drained of energy. He thinks this trip might be taxing for her constitution. She needs rest, no excitement. He wants her to return to her own home where she'll be comfortable and relaxed."

"Of course, Anna," Clarice responded immediately. "You must do what he says. You mustn't take chances with Sophia's health."

Tears came to Anna's eyes. "Oh, Clarice, I'm so worried about her."

Clarice went to Anna at once and put her arms around her shoulders. "Of course you are," she soothed.

"She's the only mother I have ever known."

"Hush, now. She'll be fine. I know she will. Did the doctor say it was dangerous for her to make the trip home?"

"No."

"There, you see? If she were gravely ill he would insist that she remain here to recover."

"I suppose you're right," Anna conceded.

"Of course I am."

Anna felt better for having unburdened. Taking a grip on herself, she stepped away and smoothed a hand over her hair. "I feel like such a mess."

"You look fine."

"Oh, I don't really care. It's just that this is so unexpected, and I have a thousand things to see to."

With what appeared to be the utmost concern, Clarice asked, "When will you be leaving?"

Anna began her pacing once more, rubbing at her forehead with chilled fingertips. "As soon as possible, in a few days, I would think. I'll have to see about booking passage on the first ship north. Sophia will need peaceful, curative accommodations. And then there's the packing. I have to send a letter to Nicholas at once."

"What are you going to do about Arturo?"

Startled, Anna's progress over the carpet halted. A burst of color suffused her face only to dissipate in an instant. The sensation was disorienting. She sat on the settee by the window.

"Arturo." Only that morning, they had clung to each other in the dappled sunshine of the park. Now, she was going to have to leave him, perhaps forever. As much as it pained her to contemplate it, she would have to write him a note and explain.

The notion did not sit well. They had become close in a

short amount of time. A few hastily scribbled sentences would never accommodate the intimate kind of relationship that had been theirs. True, she hardly knew him, but they had progressed to a point that demanded she give this her personal attention.

"He needs to be told," she said in a voice thick with regret. "I'll send a note around to his town house, asking him to meet me in the park tomorrow morning."

She waited alone, tired and drawn. She had spent the night alternately worrying abut Sophia and lamenting having to say good-bye to Arturo.

The park was much as it had been the day before, with the exception that Anna was by herself. She had decided it wasn't necessary to have Clarice along. The pretext of being chaperoned was the last thing she could contend with at the moment. Besides, she wasn't going to linger. Even though Sophia was resting comfortably under Fionna's watchful eye, Anna had decided sometime in the middle of the night that she would see this through as quickly as possible. A prolonged farewell was something she didn't think she could bear.

That assumption turned into a reality as soon as she saw Arturo striding up the path. She would miss him forever.

"What is it, Anna?" he asked, seeing her emotions clearly.

"Oh, Arturo," she began as he sat beside her. "I have the most terrible news."

"Your aunt?"

She nodded. "She isn't well. We're returning home."

He gathered her close, and she gladly laid her head on his shoulder, fighting helpless tears. She couldn't define with any accuracy what existed between them. Lust and a mutual attraction, to be sure. Beyond that, it was a mystery. A mystery there would never be time to resolve.

She *did* know that he was a compassionate man, and she liked him dearly for that.

"I shall miss you, Arturo." Her voice cracked.

Arturo shifted to cup her face in his hand. Of all the women he had ever met and liked, Anna DuQuaine was quite possibly the one he liked above all others. He found her to be as honest as she was spirited, revelling in her sexuality with a candor that was completely appealing.

At every turn, she surprised him, a rare experience for a man who was as jaded as he knew himself to be. They hadn't even begun to explore the passion that existed between them, and she was forced to leave. He felt cheated by the fates.

"I am sorry to see you go, little Anna."

"I don't wish to, but . . ."

"Don't apologize. You have to care for your aunt. That goes without saying."

"If there was only some way we could be together. If you could—" She broke off and sat straight, her eyes darting from Arturo to the nearby shrubbery and back. "You could, that is, would you be able to come with me?"

"To your home?"

"Yes, to Bellefleur." Heart in her eyes, she stared at him, hoping against hope that he would agree.

Arturo regarded her with dubious humor. "Anna, think what you're asking. You and I both know that ours is not a platonic friendship. My accompanying you would not be in the role of guardian, nor will I be relegated to such."

"I . . . I don't wish for you to be."

"Yet you expect me to be welcomed into your home by parents—"

"No, my older brother."

Arturo choked on a spurt of laughter. "A protective brother, no doubt. How do you think he's going to feel about you bringing home your lover?"

Anna winced at his blatant summation of the situation. Then she caught herself and damned her reaction. "I have every right to do as I please." Her chin came up, her gray eyes lit with a spark of indignation. "I know what Nick does when he comes to New Orleans. I know he has his . . . has his paramours."

"Does he bring them into the house?"

"Not that I know of, but why should he be allowed to . . . allowed to . . ."

"Indulge?" he offered helpfully.

"Yes, thank you, indulge, while I am not?"

A sad curve bent Arturo's mouth. "Is that why you're doing this, to prove something to your brother?"

Anna shook her head in adamant denial. "No, never. I'm doing this for me."

It was the only reason Arturo would have accepted. His smile grew to fill his face. "You are a rare one, Anna DuQuaine. It's a good thing my crops have all been planted and that I have a competent overseer."

"Does that mean you'll come home with me?"

"That means I'll come home with you."

Clarice tapped a slender finger against her lips. Eyes narrowed, she carefully thought out every possible avenue open to her.

She had been counting on Anna's downfall at Arturo's hands. That wasn't going to happen. So be it. Circumstances as they were would suffice. The old hag, Sophia, wasn't well. It would be too much to hope that she died in the next few hours. Regardless, Anna was distraught. Clarice would play on that.

A giddy rush of excitement dashed through her. Never had she been closer to Bellefleur than she was right then. Three months ago, she could have stood on the white curved steps of the mansion itself, but without acceptance, she would have been miles away. Well, she had that acceptance now, Anna's acceptance, and she was about to see her lifelong dreams and aspirations fulfilled.

A laugh of unholy delight worked its way up from her throat when she thought of what her mother would say. Probably something menial and subservient. That was appropriate. Her mother had been content to slave away for years on end, believing in a future she never had a chance at. In the end she was as dead as any other corpse and had nothing to show for it except a bullet through the heart.

Her mind skipped ahead, picturing herself ruling supreme at Bellefleur, Nicholas DuQuaine was nowhere in the mental image. Neither was Anna. The plantation would be hers alone.

The musing was so satisfying that it was difficult to shake. Even when Anna returned, it remained, a headiness warming her blood.

"I suppose you told him," she ventured, striving to keep her delight from showing.

Anna nodded, looking, oddly enough, better than she should have. "Yes, yes, and the most remarkable thing happened."

Clarice's stomach knotted with the first twinges of fire. "What is that?"

Clapping her hands together, Anna exclaimed, "Arturo plans to accompany me."

"What?!"

"I know, I can hardly believe it myself. But I asked him to come with me and he said yes."

"I don't understand." Little by little, Clarice saw her scheme falling apart. This wasn't supposed to happen this way. Anna was supposed to come back in tears.

"The thought of our parting was horrid," Anna explained. "The next thing I knew, Arturo agreed to visit at Bellefleur for a while."

Clarice's consciousness whirled, spiraling toward a mired, tottering network of impulses and sensations. At once agitated and composed, she stared at her half-sister.

She could kill Anna now . . . accompany the body back to Bellefleur. She would stay for the funeral . . . remain to comfort the grieving Nicholas.

Yes, yes, she could do this. No one would ever know. She had a knife tucked in with her nightclothes. She would explain to the authorities that she had come in to find Anna stabbed.

The most peaceful sense of calm settled in her chest. It was very much like what she felt when she had stood before her mother and shot her dead. Worries and problems seemed to disappear; the boundaries of her world closed in to one specific point.

"Oh, Anna, what have you done?" she queried gently, her tone faintly musical. She pictured her hands red with Anna's blood.

"I'm rather proud of myself," Anna sighed, missing the glassy sheen in Clarice's brown eyes.

"I'm sure you are," Clarice agreed, making her way to the wardrobe on the far wall. "I think this might have been a mistake."

"Why do you say that?"

"To have a holiday dalliance is one thing. To carry it home

with you is another matter entirely. What will your brother say?"

Anna's mouth compressed. "I don't care what Nick says."

With her back to Anna, Clarice slipped open a drawer. "What about your friends and neighbors?"

"What about them?"

"Won't they think it odd that you've taken up with a man whom you've just met?"

Scoffing, Anna plopped her hands on her hips. "Is this you talking? Where are your broad-minded notions all of a sudden?"

Where is the knife? Clarice mentally railed. Her hand made a sweep under the silk and muslin in the drawer. Would she have to use the pistol?

Anna continued unchecked. "I'm not going to stand on the rooftop and shout my personal business up and down the Mississippi, for heaven's sake. I'm not going to behave like some trollop for all to see."

"Of course not."

"Then why do you think this is a bad idea? *What* are you looking for? Can't it wait until we've finished?"

Clarice ground her teeth as fury slammed into her body to displace her dreamlike contentment. Abhorrent reality slapped her back to the present. Her stomach burned like the fires of the hell to which she damned Anna DuQuaine and their father. Francois DuQuaine, that miserable, selfish, whoring bastard, was responsible. This was all his fault.

She turned away from the drawer, eyes filled with the impotent tears of rage. "I'm sorry," she wept, and lifted a lace-edged hanky to her eyes.

Anna gasped. "Clarice, I never meant to upset you so." Gently, she took Clarice in her arms.

A bitterness Clarice had never known singed her clear to

her soul. Hatred, vile and unrelenting, stiffened her entire body. She despised this half-sister of hers. But worse, she despised herself for being so weak as to give into tears, and for being so stupid as to misplace her knife.

The revulsion she felt was unrelenting, goading her to race headlong on wild instincts.

"You have upset me," she cried. "I'm losing you, just as I lost my husband."

"No, Clarice. You can't think that way."

"It's true. You're my friend. You've come to mean everything to me." She clamped her mouth shut, fighting the nausea that gagged her throat.

Anna hugged her closer. "Don't cry so, Clarice."

"I can't help it. What will I do without you?"

"There's no need for this. Come home with me. You're more than welcome."

Clarice buried her face in Anna's shoulder, swallowing a pride she hadn't known she had. She realized that it had been important that she succeed with her plans because of her own resourcefulness. She hadn't. She had fallen apart, and gained by emotionalism what should have been hers by cunning.

As galling as that was, the results were undeniably effective. She was on her way to Bellefleur. That was all that mattered.

Nick scanned the contents of Anna's letter for the second time. Sophia was indisposed, although not seriously ill. A doctor had been consulted and had recommended that Sophia rest at home. Anna would be returning by the end of the week, bringing with her two guests.

Settling more comfortably in a deep leather chair in his library, Nick pondered the situation. He was concerned for Sophia. His first instinct was to travel south and assist in her journey. Time made that impractical. According to the date on the letter, Anna and her little entourage were at this moment steaming north. He would have to wait and trust that Sophia's condition did not worsen.

His gaze dropped to the letter in his lap. They were to have guests. Mama Lou would love that. There was nothing she enjoyed more than having a full house. Nick truly believed it was because it gave the woman a chance to throw her housekeeperly authority about. Extra servants would be brought up to help Betsy and Jessica in the house.

The slight smile tugging at Nick's mouth straightened. Up until now, he and Jessica had enjoyed relative privacy. That was about to change and he questioned how this would affect Jess. He imagined she would not be comfortable sleeping beside him at night with Anna two doors down and guests in the rooms across the hall.

"Well, hell," he grumbled, perturbed by this unwanted turn. He came to his feet and crossed the room to glare out one of the windows, fisted hands shoved into his pockets.

He would have to do his best to ensure that Jessica felt at ease. Easier said than done, especially since he didn't know how Anna was going to react to this. He had no intentions of making his personal life public, but there was no way to keep Anna from finding out.

"Damn it all." If this wasn't the most contemptible mess. Thoughts of power and command dominated his mind. This was his house and his plantation. He could do anything he damn well pleased. He didn't have to account to anyone, Anna included.

He did have to account to his conscience, and that fine faculty would not allow him to do anything to embarrass Jessica.

"Jess." He whispered her name on a sigh. What was he going to do about her? With every passing day his attraction to her grew. Her smiles illuminated his days, her passion inflamed his nights. It was becoming increasingly more difficult for him to remember that her place in his house, in his life, was temporary.

A heated denial came to his lips, but again, his conscience refused to lie still for dishonesty. In less than five years, she would be gone, and he would have to let her go.

More honesty; he could give her her freedom now, if he chose.

A profound sadness urged him back to his chair. He sat with legs stretched out, head lowered and his gaze turned inward. He wanted what was best for Jessica. Buying her indenture had been the best thing for her—months ago. What of now? She was free of her father, she was healthier, both physically and emotionally. Did he have any valid reason for keeping her?

Anyone would insist that the money he had paid for her papers was reason enough. More of that damnable honesty provoked him to admit that money was not the issue for him; he did not need another servant any more than he needed another cotton plant.

He tried to argue with himself that if she did leave, she would be penniless. It was a pitiful argument. He knew he would provide her with sufficient funds for a decent life, despite any objections she was sure to make.

Clenching his eyes shut, he damned his conscience and admitted to the most honest confession thus far. Despite any logic or rationale, he couldn't let her go. For as long as he could, he would keep her with him.

God forgive him.

"Want some company?" Mathew asked from the doorway.

Nick's eyes snapped open at the interruption. "Yes, by all

means, come in." He surged to his feet, never more glad to see anyone in the whole of his life. "What brings you out here?"

"I had business with Tom Fouchet." Mathew strode forward with his words. "I thought I would stop by."

"I'm glad you did. I heard from Anna. She'll be home in a few days."

What Nick could only describe as utter joy lit Mathew's normally serious face. "When did you find out?"

"Just a while ago." He handed over Anna's letter.

Mathew read the neatly penned missive as if it contained the secrets of the universe. When his gaze reached the last paragraph, his blond brows angled into fierce lines. "Who is this Arturo Trudeau?"

"I don't know."

"Why is he coming home with her?"

Nick shrugged. "I'm not even going to try and guess. Knowing my sister, he could be anyone from this Mrs. Johnston's latest beau to a starving artist who needs the beauty of Bellefleur to find inspiration."

"So you don't know who this Mrs. Johnston is either?"

"Never heard of her."

Mathew's gaze returned to the letter. "I'm sorry to hear about Sophia."

Taking a seat, Nick gestured for Mathew to sit. "It doesn't sound overly serious. If it were, Anna wouldn't have risked the trip."

All Mathew did was nod, clearly distracted by the sheet of paper in his hands.

"Have you decided what you're going to do?" Nick probed quietly.

"About what?"

"Asking Anna to marry you."

Shock brought Mathew's head up. "Uh . . . I . . ."

His reaction was so dazed, Nick had to laugh. "You love her, don't you?"

Mathew bristled visibly. "This is nothing to laugh at."

"Do you love her?"

"Of course I do."

Nick laughed again, stretching his long legs out before him.

"Damn it," Mathew cursed, "if I'd known you were going to sit there and enjoy yourself at my expense, I would have gone straight home."

"Oh, settle down," Nick soothed. "I'm genuinely happy for you. I think you and Anna will make a fine pair."

Mathew hung onto his annoyance for a bit. "You do?"

"Yes, I've thought so for some time now."

"I'm glad to hear it." Somewhat grudgingly, Mathew added, "I hope Anna feels the same way."

"What makes you think she doesn't?"

Heaving out a huge breath, Mathew declared, "The fact that all we seem to do anymore is argue, and for the life of me, I don't know why. I say something, she takes it the wrong way." He flung his hand wide. "Before you know it, she's in a temper and stomping off."

"That's my Anna," Nick averred, wholly unruffled.

"You might sound more concerned. I'd like to think she'll view my suit favorably."

"She will, if you handle her right."

Mathew narrowed his eyes. "What way is that?"

"That's something that has to evolve between the two of you. Just don't ever forget that Anna runs on her emotions. She's strong-willed and very opinionated. Subtlety is not her style."

Clearly confounded, Mathew assumed much the same posture as Nick. Legs shoved out and crossed at the ankles, he shook his head. "Why the hell couldn't I have fallen in love with someone less temperamental?"

"You can if you want to."

Scoffing, Mathew disagreed, "It would be easier for me to grow a second head."

"Then I guess you're stuck."

"I already know that."

"That leaves only one option, that I can see."

"I know. When Anna gets home, I'll have to ask her to marry me."

Chapter Nineteen

Jessica glared at her reflection in her mirror. She had been literally coerced into the dress she was wearing. Of a blue and white striped muslin, with rolled back sleeves and a scooped-out collar, it was similar to those that Betsy and Mama Lou wore.

In that there was nothing unusual. The garment was simple in design and made from fabric woven right there on the plantation. However, Jessica had never worn anything as fine, and that struck a raw nerve. Mama Lou had insisted that with guests arriving, they couldn't have the house staff "lookin' like they had just been out pickin' turnip greens." Jessica was sure that this was Nicholas's way of finally dressing her as he saw fit.

She had half a mind to tell him so. It wasn't that she didn't appreciate his sentiment. It was more a matter of pride. Having little else to call her own, she clung to her sense of self-esteem all the harder.

"You gonna come out of there?" Betsy called from the other side of the door.

There was nothing left for Jessica to do. She knew Nicholas well enough to know that he would brook no argument about the dress, especially since she was wearing it.

"I'm coming," she said, opening the door.

"Oooo, don't you look pretty," Betsy sighed, her brown eyes rounding.

As graciously as possible, Jessica said, "Thank you."

"I ain't never seen you in a proper dress like that before."

Jessica mentally squirmed, and readjusted the fall of her white apron covering her skirt. "Mama Lou said I was to wear this."

"Mama Lou's right, what with people acomin'. She says to get yourself out in the front drawin' room and keep your eyes open for Miz Anna. She's gonna be here soon."

An air of expectancy gripped the plantation. Nowhere was it more apparent than in the house. For days, they had been making ready, airing out linens, dusting furniture and polishing silver.

"Did Mama Lou say anything else?" she asked, well aware that Betsy had a tendency to forget Mama Lou's instructions.

Betsy thought on the matter as they walked through the house to the drawing room facing the river. "Yeah, she said that as soon as you see the carriage acomin', you's to tell Master Nick, meetin' or no meetin'."

Jessica glanced to the shut door of Nicholas's library. At present, he was deep in discussion with a banker by the name of Mr. Phillip St. James, recently up from Baton Rouge.

"All right. Anything else?"

Rolling her eyes to the ceiling, Betsy hummed and sighed, falling silent only when Mama Lou bustled into the room.

"I swear, girl," the housekeeper scoffed, "from the sounds you're makin', you'd think you was tryin' to lay square eggs." She pointed an imperious finger toward the dining room. "Get upstairs and make sure you got Miz Anna's room fixed the way I told you."

Betsy hastened off, leaving Jessica to bear the burden of Mama Lou's heavy regard.

"Is there something wrong?"

"Dress looks good," Mama Lou declared, not bothering to give Jessica a direct reply. "Should have rigged you up weeks ago." With that, she moved off toward the parlor. "You keep your eyes peeled. Master Nick sent a carriage round to the landin' to meet Miz Anna the minute she steps off that boat."

Standing a silent vigil, watching for the first sign of Anna's carriage to pull into sight was an idle job. There was little for Jessica to do except stare out through the long windows and think. Given the silence and her inactivity, her mind dragged up doubts she had been harboring of late.

How on earth was Anna going to react to the fact that her brother was bedding his bond-servant? Jessica believed acceptance and tolerance were beyond the realm of possibility. Shock, rage, indignation and or disgust were much more likely, and in all honesty, Jessica couldn't blame Anna if she did feel that way. What woman wanted to live in the same house where her brother was dallying, even if he was as discreet as possible?

Jessica liked Anna. She would do nothing to offend her. On the other hand, she doubted Nick was even considering that they sleep separately. And loving Nicholas as she did, she didn't want to.

It was a tangled, depressing quandary, posing a great many questions, which, Jessica realized with a jab of anxiety, were about to be answered. Straightening, she spotted Anna's carriage rounding the bend in the drive.

Taking a fortifying breath, she knocked on the library door and entered at the sound of Nick's voice.

"Miss Anna's carriage is coming," she announced quietly. She was as self-conscious as she had ever been. Nothing had changed between then, and yet, everything had. Where she had once been comfortable in her surroundings, she was now insecure, not knowing what to expect. She could not meet his gaze.

Nick came to his feet behind his desk. "Thanks, Jess." He searched her face for a long moment before he shoved back one side of his dark gray jacket and explained to the banker, "My sister is returning from New Orleans, Mr. St. James. Why don't you stay and meet her?"

Jessica did not remain to hear the rest of his explanation. It wasn't her place. She shut the door, missing the inquiring stare Nick sent her way. Taking up her position at the back of the drawing room, she stood silently and observed Anna's homecoming.

"Welcome home, Miz Anna," Mama Lou announced as she held the front door open.

Anna breezed into the house. Her face beaming with a smile, she gave the housekeeper a fierce hug. "Hello, Mama Lou. I've missed you."

The library door opened and Nicholas strode out. "There you are," he said, spreading his arms wide.

Anna almost danced across the space separating them and threw her arms about her brother's neck. "Yes, I'm home at last."

"How was your trip?"

"Fine."

"And Aunt Sophia?"

"Better. We left her resting comfortably at her home this morning. I'll tell you all the details once I'm settled."

Movement behind Anna caught Jessica's eye. A slender

woman dressed entirely in black stepped forward, followed by the most shockingly handsome man Jessica had ever seen.

She stared in rapt fascination. He was as tall as Nicholas, as broad shouldered, his hair brown to Nicholas's black, but this man's face was so beautifully molded, his features so perfectly harmonious that at first glance he didn't appear real.

He was the stuff of fairy tales and little girl fancies of knights in shining armor, but after several long, disconcerting moments, Jessica found herself studying the man more closely. For all of his masculine perfection, his visage lacked the character contained in Nick's face, his body the underlying power born of strength of will.

She liked the laugh lines at the corners of Nick's eyes and the slightly irregular cast to his upper lip. His jaw was a touch rugged looking, and his eyes far too penetrating for comfort, but Jessica wouldn't have changed them any more than she would have wished away the power of Nick's muscled arms or the mat of hair on his chest.

Unable to help herself, she looked to Nicholas, only to discover him staring back, those far-too-penetrating eyes boring into her with what looked like an icy intensity. Frantically wondering what was wrong, she shifted her attention to Anna as the introductions were made.

The man's name was Arturo Trudeau, the woman, Mrs. Clarice Johnston, and it was on her that Jessica found her regard lingering. Clarice Johnston was a beautiful woman, even more so when she turned her winsome smile on Nicholas.

"It's a pleasure, Mr. DuQuaine," the widow murmured, tilting her head to a becoming angle. "Anna has spoken quite often of you."

Nicholas flicked a glance to Anna before he smiled roguishly. "I can just imagine what my sister had to say."

"Only wonderful things, sir."

"Now I know she was lying."

The quip met with a round of laughter, and had Jessica biting her upper lip, every ounce of her nervousness doubling and doubling again. Miserably, she noted Mrs. Johnston's easy wit, her poise and elegance, and Nick's cheerful manner.

Feeling her stomach drop to her toes, Jessica lowered her gaze. It was bad enough to think on the heated glare Nick had given her. She didn't want to witness him bestowing his formidable charm on another woman.

"Jessica, how have you been?" Anna asked, coming forward with eyes alight.

Yanked from her misery, Jessica summoned forth a welcoming smile. "Very well."

"You look better than that." Anna peered back over her shoulder to tease Nick. "I'm glad to see my brother hasn't been running you ragged."

"I take offense to that, little sister," he averred.

"Of course you do," she shot back. "But I know how impossible you can be, arrogant, dictatorial—"

"Tolerant."

To the tune of everyone's laughter, Jessica silently completed her own list. Nick was strong, generous, benevolent, beloved, adored, cherished. He was all any man could ever be. He was everything she wanted in life. Not a man could compare with him, not Arturo Trudeau, and certainly not Phillip St. James, who emerged from the library to join the group.

Clarice's blood was racing, her senses alive as never before. After years of coveting and desiring, of being made to feel less than worthy, she was finally, *finally* where she belonged. Bellefleur.

The house far surpassed her expectations. The one glimpse she had garnered of the structure years ago in no way prepared her for the abounding elegance and costly appointments contained within. Everywhere she looked, she saw evidence of the kind of comfort and style that only the wealthy could afford.

She damned Nicholas his wealth and position. Standing there like some mighty king, he carried on without the slightest hint of who he welcomed into his home. The day would come when she would see him toppled from his throne and she would spit in his face when she made Bellefleur hers.

Satisfied by her thoughts, she noted the two servants present. The housekeeper was a mountain of a woman, tall and sturdy. She seemed to know her place. The other woman was somewhat of a surprise. Young, pretty and white. An oddity in modern times, for no one had white servants any longer.

Sensing there was something to discover in that direction, she remembered to laugh along with the others at some remark Nicholas had made. She turned to give him her most engaging grin when a nightmare erupted before her eyes.

Phillip St. James! He was there . . . in the house . . . coming forward to join them . . . to stand no more than an arm's length in front of her.

Blinking in a bid for control, she told herself it couldn't be true, that this was some horrid joke her mind conjured up to torment her. But there was no imagining the mocking smile pulling his lips to one side, or the challenging glint in his eyes. Wildly, she hoped that he wouldn't recognize her. It was a foolish, useless hope born of desperation and shock.

"Mr. St. James," Nicholas said. "Let me introduce you."

Etiquette forced her to extend her hand. It was soul-deep rage that impelled her to assume an air of utter assurance.

"Mr. St. James," she intoned politely. He had no right to be here, and she despised him for his presence.

"Mrs. Johnston," he returned.

Anna explained, "Mrs. Johnston and I met in New Orleans."

"How fascinating," Phillip remarked.

"New Orleans is also where I met Mr. Trudeau," Anna added.

To Clarice's relief, Phillip was forced to shift his attention.

"A pleasure to make your acquaintance, Mr. Trudeau."

Arturo nodded with his usual aplomb. "The pleasure is mine, sir."

Any pleasure Clarice had was shattered. *What* was Phillip doing here? A sudden ravaging fear gripped her. Was it possible that he knew about her mother? Had he somehow found out about the supposed friendship that had sprung up between Anna and herself?

This was disastrous. Phillip knew her past, her true identity. At the moment, he chose to say nothing, but how long would that last? In a matter of seconds, he could destroy everything she had achieved, and she would be left with nothing.

"Anna, dear, it's been a long trek from New Orleans. Would you mind terribly if I rested for a while?"

"Oh, Clarice," Anna fussed. "How thoughtless of me. I'll have Jessica show you up."

"No, don't berate yourself," she managed with laudable calm. "You're glad to be in your home again."

Excruciatingly aware of Phillip's taunting regard, she made her exit, unable to take a full breath until she was shown into her room. Her lungs refused to work properly and her stomach had begun to ache in fiery pain.

The spacious room was splendid, with its delicate floral

paper and canopied bed. Lilac and blue rugs complimented the drapes and the bed coverings and provided a soft compliment to the mellow tones of the cherry furniture.

Clarice was barely conscious of any of it. Her mind was consumed with a fury that made observations of any kind impossible.

"Get me some cool tea," she ordered raggedly, not even bothering to look at Jessica. "Not hot, cool, do you understand?"

Jessica hovered in the doorway. "Are you all right, ma'am?"

"Of course I'm all right, you stupid idiot," Clarice hissed, spinning about to glare her rage at one she considered worthless. "Just do as you're told."

Stunned at the virulent anger she witnessed in the woman's eyes, Jessica hurried down the stairs. She had seen that kind of frenzied anger in her father and it sent a tremor of fear skidding over her skin.

She hastened out to the kitchen and returned with a tall glass of cooled tea. A worried frown creasing her delicate brow, she made her way up the stairs, fretting over what may have put Mrs. Johnston in such a state of mind. The woman had been gracious and lovely upon her arrival, only to turn nasty for no apparent reason.

"Here you are," she said when she was bade to enter Mrs. Johnston's room.

"Give it to me," Clarice demanded. Rubbing her stomach with one hand, she made a grab for the glass with the other. She swallowed a third of the cooling drink in one gulp before stopping to catch her breath.

Jessica eyed her in a combination of worry and wariness, not daring to voice her concern nor to move from her place.

"Well?" Clarice snapped. "What do you want?"

"Nothing," Jessica assured her. "I didn't know if you needed anything else."

What Clarice needed was for Phillip St. James to be good and gone from her life forever. "No, I don't need anything else," she insisted, then abruptly changed her mind at a sudden thought. Information would be her best defense. "Yes, help me undress. I need to rest." Setting her glass aside, she turned and presented her back for Jessica's ministrations. "What do you do here?"

Surprised by the question, Jessica replied, "I'm a housemaid."

"Is that all?"

Jessica's fingers stumbled in unfastening the dress's buttons. "I . . . yes."

"You're not a personal maid or a housekeeper or a secretary?"

"No."

"That's odd."

"Ma'am?" Jessica asked, wondering what the woman was leading to.

"It's odd that you're a maid. Most servants aren't white."

"I'm a bonded servant."

Clarice looked back over her shoulder, one perfectly plucked brow arched over disdainful eyes. "You don't say."

If that required any kind of response, Jessica didn't know. She tactfully parted the back of the black moire dress and lifted the garment's hem.

"Are you the only one?" Clarice inquired as she stepped out of the dress.

"The only what?"

"Bonded servant," Clarice retorted with a snort that clearly said, "You simpleton."

Jessica flinched inwardly at the caustic response. "As far as I know."

Clarice mulled that over as she worked on the front fastening of her corset. "You see the comings and goings here in the house, then."

"Yes, ma'am."

"All the guests and visitors."

Taking the corset from Clarice, Jessica nodded, unsettled about the course the questioning was taking. "Some, not all." On the tip of her tongue was the word *why*. Why did Clarice Johnston want to know all about what in essence was Nick's private life? It struck her as deceitful to be having such a discussion, yet Mrs. Johnston continued.

"I suppose this Mr. St. James is a regular visitor."

"I don't know. I've never seen him here before, but . . ." Her voice trailed to nothing.

"But what?"

Jessica refused to say another word on the matter. "You'll have to ask Mr. DuQuaine."

Clarice's eyes narrowed with blatant animosity. To be thwarted by someone as ridiculously insignificant as a maid was infuriating. She spun away to deride. "Oh, I forgot, you're just a poor bonded white house maid who doesn't know her ass from her elbow. And as worthless as they come, if you ask me." The sigh she gave was chilling enough to put frost on her glass of tea. "Instead of standing there doing nothing, help me with this crinoline."

By the time Jessica drew the drapes to darken the room on the reclining Mrs. Johnston, her upper lip was sorely reddened, a result of her biting it in sheer nervousness. Tiptoeing into the hallway, she shut the door behind her and tried to contain her bruised emotions.

She had no business feeling hurt and degraded, she silently

reasoned. As a bonded servant, bought and paid for, she was subject to the whims of whomever. And too, she had not heard anything from Mrs. Johnston that she hadn't heard from her father.

The trouble was, in the months since her arrival at Bellefleur, she had been treated with respect. No one had stepped on her feelings, or abused her in any manner. Although she toiled and labored hard, so did everyone else. The plantation demanded that, regardless of a person's class or station. Life at Bellefleur had made her forget what it felt like to be thought of as inferior.

Horribly, just a few words had slapped home the reminder of what her true circumstances were. Nicholas might not consider her in such a light, but in the eyes of the world, she was only one rung up the ladder from a slave.

Depression settled on her with enough force to slump her shoulders. Slipping into her room, she decided that the day had not been one of her best. Her new dress made her feel conspicuous, Nick had been giving her the oddest looks and now this sobering view of herself through the eyes of Anna's friend.

She sat on the edge of her bed, but her gaze was irresistibly pulled out the window, toward the old rose garden in the distance. Just thinking of that lovely, lonely spot eased the ache that gripped her heart, and brought her a measure of comfort.

Without warning, her door opened. Startled from her pensive musings, she blinked to find Nicholas standing in the threshold, his expression unreadable.

"Nicholas." She was rattled by his unexpected appearance.

He shut the door and leaned back against its painted surface, looking as immovable and resolute as one of the live oaks sheltering the house from the sun. In his eyes was the same barely concealed iciness Jessica had seen earlier.

"Is something wrong?" she asked.

Again, his movements deliberate and unhurried, he crossed his arms over his chest, the gesture intimidating Jessica far more than any spoken answer could have.

She came to her feet, her earlier vulnerability at Mrs. Johnston's hands multiplying in the face of Nicholas's enigmatic behavior. Mustering as much courage as she could, she posed her question again.

"Nicholas, what is it?"

His jaw worked even as he thought of what he intended to say. He had left St. James and Trudeau to their own company because he hadn't been able to stay away from Jessica, not when the scene in the drawing room played again and again in his mind. Jessica standing in the far corner of the room, looking up to discover Trudeau, her face bathed in what could only be described as stark feminine pleasure and awareness.

He jeered at himself, making no excuses for his behavior. He had caught her looking at Trudeau and the green claws of a jealous beast had ripped at his flesh. Mentally, he scoffed. He wasn't the jealous type. He had never felt the need to be envious or resentful of a woman for anything, let alone something so simple as looking at another man.

But he was good and jealous now, as irrational and detestable as that was. He was reacting on pure emotion, something more suited to his sister than himself. It was a damnable feeling, and he was itching to dispel it in the only way that seemed to matter, at Jessica's expense.

"What have you been doing?" he growled for lack of anything better to say.

Studying him carefully, Jessica said, "Mrs. Johnston required my help."

"With what?"

"She wished to lie down. I don't think she was feeling well."

"And that took you all this time?"

Jessica wasn't aware that she had dawdled in any way. "She wanted some tea. I went out to the kitchen. I helped her undress."

"Is that all?" He knew he was being unreasonable, goading her for no logical reason, but he couldn't seem to stop, didn't know if he wanted to.

"Yes, that's all." Spreading her hands wide, she shook her head in confusion. "Why? Does Mama Lou need me?"

"No, she doesn't need you," he sneered.

His tone straightened Jessica's spine. She had never heard derision from him. "Have I done something wrong?"

He shoved away from the door and advanced on her. "Now there's a pretty question."

Jessica swallowed the nervousness congealed in her throat. The bed was at the back of her knees, Nicholas loomed before her. "What is it?" she asked again, her voice sounding alarmed even to her own ears.

"What is it?" he repeated, hating himself for feeling the way he did, hating himself for frightening her. "It's you."

"I haven't done anything."

"It's me."

"What?!"

He swept her up against him and breathed against her lips, "It's this."

His mouth came down on hers with a possessiveness rooted in the very depths of him. She belonged to him in ways that defied the legality of contracts and servitude. She was his in ways he couldn't begin to fathom, in ways he simply accepted and reveled in.

"I've been out of my mind," he muttered, lifting his head the barest fraction of an inch.

"I don't understand," she breathed, trying to make sense of what was happening.

"Neither do I." He kissed her again, holding her tightly. That was enough, it was all he wanted, to have her in his arms.

Jessica returned the kiss and for the first time that day, all felt right again. Her insecurities were banished by the warmth of his tongue searching out hers, the power of his body pressed close, the feel of his heart beating beneath her fingertips.

She didn't pretend to understand what had provoked him. To whatever had brought him here, she was grateful. She clung to him and held on, just as she held on to her love, for she knew forever would never be theirs.

Chapter Twenty

A dizzying headiness raced through Anna with all the potency of the wine being served at dinner. She sat at one end of the dining table, Arturo to her left, Clarice to her right. Next to Clarice sat Phillip St. James while Nick assumed his customary position at the other end of the table.

She could have attributed her excitement to the engaging conversation, or the pleasing combination of flavors offered in each course of the meal. She could have even given credit to the fact that she was in her home again. Those would all be lies.

The truth was that this was the first time since they had left New Orleans that she and Arturo had been in each other's company for an extended amount of time. She would have wished for privacy, but reasoned that would come soon enough. For now, the anticipation of being alone with him and the mixed blessing of having him so near at hand yet so untouchable was slowly quickening her senses.

"I hope your aunt is feeling better," Phillip St. James commented her way.

"She is, thank you. She rested as best she could on the way home, but even as accommodating as her cabin was, she was not entirely comfortable. I tried to see to her needs as best I could."

"You were by her side day and night," Clarice said. "I know that helped her a great deal."

Nick lifted his glass of wine. "I would have thought she would have come here to Bellefleur to recuperate."

Anna pursed her lips, her expression bordering on exasperation. "I tried to convince her to do that, but you know how *Tantia* can be."

"Stubborn."

"Exactly. Hopefully she'll recover quickly now that she is in familiar surroundings."

Arturo leaned back in his chair, his gaze as smoothly intense as French brandy. "I'm sure, Anna, that your aunt appreciated your attentions."

She returned his look, feeling her stomach flutter at the barely concealed hunger she saw in his eyes. He had been the epitome of kindness and understanding for the entire trek home. He had also made it plain to her on more than one occasion that his desire for her was like a persistent breathing thing, vital and alive, and not about to go away any time soon.

"Sophia is very dear to me," she remarked, her voice fraying around the edges.

"Sophia is lucky to have you," Clarice said. "I know I'm grateful to count you as my friend."

With what looked to Anna like an excessive amount of interest, Phillip asked of Clarice, "Just how *did* you two meet, Mrs. Johnston?"

Clarice's chin came up ever so slightly. "We have mutual acquaintances."

"Actually," Anna clarified, "Clarice is friends with my aunt's cousin, Fionna."

"That makes things cozy," Phillip commented, his tone sounding just indolent enough to prick Anna's attention.

For some reason, she felt compelled to explain, "Clarice is originally from Virginia."

Phillip's smile was all that was polite, but the look he gave Clarice seemed mocking. "Is that so?"

"Yes," Clarice returned, "my late husband's family is from Richmond."

"Now why does that surprise me?" he drawled. "I would have thought that you came from a more southern locale."

"Amusing how one can be mistaken in one's assumptions," Clarice parried.

"Oh, my dear, Mrs. Johnston, that depends on what one is assuming. Tell me, what brought you to New Orleans?"

"A steamship, Mr. St. James. How else does anyone travel through this part of the country?"

Anna followed the exchange feeling as if she had missed something. For all the civility between the two, she sensed undercurrents of emotion entwined in the layers of conversation.

And she had to wonder why Clarice had intentionally misunderstood what Mr. St. James had been asking. Clarice had never made a secret that after the passing of her husband, she had sought out the distractions of New Orleans as a sort of solace.

In any event the conversation had come to an awkward halt. As hostess, she sought to remedy that.

"Mr. Trudeau is from just outside New Orleans," she offered.

The conversation drifted to cotton and sugar cane, to the hope for good weather, and finally to a mild, socially acceptable debate on the politics of the day. Through it all, Anna felt the bite of impatience. It wasn't that she didn't care about the continued debate over California's admittance to the union. It was honestly beyond her abilities to give it consideration of any kind.

For too long, she had been held suspended, neither able to go forward nor backward in her relationship with Arturo. As a result, she felt at loose ends, as if she wasn't sure what would happen next. Tonight, her mind and body had reached their combined limits and conspired against her. If she didn't feel his lips on hers soon, she was going to crawl out of her skin.

Adjourning to the parlor took her one step closer to the end of the evening, but she still chafed to tell everyone to take to their respective beds. Thankfully, Mr. St. James departed for the inn where he was staying after only one brandy, and Clarice excused herself shortly thereafter. Unfortunately, Nick gave no indication that he was the least bit fatigued.

Sitting on a damask covered chair, her skirt billowing out about her, Anna had all she could do to keep from glaring at her brother. He and Arturo were deep in discussion on their favorite breed of horse.

She sighed and mentally threw up her hands. "If you gentlemen will excuse me, I think I will retire." She came to her feet, her movements as stiff as her words. She was angry with Arturo, with Nick, with the whole evening, and she could not sit there another second, waiting, longing, her nerves pulling ever tighter.

Both men rose as one. "Good night," Nick said, leaning down to kiss her cheek.

Arturo's farewell was taken from a book on etiquette. "Anna, the evening was wonderful. Pleasant dreams."

Anna wanted to take those dreams and chew them into little bits. She gave as fetching a smile as she could muster, than made her way to her room.

Mama Lou waited like a big, brooding hen. "About time you came up. It's been a long day for you."

"It's going to get a whole lot longer," Anna averred, her breath heaving out in aggravated pants.

"Uh oh. Somethin' go wrong downstairs?"

Anna clamped down on her temper before she shouted out the truth. Wouldn't Mama Lou love to hear that her mistress was trembling with pent-up desire.

The shrewish thought shaved a layer from her pique. She had no right to take out her irritabilities on Mama Lou, and doing so would not alleviate the situation.

"No, nothing went wrong," she muttered. She rested a hand on the nape of her neck, tipping her head to one side. "I suppose I'm tired."

Mama Lou humphed her agreement. "Of course you are. Let's get you out of your thin's and into bed where you belong. You'll feel better in the mornin'."

Anna wished it was only that simple. An hour later, she lay staring at her darkened ceiling, irritation and frustration warring inside her.

In a flurry of motion, she kicked aside the covers and crossed to one of the windows, not having the faintest idea why she was up. Peering out over the moonlit landscape was useless and it didn't make her feel better. Only Arturo could accomplish that, but he was across the hall, one door down . . .

. . . instead of there beside her.

She gazed down at her thin night dress, its lacy bodice nothing more than a teasing excuse. Yes, she wanted Arturo there, seeing her dressed—undressed—as she was.

That would require her going to him in his bed.

Her heart constricted painfully. It had come down to the point of reckoning. She had known from the start that it would. She had never harbored any delusions to the contrary. However, giving up her virginity was a momentous occasion, one that by its very nature precluded practice.

She didn't know how to go about giving herself to a man. Did she saunter up to his bed or did she knock on his door and wait for an invitation? Women weren't told these things because women weren't supposed to know about seduction.

Her temper flared for no other reason than the dictates of society were so incredibly biased toward men. When her door opened, she turned around, fire glinting in her eyes even as she realized that Arturo had stepped into the room and closed the door behind him.

"I thought you would be all tucked in," he teased in a husky whisper.

By the silvery light filtering in through the windows, Anna noted that he had divested himself of his jacket, stock and vest. His white shirt lay open to the waist to reveal a wedge of dark hair covering his chest. It was a tantalizing sight, but her nerves were stripped too finely for her to appreciate the sinewy perfection of his muscles.

"As you can see, I'm not in bed."

Arturo ignored the sting in her tone, dropping his gaze to the silhouette of her legs outlined through the sheer fabric of her nightgown. Light spilling in from the window behind gave him an unrestricted view of her gentle curves.

"I can see a great deal," he murmured.

Anna crossed her arms over her chest. Despite the fact that Arturo was where she wished him to be, she couldn't turn her annoyance off with the snap of her fingers, especially when her emotions were in such a tangled mess.

Blood pounding in dreaded excitement, she compressed her lips and smiled. "I'm glad for you. What do you want?"

There was no doubting the ire lacing her words. Hearing it

gave Arturo pause. "I got the impression at dinner that you wished me to be here." He strode toward her. "Was I wrong?"

He stared down at her, his gaze sharp, keen. He seemed to know everything while she felt like a simpleton. Her ire escalated another notch. "When are you ever wrong?" she demanded to know in a too-loud voice.

His arm snaked out to drag her into his embrace. "Quietly, little one. I like your brother a great deal. I would hate to have to shoot him dead while he was protecting your honor."

Anna was besieged by too many feelings to remain still and acquiescent. Perversely, she struggled to extricate herself from the very arms in which she longed to be held.

"If you like him so much, then don't let me stop you from joining him." She pushed at his chest to no avail. "I'll go wake him right now and the two of you can exchange views on horseflesh or what Henry Clay thinks of slavery or when you plan to fertilize your sugar cane. In fact—"

He lowered his mouth to hers, cutting off her tirade. She was in a devil of a mood. He could live with that. In fact, he rather looked forward to dealing with it.

She struggled in his arms. He answered by cupping her chin and holding her still for the sweep of his tongue into her mouth. Along the length of his body, he could feel her trembling.

He raised his head and scrutinized her expression as carefully as he studied her manner. "What is really bothering you?"

Her breath emerged as indignant pants. "Nothing's bothering me—"

The tightening of his arm across the small of her back silenced her. Nonetheless, he gave her an understanding smile. "Ah, sweet little Anna. Are you afraid?" He trailed his fingers up her neck to lift her chin. "Is that what this temper is all about?" Like the barest hint of a summer breeze caressing her skin, he brushed his mouth over hers.

His kiss both soothed and thrilled. She all but strangled on her breath. "I . . . I don't know."

Shaking his head, he stepped back to sit on the edge of a dresser, taking Anna with him. He spread his legs wide and maneuvered her so that she stood at the juncture of his thighs, her face almost on a level with his.

"All this passion waiting to be released," he said more to himself than to her as he settled his hands on her waist. "Easy, little one." He smoothed his palms down her hips and up again. "There's no need to be frightened."

Languid heat radiated out from wherever he touched. By small degrees, Anna felt her tension abate. "I'm not frightened."

"Are you sure?"

She looked into the blue of his eyes, their color shimmering like polished sapphires in the dim light. Reflected back at her was affection and patience. And beneath that a raw passion barely held in check.

"I'm sure. I don't know why I was so tense when you came in."

"Don't you?"

"I . . ." Instinctively, she knew, but she couldn't put voice to those impressions.

"This is what has you tied in knots, Anna." He raised one hand and cupped the fullness of her breast. "This is what you've hungered for until your body trembles and your temper flares."

Anna felt her bones begin to liquify. She leaned forward into his palm, seeking the pleasure that sent sumptuous spirals deep into the core of her. Dimly she acknowledged that he was indeed right. She had been longing for this, aching until she hadn't been able to claim an ounce of composure.

"Do you want me here?" he asked, noting every sign of her rising passion with a pride that was entirely male.

She closed her eyes to better absorb the sensation of his thumb caressing her nipple.

"Anna, if you don't want me, I'll leave."

Her eyes drifted open at that.

"I won't force you, little one." He stilled his hand, his expression sobering. "But neither will I remain to dangle on the end of your lovely thread."

She knew what he was saying. Without reproach of any kind, he was willing to walk away from her forever if she so chose. But if he did stay, it would be in her bed. He was a man and there was only so much he would endure.

The moment took on an unreal quality, where existence was blurred by the necessity to know, to experience this to its natural conclusion. If she didn't, she would live for the rest of her life wondering, asking herself *what if,* berating herself with *if I had only.* To whatever end, no matter the consequences, she had to have this moment for the sake of the woman she was.

In answer, she lifted her chin and kissed him fully, hotly, open-mouthed as he had taught her.

"I will take that to mean that you want me to stay," he murmured around a thick chuckle.

"Yes."

He narrowed his eyes. "I won't give you another chance to change your mind."

She took his last warning and calmly laid her hand along his jaw. "It's what I want, Arturo."

His eyes glittered like a thousand cobalt stars. He was more than glad for her reply. If she had said otherwise, he would have turned and left her untouched. It would have been the most difficult thing he would have ever had to do.

Spurred by a rich passion to please and be pleased, he cupped her bottom and pressed her into the straining bulge beneath his pants. "Then let yourself go, Anna. Don't think of being shy or confused. Your body will tell you what to do."

He slowly raised her gown, inch by inch, up her legs. The fabric slid over her skin in an arousing caress. Anna held her breath, all the while unable to look away from his eyes and dimly marveled at how sensitive her skin had become.

"Just feel what I can make you feel," he told her.

He brought his mouth and tongue into play, kissing and laving a seemingly random path along her shoulders to the slope of her breasts and up to her neck. Still, his hands continued to inexorably bare her legs of all clothing.

A cooling breeze from the window stroked her heated flesh and she realized that the hem of her nightgown was at her waist. She shivered in shock and embarrassment and reckless abandon.

"It's all right," came his steady dark voice. "Don't reject this small sensation. Absorb it, make it yours."

Anna licked her dry lips, trying to do as he said.

"Relax," he coaxed. "Breathe deeply."

Automatically, she sucked air into her lungs, past her parched throat, and felt better.

"You see?" he smiled. "Don't fight what you feel." He nuzzled the line of her neck. "Do you like this?"

Her eyes drifted shut as his lips nibbled below her ear. "Yes," she sighed.

"And this?" He bit the curve of her shoulder with exquisite care.

"Yes."

His head lowered to her breast, full and expectant beneath

the lacy bodice. "And this?" he breathed, touching the nipple with the tip of his tongue.

Heat exploded out from that one tiny spot, and if her life had depended on it she couldn't have summoned an answer. She slipped her arms about his dark head and held him close, instinctively seeking to increase the contact and find some kind of relief for the tension his caresses were creating.

"Anna?"

"Yes yes yes yes yes," she murmured in a litany that finally halted when his mouth closed over her breast through the thin barrier of lace. She arched helplessly and clung tightly. It was what her body demanded she do.

"Ah, sweet, sweet Anna." Wanting her to revel in her own sensuality, he increased the pressure of his mouth, first on one breast then the other. Within the circle of his arms, her body began to writhe in a timeless, intoxicating rhythm. "Yes, let it happen. Your body knows."

It did. Her blood pulsed, her heart raced, her limbs quaked. All urged her hips to his.

He drew in a strained breath, raised his head and kissed her as fiercely as her hands clung to his arms. She was everything he knew she would be. Fiery, sensuous, filled with a rare kind of courage in this erotic skirmish. She was more woman than any man had a right to claim as his own. She was the absolute best that womankind had to offer, and he wanted to bring her as much pleasure as she could bear.

His movements quick and sure, he grasped the back of her thighs and lifted her so that she straddled his lap. When she settled, her most sensitive flesh was pressed to the rigid length of him.

The shift in position startled her into breaking the kiss. She stared down at her lap, at his. Her gown was draped over her thighs, but only for a second. He tugged it away then up over her head, leaving her naked.

"Arturo," she gasped. He didn't give her time to panic. His mouth captured hers as he urged her into a closer embrace, her exposed softness cradling him through this pants. The shocking contact created ripple after ripple of the sweetest pleasure, tearing a low, sweet moan from her lips.

It was a purr of satisfaction to Arturo's ears. He stroked the delicate line of her back, deepening the kiss until it was out of control, untamed, pagan in its intensity to claim. In wild abandon, Anna met each stroke of his tongue, inflaming the need that coursed between them.

In one lithe move, he came to his feet, taking her weight as though it were nothing. Anna's legs, already straddling his hips, circled his waist while her arms clung to his powerful shoulders.

And still, she continued to kiss him, taking as fiercely as she gave, feeling alive to the very ends of her toes. The heat from his body seared her skin, reaching deep into the marrow of her bones with the kind of intensity that had her gasping for breath.

Her head fell back, her nails digging into his back. He took one nipple into his mouth at the same moment he lowered her to the bed. She gloried in his weight covering her and eagerly twisted beneath him.

"Jesus," he muttered, rearing back slightly. "You make me forget you're a virgin."

"Don't treat me like a virgin," she rasped. Her entire being was saturated with a primitive hunger that had to be appeased.

"You don't know what you're asking for," he ground out.

"I know, but I don't care." She pulled his shirt from his pants and ran her hands up the plane of his chest. "I want it all. I don't want to wait." Aching from the coil of tension centered in her womanhood, she ground her hips against him. "Show me everything there is to know."

Arturo exhaled sharply. He had never met anyone like her. Rolling to his feet, he quickly yanked off his clothes. Anna stared in rapt fascination at the body bared to her view.

He was more magnificent than she could have ever dreamed. Long-limbed, broad-shouldered, his body was a sculptor's study of muscle and bone. A dark mat of hair covered his chest, tapering to a thin line as it ran down the flat plane of his abdomen, flaring again to frame his manhood.

She swallowed with difficulty. He looked huge. To think of how her body was suppose to accommodate . . . that . . . was staggering. It was thrilling.

Lifting her arms, she silently beckoned him back and gave herself up to him, to herself, to the night that belonged solely to them.

The pleasure was breathtaking. That her body was capable of such stunning ecstasy was nothing short of a miracle. Again and again, she was claimed by the kind of joy that wracked her body and numbed her mind.

She was glad for that. Glad that she gave Arturo as much pleasure as he gave her, glad for his expertise that took them to fervent heights. He taught her more about a man's body than she had ever thought possible and in the process, opened up a new world of discovery about herself.

Long into the night, she poured out every ounce of pent-up emotion that had ridden her for years. She offered of herself fully. She accepted all he had to give without reservation.

Dawn found her sprawled on top of him, her skin bathed in sweat, her breath mingling with his. Against her chest, she felt the pounding of his heart. She rested her head on his shoulder and closed her eyes, content.

The most remarkable peace pervaded her, to the point that she couldn't lift a finger, could not even think of a single problem she might have.

"I have to leave you, princess," Arturo whispered.

Princess. An endearment created sometime in the middle of the night. He had used his hands and mouth to tease and torment her until she had demanded, like some imperious princess, that he take her. He had complied with laughing fervor.

She smiled into the hollow of his neck. "I know. The house will be up soon."

"You should sleep today."

"I don't think I'll be good for anything else."

Carefully, he rolled to his side, bracing his weight on a forearm to gaze down at her. "You are magnificent, princess."

She looped one arm about his neck. "So are you."

Tenderly, he kissed her. "Make sure you take a long hot bath today. It will help ease the soreness from your muscles."

The smile that came to her lips was sleepy, sated. "I will."

He kissed her again, then rose and dressed before tidying the bed. Through half-closed lids, Anna watched. One sheet was strewn haphazardly on the floor, the pillows resting where ever they had been tossed. Netting had been released from its canopied mooring and draped one side of the bed.

She drifted to sleep, knowing that Arturo would set it all to rights. He would make things perfect, just as he had made the night perfect. And it had been. There was no doubt of that, nor of the fact that she was a changed woman.

With absolute certainty she knew that her life would never again be the same.

Chapter Twenty-one

She would kill him if she had to. There was no question in Clarice's mind that if Phillip interfered with her plans in any way, she would see him dead.

Adjusting the angle of her parasol, she strolled along the path behind the house, having no particular destination in mind. Nervous restlessness had her insides in a tremble. If she was going to sit down to breakfast with any composure at all, she had to get herself together.

Last night's dinner had been a nightmare. Phillip's smug glances and subtle challenges had torn at her self-control. She had spent half the time waiting for him to expose her lies and the other half anticipating how he was going to use them against her. Sleep had been futile. The long hours of the night had been an agony of dread.

She stuck a finger between the high collar of her dress and her neck to alleviate the discomfort brought on by the moist heat of the day. It was barely eight o'clock, and the morning air hung heavy and hot. Beneath the layers of her clothing, her skin was damp and sticky.

She damned Phillip for her discomfort. He had her so tense, she hadn't been able to remain inside where it was cooler. Instead, she was curving her way around magnolia trees and lilac bushes, swatting at an occasional bee as she tried to foresee what he would do next.

Her thoughts boiled and fumed and seemed to conjure the bastard up out of spent energy alone. Gritting her teeth, she spotted him standing beneath a moss draped oak, smiling as if he alone ruled the world.

He looked as he always did; medium height, light brown hair and an angular face. Perfectly groomed, cocksure, he cut an impressive figure. His dark brown eyes held a complacency she had at one time found attractive. She slashed her gaze over his broad smile and casual stance and thought him a poor excuse of a man.

"Good morning, *Mrs. Johnston,*" he mocked, his smile pulled to one side.

Clarice strove to keep her rage hidden. "What are you doing here?"

Phillip spread his hands wide in a gesture of supreme innocence. "Visiting with an old friend."

"I'm not your friend."

"No?" He made a show of scratching the back of his head. "I could have sworn, *Mrs. Johnston,* that you and I knew each other intimately enough to consider each other friends."

"You don't know a damn thing."

"I know everything there is to know about you."

"I have no idea what you're talking about."

He reacted with a laugh that ignited the heat of pain in her stomach. "Poor little, Clarice. You never were any good at pretending." He leaned against the oak and cocked his head to one side. "If I remember correctly, you tried to pass for my mistress, but you showed how pitifully worthless you were at that. Now, you're play acting at being a widow. Personally, I think you're a bit merry around the edges." He shoved away from the tree. "And we mustn't forget your ultimate pretense, your trying to pass for white."

He threw back his head and laughed. The second he looked her way again, she slapped him full across the face.

"You bastard," she hissed, giving up all attempts to maintain an unaffected facade. She loathed him for everything he had ever done to her and she despised him for inflicting himself on her now.

"Get out of my way," she spat, fully intending to rush past him.

"Oh, no you don't," he growled, gripping her upper arms to keep her from escaping. Despite the red hand print on his cheek, he gave her a wicked grin. "We haven't finished our little discussion."

"We have nothing to say to each other," she got out from between gritted teeth.

He paused for a long moment. "As you wish." Dropping his hands away, he gave a short, quick bow. "If you don't want to chat with me, I can always chat with Nicholas DuQuaine."

The threat was everything Clarice feared the most. "No."

"No?" he mimicked, his chin thrusting forward. "What was that? No, you don't want me to sit down with the master of Bellefleur and tell him that the woman he has welcomed into his house is a murderess?"

Clarice dropped her gaze to the ground, feeling trapped and desperate. "I . . ."

"Don't bother to protest your innocence, Clarice. The authorities may not think the murder of one former quadroon slave is important, but that doesn't make your mother any less dead or you any less guilty of killing her."

"You don't have any proof," she averred.

"No, you're right, I don't. It doesn't matter. To these high-minded planters, the hint of scandal is bad enough. A rumor here, a whisper there would suffice in ruining you. And if that doesn't work, there is that interesting little fact that your ancestors came from Africa."

I'm going to have to kill him. There's nothing else for me to do.

It was funny how that decision struck the fear from her heart. She could actually feel the dread washing from her body, as if someone had dumped a bucket of cleansing warm water down from above.

Yes, she would put Phillip in his grave. Soon. Not now. The timing was all wrong, and she had no weapon with her. But soon, tonight, tomorrow ... before he had a chance to say anything to Nicholas. She would lure Phillip away to meet her ... an isolated spot was needed. It would be simple enough after that.

The brown of her eyes glassed over, one corner of her mouth wobbled. "What do you want?" she asked, her voice taking on a musical quality.

Phillip's mien of casual indifference came back full force. He leaned against the tree again, his bearing that of a very satisfied man. "I see you've finally decided to cooperate."

"You haven't given me any choice."

"Of course I have. The problem is that you don't like the choices, but I'll forgive you that. Now tell me what you're doing here?"

As cool as shaved ice, Clarice replied, "Anna and I met in New Orleans. She invited me home with her. I accepted."

"Why would you do that?"

"Why wouldn't I?"

"Because I know you Clarice. You hated the staid everyday life you had in Baton Rouge. You did everything you could, including trying to get me to marry you, just so you could escape the boredom of being a seamstress. You wouldn't willingly give up the glamor to be found in New Orleans to come here and rusticate unless you had a damn good reason. What is it?"

"I've already told you—"

"And I've already warned you," he shot back.

A tiny frown creased lines above her left eye. She wasn't going to be able to bluff her way out of this. Phillip was not going to be satisfied unless she told him something he thought was suitably vile or suspect or illegal.

That was so like him. He had always thought the worst of her. "Why are you so interested in what I do? For that matter, why are you here?"

"Me?" he shrugged. "I have business to discuss with Nicholas, not that I owe you any explanations."

She could debate that with him. She didn't. His expression demanded that she tell him what he wanted to hear.

"Anna was of a mind that her brother and I would suit," she lied. "I am not adverse to the idea of marrying, so when she suggested that I return here with her, I agreed."

"Of course, Anna DuQuaine has no idea of your lineage." He waved her protest away. "Never mind, I already know the answer to that." He paced for a short distance, his hands behind his back, his gaze directed at the pure blue of the sky.

"Are you going to ruin this for me?" Clarice asked.

He faced her from a distance. "No."

She eyed him carefully, suspiciously. "Why not?"

"Because, Clarice Bouchard *Johnston,* it suits my purposes not to. If you want to be the next Mrs. DuQuaine of Bellefleur, be my guest."

"I don't need your permission."

"But you do need my silence . . . which you can have. For a price."

Clarice's hand tightened on the handle of her parasol. "You think to threaten me for money?"

"No, no, Clarice, the correct term is blackmail. Get it right."

I'm going to kill him. "I don't have any money."

Her avowal met with more of his humor. "Of course you do," he laughed. "New Orleans isn't cheap, but that isn't the money I'm referring to." He sauntered back to her and raised a finger to flick the fringed edge of her parasol. "I'm talking about the money you'll have as the next Mrs. DuQuaine."

As tidy as some nut in its shell, he had planned out her entire life for her. The arrogance in that made her wish she had her pistol in her pocket. She would blow what little brains he had right out of his thick, conceited head.

"That's all you want?" she asked, feeding off the anger pent up within her.

He gave her one of his smug grins. "That's all I want."

"How much?"

One of his shoulders rose. "That remains to be seen."

"Why?"

"Why what?"

"Why are you doing this to me?"

"You? Oh, please, Clarice, don't delude yourself into thinking that this has anything to do with you. This isn't for your benefit or failing. You're nothing but a means to an end. I'm a businessman and money is money."

"Regardless of how you come by it."

"You should heed your own words. I may want to take some of what Nicholas DuQuaine has, but I wouldn't go so far as to kill him for it. Pity the same can't be said of you."

His laughter sounded behind him as he strolled away. Clarice didn't bother to watch him leave. She concentrated on exactly how she was going to send him to hell.

* * *

Jessica set the platter of eggs on the buffet, thankful that breakfast was a casual affair. She didn't think she would be able to make her rounds about the table with Mrs. Johnston's melodious laugh sounding in her ears. It was bad enough to have to enter the dining room as often as she did, clearing away empty dishes or setting out bowls of beignets or candied peaches or grits.

She glanced to Nicholas seated at the head of the table. As usual, he was dressed to spend his day outdoors. As usual, her heart flipped over in her chest at the sight of him, only this time, instead of her feeling the resulting joy she normally experienced, she was swamped by grief.

There was absolutely no mistaking Mrs. Johnston's pointed attention to Nick. His response to the widow was polite, charming and attentive. Jessica wanted to cry.

"Your home is impressive, Mr. DuQuaine," the widow exclaimed, smiling her very best smile for all to see. "A true reflection of its master."

Nick acknowledged the compliment with a brief nod of his head and a smile Jessica found as smooth as warm honey. "Bellefleur is at its best when it is graced by gracious company."

Jessica stacked an empty bowl and two cups on her tray, not wanting to hear more of the polished, civilized, socially correct banter.

"It's a shame that your sister couldn't join us this morning," Clarice commented. "I do hope she hasn't taken ill."

Nick's assurance came readily. "I'm sure it's nothing serious. She's probably tired from all of yesterday's excitement."

"Yesterday was more than exciting. It was wonderful." Clarice laid aside her fork, giving Nick a solemn, dreamy-eyed look. "My first glimpse of Bellefleur took my breath. I felt as if I had been transported."

Jessica spun and headed for the door, the conversation echoing harshly in her ears. China and silver rattled on her tray, seeming to jeer her as she marched toward the kitchen.

Emotions assailed her from every direction. She tried to tell herself that she had no business feeling hurt by the friendship between Nick and Mrs. Johnston. They were both attractive, well-bred, from the same social standings. They were bound to be comfortable and witty with each other.

That was what she told herself, that and the fact that she had always known that some refined lady would come along. If not Mrs. Johnston, then someone equally pretty and genial. However, reminding herself of all this and having to accept it were two different things entirely.

She stepped into the blazing heat of the kitchen, white-faced and tight-lipped. "They'll need more ham," she intoned, her voice as flat as the light in her eyes.

Pearl waddled from the fireplace to the work table, her round, coffee-dark face glistening with sweat. "Got dem some ham right here." She arranged a neat pile of sliced meat on a clean platter, pausing to cast Jessica a curious glance. "What's ailin' you?"

"Nothing," Jessica replied too quickly.

"You don't look like nothin's wrong. You look sick. You feelin' poor?"

"No."

Pearl pursed her lips, making her puffy cheeks appear rounder than normal. "You take care in de heat. Roll back dem sleeves. Don't want you droppin' to yo knees."

"I'll be fine." As soon as her heart stopped aching.

"You don't look fine. Never saw anyone so white, even for a white person."

Jessica endured the well-meaning concern, but it was a battle not to give way to tears. "It must be the heat of the day."

"I told you so. Goin' to be a sticky one." Pearl shifted the plate onto Jessica's tray. "Dere you go. Get dat on up to doze hungry folks. Here tell dat Mrs. Johnston has her a fine appetite. Does my heart good to see a pretty gentry lady what knows how to eat."

Jessica wished she could refute the cook's assessment of Clarice Johnston. It wasn't possible. The woman was pretty and genteel, everything Jessica believed she herself wasn't.

Entering the dining room again to the sound of Nick's laughter, she hastily placed the platter of ham on the buffet, refusing to linger there in attendance. The cost to her heart was too dear.

Choking back heartache, she turned to leave, only to be brought up short by Nick's discerning gaze. Her feet stumbled in place. He stared at her with a look she couldn't fathom, one that made her pulse trip and her stomach twist.

"Jessica, are you all right?"

She wasn't well at all. In her naiveté, she had thought she could have her time with Nick, free and unfettered by the harsh realities of life. She had been woefully mistaken, for before her sat a woman whose presence was like a cold hard slap in the face.

Never was her position in life more apparent. Mrs. Johnston's cajoling and Nick's affable flattery brought home the truth as never before; that she was a nothing except a bonded servant. Her place in Nick's life was temporary at best. She shared his bed, she cleaned his house, served his meals, but it was Mrs. Johnson who was free to sit down to the same table with Nick, free to openly tease and converse.

She didn't bother giving him a reply, in truth, one was beyond her. Almost blindly, she ran from the house, letting instinct take her where it would. It came as little surprise that she found herself in the old rose garden. The serene spot had come to be a special place to her, and from its solitary hush, she garnished a measure of peace.

She knew her ultimate course of action even as she sank to her knees on a mossy knoll. She had known from the moment she had first given herself to Nicholas that this day would come. Plucking at a stray wildflower, she admitted, though, that she hadn't expected this day to come so soon. Or that she would hurt so badly.

It wasn't possible for her to continue as she had. She would love Nicholas forever, but loving him was tearing her apart.

The sun-dappled isolation bore witness to the tears that trailed over Jessica's cheeks. She let them fall and wished she could hate Mrs. Johnston. She couldn't. It was the woman's *presence* in the house, her place at a table that was denied to Jessica herself that she couldn't endure. It served to remind Jessica of all that would never be hers.

That was a bitter reality to face and she didn't even have the satisfaction of being able to hate Nick. A trickle of resentment *did* worm its way into her brain, however. She wanted Nick to see past her papers of indenture to the woman who loved him, to a woman who could be his wife.

Drawing her knees to her chest, she wrapped her arms about her legs, unable to hold onto her puny asperity. Nick had never lied to her. He had never pushed her into his bed. She had gone there because she loved him.

A torrent of tears came and she cried until her throat was raw, damning her practical outlook on life, damning her less-than-perfect existence, damning her doomed love. In the end, she sat straight and was left with that same pragmatic attitude, the very same set of circumstances and a love for Nick that would endure until this pretty rose garden was so much dust.

She filled her lungs with a cleansing breath and looked about, feeling as if everything in life had changed. All about her appeared the same. Only her heart's perceptions had been altered. She hoped they would stand her in good stead. She was going to need all the courage and strength she had to go on from here.

It wasn't easy avoiding Nick for the rest of the day. Their paths seemed to cross more frequently than was normal. At those times, she found his hard pewter gaze riveted to her and it was all she could do to remind herself that she had to begin anew. What they shared was over, she would have to tell him so.

The question of when frolicked about in her mind like some recalcitrant child. As much as she knew she was going to have to talk to him, she didn't want to. Given that it was inevitable, she preferred the little bit of security the privacy of night provided.

Still, she lingered in Pearl's kitchen long after the place had been set to rights that evening. Listening to the night sounds float in through the doors and windows, she silently called herself a coward for sitting there culling dried beans.

Thankfully Pearl didn't mention whether she found it odd that Jessica would assume such a task. Nor did the huge woman make any kind of comment as to why Jessica was there instead of in the house. It was certainly past the time when she should have been. Nick was bound to be looking for her.

"Nice night," Pearl offered, shifting her huge bulk in her wooden chair.

Jessica looked up from her bowl. Pearl was leisurely sipping a tall glass of lemon water. "It's cooled down."

Pearl nodded slowly. "Only goin' to get hotter. M'skeeters goin' to be makin' mince meat of us in no time."

"They've already begun." Jessica resolutely avoided scratching the inflamed bite on her left wrist.

Leaning forward, Pearl examined the reddened spot then sat back. "You didn't drink you yo tea tonight."

Jessica wasn't prepared for the comment. It had become a matter of routine for Pearl to brew up the foul-tasting tea each dusk. No word had ever been spoken one way or the other about the matter until now.

Studying the pale oval beans in her bowl, Jessica shook her head. "No. I won't be needing the tea any longer."

"Not ever?"

"No."

"You gonna have you a babe?"

"No."

Pearl seemed to absorb that. She remained silent for a long while then hefted herself out of her chair. "Thin's gone bad for you?"

Jessica looked up into the concerned face. "Things have . . . have changed."

"Don't dey ever. Dat's de way of life." She patted Jessica's knee. "No use frettin'."

From the open door came Nick's deep voice. "Fretting about what?"

Jessica started so badly, several beans jumped over the rim of her bowl. Lips parted, heart wedged against her ribs, she stared at Nick leaning causally against the door frame.

"Are you worrying about something?" he asked, the gray of his eyes boring into her with an unwavering intensity that speared straight into her, searching out secrets deep and private.

She mentally scrambled around for her voice. What came

out sounded like a croak. "I . . . I suppose." Out of sheer self-defense, she glanced to Pearl.

The cook looked from Jessica to Nick and back again. "Dat tea's warmin' by de coals."

Jessica rolled her lips inward as she watched Pearl leave. Nick moved away from the door and advanced with long, lazy strides.

"I've been looking for you," he said, never once taking his eyes from her. "What are you doing in here?"

His unbroken attention was unnerving, especially since she didn't know how he was going to react to the decisions she had made. Nor did she know how best to tell him. For the most part, she had hidden from this very moment all day. Now she could either continue to run or simply get it over with.

"I . . . I was av-voiding you," she whispered.

"I know that," he replied smoothly.

"You do?"

He stood directly before her, legs parted, hands riding low on his hips. "What I want to know is why."

She tipped her head back, incapable of looking away.

"Jessica?"

He was waiting for her to say something. Mouth as dry as the beans in her bowl, she tried to begin. "I can't—" She gripped the bowl with all her might. "I—don't—think—" Each word came out separately spaced, a grating murmur filled with regret and anguish.

"You don't think what?" he growled, his face taking on lines of annoyance and suspicion.

"It would be best if . . . if I we didn't . . ." She caught herself and finally blurted out, "I won't be coming to your bed again."

The words hovered in the dreadful silence that saturated

the room. Having used up her bravado, Jessica sucked in a shallow breath and lowered her head, trying her best not to cry, not caring that Nick stared down at her.

He silently swore. He had known something was wrong. She hadn't been herself all day, and he knew that it was due to having guests in the house.

It was only natural for her to feel insecure and uncomfortable. Hell, he didn't like the arrangement any better than she did. He anticipated that she might be jittery or confused or even angry, but deciding not to give herself to him was the last thing he had expected.

And it struck him with all the force of being kicked in the gut.

"When did you come to this decision?"

"Today." She continued to stare at her lap, his taut voice adding to her anxiety.

"Why?"

"I thought it would be best."

"For whom?"

"For both of us." No, that was a lie. She couldn't begin to guess what was best for him. "Um, it was best for me."

"Why?"

His blunt questions were difficult to take. "What?"

"Why has it suddenly become better for you to end what we have?"

"It was bound to happen eventually."

"Eventually isn't now," he insisted.

She scrubbed her damp palms over her muslin covered thighs. "That's what I thought. I was wrong."

They were talking in circles. Nick shook his head in a bid for a patience he was sorely lacking at the moment. "You were fine until this morning. I can only assume that this sudden change of heart is due to Mrs. Johnston."

"You're right."

"She has nothing to do with us."

"Yes, she does."

"What gave you that idea?"

She drew a steadying breath and lifted her eyes to his. "Don't you see, Nick? She could be a hundred different women and I'd feel the same way."

"Which is?"

"Wrong, out of place, common. I'm allowed to share your bed, but as long as there's another woman in the house, I can't even eat breakfast with you. At every turn, I'm faced with the truth that I'm your servant." She dropped her gaze away, not wanting him to see the resentment boiling within her. She would never be able to abide any woman who came into his life. Her love wouldn't allow for that.

Nick exhaled a string of curses and paced away in frustration. He should have known this was going to happen, but once he had given into the need to have her, he rarely allowed himself to question the right or wrong of the thing, let alone the problems involved. His desire for her had always been, and still was, all-encompassing.

He turned and stared at her from across the room and damned himself for putting that wounded expression in her eyes. She was completely justified for feeling the way she did. He wouldn't argue the point for he himself couldn't remember the last time he had thought of her as his servant. And he had never thought of her as his mistress.

Whatever status she did hold in his mind and life, she didn't deserve to be denigrated by anyone.

"I'm sorry."

"For what?"

"You shouldn't have been put in such an awkward position."

Her blond brows rose in a meager shrug. "As you say, it is awkward. That's why I can't go on as we have."

It made sense. Nick knew it made sense, but sense had nothing to do with what he was feeling. "You can. We can make adjustments."

"To what?"

"To your duties around here."

Jessica sat straighter. "What would I do?"

"I don't know," he snapped, irritated because he knew he was grasping at straws and couldn't seem to stop.

"Would I work here in the kitchen or in the fields?"

"No." He'd be damned before he allowed her to toil in the cotton. And while the kitchen was more suitable, he didn't want her there either. He wanted her in the house.

How many times had he heard the gentle sound of her laughter echo from one room to another? How many times had he looked up to see the fragile beauty of her face smiling back at him? Her spirit was everywhere, from the special care she bestowed on each pane of wood to the elusive scent of her hair that clung to his pillows.

He had come to think of her as belonging within the grand white structure. Especially in his bedroom at night. Beside him.

"We'll think of something, Jess."

"There's nothing to think about." She came to her feet and set her bowl aside. "Regardless if I spend my days doing laundry or weaving baskets, my place in your life will still be the same."

Gray eyes glittering with his rising ire, he averred, "That hasn't bothered you before now."

She met his temper with a sad dignity. "No, it hasn't. And I don't regret for a moment having given myself to you, but I've known all along that this wasn't forever." She tipped her head to one side, hoping to make him see reason. "It's better to end this now and be glad for . . ." *The love we shared?* It had never been that on his part.

Blinking rapidly, she finished, ". . . glad for the happiness we had together."

Her voice trailed to a sigh that scraped Nick's nerves. He wanted to dispute every word she said. He couldn't. But neither could he agree and that sent his temper flaring right out of control.

What in the hell was he going to do? Life had become murky, its normally well-defined precepts blurred by feelings that made clear thinking impossible. Custom dictated one role for Jessica, pride and honor and a tender affection demanded something else.

He jabbed a heated glare at her, his emotions soaring with his temper. The entire situation had suddenly become too complicated to define. He wasn't going to even try. All he knew right then was that he would be damned if could let her go.

Three long strides and he had her in his arms. "You're mine," he grated, not caring that his move snatched her breath.

"Nicholas, please," she gasped, catching hold of his arms to steady herself.

"Please, what? Let you go? Give you up?"

"In bed, yes."

He snared the coiled braid at the back of her head. "You want to be there. You can't tell me differently."

"No, I can't, but it doesn't matter."

"Like hell it doesn't." He kissed her with brutal force, driven by a frustration and anger that tore at his mind.

"Nick, don't," she cried, yanking her mouth from his. "Think what you're doing."

"You think. Think about how your body responds to mine. Think of all pleasure we've given each other." *Think of how perfectly right it feels to lie in each other's arms, taking comfort and bestowing utter contentment.* "Think of your future without that, without me."

"I have thought of my future."

"Not very hard. What if you're pregnant?"

"What does that have to do with anything?"

"Everything." His arms tightened. "Do you think I'll allow you to slink off somewhere while you carry my child?"

"I'm not pregnant."

"You can't be sure."

"I am. And I'm not."

He actually mustered a laugh. There was nothing humorous about the fire in his eyes. It pierced with scorching force. "Don't be naive and don't take me for a fool. You've been in my bed long enough for me to time your monthlies and I know you can't be certain one way or the other if you're carrying my baby."

Jessica's lips parted. No sound came forth. She stared unflinchingly, remorse and misery filling the blue orbs. "Nick," she whispered in a hint of a voice. "I am certain."

"You ..." He wanted to repeat that she couldn't possibly be sure, but there was absolute conviction in her words. And her gaze ... "What are you saying?"

All the anguish she had felt when she had chosen this path swamped her anew. Her beggar of a heart pleaded for surcease from the hurt. What she was given was a simmering pot of tea and the unrelenting anguish of a motherhood lost forever.

With surprising ease, she stepped out of Nick's embrace to stand several feet off. Shoulders slumped, lines of fatigue and heartache marring her features, she faced him squarely.

"I'm not pregnant. I've been ta-taking, drinking something to prevent that."

As difficult as it was to get the words out, it was more difficult to watch comprehension strike Nick. No scowls or frowns met her confession, no tightened jaw or clenched hands. Yet the change in him was profound and unmistakable.

It was there in the utter stillness that claimed him, an austere hardness that was frightening. For long seconds, he didn't move.

"Tell me." He gave the order, compelled to hear the explanation he already despised. *"Tell me!"*

Jessica flinched at his harsh demand, wondering if he could understand her reasons for doing what she had done. "Any children we had together would have been bastards."

"Don't you dare call them bastards," he spat.

"Why? That's what they would have been. Life is hard enough without a child having to bear that burden."

"My children would want for nothing.'

"Would you have loved them, given them your name?"

"Of course. How can you think otherwise?"

"I didn't really." A ragged sigh escaped her. "In my heart I think I knew you would never turn any of your offspring away. The same couldn't be said for me, though. I would have had to leave them, my own flesh and blood, behind. How could you expect me to do that?"

Something like betrayal gripped Nick's insides, chilling his blood and filling him with a rage rooted in his soul. Somehow, it had all become enmeshed; him, Jessica, the land, the bond between one and all. Yet in one breath, she spoke of the babes they would never have, and in the next her eventual leaving.

He cursed for having allowed himself to be snared by her in the first place. It had been a foolhardy thing to do, and only now, feeling as if his world were coming apart, did he realize just how foolish and dangerous their involvement was.

Muscles clenched, he dropped his gaze to the flat of her stomach, as if the soft expanse was the fertile earth to his seed, and felt the most hideous sense of violation.

Choking on curses too vile to utter, he stormed from the kitchen, leaving Jessica to stare and weep.

"I'm sorry," she told the night. "I love you, Nick, and I'm so sorry."

Chapter Twenty-two

The subtle ache between Anna's legs was sobering. As she lowered herself to one of the benches on the perimeter of the herb garden, the unaccustomed twinge served to remind her of Arturo's passion.

Her stomach flipped over at the thought of the things they had done. There wasn't a spot on her body that he hadn't touched in some manner. His mouth and hands and body had brought her the most remarkable pleasure, and he had taught her countless ways in which to please him. In the pleasing, her own enjoyment had been enriched.

Not perfected, though.

She looked askance at nothing in particular. For all of the magnificence of their making love, it hadn't been perfect. Love was needed for that and love didn't exist between them. She wished it did. She could easily spend the rest of her life with Arturo. Lord knew he was handsome enough to make her knees go weak, and she truly liked him.

If love between them was possible, she couldn't guess. He'd made no secret of the fact that he didn't believe in marriage. That didn't necessarily mean that he didn't believe in love or that he was incapable of loving. However, if he loved someone, wouldn't he *want* to marry her?

That was a tangled quandary with answers, she sensed, lying somewhere in Arturo's past. Her woman's intuition told her that something terrible had happened to influence his opinions to such a degree. Common sense confirmed that. No one, especially of his ilk, decried matrimony on something as simple as a whim.

She shielded her eyes from the sun as she looked up to the windows of his room. She hadn't seen him since he had left her bed near dawn yesterday. It was no wonder, since she hadn't risen until late in the afternoon, and then only to venture as far as her bathtub. The energy to dress and face the world had been beyond her.

A pang of guilt nibbled at her conscience. She had been a terrible hostess, leaving poor Clarice to fend for herself. Thankfully, according to Mama Lou, nothing untoward had happened and Arturo and Clarice had carried on quite well. That wasn't surprising. Bellefleur had a way of taking care of people.

A sense of satisfaction engulfed her and that gave her pause, not because she didn't recognize the plantation for what it was, but because it had been so long since she had not taken it for granted. It was the only home she knew, and she realized that she couldn't remember the last time she had truly appreciated the splendor and spirit of the place.

She scanned the garden with its backdrop of flowering trees and mantles of moss. The scent of earth and crepe myrtle mixed with sage and mint and sunshine. Moisture saturating the air added its own unique fragrance, reminiscent of the river nearby, and evoked mental images of indolent currents giving way to even lazier rolling fields.

This was Bellefleur at its best. In her mad dash for excitement, she had somehow overlooked that. How sad. The land could not be ignored, it didn't deserve to be.

She was glad for her renewed understanding, and knew that no matter where she went, whether her future lay with Arturo or not, Bellefleur would always be a part of her.

Her musings brought a laugh to her lips. She hadn't been this whimsical in a very long time. It felt remarkably good, but at present, she needed to be a bit more practical. Among other things, the night's menu had to be planned and there she sat philosophizing.

She came to her feet with a smile and headed for the kitchen. Two paces off she saw Mathew approaching from the other end of the garden path.

"Matt," she exclaimed, her smile broadening. The comfort of their long-standing friendship warmed her heart. She was genuinely glad to see him. "How are you? I didn't know you were coming by today."

"I heard you had returned," he said, coming forward to take both her hands in his own. "Welcome home."

"Thank you. I admit, it feels good to be back."

"Nick told me of your aunt. I hope she is better."

"Much. She's at her home resting. I expect to see her here any day, bossing everyone around, issuing orders in French."

Mathew shook his head slowly. "I can't imagine anyone ordering you around, Anna."

"It is rather useless." She gave him a jaunty smile and teased, "You should know."

To Mathew's chagrin, he felt his face heat up. He didn't have her flair for raillery and even if he did, teasing was the last thing on his mind right then.

He stared at her, visually consuming the sight of her. If possible, she had grown more beautiful in her time away. It wasn't anything he could put his finger on, but there seemed to be a radiance about her that made his blood run hot.

"You look wonderful, Anna," he observed, his voice a husky vibration.

"Thank you. I feel wonderful."

"Did you enjoy yourself in New Orleans?"

"Every day. It's the most grand place. There's so much to do, and I swear, I ate from one end of the city to the other."

"It doesn't show," he told her, scanning the trim line of her waist.

"It doesn't?" She linked her arm through his to lead him toward the house. "You're just being kind, but then you always have been."

Mathew cleared his throat. "I'm glad you think so. After my last visit, I wasn't sure you'd even want to talk to me again."

Anna's humor dissipated. "I've felt awful about that. I hate it when we argue."

"So do I."

"You aren't mad at me?" She peeked out the corner of her eyes at his serious profile.

"Of course not. I would ask the same of you."

"I can never stay mad at you, Matt. After all these years, you should know that."

He should have known, but where Anna was concerned, logic and reason tended to escape him. The touch of her hand on his arm was making it difficult for him to think clearly.

"I thought a great deal about you while you were gone."

The gray of Anna's eyes lit again. "Did you? Good things, I hope."

"I'd like to think so."

"Tell me."

They had reached the curved stairs leading up to the house.

Mathew came to a standstill and glanced about with a certain amount of irritation. This was not where he would have them be while he declared his heart. Privacy was needed.

"Why don't we go inside," he suggested.

"If you like." One of her dark brows quirked upward while a lopsided grin flitted over her lips. "Is everything all right?"

"Yes, of course. Why?"

"You seem tense suddenly."

"No, I'm fine," he lied.

"Are you sure? I worry about you sometimes, Matt."

Even though he didn't want her chafing on his account, he was inordinately pleased that she did. His confidence bolstered, he asked, "Did you miss me at all while you were away?"

"I did. Our parting was horrid. I wouldn't have you angry with me."

"Did you think of me in any other way? That is, in terms other than remorse?"

She didn't have a chance for a response. The doors at the top of the stairs opened and Anna turned to see Arturo step out.

"Good morning, Anna."

With all the fluid masculine grace that Anna had come to associate with him, Arturo descended the stairs, looking as virile and potently male as ever. More so, for now she could envision beneath the layers of his clothing.

"Arturo . . . good morning," she stammered, picturing her hands trailing down the flat plane of his stomach. Instantly, she dragged her mind away from that avenue of thought and hastened to introduce Mathew. "Arturo, this is a dear friend, Mathew Bennett, of Hartford Grove."

Mathew swallowed the string of curses that were balanced, just waiting to be shouted out in frustration. Instead he was forced to go through the formalities of exchanging names and handshakes.

"We were just about to come inside," Anna explained to Arturo. "Why don't you join us?"

She didn't give either man a chance to object and within moments was seated in the drawing room, telling herself that it was only normal that she should feel so agitated. Seeing Arturo for the first time since their shared intimacy was disconcerting. Having to do so in front of Mathew in particular was almost unnerving.

She didn't know why it should be so. Mathew was her friend, although she doubted he would understand her actions. In fact, she knew for a certainty that he would object, strenuously, adamantly. She could practically hear his condemnations in her head.

In his defense, she told herself that Nick would react in the same manner. Of course, Nick was entitled to his brotherly concern. No such reason or excuse existed for Mathew.

Her shoulders squared ever so slightly. "I'm glad you two have a chance to meet," she said, wondering how Mathew could make her feel so self-conscious when he was doing nothing more than sitting there.

"It's not often that we have visitors this far north," Mathew said, then turned to Arturo. "Is your stay to be extended, sir?"

Arturo leaned back in his chair and raised a brow Anna's way. "For as long as Miss DuQuaine will have me."

Anna did not miss the double meaning underlying his words and fought to keep her face straight. She could do nothing about the melting dewiness in her eyes.

"You are welcome here for as long as you like." Belatedly, she smiled for Mathew's benefit. "Bellefleur's doors are always opened to friends, aren't they Matt?"

Mathew's answer was as stiff as the angle of his brows. "Always."

Anna considered his air, wondering what had caused his sudden scowl. "I've believed for a long time that friends are as important as family."

"Do you have a large family, Mr. Trudeau?" Mathew asked, studying the south Louisiana planter with special interest.

"Three brothers, three sisters."

"No wife, then."

"No wife." A small flicker of amusement creased Arturo's left cheek. "And you?"

"None at the moment." Mathew's gaze seemed to challenge before it slid to Anna.

She gave him a grin that was stretched taut. The discussion, for all of its decorum, seemed laden with tension. "All these wonderfully handsome bachelors running about unchecked," she teased. "Women up and down the plantation road will be giddy with delight."

"One can only hope," Arturo teased back. "Makes life so much more interesting, wouldn't you say?"

"That depends on one's outlook," Mathew concluded, as serious as ever. "On one's experiences and what one is looking for."

"And what exactly would you be looking for, Mr. Bennett?"

"What any man wants," Mathew answered with just enough sting in his voice to make Anna hold her breath. "A woman of substance and character."

Arturo winked. "Not to mention beauty." With obvious relish he encompassed Anna with one long look.

She exhaled a brief, choking breath, dismissed the flattery and nearly suffocated on the heat she saw in his oh-so-blue eyes. "Would either of you like something to drink?" she blurted out, feeling in dire need of healthy dose of sherry.

"Nothing, thank you," Arturo returned.

Mathew's response was more pointed. He surged to his feet. "No. I have to be leaving."

Anna's eyes rounded. "So soon? You only just arrived."

"I have to be getting back. It was a pleasure, Mr. Trudeau."

In less time than Anna thought seemly, Mathew took his leave. Standing beside Arturo, she wondered what on earth had happened.

"You didn't tell me," Arturo said with mild reproach.

She turned to face him. "Tell you what?"

He nodded to the door through which Mathew had just passed. "That there is something between the two of you."

Anna stared, stunned. "Between Mathew and me? That's silly. We're friends."

A wry smile pulled at the firm line of his mouth. "Are you sure?"

"Of course. I've known Mathew forever, although I don't always understand him. He was certainly in a mood today."

He thrust his face close to hers, his smile stretching. "I wonder why that was?"

She blinked repeatedly, all eyes and innocent wonder. "I wouldn't know."

"Little Anna, it's obvious."

"What is?"

"That he's in love with you."

Her mouth actually dropped open. "Mathew? No . . . no . . ." She grimaced in disbelief as she looked to the empty doorway. "You're mistaken, Arturo. I'm . . . I'm sure of it."

He didn't say anything more. His hands circled her waist and drew her close. "I won't push the matter. It's your business, but I'm glad you don't think of him in that way, princess." He moved her hips ever so slowly against the length of him. "I've become very *fond* of you, and I'd like to be selfish for a while longer. I missed you, yesterday."

Her hands settled on his arms. "I missed you, too."

"How are you feeling today? Any ill effects?"

"None to mention."

"Good. I would not have you suffering in any way."

As always his concern touched her. "You're very sweet to worry about me."

"You're very easy to worry over." He brushed his lips over hers. "Now, why don't you show me this beautiful plantation of yours."

Mathew was held in the grips of a fury so blistering, he could actually see his pulse pounding before his eyes. His blood hammered, his hands shook, and the legs that gripped the barrel of his mount clenched until the horse sidled nervously, trying to escape the punishing hold.

"Bloody hell," he spat, riding along the edge of the river toward Hartford Grove. He cursed fluently and savagely, damning himself, Arturo Trudeau and Anna.

Mostly Anna. If he had her before him right then, he would be tempted to . . . He couldn't finish the thought. Visions of shaking her silly infiltrated his mind. So did spreading her legs and pounding his body into hers.

He shook off the images. The vicious anger remained, impossible to relinquish as long as he recalled Anna and Arturo Trudeau together. He had wanted to smash his fist into the man's face for casting his looks at Anna, gazes and stares that had been polished smooth by years of practice. And Anna, the little fool, had blithely looked back, smiling that smile of hers that never failed to act on his senses.

Those very same senses were tortured at the moment, useless to see anything but Anna's beautiful face, hear anything but her low, soft voice, taste anything but the bitterness of a jealously that knew no bounds. He loved Anna and he resented Trudeau or any man who would see himself at her side.

He reined in on his horse so unexpectedly, his animal fought the bit. Silently, he stared down at his clenched hands.

"I love you, Anna." He repeated the words again and again, a litany torn from the depths of him.

He had gone to her today to ask her to marry him, to tell her of all the love he harbored in his heart. Instead, he had had to sit there and watch some other man cajole Anna with his beguiling words and flashes of wit. It had been enough to try a saint, and Mathew knew he was no saint. The way he was feeling he was closer to landing in hell than in Heaven.

Damn, he was a fool. Knowing that Anna was an earnest, emotional woman, he had foolishly anticipated being the recipient of all her energies and passions. A true folly on his part, since it seemed she was enamored of Trudeau.

His shoulders hunched forward as his eyes drifted shut. The reflexive moves did nothing to alleviate the pain churning in his gut. He didn't think there was anything that could help, not even the bottle of hundred-year-old brandy he was keeping for a special occasion.

His marriage to Anna, their tenth wedding anniversary, the christening of their first child. Those were the kinds of special occasions for which he had been saving the brandy. He might as well drink the liquor and get good and stinking drunk. It wouldn't remedy anything, but it would make him forget, if only for a while.

With an uneven breath, he straightened, feeling as if his insides had been wrung out. As useless as it seemed, he should simply go home and consider whether he would ever have a chance of winning Anna's love.

He started to laugh at the notion, only to have the grating sound catch in his lungs as his gaze fell on the river's edge and the bloated, dead body of Phillip St. James.

Chapter Twenty-three

"Whoever wanted St. James dead, wanted him good and dead."

Nicholas squinted against the sun as he considered the sheriff's statement. "What makes you think that?"

Sheriff Beaumond shifted his bulky weight from one foot to the other, his body brushing against one cotton plant and then another. "Well, hell, Nick. You've heard the rumors."

Nick angled him a narrow glance. "I have and in the end, they were rumors."

"Meaning you don't believe in local gossip."

"When have I ever?"

"Yeah, I know, but in this case, believe what you heard."

"What I heard was that St. James was butchered."

The sheriff sputtered a curse. "That's putting it mildly." He scrubbed a hand over his layered chins, his expression becoming pained. "Someone took a knife to him."

"I also heard that he had been shot through the head."

"He was that. Clean through one side of the head and out the other, but he was slashed up pretty bad, too, like someone went a little crazy stabbing away." He lowered his voice.

"Damn it, Nick, someone took off his balls. Gives a man the willies just to think about it."

Nick watched Andre Beaumond mentally wrestle with his intrinsically male discomfort, feeling both empathy and annoyance. Given that his temper was as frayed as it was, the annoyance seized hold of him.

"Why are you telling me all of this, Andre? You didn't track me down in the middle of my cotton fields just to add to the gossip."

"Take it easy, Nick. I'm just trying to find out what happened. The man was visiting these parts. I thought you might be able to shed some light on the whole thing."

"As in who might have wanted his balls?"

"Something like that."

Nick set his arms akimbo and swung his gaze out over Bellefleur's acres, clamping down on his ire. He was being uncharitable. A man was dead, Beaumond was only doing his job. Nick had to remind himself that tolerance and compassion were in order here.

"I don't know of anything that might help. St. James and I met a couple of times over business."

"Heard tell he was thinking of setting up a bank of his own in these parts."

"That was his plan. We discussed it, but not enough to make a difference one way or the other."

"Did he ever say anything about enemies, anyone who might be out for blood?"

"Not a thing, but I wasn't his confidant. For all I know, he could have left an entire city aching to have his head."

"Or some other bodily part a little further south." Beaumond heaved a sigh of exasperation and wiped at the sweat on his forehead with a handkerchief that looked as if it hadn't been washed in six months. "None of this makes sense."

"Murder usually doesn't."

"That's for damn sure." He shoved the soiled cloth back into his pants pocket, patted his chest a few times and then nodded. "I guess I'll have to send word down to Baton Rouge. In the meantime, let me know if you hear anything."

"I will."

"Someone has to know something."

"Do you think it's someone local?"

Beaumond screwed his mouth to one side. "I want to think that whoever done this thing was just passing through on his way to somewhere else. I sure as hell don't wish bad on no one, but I'd hate to think that we had us a killer attending church with us every Sunday."

Beaumond left Nick with that parting comment, and a temper once more in jeopardy of erupting. That had become a common occurrence during the past several days. Ever since Jessica had made her confessions to him in the kitchen, his forbearance for even the simplest plight had been reduced to nil.

A murder in the area tested his temperament to the limit. He felt concerned, but not in any manner he would have expected from himself. His interest and disquietude were detached, much like the sounds and sights of chopping cotton going on around him. All were real, but their importance dimmed. His mind was absorbed with Jessica, not with Phillip St. James nor with slaves hoeing weeds out from under cotton plants.

Jessica. As if he could escape the thought of her, he spun and headed for the house. What an ass he was. Why had he ever given into the feelings he had for her, and why wasn't he now able to shake them? All he knew with damnable certainty was that the lines of master and servant should have never been crossed.

For all the good it did, he blamed himself for that mistake. They would have both been better off if he had ignored his attraction to her. Jessica would have been satisfied with her lot in life, and he would have gone his way as he had intended, looking for a wife.

What a sour notion that had become. A wife. Reason told him it was the only way to continue. His emotions didn't give a damn. Again and again, he was plagued by an overwhelming sense of loss that even Bellefleur couldn't assuage.

That realization stopped him cold. Turning, he scanned the entire landscape, as far as his eyes could see. The trees, the buildings, the fields, streams, people, animals, stacks of hay, fences. This little world within a world had always been his strength. From the day he had been born, he had drawn his sense of self from everything from the gritty dirt to the scent of smoke in the air.

Purpose had meaning as defined by the land. His values and beliefs may have been molded by his parents, but they were rooted *in the land*. To suddenly feel bereft of that bond infuriated him beyond all that was holy.

He gained the house, a black, menacing glint in his eyes. If his mood had been testy before, it escalated to a dangerous level now. And he didn't give a good goddamn if everyone knew it.

In the ensuing days, he kept a civil tongue for the sake of their guests, managing even to converse politely. But beyond that, he didn't care if they stayed or sailed away on the first steamship to hell. He felt as if the fabric of his life was shredding apart and he was helpless to do anything to stop it.

The land, that core of his being, became his salvation. He worked it, tended it, loved it, poured out his every frustration on it. He was on horseback and in the fields before first light and only at Anna's insistence did he stop for the last meal of the day.

What Jessica was about, he didn't know. He told himself he didn't care. She was wreaking havoc on his life and he preferred that she keep her distance. In fact, he wished that everyone do so and went out of his way to insure that very thing. Unfortunately, his wishes were for naught when Clarice Johnston decided to make a point of engaging him in conversation after dinner one evening.

"Your crops will be the best ever, Mr. DuQuaine," she said.

Standing at the fireplace in the parlor, Nick swirled the brandy in his snifter and gave her a bland look. "What makes you say that, madam?"

She lifted her hands to shrug delicately. "Why, because you've spent so much time tending to them."

"This plantation does not run itself."

Clarice's lips curved into a becoming smile. "I meant no criticism. Quite the opposite. I admire your dedication."

Anna set her tea cup down. "Nick lives for Bellefleur. I swear, it's become his mistress."

"Land," Arturo teased lightly, "can be a more satisfying mistress than any woman."

Anna reacted with a good-natured gasp of effrontery. "What a perfectly male thing to say, Arturo."

"But he is right," Clarice offered. "Women, men, people don't always measure up to our expectations, wouldn't you agree, Mr. DuQuaine?"

Nick wanted to be anywhere but standing there pretending to enjoy himself. "The land is enduring, steadfast."

"Do you mean to imply that women are not?" she quipped with a laugh.

The gray of his eyes took on a challenging glint. "You may take that any way you wish, Mrs. Johnston."

Clarice surrendered to another lilting giggle. "I will assume, then, that you have a true love for the land that is to be envied. Tell me, what is it that fascinates you so?"

Nick took a firm hold on what little tolerance he could claim as his own. "What I feel for my home is what any man might feel. It's made up of a series of intangibles."

"How perfectly philosophical."

"I've always thought of it as practical," he countered just to be contrary. If he was going to have to endure this banter, he would take what enjoyment he could. To be just short of disagreeable suited him perfectly at the moment. "I'm a very practical man."

"Oh, you're far too humble, sir. In the short time that I have been here, I've come to the conclusion that you are quite the visionary. One sees your influence on every aspect of Bellefleur."

Anna pouted prettily. "I hope you have noted my personal touches. I take great pride in the formal garden. Nick says it's a showcase."

Clarice gazed directly at Nick. "I would love to see it."

It was a bad hint. Coupled with the dreamy-eyed stare meant to entice, Nick ground his teeth, then silently swore to the heavens above. The widow was obvious and annoying.

He damned her, damned the moment, and damned the social dictates which made it impossible for him to ignore her thinly disguised request.

"Of course," he muttered. "Will you need a wrap?"

He didn't even wait for her answer. Setting aside his glass, he crossed to the doorway and called out for Betsy, already anticipating having to call out to the deliberate, unhurried girl again.

Surprisingly, detestably, it was Jessica who answered his summons. "Where's Betsy?" he grated in a hushed voice, resenting her for being there, resenting himself for reacting so strongly to the sight of her. She looked as beautiful as ever, more so with lines of gentle fatigue making her appear more fragile than usual.

"Betsy isn't feeling well. She's gone to bed."

An appropriate reply, if he had been in the mood for such. "If I had wanted you, I would have called for you."

Jessica exhaled slowly, her discomfort clearly visible. "Please, Nick," she whispered. "Don't make this any harder than it already is."

"Has life suddenly become difficult for you?" he sneered, wanting her to hurt as much as he did.

From behind him, Anna asked, "Is there a problem, Nick?"

"No," he averred before he lowered his voice again. "Is there a problem, Jess?"

She gaze wavered from his. "You tell me. You called for Betsy."

"So I did. Mrs. Johnston needs a wrap from her room."

Jessica nodded and hurried off. He watched her flight, feeling his lungs wrap themselves about his heart. God above, he missed her. They were in the same house, yet miles apart.

He shoved away from the thought and took up his stance at the fireplace. All too quickly, Jessica returned, her face more pale than it had been minutes ago.

"I hope this one is all right," she said to Clarice, her voice low and strained.

"Yes. It's fine."

Jessica practically raced from the room, capturing Nick's attention to the distraction of all else.

"Mr. DuQuaine?" Clarice prompted.

He blinked to find her standing, her black brows arched expectantly. Snared by courtesy, he extended his elbow and escorted her from the house.

"You seem distracted, sir," Clarice began.

"If I am, I offer my apologies."

"But no explanations," she responded, her voice laced with humor.

Directing her between the rows of clipped shrubs, he glared at her through night's concealing darkness. "No, madam. No explanations or excuses."

He had intended his words as a rebuke. In response, he was berated with more of her laughter, which seemed to be in overabundance tonight.

"How very much like my dear husband you are, sir. Like you, he, too, chose a more private course for life's little quandaries. It must be the way of powerful men."

Nick had never considered himself in that light. "I'm sure I wouldn't know."

"I think you are very powerful."

"Why would you think that?"

"Bellefleur speaks for itself. The plantation is thriving, well-cared for. It takes a powerful man to insure all of that. Then again, one has only to look at you to know how strong you are."

Her flattery did not sit well. Instinctively, Nick drew back from the compliment and the woman, only to have her advance yet again.

"Forgive me, sir, if I am too forward, but you have made me feel so very much at home here." She hugged his arm close. "I feel as if I've known you for years instead of days."

She sank onto a stone bench and turned her face up to his. A sliver of a moon cast enough light for Nick to see the loneliness in her shadowed eyes.

His conscience pricked him. She was an attractive woman in need of conversation, doing what she considered her best to entertain him. Certainly he could put aside his rancor long enough to indulge her for a few moments.

"I'm glad your stay has been pleasant," he told her levelly.

"How could it not be? Anna is so very dear to me. And Bellefleur is . . ." She let out a heavy breath and gazed wistfully toward the fields. "Bellefleur is everything a person could want for in a home. Gracious and splendid. The kind of home everyone wishes for. My husband had dreamed of owning something half as fine."

"Were you married long?"

"Several years. Long enough to have a taste of happiness. When he died, I was . . . I was lost. The distractions of New Orleans helped ease the pain of his passing. And then fate smiled and brought me Anna as a friend." She paused and murmured, "And you, too. I hope I may count you as a friend, Nicholas."

"Of course."

A huge smile creased her face. "Thank you. You don't know how much that means to me."

For a long moment, she stared up, and then visibly collected herself. As if she had suddenly remembered the time and place, she rose and linked her arm through his.

"We should be getting back. I'll have to tell Anna that the garden is beautiful."

Hours later, in the silence of her room, Clarice hugged her knees to her chest and laughed. Sitting in the chair before her window, she congratulated herself on her time spent with Nicholas.

The ground work was laid. A "friendship" had been established. A little more time, a little coyly staged seduction on her part and she would have him asking her to marry him.

She wouldn't entertain the remotest possibility that it would be otherwise. This was destiny. It was meant to be. She would marry Nicholas as easily as she had killed Phillip.

She laughed again, not hearing the odd quality in the chuckling vibrations. Killing Phillip had been like child's play. And as enjoyable. Another laugh tickled the back of her throat when she thought of the note she had sent to him asking him to meet her.

In his arrogance he had assumed it was for carnal purposes. A tryst in an out-of-the-way spot. She could still see the shock and disbelief on his face when she had pulled the pistol from her pocket and fired it right into his skull.

Closing her eyes, she lived the moment again. The night had been as black as this night, the air thick with the river's murky scent. In his attempts to kiss her, Phillip's heavy breathing had sounded too loud in her ears. Her skin had been bathed in sweat, her heart had pounded, anticipation and a thrilling kind of energy had churned through her body.

And then the jolting blast of the pistol and blood everywhere . . .

Supreme satisfaction warmed her now as it had then. She clasped her jaws with fingers spread wide and slowly angled her palms up the sides of her face and into her hair. Phillip was dead, dead, dead. The headiness of that was pure bliss.

Her head tilted to one side as she envisioned the knife slashing into his neck and chest. The steel had dragged sluggishly through his skin, the blade's handle jerking in resistance in her fist.

She lowered her hands to stare at them now. Her beautiful white skin had been sticky with his blood. She hadn't minded . . . she had sought more . . . in the one way she knew Phillip would have abhorred the most.

Another giggle bubbled up past her lips, her mind still

firmly caught in another time. A quick slice had rended his pants, another had emasculated him forever. It didn't matter that he hadn't been alive to suffer. It was enough for her to know that she had had her revenge.

With movements languid and sleek, she draped her arms over her head and slouched into the chair's cushions, brimming with pleasure. Nonetheless, a niggling little doubt surfaced from the back of her mind.

She didn't like the exchange between Nick and that little blond maid. Their conversation had been too low to overhear, but the tension between them had been unmistakable.

Were they lovers? She didn't care what they did or didn't do. As soon as she was mistress of the plantation, she would have the chit sold off somewhere. Or maybe the girl, Jessica, would meet with her own accident.

Whatever. It didn't matter . . . as long as Jessica didn't interfere. As long as she and everyone else did nothing to keep her from Bellefleur, they were safe. If not . . .

She smiled at the armoire and its hidden pistol.

If not, she would do what had to be done.

Chapter Twenty-four

"Short of lay-by day, this party is the grandest thing we've had in a year," Mama Lou declared.

Jessica set out another arrangement of freshly cut flowers in the drawing room just as Anna had instructed. The room, like every other room in the house, was in readiness for the party Anna had decided to have.

"What's lay-by day?" she asked, giving the housekeeper a quizzical look.

Mama Lou lit the tapers set in the wall sconces. "Girl, that's the day when most of the plantations in these parts stop for a day. Folks kick up their heels and everyone has themselves a fine time."

"Why?"

"Because it's the day the crops are able to fend for themselves. When that happens, it's cause for celebratin'."

Jessica could understand that reasoning. As much time and energy as the young cotton plants required, it had to be a blessed relief to find them sturdy enough to survive until harvest. The moment had to be well worth a party not unlike tonight's gala.

The cause for this evening's festivities had nothing to do

with crops and everything to do with Mrs. Johnston and Mr. Trudeau. The party was Anna's way of introducing them to the neighbors and for nearly a week, the entire household had been preparing for this very night.

Invitations had been sent out, rooms readied, musicians hired. A festive atmosphere vibrated about the house, epitomized by the fact that Sophia had fully recovered from whatever had afflicted her and was due to arrive at any moment.

"You done in here?" Mama Lou inquired, checking every corner of the room.

"Yes."

"Good. I'm goin' up to see if Miz Anna needs anything." The housekeeper headed for the dining room and the stairway. "You go on out to the kitchen and tell Pearl that she best have plenty of ice on hand. Miz Sophia's comin' and she always likes a heap of ice in the bottom of her cups."

"Yes, ma'am."

"Then you go find that Betsy and make sure she ain't grown roots. If she moved any slower, she'd be goin' backwards."

Jessica did as she was told, up to a point. She hastened out to the kitchen, but she wasn't about to *tell* Pearl anything, especially as phrased by Mama Lou. As always, tact was in order when Jessica found herself between the two women.

"Is there anything I can do?" she asked, stepping into the noisy bustle of the sweltering cook house.

Without looking up from the roast she was carving, Pearl smiled. "Not a thing. We're doin' fine. Food's gonna be de best anyone done ate."

Of that Jessica had no doubt. "Do you need for me to set out plates or get more ice from the ice house?"

Pearl shook her head to the negative. "Nope. Got us plenty of ice all chopped up, just waitin'."

Jessica smiled inwardly as she dabbed at the sweat dotting her forehead. "That shouldn't be too long. I thought I heard a carriage coming up the drive."

"Den it's time." Knife in hand, Pearl swung about and pointed her blade to a boy of about nine, standing near a window. "You take dat tray of sweets up to de house."

The boy nodded and lifted the indicated platter.

"And I want to hear you whistlin' all de way up de path, you hear?"

"Yes'm," the boy mumbled.

Jessica suppressed her smile for the boy's sake. "Why does he have to whistle?"

Pearl went back to carving. "Oh, dat," she grinned again. "Let's me know he ain't snitchin' something he ain't ought to. If his mouth's full, he can't make no whistle. B'sides, he'll get his fill when de night is over. I'll make sure of dat, but for now, I got to worry about de folks dat's comin'."

Jessica did, too. She went in search of Betsy, and finally found the girl in one of the corner bedrooms, staring down through a window at the carriages that had begun to arrive in a steady stream.

"Ain't they pretty?"

"Yes, very." Jessica's reply was gentle but abrupt. There was simply too much to do for them to be standing there. "Betsy, Mama Lou wants you downstairs."

It took a little more coaxing to pry Betsy's attention away. The girl finally left when Jessica mentioned that she would have a better view of the pretty dresses downstairs.

Jessica lingered in the room only long enough to smooth the counterpane on the bed. In her mind, she could hear Mama Lou fussing, wanting to know where she had gone off to.

Head lowered, intent on hastening below as quickly as possible, she sped down the hall . . . and slammed right into Nick as he emerged from his room.

"What . . ." He grabbed hold of her shoulders to steady her.

"I'm . . . sorry . . ." she began, her stomach knotting in instant tension.

"Are you all right?"

"Yes." She wasn't. She couldn't even peer up at him. It had become a habit of late, a habit formed to spare herself the bite of his angry glares. "I'm sorry. I wasn't looking where I was going."

"Obviously," he intoned dryly.

His tone scraped her nerves. She told herself that she should be used to it by now. He rarely spoke to her anymore, but the few times he did, it was with a barely controlled irascibility that buffeted her heart.

A quivering sigh shook her body. "I have to go downstairs."

As if he had unexpectedly become aware that his hands still held her shoulders, he jerked them back to his sides.

"By all means," he scoffed, sweeping one arm out in a grand arch. "Don't let me stop you from doing what needs to be done."

His sarcasm bit deep. "Mama Lou is expecting me."

"Of course." His mouth turned up into a cold smile, its chill reflected in the steel of his eyes. "Run off, Jess. You're good at doing that."

She clamped her eyes shut, wounded and angered by his attack. For days and days, she had been walking on egg shells, afraid of displeasing him, of angering him, wary of his ever-present temper seething just below the surface of his controlled exterior.

She couldn't go on taking the brunt of his displeasure, she didn't think she deserved to. From the very start, he had told her that their relationship was that of a man and a woman. He had let her decide, as a woman separate from the bonded servant, what course they would follow. Her choice had been to go to his bed.

Now, for what she considered to be valid reasons, she chose not to be his lover, and he was as belligerent as some stallion who had been denied his favorite mare in heat. Clearly it was obvious that as long as her actions suited him, he was content and happy, but the minute she chose to do what she knew was best for her, his tolerance disappeared.

That riled her to no end, and she was tired of meekly accepting his behavior. Her eyes snapped open and she lifted her chin to glare right back at him.

"You make me sorry I ever gave myself to you. I've tried to explain, I've done my best to apologize. I don't know what else to say or do to make you understand."

Before she drew her next breath, his arm snaked about her waist and he swung her into his room. Silent, commanding, towering over her with eyes glittering darkly, he locked his fist into her hair, angled her head up and kissed her, hard.

Her world was tilted off balance, and she clung to his jacket, scrambling internally to find her equilibrium. It wasn't possible. His passion was fierce, wild, stunning her into immobility while her mind sought to make sense of the moment.

To be in his arms was a wonder she thought never to experience again. The lonely nights and tense, sad days dissolved as his hands played over her hips pulling her tightly against him, demanding that she respond. She wanted to. She loved him and wanted him.

"This is what you can do," he growled roughly.

The lure of that ate at her willpower. How easy it would be

for her to surrender to him, to the desire he so effortlessly created within her.

"No," she choked out, struggling to free herself even as her body yearned to remain. "We can't do this. Let me . . . go."

He went utterly still and for a long moment, he stared down at her, saying nothing, doing nothing, his fingers biting into her flesh. Before her dismayed gaze, his face hardened, and then he swore viciously and shoved her away. In his eyes, she saw accusation and something that looked like pain.

"Stay away from me, Jess." He ground his teeth, and rasped, "If you know what's good for you, you will stay the hell out of my way."

He stormed off, leaving her paralyzed with alarm. His fury was beyond anything she had ever witnessed and it frightened her. Shaken, she pressed the back of her hand to her lips and dragged in a teary breath before she slowly closed the door to his room and went below.

Thankfully, it was easy enough to do as he had demanded. Her duties for the night were primarily assisting any of the ladies who might need help with a torn hem or drooping curls. As she hurried up and down the stairs, her path never crossed his. She didn't think her benumbed nerves could have survived if she had. Her heart tugged her in one direction, common sense in the other, her rare temper in yet a third. To have withstood more of his anger would have only added to the strain of her internal battle.

As it was, a nauseating headache pounded across her forehead and she had to fight off the nervousness that hounded her every move. The gaiety surrounding her became abrasive. The music and voices seemed too loud, the laughter raucous. The combined scents of flowers and perfume turned stifling. She had to take a few moments for herself and treasure the solitude she so needed.

Making her way along the length of the upstairs hall, she anticipated the calming effects of the sable darkness to be found outside beneath the elms. She would have preferred the old rose garden, but it was out of the question for tonight.

She descended the first three steps of the stairway only to look down and find Sophia Marcheaux coming toward her, her wide, unattractive face drawn into disapproving lines.

"I've been looking for you," she declared.

Jessica stopped where she was. "Good evening, Mrs. Marcheaux."

"Bonsoir, bonsoir," Sophia retorted, waving the greeting away with an impatient hand. All the while she continued her way to the landing.

Jessica joined her and faced her squarely. "I was glad to hear of your recovery."

"Merci. A *petite maladie,* nothing more." Her hand fluttered about dismissively. "The doctors know nothing. They look, they poke about, they make their diagnosis. In the end . . ." She finished with one of her shrugs. "Let me look at you."

She made her inspection with an eye critical enough to make Jessica bite her upper lip. "You look terrible. *"Qu'est-ce qui s'est passé?"*

"Excuse me?"

"What happened? There are shadows beneath your eyes and you've lost weight."

Jessica didn't need to be told that she looked tired. "There's been an awful lot to do lately."

Sophia folded her arms over her chest and drew in her chins. "An excuse if I've ever heard one." Her gaze narrowed. "Now, tell me the truth. Something that will explain your appearance and Nicky's mood."

Jessica's brows lifted over rounded eyes. "His mood? I . . . I don't understand."

"Yes, you do. The last time I was here, Nick could hardly keep his eyes off you. He was in a grand mood. Now . . ." She threw her hands into the air. "Now, he is as vile as I have ever known him to be. Something is going on between the two of you. I want to know what it is."

With all her heart, Jessica did not want to delve into this very private matter. It hurt enough to have to live with it. To have to discuss it would dredge up the pain she was striving so hard to keep at bay.

"It's personal."

"Of course it is. Which is why I'm coming to you. If it weren't, I could have asked Anna."

The logic in that could have been humorous. "Mrs. Marcheaux—"

Sophia took hold of her arm and ushered her into the first room, Nick's.

"I don't think we should be in here," Jessica began, only to be cut off again.

"This is most likely the perfect place for us to be. I would say your troubles began in here."

Jessica dragged her gaze away, unwittingly to the bed. The huge four-poster stood as silent testimony to the truth of Sophia's words.

Her shoulders slumped in defeat as she turned and crossed to sit on the edge of the bed. "He's furious with me," she admitted in a low voice.

"I thought as much."

"Has he said anything?"

"No, but he's positively irate, although he's doing a good job of hiding it. I suspected you were responsible."

It didn't sit well with Jessica to be blamed for Nick's disposition. "A person makes his or her own happiness. Nick choses to be the way he is."

"And what way is that?"

"Unreasonable." Her indigo eyes flashed then unexpectedly filled with tears.

Sophia heaved a sigh that expanded her huge chest to enormous proportions. "Ah, Jessica, *petite,*" she crooned, coming to sit beside Jessica on the bed. "Has he made you so unhappy?"

She wanted to say yes, but she couldn't.

"Tell me what has happened?" Sophia coaxed.

Surprisingly, Jessica found it remarkably easy to confide. Once she began, the words came forth in a steady stream that related everything up until that night.

"No wonder he's put out," Sophia exclaimed. "You've afflicted him where he's most vulnerable."

Jessica's head snapped about and she stared opened mouth.

"No, not there," Sophia muttered. "Although, after having had you, he's sure to be uncomfortable these days. No, you've managed to strike him where it really counts, his beliefs."

"I don't understand."

Sophia wiggled her squat figure about, as if settling in to do battle. "Do you remember the talk we had when I first met you?"

How could Jessica ever forget it. The woman had nearly knocked her off her feet with her generous, albeit, unusual ideas. "Yes."

"Among other things, I told you that Nicholas is a man true to his beliefs. Unfortunately, his convictions about women are deeply rooted. You didn't then, nor do you now, adhere to any of the usual categories he expects of the women in his life. He's angry because of that."

"I don't mean to be rude, Mrs. Marcheaux, but your nephew is angry because I won't lie down for him."

"Of course he is. He's a man. What do you expect?" Sophia's face softened. "But if that was all he wanted, he could find it anywhere and save himself a great deal of aggravation."

"He's just being stubborn."

"True."

"And single-minded."

"True."

"I've become a challenge to him and he thrives on challenges."

"You're right again. And again I tell you, if Nicky didn't care, truly care, he wouldn't bother. He's too busy with life in general to expend energy on something that's meaningless."

Jessica wished she could believe Sophia. In her heart she couldn't. "I don't know."

"You love him, don't you?"

"Yes."

"Good."

"I'm glad you think so. It's brought me nothing but heartache."

Sophia rose and jerked her bodice into place. "Life is long, Jessica. Love is never wasted."

Normally Jessica would have agreed, but long after Sophia had bustled from the room, she considered the worth of the woman's statement. Thinking of Nick, she was of a mind that love was useless.

Mathew watched Anna smile up into Arturo Trudeau's face and decided that love was a futile, useless affair. He gripped his hand about his drink and swallowed the curse that threatened to explode.

Bloody hell. He should have never accepted the invitation to attend, but he hadn't been able to force himself to decline. Even knowing that Anna's attentions were elsewhere, he had wanted to be with her.

The best he had been able to manage was a quick hello and then fleeting glimpses of her as she flitted from one room to the next, the quintessence of feminine energy and charm. More often than not, Trudeau was on the receiving end of all that attention.

What did you expect? he asked himself. He had seen the way she had behaved with the man, her eyes glowing, her manner exhilarated. Still, he loved her, desired her. So he had scribbled his acceptance to the invitation on a note and sent it back, damning himself all the while.

He turned from his thoughts and from the sight of Anna's smiling face. He glanced down at his glass. He needed another drink if he was going to make it through the night.

"That's my best bourbon you're frowning at," came Nick's irritable voice.

Mathew looked up, seeing a touch of his own dissatisfaction reflected on his friend's face. "Don't take offense. The bourbon's as good as it always is. I'm not in the right frame of mind to appreciate it, though."

Nick shoved one hand into his pants pocket. "What's wrong with you?"

"Nothing that this won't cure." He lifted his drink in a silent toast.

"You look like hell," Nick observed.

Mathew angled his blond head to one side, too disgusted to tolerate such honesty. "Don't mince words, Nick," he grated, his words saturated with sarcasm. "And you have no room to talk."

Nick's eyes narrowed. "I have my reasons."

"Well, so do I."

"Anna."

It wasn't a question, but a statement of fact that pricked Mathew's ire further. "Am I that obvious?"

The broad line of Nick's shoulders arched with a shrug. "Let's just say that I know you and I know the situation."

"That's a fine way to describe what's happening."

Nick sent his gaze to his sister standing beside Trudeau. "Does she know how you feel?"

"No." Bitterness rose up in Mathew at the confession, a bitterness he turned on Nick. "And I bloody well do not need any advice from you."

"I wasn't about to give you any," Nick returned in a nasty tone.

"What's this?" Sophia demanded to know.

She sidled up to them, all smiles and shrewd eyes. Mathew sucked in several breaths in an attempt to get a grip on his temper.

"You two look like the dregs of the earth," she stated gaily.

Nick scoffed and turned his head to glare at the far wall. Mathew gave into the sarcasm that seemed to come so naturally. "Flattery must run in the family."

"Don't take that tone with me, Mathew Bennett," Sophia admonished in a manner that spoke of familiarity. "If you feel as bad as you look, you had best run on home."

"I might very well do that."

"What's keeping you?" She didn't bother to wait for an answer. "I suspect it's something, or rather, someone that's holding you here."

"Sophia, if you please," Nick muttered.

"I don't please. You two should see yourselves, *mes amis,* standing here, glowering at the world." She gave into a hearty laugh. "Ah, the follies of youth. You waste precious time and energies on such trivialities."

"Tantia, what are you going on about?" Nick demanded to know.

She screwed up her face until it resembled a pugnacious bulldog. "I never took you to be stupid, Nicky. Nor you either, Mathew. But you're both so caught up in your own misplaced pride that you're blind to the obvious. Heaven help the women in your lives."

With that, she moved on, her laughter trailing behind her and igniting Mathew's fuse. "God damn it." Not caring who saw or heard him, he shoved his glass into Nick's hand and stormed from the room. If he didn't get some air that second, he would explode.

The pewter gray night was calming in that its distorting qualities distracted him. He found a bench on the edge of the formal garden and sank down, feeling as exhausted as he had ever felt. Just as suddenly as he sat, he stood, deciding that he should follow Sophia's suggestion and go home. That pride she had so cheerfully condemned refused to allow him to linger any longer.

He stalked toward the front of the house, intent on having his carriage summoned. With every step he took, his mood darkened, until the heat of his anger was near scorching. He thought it grotesquely humorous that Anna should choose that very moment to put herself in his path.

"Mathew, where are you going?" she called, advancing quickly.

"Home." He brushed past her.

"Why?"

He ignored her query.

"Mathew, I saw you leave. You looked angry."

"I am angry."

She ran to catch up, retracing her steps. "Wait. What's wrong?"

He continued, knowing that if he stopped, he would vent every thought, every feeling tearing him apart.

"Why are you angry?" she panted, catching hold of his arm.

He shook off her fingers, praying for control. "Go back to your party, Anna."

"No," she retorted, reaching for him again. This time, she managed to take a firm grasp on his jacket. Her intent was obviously to spin him about to face her. His momentum and greater weight turned the motion to the opposite and she was whirled around to stand before him. He was forced to come to an abrupt halt.

"What is the matter with you?" she demanded, planting her hands on her hips and tilting her angry face up to his.

That was all it took. That delicate expression of pique pushed him over the edge.

"I'll tell you what's the matter," he stated through clenched teeth. "You're willful and headstrong." Shaking with each word, he raised a hand and pointed a finger just below her nose. "You react on pure emotion, disregarding logic and reason. You're a plague to mankind, with your easy smiles and your careless manner and you wouldn't know what's good for you if it came up and bit you on your ass, which is probably just as well since you're blind to boot."

"Blind!" Her eyes flashing even in the dimmed light beneath the surrounding trees, she yelled, "How dare you? Who do you think you are calling me all these names?"

"I'm your friend."

"No, you're not! You're not behaving like my friend. You're going on like some crazed maniac."

"Crazed." He nodded, an unholy light glinting his eyes. "Crazed. Yes, I'm feeling crazed and with some very good reasons."

"I don't want to hear them." Unexpectedly, she spun about and began to leave.

He caught her before she could take a single step. "Oh, no you don't. You started this and I'm going to damn well see that you finish it."

"Finish what?" she railed back, her chest heaving. "Let me go."

"No. I've let you go too many times. But not tonight. To-night, you're going to stay and reap the consequences of your idiocy."

"Idiocy?!"

She was infuriated and he didn't care. There was only one thing that mattered.

He crushed her to him, pinning her body to his with a force that brooked no argument. His mouth came down on hers and he finally . . . *finally* kissed her with all the emotions he had kept hidden for months.

Love warred with fury, desire with frustration. Slanting his mouth over hers, he poured his heart and soul into the kiss, wanting her to feel all he was feeling; the pain, the confusion, the hunger and the love. Most especially, the love.

His arms tightened, wringing a stifled moan from her. The sound was like so much debris in the night, a meaningless nothing before the onslaught of his passion. That passion had held his mind and body in thrall for countless days and nights, a passion he would carry with him until the day he died. And maybe even beyond that. His love for Anna was boundless and all-consuming.

"Mathew," she managed to gasp around frantic little breaths. "What . . . what are you doing?"

"Kissing you." He matched actions to words again, this time breaching the sweet barrier of her lips to plunge his tongue into her mouth. Her body became limp in his embrace and he pressed her indecently close, letting her feel the proof of his desire.

"You little idiot," he rasped, his mouth hovering over hers. "How long did you think I could go on?"

Blinking again and again, she struggled for coherency. "I . . . I didn't think. I didn't . . ."

The truth of that stung, so much so that he shoved her away. "Well, think about this the next time you decide to exercise what little brains you have."

He stalked away, wanting more than anything else on earth to continue kissing her, but he denied himself that pleasure. He was only human, a man with very definite limits. He had reached his for the night, and possibly for every night to come.

Chapter Twenty-five

Anna's stomach lurched, her lips burned. Rage and wonder and a sense of helplessness assailed her, churning her emotions into a spiraling tempest. Pressing trembling fingers to her mouth, she stared through the darkness to Mathew's retreating figure and thought to call him back. She wanted to rail at him, to pound her hands on his chest and demand explanations for his behavior.

He had kissed her . . . after he had accused her of all manner of things. The cad! The insufferable, arrogant cad. How could he call himself her friend and then do as he had?

"I hate you," she burst out, clenching her hands into fists. "You make me so angry I want to . . . to . . ." She whirled about, not certain what she wanted to do.

Her pace marked with her ire, she hurried back into the house, not stopping to talk to anyone until she found Clarice in a quiet corner of the parlor.

"Do you know what that man did?" she asked, her hushed voice vibrating.

Clarice gave her a pleasant smile. "I assume you mean Arturo."

"No, I mean Mathew Bennett."

"Who?"

"Mathew Bennett."

"Oh, yes, that neighbor of yours. Tall, blond hair, handsome in a serious sort of way." Clarice's eyes narrowed. "He's apparently done something to upset you."

"He's done more than that. He's . . ." Anna broke off when several couples wandered in amidst a round of laughter. Out of politeness alone, Anna was forced to exchange pleasantries, but as soon as possible, she excused herself and Clarice. The latter she led into Nick's library.

"What is this all about?" Clarice asked when Anna shut the door.

"I wish I knew."

"Well, something has happened."

Anna swept across the room, flexing her fingers as if that small motion would alleviate the tension rifling her nerves of strength. "Yes, something has happened." At one of the windows, she turned to face Clarice. "He kissed me."

Her declaration met with a casual one-shouldered shrug. "So? It isn't as if you haven't been kissed. And more."

"I know that," Anna insisted. "But this is Mathew, for heaven's sake. He's never kissed me before. He's never done anything like this."

"I see." Clarice took a seat in one of the chairs set before Nick's desk. "This bothers you?"

"Of course it bothers me. I wasn't expecting it."

"Some surprises are nice, I think."

"Not this one. He accused me of being stubborn and willful. He was incensed." She closed her eyes briefly as she shook her head. "And it wasn't a casual, brotherly kiss. He was in the throes of a terrible passion."

"Do tell? This *is* interesting."

"It isn't, Clarice. It's absurd. It's . . . it's ridiculous. . . ."

It's . . ." She sputtered to a stop, unable to find the words for what she was feeling.

She wished she could understand what had happened. There was no doubt that Mathew wanted her. She could still feel the hard evidence of his arousal as it had pressed against her belly. Her insides braided tautly at the memory.

It was difficult to think of him in that manner, earthy, sexual, driven by desire. All her life, she had accepted Mathew as a calm, staid friend. She had never attributed passion to his nature. Mentally she gave a scoffing laugh. Apparently she had been horribly mistaken in her impressions. Mathew was most certainly capable of raging, consuming emotion.

Was it love, as Arturo had claimed?

Mathew was not one to give his emotions lightly. He got riled with her often enough, but not like tonight. She had never seen him in such a state, his body shaking, a scalding fire in his eyes. And the straining length beneath his pants had been telling in and of itself.

The stain of a rare blush heated her face. Imagine Mathew reacting to her that way. As serious and faithful as he was, it was disconcerting.

A stirring sensation raced over her skin, bringing with it a shocking suspicion that Arturo had been right. Could Mathew, who had always been so dear and so infuriating, truly love her? He hadn't said as much, but what other explanations could there be for his actions of late and particularly tonight?

Out of nowhere, came a headiness that took her by surprise and confusion set in once again. She gripped her head and moaned right out loud.

"Now what's the matter," Clarice queried.

"I'm so bewildered. I swear, I don't know what to do."

Clarice rolled her eyes. "Why do you have to do anything?"

"I can't leave things as they are."

"Why not?"

Anna dropped her hands. "Because he's my friend. I feel *something* for him."

"What?"

"I . . . I don't know. That's the problem."

Coming to her feet, Clarice contained a sigh of barely concealed annoyance. "The only problem I see is that you've let this go to your head. It's just a kiss, Anna. You're making too much of it. Come back to the party and cease this childish nonsense."

Anna drew her brows into a insulted frown. "There is nothing childish about this, Clarice."

"Perhaps, but think of what has you so worried. A kiss, Anna, nothing but a harmless kiss."

It wasn't harmless. Not to Anna. Mathew had upended her entire life, and she resented Clarice making light of what amounted to an extremely important matter.

"You're right about one thing," she commented, put off by Clarice's attitude. "I will definitely think about it."

"You do that." Clarice came to her feet, her smile fixed, her gaze harder than Anna had ever seen it. "I'm going to return to your guests and have a good time."

Clarice swept from the room, doubting that a good time was possible. She had a wicked headache and everything she ate ignited her stomach. Even though the windows were opened to allow for the cool evening air to circulate, she was excessively uncomfortable. She had lost her patience hours ago, and it was all she could do to tolerate any more of the entire wretched affair.

She hated this so called party. Everywhere she looked, peo-

ple were milling about *her* house, scuffing the polished
floors, staining the table cloths. She fumed at their careless-
ness and resented their presence.

Hiding her rancor behind a pleasant facade, she surveyed a
group in the dining-room. She didn't know these people, she
didn't want to. Yet there they stood, eating her food and
drinking her wines.

The food *was* hers. Just as Bellefleur was hers. Even
though it wasn't legal as yet, she was through with waiting to
claim it. In her mind, the land, the house, the food, all of it
belonged to her, the legacy Francois DuQuaine should have
given her. His daughter.

Can you see me, Papa? she silently asked. Thinking of him
filled her with hate, and strangely enough, a humorous languor that bubbled up and seethed in her brain, suddenly making it difficult to concentrate. She lifted her wandering gaze
to the ceiling, then caught herself in the act and lowered her
eyes to the floor. Her father would be in hell. A fitting place
for him . . . and all these people.

Raking them with a narrowed glare, she silently decreed
that if the power were hers at that moment, she would have
them all thrown out. Of course, Nick was the only authority
that counted. He and Anna.

She suppressed a scoff. Damn the sniveling little twit, going on about a kiss as if it were the end of the world. Her
half-sister's head had to be stuffed with manure—Bellefleur's
best, straight out of the barn.

A chuckle parted her lips, easing some of her tension. She
had had enough of Anna's histrionic whining. She had had
enough of everything. She was going to find Nick.

Absently rubbing at the ache in her stomach, she mean-
dered from one room to the next, finding Nicholas at last in

the plantation office, one of the few rooms not overrun with the night's diversions.

"Oh, hello," she began, feigning surprise. "I didn't mean to intrude."

"What is it?" he asked, turning away from the window and his study of the night.

His reply made her bristle. He hadn't denied that she was indeed intruding on his privacy. "I was searching for a quiet place." Stepping into the office, she shut the door and affected a sigh of relief. "I see you have managed to find a few moments of respite yourself."

Unexpectedly, visions of her mother's dead body flashed through her mind. She blinked them away, momentarily startled and then oddly amused by the bloody images. "Do you mind terribly if I join you?"

Nick's jaw worked and for a few seconds, Clarice thought he was going to tell her to get out. "No." He gestured to one of the chairs. "Sit, if it pleases you."

"Thank you." Her movements a study in feminine grace, she sat, taking the time to arrange the folds of her skirt with exacting precision. That seemed to be an important thing to do, although she couldn't imagine why. When she looked up, it was to find Nicholas watching her every gesture.

"You don't seem to be having a pleasant time," she said, remembering to force sympathy into her words.

"It's been a long night."

"I think it's going to get longer. Your friends and neighbors are enjoying themselves."

"Bellefleur has always been known for its hospitality."

"I can attest to that. I would have thought, though, that you would be out there with them, having a good time."

"One would have thought that." His black brows lowering he added, "My mind is on other things tonight."

Clarice leaned back in her chair, wanting to give into the most irrepressible urge to laugh. Clamping down on the impulse, she said, "That explains a great deal."

"Such as?"

"Why you're frowning the way you are, why you're in this office instead of dancing." She didn't have a clue as to what was gnawing away at him. She didn't give a damn. It suited her purposes to have him think she was commiserating with him. Sitting forward, she gave him her best imitation of concern. "I understand how you feel."

His eyes narrowed. "Somehow, I doubt that."

"You shouldn't. I've had my share of grief and vexation. There have been times in the past when I have done exactly what you're doing now."

"And what, exactly, is that?"

She ignored the steely edge to his voice. "Seeking privacy in order to maintain." She let a smile soften her face. "It's very effective in controlling an unruly temper."

Nick shoved away from the window, disdain glazing his eyes to a flinty gray, indifference curling the corners of his mouth into a snide grin.

"Ah, yes, my unruly temper. It has been getting the better of me lately."

"I haven't wanted to mention it," she teased.

"You just did."

"Only because I care about you. We're friends."

Out of nowhere, Phillip's bloodstained face swam before her eyes. Like the image of her mother, it seemed real. Laughter welled up in Clarice's chest. How unusual that this should be happening. It was even more amazing that she wasn't frightened. In fact, she didn't feel anything in particular. Part of her mind felt slightly numb.

"Did I say something humorous?" Nick asked.

"No." She yanked in on her concentration. "I was just thinking that perhaps we can both get through the evening if we join ranks." Standing, she extended her hand his way. "I'll keep your mind from whatever is bothering you and you can keep me company amidst the throngs."

She knew she hadn't given him an alternative. Short of insulting her, he had no choice but to accept her offer. He did so, shaking his head as he tucked her hand into the crook of his elbow and escorted her from the room.

"If you can alleviate my mind, tonight, Clarice, than you are to be congratulated."

"Thank you, sir." The heady promise of success flowed through her. Giggling like a child, she pledged over the din of voices, "I will appease the demons that besiege you."

Phillip's image was suddenly there again to accompany her, his hacked up face loitering over her right shoulder. If she peered out the corner of her eye, she could make out the edges of his brutalized profile.

You're an idiot, Phillip. You're dead. Go back to hell where you belong.

"Clarice?"

Nick's voice jerked her back to herself. "I'm sorry. What did you say?"

"I asked if you would like something to drink?"

"Yes, thank you." Her throat was unaccountably dry, her skin overly sensitive. The pounding in her head had begun to worsen and the noise was reaching an unbearable level.

The champagne punch went far in helping her thirst and even seemed to help ease her headache. As for the music and unrelenting voices, there didn't seem to be anything she could do about that except go outside or upstairs.

The softness of her bed beckoned with its comfort offering a haven for her mind, a place where she could dream and . . .

She peered about, shaken that her thoughts had wandered so haphazardly. Instantly, she collected herself and forced herself to pay attention.

Going to bed was out of the question. She couldn't leave Nicholas. He was where she wanted him, by her side. The obvious solution was to take a stroll in the dark, a move she could use to her advantage if she was ever going to begin her seduction.

"Why don't we leave all this for a few minutes?" she suggested. "The night is cool enough to lighten your mood." She lifted her gaze to Nick's, only to find that his face was drawn into a frightful mask, his jaw rigid and unyielding. Beneath her fingers, the muscles of his arm coiled with an iron tension.

Drawing in a quick breath, she followed his line of vision and damnably, found it focused on the maid, Jessica, as she made her way toward the stairs.

"Nicholas?" He didn't so much as glance her way. "Nick? I could use some fresh air."

With what looked like a supreme effort, he turned away from the sight of the maid, shocking Clarice with the cold virulence chiseled into his face.

"I'd like to step outside for a while," she whispered, exercising every bit of her self-restraint to keep her voice level. It was for naught. Nick calmly, carefully disengaged her fingers from around his arm.

"You'll have to forgive me, Clarice," he snarled. "I'm terrible company tonight."

Fury, raw and unbridled ripped into Clarice's body, tearing at her sanity, ripping away at her self-restraint. She stared at Nick, hating him as she hated their father. Instinctively, she reached for the pistol that she wished she had in her pocket.

Silently, she swore and cursed, and damned Nick to an everlasting abyss of pain and suffering. He had been manageable, responsive to her wiles. Then a single look at Jessica and he had turned cold.

"You're wonderful company," she contradicted a little shrilly, willing to say anything, do anything to prevent his departing. "I wouldn't want to be with anyone else." She tried to tug at his arm once more. "Come outside with me, or we can go up to my room if you like. You'll be more yourself away from all these distractions."

"Not tonight." He jammed a hand back through his hair. "Perhaps another time."

In a blazing rage, she watched him stalk off. If she could kill him now, she would be a happy woman. Just thinking about his warm blood on her hands made her draw in a contented breath.

His time would come soon enough, after they were *married*. The trouble was, she would never be able to seduce him if all he could think of was some stupid, insipid girl.

Damn her, damn her, damn her!

Clarice whirled, and came face to face with her mother. Mouth slack and bloody, the transparent visage swayed before her eyes while it swirled through her mind. The sensation was disorienting and yet amusing in a bizarre way.

Not caring what anyone thought, not even aware that people were about, she bent over and laughed, venting the absurd humor that had plagued her ever since she had killed Phillip.

Poor little Jessica. You're going to have to die. Poor, poor little Jessica.

Her brain repeated the phrase again and again, the unspoken words marking a perfect cadence to the rhythm of her chuckles. Oblivious to the curious stares of those around her, she left the room, feeling a comforting heat rise up to bathe her skin.

The silence was to be treasured. It soothed Jessica's jumpy nerves as she and Betsy finished setting the parlor to rights. Dawn was just making itself known through the windows and Jessica longed for her bed.

She had never seen such revelry as had gone on last night and into the early morning. The food had been plentiful, the wine even more so. People had laughed and danced and carried on with a fervor that had to have been exhausting.

She felt her own exhaustion. In the wake of everyone's departure, she and Betsy and Mama Lou had spent the hours cleaning. Now, the muscles in the small of her back ached, and she smothered one yawn after another.

The anticipation of sleeping, if only for a little while, was tempting. She hoped it would be possible. Thoughts of Nick were constant, infusing her mind with lost dreams and her body with a restlessness that made true rest difficult.

"If it's all right with you, I'm going to lie down for a bit," she told Mama Lou.

"Sounds good to me. We're goin' to have to be up soon enough."

Too tired to say anything more, Jessica made her way to her room, not even bothering to remove her shoes before she slumped onto her narrow bed. In seconds, despite her disquieting dreams of Nick, she was asleep.

The touch of a hand on her shoulder roused her. She awoke groggily, disoriented and sluggish. It took her a long moment to realize that Clarice Johnston stood beside her bed.

"What . . . is there something wrong?" Blinking against the remnants of sleep, Jessica sat up, her muddled mind striving to make sense of the woman's presence. "What are you doing in here?"

Clarice smiled a serene smile. When she spoke, her voice was soft and lilting. "I've come to talk to you."

As sensible as that sounded to Jessica, it was extremely unusual. In her dealings with Clarice Johnston thus far, she had never know the widow to seek her out for anything. More often than not, the woman didn't even acknowledge her.

"You have to hurry," Clarice insisted.

Jessica sat straighter as she swung her legs over the side of the bed, noticing for the first time that the day was fairly new. She hadn't slept for very long. "Is there something wrong?"

"Yes. Come with me. Now."

Instantly, dread assailed her. Had something happened to Nick? Or Anna? "Mrs. Johnston—"

The widow grabbed hold of her arms and pulled her to her feet. "Get up you idiot and stop this nonsense." The gentle tones of her voice were replaced with a whiplash resonance. "There's no time to waste."

"For what?" Jessica's alarm grew, making cold fingers of fear trace up and down her back. "Mrs. Johnston, what is going on?"

"I'll tell you later. It's imperative that you come with me before the rest of the house wakes."

Instinct impelled Jessica to refuse. There was something wrong, but she sensed it had nothing to do with Nick or anyone in the house. Staring into the brown eyes, she saw a faraway, feverish look that was disturbing.

"Are you feeling ill? Do you want me to get you some tea?"

"No, no, no no no," Clarice muttered impatiently, digging her fingertips into her cheeks. "I don't need tea."

"Perhaps I should send for the doctor and—" She finished

on a gasp, shocked to that painful silence by the sight of a small pistol pointed at her head.

"You should shut up and come with me." Clarice's face tightening with ragged, ugly lines, she thrust the pistol up under Jessica's chin. "Do you understand?"

Every muscle and nerve in Jessica's body froze, held immobile by the worst terror she had ever experienced. The blood drained from her head with dizzying speed while her heart lurched and pounded furiously.

She could not believe this was happening, she could find no cause for this woman to hold her at gun point. A moan trembled in her throat. A gun!

The woman was crazed. Jessica had only to look into the brown orbs to see the burnished wildness that shimmered there as though focused on some inner sight.

"Please—"

She managed no more. The gun was jammed with cruel force into her throat, choking off precious air.

"We're going outside," Clarice instructed slowly. "And you will not make a single sound."

Afraid to nod, frightened to take a breath, Jessica did as she was told. She made her way from the house, Clarice's body a snug shadow behind. With her every step, she silently called to Nick, pleading with him to save her from this madwoman.

Clarice nodded toward the river. "That way."

Jessica swallowed hard, all the while furtively casting glances about. She could see no signs of activity anywhere. Everyone was still in the process of rising for the day.

"Where . . . where are we going?"

Silence.

"What . . . I don't understand."

More silence.

"Mrs. Johnston, please, if you'll tell me what's wrong."

It was useless. Jessica was left with her questions and fright and the longer they walked, the more desperate she became. Her mind, tormented by unreasoning fear, discarded the overall, and narrowed its focus to the minutest of details.

Mournful doves sang in the trees, dampness from the humid air chilled her skin, the widow's expensive shoes moved over the land in a crunching sound. She could smell the river in the distance. Everywhere, there was a sensation of solitude and stillness.

She was going to die.

The realization slammed into her consciousness like a heavy fist. On this beautiful, bountiful land, where she had come to know love and laughter, pride and self-respect, she was going to end her life ... without having told Nicholas that she loved him.

Tears flooded her eyes, doubling when she discovered that Clarice was herding her into the seclusion of the old rose garden. A sorrow of the soul crippled her heart, wounding her more deeply that she would have ever thought possible. Of all the special places on the plantation, the rose garden had come to mean the most to her.

How long ago had she picked that perfect bloom? The flower was to have heralded the coming of a new bride for Bellefleur, a fateful, fanciful symbol of the permanence and goodness the land. She had gained strength from the legend just as she had taken courage from the plantation. How pitiful that she should die in the very spot cherished for the essence of life.

"That's far enough."

She shut her eyes against Clarice's dictate, but she came to a stop and turned around to face her. A crazed, unearthly gaze peered back at her.

"Why are you doing this?" she got out in a choked whisper.

The gun dipped and wavered about as Clarice lifted her chin to an awkward, off-centered angle. "You have to go away, Jessica. You can't be here any longer."

"I haven't done anything wrong."

"You've upset Nicholas."

Hearing Nicholas's name mentioned now sent agonies of new regret through Jessica. "I . . . I didn't mean to."

Clarice's high pitched giggle rent the air. "You have to join my mother and Phillip."

Jessica flinched. "Phillip? St. James?"

"I can't allow you to interfere." As though speaking to herself, Clarice mumbled, "Everyone is always interfering. They won't leave me alone to let me have my due. That's all I've ever wanted, what was coming to me." Her mouth skewed to one side, her eyes to the other. To Jessica, she looked as demented as she sounded.

"I haven't interfered," she tried to explain.

Like a ferret singling out its prey, Clarice trained her slitted eyes on Jessica. "You have," she hissed. "And just like Phillip, you're going to die."

Horrible realization hit Jessica, stripping away whatever hope she had left. "You killed him. It was you!"

"Of course it was. The bastard shouldn't have been here."

"Oh, my God."

"Go ahead and pray. It won't do you any good."

If Jessica had any doubts that Clarice wouldn't pull the trigger, they were gone now. With all her might, she frantically sought some means of escape. "You don't have to kill me. I'll go away."

Mouth twisting from side to side, Clarice gave every appearance of considering the suggestion. "No," she finally said in the kind of conversational tone used when sitting down to tea. "No, this way is best. For you and for Anna, too, I think."

"Anna?" Jessica's horror was joined by disbelief and then a cold, raging anger. "No, you can't do this."

"I can do anything I like."

"But not to Anna." Anna was all that was good and kind. She didn't deserve to be murdered.

Breathing in great gasps, Jessica stared at the pistol, refusing to let this happen. Forsaking the certain danger to herself, she darted forward, managing to grab hold of the barrel of the gun. For the briefest moment, she caught Clarice by surprise. But only for those few short-lived seconds.

In the next heartbeat, the report of the pistol exploded into the clearing. Jessica's breath left her in a single exhale and she fell to her knees, stunned by the pain in her chest and the hideous realization that she was as good as dead.

The world whirled away from her as she fell forward. Gray mists covered her vision while she fought off the burning that consumed her body. From a distance she heard Clarice's demonic laughter and tears collected behind her closed eyelids.

Her last thought was of Nicholas.

Chapter Twenty-six

Nicholas came awake cursing. Sweat glistening his naked form, he sat up in a single move and shoved the tangled sheets from his legs. Angered with whatever had pulled him from sleep, he ground the heel of his hand into his forehead, the gesture doing nothing to alleviate the ache centered behind his eyes.

He had had an accursed night. He didn't begrudge Anna her party, but he hadn't been of a mind for entertaining. He hadn't been in a civil mood for days and it was Jessica's fault.

The little witch. Time and again he had caught sight of her last night. She had looked pale and tired. That had set him off. Having to watch her fetch and carry had been worse. His insides had knotted whenever she had come in sight. By the end of the evening, he had quite illogically wanted to strangle her for performing the duties to which she had been assigned. His ire had been such that he had turned and walked away from Clarice Johnston in the middle of a conversation.

His reasoning was gone. He was making no sense. He was tired and fed up and he didn't need to delve any further into the issue to know why.

"Jessica, you stubborn, self-righteous little witch." Every problem he had, starting with the hunger in his loins and ending with his inability to function with any semblance of normalcy, began and ended with her.

He'd had enough.

Flinging back the netting draped from the canopy, he hurried through his washing and dressing. Quickly, he pulled on his clothes, berating Jessica all the while. If she thought she had had the final word last night when she had put a stop to his kissing her, she could damn well think again.

In minutes, he was down the stairs. He was primed and ready to settle this mess between them once and for all. He refused to continue as he had, listening for the sound of her voice, unable to sleep or eat, dying a little every day with want of her. She had come into his life with her innocence and optimism and ripped his existence to shreds.

He thrust open the door to her room, heated words already forming, only to find that she wasn't there.

"Damn it." Where was she? The answer came at once.

"There's no hiding this time, Jess." He uttered the words on his way to the stables, his stride as purposeful as the stormy gleam in his eyes. Once mounted on his powerful stallion, he set off with every intention of hauling Jessica back to the house and making her understand exactly how things were going to be.

For the first time in days, he smiled. It was a nasty smile, its humor grounded in a purely male sensation of triumph and absolute command. He was going to make sure that Jessica understood that he wasn't one to be trifled with and he was going to enjoy every minute of it.

The sound of gunfire tore the grin from his face. Even over the thud of the stallion's hooves, he heard the single shot from a close distance, too close to be from anywhere other than the rose garden.

He sent the stallion into a full run, fearing suddenly for Jessica's safety. Ordinarily, there would be no cause for alarm, but St. James' murderer had yet to be found. A gruesome mental image of Jessica began to take shape. He shook it off, unwilling to picture her lying dead.

The stallion plunged into the clearing with its legendary rose bushes and what Nick saw was more hideous that any imagined vision. Jessica's was covered with blood, lying white and limp as Clarice struggled to drag her away.

Icy alarm tore at his soul and he hauled back on the reins, a mighty snarl tearing up from his chest. Clarice looked up then, and hovered in place, dropping Jessica's arm as if it had stung her.

"Jessica." Her name was a prayer as he ran to her side and went to his knees. Hands quick and sure, he checked her neck for a pulse, holding his breath, praying for her life, shaking with murderous intent.

The pulse was there, her chest rose and fell with her erratic breathing, but he didn't surrender to relief. That was beyond him.

Impaling Clarice with eyes as black as onyx, he surged to his feet. "Why?" There was no question that she was responsible. Goaded past caution, he grabbed hold of her arms and shook her until her hair tumbled down in chaotic disarray. "Why in God's name have you done this?"

Clarice's chocolate eyes filled with tears. "Stop it, you're hurting me."

"I should kill you now." By everything he held dear, he was tempted, but he wouldn't waste another fraction of a second on her. Throwing her to the ground, he spun back for

Jessica, going down on one knee to tenderly lift her into his arms.

"It's all right, love," he whispered. "I'll get you home."

From behind him, Clarice screamed and Nick had just enough time to see her attack with a knife clenched in her fist. He instinctively turned to shield Jessica from further injury and his arm caught the brunt of the blow, the blade slicing into his forearm before he could shove away to a safe distance.

Pain slashed up his shoulder and into his fingers. He ignored the scorching agony, scarcely able to settle Jessica on the mossy ground before Clarice came at him again.

"You've ruined everything," she screamed, her maniacal screech causing the stallion to rear and prance in a tight circle.

Nick deflected her blow with his arm, then captured her wrist. Even injured, his strength was superior to hers and he yanked the knife from her grasp and flung it away. Still, she continued to attack, curling her fingers into talons aimed at his face.

"You ruined it all," she spat, doing everything she could to extricate herself from the punishing grip of his hands. "It was going to be mine. It's supposed to be mine."

"What the hell are you talking about?" Not that he cared. She could rot in hell as far as he was concerned, but as long as she was intent on killing him, he was forced to endure her tirades.

"Bellefleur. It's mine!"

He stared at her in absolute awe, stunned by her claim. She was insane, deranged. In a quick, brutal move, he thrust her to stand at arm's length. "What madness is this?"

She wrapped her arms about her waist, gasping for breath. "It isn't nonsense. Bellefleur should have belonged to me."

Nick swore viciously, too angry and disgusted to tolerate more. With a last look at Clarice, he started back for Jessica.

"No. Leave her alone," Clarice commanded.

Into the silence came the sound of a pistol's hammer being cocked into place.

"Leave her alone or I'll put this last shot through her head."

Slowly he faced Clarice and the gun she held pointed straight at Jessica from several yards off. The distance was close enough for her to finish what she had begun.

Lethal, soul-rendering fury threatened to swamp him. His reflexes urged him to charge the pistol and end this now. Every instinct he possessed would let him do nothing to cause Jessica more harm. Forcing himself to a caution he did not want to tolerate, he remained where he was, considering the situation in its entirety.

He had no way of knowing if the pistol Clarice held was the same weapon she had used on Jessica. If it was, then it stood to reason that it was empty, its single shot already fired. That was of course, if it was the same weapon. He could see no other pistol lying about, but then again, he hadn't been aware that this one had been hidden in her pocket.

Common sense told him she held the same gun, and that she hadn't reloaded. However, he wasn't going to gamble Jessica's life on something so flimsy as an educated guess.

"What do you want?" he asked.

"I told you, the plantation."

"Why should I give it to you?"

One of Clarice's shoulders rose to meet her ear as she pulled her chin into her chest. "Because our father would have wanted it that way. He owed me that much."

Nick didn't think he heard correctly. "Our father?"

She nodded, blinked, nodded again. "You didn't know. You weren't supposed to. You were supposed to marry me."

The more Nick heard, the more confusing her tale became. "I never gave you any reason to think that we would wed."

"But you would have, you would have." She tipped her head from side to side. "Then I would have been mistress of Bellefleur. Now it's all for nothing."

Her reasoning, as far as it went, was seriously flawed. He would have never married her . . . had never entertained the slightest notion to take her to wife. How she could have imagined such a thing was beyond him.

"What does any of this have to do with my father?"

"He was my father."

"Who was?"

Clarice repeatedly clicked her teeth together, the sound accompanying a low humming in her throat.

Nicholas studied her carefully, wondering what had happened to this woman to send her over the edge. She was well and truly doddering, infantile sounds emanating from her lips, her mannerisms oddly aimless.

"Who was your father, Clarice?"

His query met with a burst of unbridled laughter. "Francois DuQuaine."

"The hell he was," Nick averred, gray fire glinting in his eyes. "And I'll be damned if I'll let you can lay claim to Bellefleur with that paltry means of extortion."

"It's true."

"Why the hell should I believe anything you say?"

"I'm not lying."

He scoffed and shook his head in disgust. "You're insane."

"I'm not insane!" she screamed, trembling with visible rage.

Off to Nick's side, the stallion shied nervously at the sudden noise. Nick spared him a quick look then drilled his gaze back to Clarice.

"If you're not insane, then put the pistol down. Let me take Jessica back to the house."

"No. It's time you learned that the same dear dead daddy that sired you and Anna sired me." Her hand shook with her uncontrolled trembling, but it never strayed far. It remained aimed at Jessica's head. "Francois was my father, only my mother never told him about me. Oh, no, not my sanctimonious mother. She was content to spread her legs for the bastard, give him her body. When he left, she was pregnant."

"Where was all of this supposed to have happened?" He was becoming increasingly frustrated. With each passing second, Jessica's life was ebbing away.

"In Baton Rouge." Squinting ever so slightly, she purred, "Months after your mother died, your father traveled there and found my mama. Did he ever mention her? A quadroon seamstress by the name of Josephine Bouchard?"

Nick stilled, his body tensing at the mention of the name. "Josephine Bouchard." He couldn't refute the importance of that woman in his father's life. "Your mother was Josephine Bouchard?"

"So you've heard of her. I wondered if Francois had ever confessed to anyone."

His father had, but he had never said anything about a daughter. Damn it all, a daughter. If what Clarice was saying was true, than he was facing his own half-sister.

He wanted to refute her assertions. His conscience would let him. Clarice had all the facts concerning his father's time in Baton Rouge correct, and as far as Nick knew, his father had told no one else of Josephine.

Questions clashed with myriad emotions . . . none of which he had time for. He clamped down on his inner turmoil and shoved away any extraneous notions. The process gave rise to a clear and sudden insight.

"You planned this from the start. Your meeting Anna was some sort of contrivance to get you here."

With her free hand, she plucked at her mane of hair. "Rather clever, don't you think?"

"How did you know she was going to be in New Orleans?"

"I didn't. Luck was with me. And if it hadn't been, I would have managed another way. All that matters is that I'm where I belong." Her smile slipped, her gaze dulling with all the appearance of it pulling in on itself.

Nick lunged for her in that second, slamming his body into hers. The force of the impact sent them crashing to the ground, the pistol flying free of her hand.

Again and again, she shrieked and cried out. Using every bit of her energy, she squirmed and twisted until Nick levered himself to his feet, dragging her with him.

"See what you've done," she shouted. "I hate you. I hate you!" Low, rumbling sounds spewed from her throat. "Go away, Phillip, you're dead, you're in hell."

Nick held her tightly only to have her sink her teeth into his hand. With unexpected strength, she wrenched away and flung herself wildly about the clearing, never seeing the stallion in her path. The skittish horse reared, adding his enraged shrieks to Clarice's.

"Look out!" Nick yelled.

She fled from the voice, tried to escape the horse. Stumbling in her confusion and haste, she collided with the hooves pawing the air. Her head took the worst of the blows, and she crumbled into a heap. The stallion screamed, arched his neck for attack and finally landed with all his weight on her still form.

Nick grabbed hold of the reins, trying to calm the beast.

Ears flattened to his head, the horse quivered, reared again, and then settled beneath Nick's soothing hand. Only then did Nick look to Clarice.

It wasn't necessary to check if she was dead. Her head was bent at an impossible angle, her eyes open and staring at the sky.

Deep rooted compassions tugged him toward sorrow. A person was dead, his *half-sister* was dead. . . . Anger buffeted him from all directions, he staved off his questions and his mourning for another time. Jessica was hurt, she needed him *now.*

To his utter relief he found her still breathing. As carefully as he could, he gathered her close, mounted the stallion and rode for home. As never before, he prayed.

Mama Lou and Aunt Sophia met him as he came through the front door.

"Oh, my Lord above," the housekeeper cried.

"Send for the doctor," Nick instructed, holding his precious, precious burden close to his heart.

Mama Lou rushed off to do as she was told, leaving Sophia to ask, "What happened?"

"Clarice tried to kill her."

"Mon Dieu!"

"I'll need your help, *Tantia."* He took the stairs two at a time, Sophia close behind.

"Cela va sans dire, of course, of course." She sped down the hall to open the door to his room.

Between the two of them, they removed Jessica's clothes and found the bullet wound in her right shoulder.

"This doesn't look good, Nicky," Sophia whispered.

Sitting on the edge of the bed, Nick took one of Jessica's hands in his own, appalled at how chilled she was. Tenderly, he smoothed her hair back from her face, willing her to open her eyes.

Anna's voice sounded from the doorway. "What's going on? Mama Lou is crying and carrying on about blood, and . . ." Her words choked off as she neared the bed. White-faced, she stared from Jessica to Nick, her shock and confusion plain to read.

"There was a problem . . . I don't know what," Sophia explained gently. "Clarice tried to kill her."

"Clarice?" Anna's horrified gaze riveted to Jessica again as if she could find answers there. "I don't understand."

"I'll tell you later," Nick said.

"Where's Clarice now?" Anna demanded.

"Dead." He wouldn't say more. It wasn't the right time, and he couldn't think past Jessica. "Wake up, love." Thankfully, the bleeding had stopped. "Can you hear me, Jess?"

"Let's get her washed before the doctor arrives," Sophia suggested.

The minutes crawled by, becoming eons before a half hour had elapsed. Nick remained at Jessica's side, peripherally aware that his aunt and his sister came and went, readying the room with bandages and hot water for the doctor. And with each expired second, for each minute that Jessica lay unconscious, his heart shrank and shriveled until tears came to his eyes.

"Where the hell is the doctor?" he grated, after what felt like forever.

Jessica stirred, turning her head as she moaned.

Nick exhaled in a single breath, his heart pounding, his fear slaked just enough to allow for normal breathing. Bending low, he held her hand and whispered, "I'm here, Jess. I'm here."

"Nick." She sighed his name even before her eyelids fluttered.

"You'll be all right."

Her eyes slowly opened, the blue orbs dulled by pain and fever. "Nick."

That seemed to be all she could say. It was enough for Nicholas.

"You've been shot, love, but you're going to be fine. I've sent for the doctor."

She nodded and held onto his hand as tightly as she could. "Clarice . . ."

"I know." He didn't want her using her energy by talking.

"No . . . no . . ." Her face pulled into a agonized grimace, her teeth gritted, her eyes clenched shut.

"Easy, love. Breathe deeply."

She ignored his command, struggling to get the words out. "She killed Phillip St. James."

Anna's breath caught.

"She . . . she's going to kill Anna."

Anna crossed to the bedside and, sitting, ran a soothing hand over Jessica's forehead. "I'm here, Jessica. She hasn't hurt me."

Jessica lifted her gaze to Nick. He saw the seeking, probing query in her gaze, silently asking him for the truth.

"Anna is safe, I promise. Clarice won't be hurting anyone again."

The pressure of Jessica's grip on Nick's hand lessened. The sigh she gave could not be mistaken for anything other than relief. "Are you all right?"

"Yes. Don't worry about me."

She smiled weakly, tears pooling in her eyes. "I'm glad you're unharmed. I was so afraid . . ." She broke off as another seizure of pain gripped her. "Nick." His name was torn from her lips, issued on a rasping, suffocating moan.

He sank down beside her and gathered her into his embrace. "I know, love, I know. There's nothing we can do until the doctor gets here." If he could take her pain upon himself he would, a hundred times over. All he could do was hold her and give her his strength.

It wasn't nearly enough, and nothing at his disposal, not money nor position nor power, could ease her suffering. Never in his life had he felt so useless. Feeling the frightful trembling in her body, he knew he would sacrifice all he had to insure her well being.

The spasm dimmed enough to allow Jessica a deep breath. She lay back in his arms and tipped her face up toward his, her expression one of desperation.

"I have to tell you."

"Save your strength, Jess."

She shook her head, feebly clutching his shirt with her left hand. "No, I don't want to . . . to die without you knowing."

"You're not going to die," he insisted, his voice as rough as hers, his face rigid and drawn. "Do you hear me? I won't let you die."

Her words tumbled forth as if he hadn't said anything. "You have to know. . . ." Her fingers tightened. "I love you. I love you and I wish I could have been the kind . . . the kind of woman . . . you needed."

Nick stared into her ashen features, the face that had become so dear to him. Her declaration tore at his heart. Too late, he had come to realize that she was everything to him.

"Jessica, listen to me—"

"No, let me say . . . what I have to say." Her gaze frantically searched his, willing him to see and understand. "Too often, we go through life . . . unsure of what is real and what isn't ... afraid to speak the truths we do know. I ... I can't go on ... without telling you ... You gave me everything ... happiness, friendship, self-respect ... a home." A soft smile curled her lips. "Bellefleur is the first home I've ever had." She coughed, her voice wavering to a mere hint of sound. "If I could stay here forever, I would, loving you. Always, loving ... you ..."

Before she could finish, she went slack in his arms.

"No!" Nick yelled, laying her on the bed, afraid to see death's stillness claim her.

He didn't bother blinking back the tears that gathered. When the doctor arrived, he turned to the man with rare and burning emotions crystalizing his eyes.

"How is she?"

At the deep sound of Arturo's voice, Anna looked up from her lap and nodded. "Sleeping peacefully. Nick is with her now. The doctor said she'll be fine in a week or so."

He entered the parlor slowly, his gaze probing through the curtain-dimmed afternoon light filtering into the room. "I'm glad to hear that. She was most lucky."

In more ways than one, Anna thought. Feeling slightly uncomfortable, she watched Arturo as he sat beside her on the settee and couldn't help but be reminded of Jessica's words. She had spoken of truth and love and what was real and what wasn't.

"You look tired," he said.

"I am. It's been an awful day. First with Jessica and then with ... Clarice." In her heart, she blamed herself for having brought Clarice's madness to Bellefleur.

"Your brother told me of the mishap."

"I'd call it a disaster. Jessica is wounded so terribly."

"And your brother's arm?"

She lifted her hand in a vague gesture. "The doctor took several stitches."

Arturo laid a comforting hand along her shoulder. "You had no way of knowing."

She smiled a little bitterly, wondering if she wore her guilt for all to see. "I'm trying to convince myself of that. I keep thinking, though, that I should have seen the malice in her."

Nick had taken a few minutes to relate all that had happened with Clarice. Anna still found it hard to believe that anyone would go to such extreme, reckless lengths.

"I should have detected something that hinted at what she was really trying to do. Aunt Sophia did. She said that Clarice was peculiar, but I was too bent on believing what I wanted to believe."

"That wasn't your fault, Anna."

"When I think of how blindly I trusted her, I want to kick myself. It was stubborn, vain pride on my part."

"Oh, Anna, you are too hard on yourself."

She lifted a dark brow his way. "I don't think so. If I hadn't been so eager to have things my own way, perhaps I would have listened to Aunt Sophia, maybe I would have been more observant, less trusting. Clarice would have never come here to Bellefleur."

Arturo stroked his fingers up her neck in a soothing motion. "Someone as deranged as Clarice would have succeeded in any way she could have. If not through you, then in some other way. Through no fault of yours, you were the victim of her insanity, too." When she looked unconvinced, he added, "She had everyone fooled, Nick included."

What he said was true. She hadn't been alone in her ignorance. There was some solace to be had in that. "I suppose you're right. At least I'd like to think so."

"Clarice was a cunning, shrewd, insane woman. You couldn't be responsible for her actions, only your own."

She sighed heavily, gazing into his ocean blue eyes. He was so good to offer comfort. He was a good man, as good as he was handsome.

In an abrupt move, she rose and paced to one of the windows, levering the thick curtain aside to stare out over Bellefleur's lawn. The scene was a perfect harmony of colors and textures, lines and forms. Taken as a whole if offered a sense of serenity that had always been there, but one that Anna had never accepted.

"Have you told him yet?" Arturo asked from behind.

Letting the curtain fall, she faced him. "Told who what?"

His stride as powerfully male as it always was, he came forward. "Mathew Bennett. Have you told him yet that you love him?"

Anna stared in absolute amazement, her eyes rounding to enormous proportions. How had he discerned such a thing? She had only made the discovery herself hours ago. Jessica's heart-wrenching avowals about what was real in life and what wasn't had made her realize the truths that had lain dormant within herself.

She loved Mathew. As impossible as that was for her to admit, she did, and with such a sense of joy that she wanted to twirl about in gay abandon. She hadn't seen love for what it was.

She had viewed her fury and annoyance with Mathew as bothersome emotions, nothing more. It had taken that tempestuous kiss last night for her to even begin to suspect that he loved her, and that she loved him. That and the confessions of a woman who thought herself dying.

"How did you know?" she finally asked.

Arturo spread his hands wide, letting them come to rest on

her arms. "I've known for a while. It was simply a matter of time before you realized it on your own."

She gripped her hands together and stared at the lacing of her fingers. It was extremely disconcerting discussing the man she loved with the man who had taken her to bed. "I'm just beginning to realize a great many things, things I should have known a long time ago."

"That's all part of life, little one. What do we have to say for ourselves if we do not learn as we live?"

He was impossibly understanding, and she liked him more now than she ever had. "I'm sorry," she said, giving him her first smile of the day.

"For what?"

"For having it end this way between us." She wouldn't be human if she didn't wish that it could have been different for them. Try as she may, though, she felt no feelings of love for him.

"This is the best way for it to end, princess, with no rancor or hostility. Besides, we both knew it wouldn't last forever."

Yes, she knew that. Arturo, with all his sensual charm and gracious wit, was not a man to marry. "I'd like to think of you as my friend, if you'll let me."

Taking her chin in his hand, he raised her lips to his. "You will always have a place in my heart as my very dear friend." Ever so lightly, he brushed his lips over hers one last time.

She accepted the kiss for what it was, a token of their time together, a memento of the regard they held for each other.

"Promise me something," he asked.

"If I can."

"If you ever need anything, if there is ever anything I can do for you, promise that you will send word."

Helpless tears came to her eyes. "Will you promise me something in return?"

"If I can."

She laid a hand along his cheek. "Promise me you will find someone to love, someone who will love you the way you deserve to be loved."

In answer, he hugged her close. When he released her, he tucked her hand into the crook of his arm and walked with her to the door.

"If you'll have someone see to my things, I'll make arrangements to leave sometime in the next day or so," he said.

She would be sorry to see him go. He would always be special to her. But she knew finally that her life was with Mathew. If he would have her. She could only hope that his love for her was great enough to accept her as she was, so very less than perfect.

Chapter Twenty-seven

Shivers of dread mingled with quivers of anticipation as Anna stepped down from her carriage in front of Hartford Hall. She tried to draw some kind of strength from the knowledge that Mathew loved her, but that was still a large supposition on her part. In her heart she believed he did, and she had Arturo's assurance that it was so. Still, climbing the stairs to the door of Mathew's house and casually allowing herself to be escorted into his study required all her courage.

"What are you doing here?" Mathew asked, doing nothing to hide his irritation.

His tone scraped her nerves. Secretly, she had hoped that the dark quiet of the night had eased his ire. It hadn't, and a single look at his face proved that. His mouth was a grim line, his tired eyes shadowed with recrimination.

"I . . . thought, that is, I needed to talk to you," she said after the housekeeper had shut the door.

"About what?"

The chill in his eyes was enough to freeze what little spirit she had left. "We've had some trouble at home." That wasn't what she intended to say straight off, but she didn't know how to broach the subject that had brought her here.

"What kind of trouble?" He frowned deeply, his gaze sharpening with concern.

Oddly, it was that ever-so-slight warming of his eyes that robbed her limbs of energy. The last few hours had taken an immeasurable toll. She expected the hours to come would prove to be worse. Feeling more vulnerable than she ever had, she asked, "Could I sit down?"

He slapped a hand against his thigh, all the while taking in every detail of her appearance. Finally, he tipped his head toward a grouping of chairs by the fireplace.

"Have a seat."

She lowered herself to one of the chairs, finding little comfort there, and even less fortitude.

"What's wrong?" he asked, choosing to stand instead of sit.

"Jessica was shot, Nick stabbed."

"What?"

She nibbled on the inside of her cheek at his exclamation, knowing she was handling this badly. "I'm sorry, I shouldn't have blurted it out that way. I swear it's been a frightful morning." Her movements suddenly reflecting the collision of too many emotions, she removed her bonnet and set it aside.

The listless gesture was telling. "Can I get you anything?" Mathew asked.

His gruff question surprised her. There had been a time when she would have taken his polite regard for granted. Everything was changed now. She didn't know what to expect from him or their future, if indeed they had one. They had several critical bridges to cross first, the most important one being the issue of love.

Did he love her? She dearly hoped so with all her heart. Would his love be strong enough to accept the fact that she was no longer a virgin? She had no answer.

"Some mint water would be nice," she murmured.

Minutes later, he was seated in the chair opposite her while she sipped at her drink. The water helped to a small degree to reestablish some of her composure.

"Now, tell me what has happened," Mathew coaxed when she appeared more herself.

In exacting detail. she related all that had occurred at Bellefleur since early that morning. Through her gruesome recounting of the facts, Mathew remained silent, giving vent to his question only when she had finished speaking.

"How is Jessica now?" he queried.

"I left her sleeping. She should recover nicely."

"What about Nick?"

"He'll be fine. The knife did no permanent damage."

Mathew shook his head, disgust and disbelief lining his face. Coming to his feet, he muttered, "Who would have thought she was capable of something like this? It stretches the boundaries of decency."

"We're all feeling violated."

"I should think so. She came into your house under false pretenses, abused your hospitality, hoodwinked everyone she met. And then she tried to kill not only Jessica and Nick, but planned to murder you as well." Gripping his head, he grated, "Bloody hell, if the woman wasn't already dead, I'd see her in hell myself."

Anna grimaced at his temper. "I didn't tell you this to make you angry, Matt."

"How the hell did you expect me to feel?" He paced to the fireplace.

"Well . . . not angry."

He swung around and gave her a hard stare. "You come in here and tell me that my best friend is stabbed, one of his servants nearly killed and that you were supposed to be next on the list and you expect me to feel nothing?"

In her emotional agitation, his words sounded like a censure. "I didn't say I expected you to feel nothing." She rose to her feet with her mounting pique. "I just didn't want you to get upset about this. It's over and done with."

"For you, but not for me."

"What do you mean?"

Frustration riding him hard, he glared at the ceiling for a full thirty seconds, fists planted firmly on his waist. "I mean, Anna, that you've had time to adjust to this. I'm still trying to cope, so please, allow me my anger and my incredulity and anything else I might be inclined to feel."

He strode to the far end of the room to pour himself a drink. Anna watched him with troubled eyes, rubbing at the knot of strain centered at the nape of her neck. She had muddled things up. He was tense and irritable, something that did not bode well if they were going to discuss last night.

The memory of his kiss still made her stomach turn over with sweet desire. The realization of her love fluttered in her heart. How did she go on from here? The easy self-assurance she normally had in such abundance when dealing with him was absent.

"Are you all right?" she asked at length.

"No."

"Is there anything I ... I can do?"

From across the room, he shook his head.

She told herself that it wasn't unusual for him to be taciturn. Mathew was a serious man, and he had just received some very shocking news. He was entitled to be close-mouthed and strained.

It was good, sound reasoning. She even congratulated herself for exercising such unemotional self-restraint ... just before apprehension sapped the last reserves of patience and she gritted her teeth.

"If you want me to leave, why don't you come right out and say it," she accused, swept away by fright and confusion.

Slowly setting his glass aside, Mathew lifted his chin at her tone. "What are you talking about?"

"I'm trying to make amends for upsetting you and you're behaving like I've got the plague."

"I've done no such thing. Don't be unreasonable."

"I'm being very sensible."

He gave a scoff as he crossed back to her. "Anna, I'm beginning to think that you don't know the meaning of the word."

Her eyes flew wide at his insult, and her good intentions began to crumble. "Fine, if that's the way you feel, then I'll go home." She scooped up her bonnet and muttered, "I don't know why I came here in the first place."

"Why *did* you come?"

Hat in hand, she whirled to face him . . . and stopped, her love surging up to steal her ire. In the next second, insecurity of the worst kind set her limbs to trembling.

Feeling as if her lungs were trapped behind iron bars, she said, "I came about last night."

His entire body stiffened. "What about last night?"

"I wanted to know why you . . . why you . . ." Her words dried up and she silently swore. She wasn't one to stutter. "Why did you kiss me?" she forced herself to ask.

For a long moment he didn't say a word, forcing her anxiety up another notch. Instinctively, she started to rail at him, then caught herself in time to temper her words.

"Mathew, please, you said some terrible things last night, and I'm trying to understand."

"Why?"

"Because it's important to me. You're my friend and I've never seen you behave the way you did."

A look of cynicism added creases to his forehead. "And now you want to tell me that you're worried."

"Yes, I'm worried, and . . . and confused. You've never kissed me before." Unconscious appeal turned her eyes to a smoky gray. "I thought you might tell me why you did that."

Giving her his back, he started for the other side of the room again, but stopped several steps off and shook his head slowly. When he spoke, his voice was rife with as much resignation as resentment.

"Why do you think I kissed you?"

She stared at his back and realized for the first time that this was as difficult for him as it was for her. If he did love her, then his pride was balanced on a very precarious edge.

Ever so softly she said, "I'd like to think you kissed me because you love me."

The words were out—she wouldn't have recalled them for anything, but by not so much as a single move, did he betray what he was feeling. Anna waited . . . and waited, anticipation growing, doubt festering until her heart lodged at the back of her throat and tears welled in her eyes.

"Mathew?"

He turned, his face looking far older than his years. "What would you do if it were true?"

At this guarded response, she gripped her fingers tightly. "I would tell you that I love you, too."

"Do you?"

"Yes." She bowed her head, blinking back the tears. "I love you, Mathew. You were right when you called me blind. I didn't recognize my feelings for you and I never knew how you felt about me." Peering up at him, she added, "I hope it isn't too late."

He closed the distance between them, swept her into his arms and she had her answer. When his mouth took hers, she knew that he loved her, and her heart soared.

"I've loved you for so long," he muttered against her lips.

"I didn't know," she whispered, gazing into his beloved eyes. "You never said anything."

He grimaced as if in pain. "Don't remind me. We've known each other for so long. In my mind, you were a little girl and a pest and my best friend's sister." He laid a tender hand along her cheek. "I didn't know how to tell you that somewhere along the way all of that changed. You grew up on me and I fell in love with you."

He claimed her mouth again with a near desperate urgency. Anna willingly, ardently returned his passion and love. But beneath the surface of her desire lay more of the truth, a truth that could destroy the promise of their love.

"Mathew, we need to talk."

His smile stretched free and unburdened. "Your timing isn't wonderful, but if you insist, we'll discuss anything you like, as long as we begin with the issue of marriage."

"Marriage?"

"Of course. Love, marriage, they go hand in hand."

With each word, he was killing her inch by inch. Frantically, she sought of how best to continue.

"What is it?" He searched her suddenly tremulous expression.

Carefully, she stepped away, instantly wishing to be back within the loving circle of his arms. "I can't be dishonest with you . . . you have a right to know." If she could spare him this, she would. "I've . . . I'm not . . ." All the color drained from her face. "I'm not a virgin."

His eyes narrowed. "What?"

"I'm not a virgin, I'm . . ." Helplessly, she lifted her hands.

"Before you start making plans for us, you had to know that." She tried to gauge his reaction and saw only a fathomless stare. Her insides dropped to the soles of her feet.

She lowered her gaze, raised it to the door behind Mathew, dragged it to the window. Everywhere she looked, she saw her happiness slipping away in a misguided world where the rules for men and women were completely different and ruthlessly unfair. The injustice of that kind of prejudice made her look at Mathew with love, but with candor as well.

"I know how men feel about wanting their wives to be pure and innocent. I'm neither. If you want me to apologize for that, I can't. I don't regret what I've done."

She paused for a breath, licking her lower lip in her nervousness. "I do apologize if my lack of virtue hurts you. You don't deserve to be hurt. You're honest and sincere and proud and I love you. You may not think my actions prove that; until this morning, I didn't know that I loved you. If you hadn't kissed me, I would have gone on for a long time not knowing."

A blunt, unrelenting silence dropped into the space between them. Anna returned to her chair, suddenly bereft of any kind of energy.

From behind, came Mathew's harsh voice. "Who was it?"

Staring at her hands in her lap, she countered, "Does it matter?"

"I have a right to know," he snapped.

"Do I have similar rights?"

"What the bloody hell does that mean?"

His anger always had a way of setting her off. She was strung too tightly now to have any kind of defense against his ire. She turned her head, just enough to see the virulence extinguishing the blue of his eyes. Through set teeth, in precise tones, she asked, "I mean, are you going to tell me the names of every woman you've ever bedded?"

"Of course not," he sputtered, all outraged male sensibilities. "It's a private matter."

She surged to her feet, her energy restored with such vigor that her cheeks took on a ruby stain. "Then allow me the same courtesy! If you respect me enough to love me, if you care enough to love me, if you believe in me at all, then you will not condemn me for my actions and you will allow me my privacy just as I allow you yours."

Not caring that tears coursed from her eyes, she clenched a shaking hand to her chest and railed, "I love you, Mathew, more than I ever thought it possible to love anyone. I can't think of a time when you haven't been a part of my life. I don't even want to contemplate the years ahead without you. But I am who I am, with all my flaws—my temper, my stubbornness, and yes, the loss of my virtue. Either you love me despite all of that, because of all of that, or don't love me at all because—"

He moved so quickly, she never saw him coming. All she knew was that he jerked her forward and crushed his mouth on hers with such brutal strength that her knees buckled.

She clung to his shoulders, giving him her mouth, surrendering to his passion.

"Shut up," he ordered, kissing her temple, her forehead, her eyes. "I'll always love you, and I don't care what you've done. I despaired of ever making you mine. I can't turn you away, I *won't* turn you away."

His mouth moved fiercely over hers again, his arms banding her to him until she thought their bodies would meld.

"I love you," she got out between her tears and her choked breathing. "I was so afraid."

"Of what?"

"Of losing you, of having you hate me."

He raised one hand to capture her chin. "Never. I won't lie and say I don't care that I wasn't the first. I wish I could have been. But I can't hate you for that. I love you too much. You're in my blood, my every waking thought. Oh, God, Anna, as long as you love me, I can accept anything."

Fresh tears rose to cloud her vision. There was nothing vague about her perceptions, though. Pressing her face close to his chest, she knew that she had found everything she had been searching for. Her life and her love, her future was Mathew.

Jessica opened her eyes to find herself in Nicholas's room. Several seconds passed where she couldn't imagine why she was there. Levering herself upward, a biting pain lanced out from her shoulder and memory promptly returned.

She lay back and expelled a ragged sigh, drained and yet, so relieved she wanted to weep. Nicholas was unharmed, Anna was safe. Clarice would never hurt anyone again.

Those were Nick's words. She remembered waking up and warning him about Clarice. He had soothed her fears about the widow, but he hadn't elaborated. Jessica had to wonder where Clarice was now, what had happened to her. All she knew was that both Anna and Nick had seemed well, secure and at ease.

She took great faith in that, tired enough to relegate her questions to another time. Her arm and shoulder ached terribly and she felt as if every inch of her body had been bruised. Under the shirt she wore, she could feel the pressure of a binding.

Belatedly, she thought to consider the shirt. It was obviously Nick's, and fit her like a nightgown three sizes too big.

She fingered the rolled back cuffs, suddenly discomfited and unsure of herself. She was lying in his bed, clothed in one of the same shirts that had covered his torso. Given the circumstances, it wasn't terribly surprising. Given that she had poured out her heart to him, it was horribly unsettling.

She let her eyelids drift shut, overcome with rioting emotions. She hadn't meant to confess her love the way she had. Her only excuse was that she had truly believed herself dying. Telling him how she felt had been the single most important thing for her to do, her mind had been consumed with the need.

She loved Nick, she always would. In that she had no regrets, but loving him and having him know about it were two different things entirely. There was no telling how he was going to react to her, how he would treat her. Regardless, it was embarrassing and disheartening to love someone and not be loved in return.

Pride forced her eyes open. Dogged determination got her to her feet. That was as far as she got. Dizziness assailed her just as the door opened and Nick came in.

"What are you doing?" he demanded to know, rushing to her side. He steadied her as she swayed then lowered her back onto the bed. "Lie down," he ordered.

She didn't have any choice. Even if her legs had been able to carry her anywhere, Nick prevented that. He tucked her under the covers and smoothed her hair from her forehead before he took up a very unmovable stance.

His face a study of uncompromising lines, he stood there and shook his head. "Where did you think you were going?"

"I . . ." She hadn't thought about it. Her only impulse had been to flee so that she wouldn't have to face him right then. At another time, she would feel strong enough, more composed. As taxed as she was, both physically, and emotionally, she was feeling far too vulnerable to deal with him. "To my room, I suppose."

He gave a scoffing laugh. "I don't want you supposing anything, I don't want you *doing* anything except getting better. And that means staying right where you are. The doctor says you'll be all right, but he gave orders that you are to rest." His eyes narrowed. "How are you feeling?"

She was thankful for the mundane question. It helped take her mind off the chagrin shivering within her. "I'm a little dizzy."

"That's to be expected." He sat on the edge of the bed facing her. "Does your arm pain you a great deal?"

"It throbs."

"Getting up didn't help. I don't want you moving about for at least another day."

His nearness was a sweet agony, more painful than the wound in her shoulder. Against her thigh, she could feel the hard length of his leg. "I would prefer to rest in my own bed."

"No, I want you here."

Her gaze jerked to his. "But this is your bed. I can't stay here."

He returned her stare calmly, steadily, never once blinking as the light of challenge began to glisten in his silvery eyes. "Why not?" he asked as carefully as he watched her.

She swallowed, not liking his expression. It boded of stubbornness and his irrefutable air of power. "I . . . I can recuperate just as well in my own bed."

"But I don't want you recuperating there," he countered, his voice low and succinct. "I want you in my bed."

In a kind of dread, she heard the meaning underscoring his words. "I can't."

One of his black brows flicked up. "Can't or won't?"

"Both."

"That's odd, considering you love me."

She shut her eyes, swallowing the moan that began in the region of her heart. She should have realized this was going to happen. Knowing that she loved him, he was not above using that knowledge to bend her to his will.

It would be so easy to give him what he wanted, to lie next to him and pretend. She couldn't. If given the choice, she wouldn't yield again to the kind of one-sided love that tore at her soul. She had had that and it was too painful to bear. Somehow, once and for all, she had to make him understand.

"Nothing has changed, Nick," she whispered, tears gathering on her lids. "I can't go on giving you my body and receiving only snatches of momentary pleasure. Don't ask me to do that. It hurts too much, loving you and . . . and wanting more, wishing that you . . . that you loved me in return."

Her misery was complete, draining her of the last of her strength. "If you have an inkling of regard for me, if you feel the slightest bit of concern, then leave me alone."

She gave herself up to her tears, not caring if he watched or not. As exposed as she felt, his glowering stares didn't matter. Nothing mattered. Her pride and her dignity were in shreds, her chance at love gone.

"You're a little fool," he muttered a second before he slipped his arms about her and carefully drew her into his embrace. "And I'm an even bigger fool."

His words didn't make any sense to her. She laid her head against his shoulder and wept.

"I'm sorry, love. Don't cry. I shouldn't have put you through this."

In the back of her mind, she thought to lever herself away. She remained where she was, taking the comfort he offered while her heart wilted.

His arms tightened and he caressed the top of her head with his jaw. "Don't cry, I can't bear to see you so upset. Hush, love."

"Let me go, Nicholas," she pleaded. "Sell my papers to someone else."

Pain speared through his gut. He ground his eyes shut in an attempt to control the anguish brought on by her words. He had almost lost her to a mad woman's revenge. He couldn't even begin to think of voluntarily relinquishing her to another man, to another place away from him.

"I can't let you go. Not ever." His face mirrored every emotion that had been gripping him for hours, days, months. Fear, anger, frustration, hope, concern, bitterness; all those and so many more. They all warred and combined and emerged as love. "I love you, Jess. You're mine, I won't ever let you go."

Through the mist of her sorrow, she heard his voice. She lifted her head, not certain she had heard correctly. "What?"

He captured her face between his palms, his gaze delving into hers. "I love you," he grated, his throat tight. "I didn't realize it until I saw you covered in blood." If he lived forever, he would never forget that moment. He would go to his grave feeling the hopeless rage and terror when he thought her dead.

"My heart stopped, my whole life seemed worthless." He lowered his mouth to hers. "I knew then that I loved you, that I didn't want to go on living if you weren't beside me."

He kissed her with tightly leashed passion, drawing a gasp from between her lips. Shock held her immobile, incapable of responding to the sweet pressure of his mouth.

"You . . . love me?" she asked, tearing her mouth away.

"Yes."

"I . . . I don't . . ."

He kissed her again, his tongue urging her to give him the kind of response he longed for, needed, had to have.

"Nicholas, no," she breathed. "Wait, I don't understand."

"I love you," he told her. "I want you for my wife."

"Wife?" Stunned, she gazed at him in complete amazement. "You want to marry me?"

Raising her hands, he kissed the center of each palm. "Yes. If you'll have me."

She felt as if she had walked into a dream. An hour ago, she hadn't been aware that he had harbored anything for her but rage and lust. Yet there he sat, declaring his love and doubting if she would accept him as a husband.

If she would accept him. How could he think such a thing?

"You really love me?" she asked, still amazed that it could be true.

He stroked his knuckles over her cheek, the gesture as delicate as it was pensive. "I don't blame you for finding this hard to believe. I never gave you reason to think that I loved you." He swore harshly. "I was a blind fool, an ass. I saw you as a woman, but only at my convenience." Remorse lined his face. "I know I hurt you terribly, but I didn't know that what I was feeling for you was love. All I knew was that you had become a part of me, and I wanted you. When you turned me away, I didn't know what to do." He blinked against the tears that threatened. "When you told me you wouldn't have my children, I wanted to hate you. In the end, I hated myself and my life."

His every word filled her with the most profound tenderness. In his own way, he had suffered as much as she.

Lifting a hand, she traced the curve of his upper lip. "Don't berate yourself so."

"I'll carry the regret with me forever." He turned his head

to kiss her fingers. "Please, forgive me. Tell me you love me. Tell me you'll marry me."

Her heart soared, her soul flew. She leaned into him and lifted her mouth to his. "Yes. Yes, I love you, yes, I'll marry you."

He crushed her to him, forgetting her injury. She didn't care, the hurt was nothing in the face of their love.

"God, I love you," he grated. He pressed his mouth to her eyes, her nose, her forehead. "Tell me again."

"I love you."

On the tail end of her declaration, the door opened and Mama Lou came in carrying a heavily laden tray. Jessica remained where she was, glad for the whole world to know that she loved this man.

"I would ask how you're feelin'," the housekeeper said, "but I can see that you're doin' fine."

Smiling with pure joy, Jessica leaned into the support of Nicholas' arms. "I feel wonderful."

"Good. Do you think you might want to eat a little somethin'?"

Nick gave her a gentle squeeze. "You should if you're going to gain your strength."

"Will you stay and eat with me?"

He brushed his lips over hers. "You won't be able to pry me from your side."

A beaming Mama Lou left the tray on the bedside table. To Jessica's delight, a small vase of flowers decorated the large salver.

"Flowers," she exclaimed touched by the thoughtful decoration.

Nick plucked one bloom from the arrangement and fingered the petals with great care. "For you."

Jessica held the rose and breathed in its sweet scent. "It's beautiful."

"If should be."

"Why?"

He gave her a long, gentle look. "Can't you guess where it came from?"

She dropped her gaze to the single red bloom and pure happiness raced through her. "The rose garden?"

"Bellefleur's rose garden. This was the last rose. It was nearly hidden, almost forgotten." He slipped his hand about hers, entwining their fingers so that they both held the stem. "Take a long look, love. You and I will never see Bellefleur's rose bushes blossom again."

Gazing into Nicholas's face, she silently agreed. She believed in the legend of the rose with its tale of everlasting love. How could she not?

She had found her home and her love in Nicholas. Both were enduring and genuine, as rich as the land, as real as Bellefleur.

EVERY DAY WILL FEEL LIKE FEBRUARY 14TH!

*Zebra Historical Romances
by Terri Valentine*

LOUISIANA CARESS   (4126-8, $4.50/$5.50)

MASTER OF HER HEART   (3056-8, $4.25/$5.50)

OUTLAW'S KISS   (3367-2, $4.50/$5.50)

SEA DREAMS   (2200-X, $3.75/$4.95)

SWEET PARADISE   (3659-0, $4.50/$5.50)

TRAITOR'S KISS   (2569-6, $3.75/$4.95)

Available wherever paperbacks are sold, or order direct from the Publisher. Send cover price plus 50¢ per copy for mailing and handling to Penguin USA, P.O. Box 999, c/o Dept. 17109, Bergenfield, NJ 07621. Residents of New York and Tennessee must include sales tax. DO NOT SEND CASH.